The Department of Off World Affairs

Printed in the United States of America

Published by Silverthought Press
www.silverthought.com

Cover design by E.B. Lutz

Author photograph by Leslie Brown and Stephanie Spahlinger

Grateful acknowledgement is made for permission to include the following copyrighted material:

Lyrics from "Weight of the World" by Daniel Hines and Todd Faulkner. Copyright © 1997 by BAMACTS Music. Used by permission.

"Brianne's Hand" font designed by Jeni Hopewell. Copyright © by Jeni Hopewell. Used by permission.

ISBN: 978-0-9815191-7-3

The Department of Off World Affairs
by Russell Lutz

[silverthought]
Philadelphia | New York

Acknowledgments

It occurred to me very late in the publishing process of my previous novel, *Iota Cycle*, (after it was, you know, done) that I hadn't included any acknowledgements. These, then, are the people I wish to thank for that book, this one, and pretty much everything else I've written. I list them in roughly the order I met them...

Eloise Lutz, E.B. Lutz, Rip Rowan, Byron Glickfeld, Tawny Kilborne, Leslie Brown, Paul Alanis, Heather Alanis, Max Plotsky, Scott Lyerly and Paul Hughes. You're the ones who read my writing before it was published, and you gave me your feedback, both positive *and* negative. Every little bit helped, believe me.

And don't think this means you're off the hook.

also by Russell Lutz

Iota Cycle
Silverthought: Ignition ("Athens 3004")

Heliopause

The Pythagoreans bid us in the morning look to the heavens that we may be reminded of those bodies which continually do the same things and in the same manner perform their work, and also be reminded of their purity and nudity. For there is no veil over a star.
—*Marcus Aurelius Antoninus, Meditations, XI, 27*

Vanessa Hargrove's hobby didn't make sense to anyone outside the field of astronomy. She accepted that, finally, while having dinner with a friend of a friend of a friend. Her date—a man with the unfortunate name of Trevor—had some sort of god-awful consulting position, traveling from city to city, telling retail corporations how to reduce costs. Ironically, he seemed willing to charge exorbitant rates for this information.

"I study the heliopause," Vanessa told him between sips of a very mediocre red wine. Their pasta had not yet arrived. By extreme force of will, she hadn't devoured the entire basket of breadsticks while listening to Trevor's consulting anecdotes.

"Is that anything like the *menopause?*" Trevor smirked. Vanessa choked back a nasty comment. She needed reminders of her advancing age like she needed another breadstick. However, the disdain she now felt for Trevor did not diminish her innate need to *teach.*

"The heliopause is like a bubble around the solar system. It's where the solar wind finally slows down as it brushes up against the interstellar medium of gas and dust."

Trevor's blank stare was pointed directly at her breasts. Only three-plus decades of experience maintaining generally pleasant and conflict-free interaction with other humans kept Vanessa from tossing her wine in Trevor's face and storming from the restaurant.

That and the fact she had a free plate of chicken alfredo on the way.

On September 5, 1977, NASA launched *Voyager 1* to the heavens. The probe's primary mission was a tour of Jupiter and Saturn, sending back to Earth unprecedented imagery of the two largest planets in the solar system and their rings and moons. After that, assisted by the gravity of Saturn, it shot off, out of the plane of the ecliptic, toward interstellar space, soon to become the most distant man-made object in history.

On September 12, 2006, two days before Vanessa's eighteenth birthday, she attended her first class at the University of Washington. She was one of only one hundred eighty-two entering freshmen that year who graduated with a degree in their declared major. Her chosen field was astronomy.

Now, in April of 2021, *Voyager 1* was about to make history as the first human-built object ever to cross the largely theoretical border of the heliopause. Vanessa's models and data analyses put her in the vanguard of scientists interested in this distant, ephemeral phenomenon, which averaged something over 150 AU in radius around the Sun.

This obscure topic garnered only slightly more interest within the scientific community than it did for laymen like Trevor. Vanessa believed herself to be the only person on the planet currently interested in *Voyager*'s continuing progress out of the solar system. She had watched, horrified, during her junior year at UW as JPL finished a complete shutdown of the *Voyager* project. Vanessa had written a passionate letter to the director of JPL, making a plea for continuation of operations at *least* until the spacecraft crossed the heliopause. The letter she received in response was as polite as it was disheartening—they saw no future in monitoring the aging spacecraft.

Now, at the age of thirty-two, Vanessa had made it into JPL herself as an analyst. Her duties involved monitoring data from a necklace of interconnected orbital telescopes that sought to answer the most vexing questions of star and planet formation in the local region of the galaxy. It was interesting work, even rewarding. But Vanessa still longed for a more direct connection to the cosmos. Passively receiving electromagnetic radiation didn't seem nearly as thrilling as building a real *spacecraft* and flinging it to the stars. In the six decades since man escaped the gravity of the

Earth far enough to orbit the planet, only *four* interstellar craft had ever been built. Only *four* times had something designed and built by human hands left the gravity well of the sun. To Vanessa, that was more than a shame; it was a crime.

Two years ago, Vanessa carried out a plan that had been a childhood dream. First, she searched through the archives at JPL, looking for the original frequencies and control programs for *Voyager 1*. Even eleven years after the official end of the project, the pack rat mentality common to most scientists held sway; she found everything she needed to resume contact with the forgotten probe in the dusty back rooms of JPL.

Next, in the attic of her modest Pasadena home, she built transmitter and receiver hardware from scratch. The transmitter weighed only a pound and sat on the north end of her roof, pointed to the sky over the branches of a severely pruned mimosa. Designing the receiver took a bit more ingenuity. The signals from *Voyager* were very faint and not particularly directional at this distance. She needed the equivalent of a hundred-foot-wide parabolic dish to get any kind of clarity of reception at all. She solved the problem by creating a web of tiny receivers—connected through a standard wireless networking scheme—which she spread all through her neighborhood. Each receiver measured only inches and looked quite a bit like the roofing material used by most of the homeowners in her neighborhood. Her neighbors never questioned the little squares she had secreted on their roofs over the course of a couple of weeks.

It was a small wonder Vanessa didn't have a boyfriend when she spent her nights sneaking onto her neighbors' roofs, installing electronic devices she had designed and built herself. And, on top of that, the love of her life was a dying spacecraft from the 1970s, flying through space, several billion miles away.

The day was Thursday, April 22, 2021. Vanessa devoted this evening to reviewing last week's transmission from *Voyager*'s CRS. The cosmic rays hitting the spacecraft had been growing of late, a possible indicator it was nearing the heliopause. She hadn't fired up any of the other instrument packages in months. *Voyager*'s power had dropped so low only one instrument at a time could function. The CRS tended to give her the most reliable results, so she left it on.

As Vanessa reviewed the recording from last week, tonight *Voyager* sent her an update of the probe's systems, primarily a report of the power remaining in the tiny reactor. She switched to her receiver program and saw that the binary code was trickling in at the normal, glacial rate. She almost turned away, almost minimized the window, almost missed it.

The signal stopped mid-word. A pause like that was common enough with hardware this antiquated. *Voyager* often had to stop and resend entire messages. Vanessa sighed. Then the transmission restarted…

Except something was wrong. The signals were too fast. *Voyager's* computer shouldn't have sent its pulses like that. They accelerated. The pings of binary code, represented by 1's, ran left to right across the screen, filling line after line. Faster still, whole screens of 1's flowing past every few seconds.

Vanessa knew what had happened. She lived in constant fear of her *Voyager* frequencies being sold off to a cellular phone company, or a communications company for one of their satellites. They might have been handed over to an airline or the military for communications with their planes. How would she ever find the heliopause now?

Was there any point in trying to fight to retain her radio frequency? Did she have the slightest chance of changing the mind of Verizon or Southwest Airlines or the US Navy? No. Pure and simple.

She imagined *Voyager* out on the edge of interstellar space trying to sort through a howl of nonsense signals coming from Earth. Pitch and yaw telemetry from a commercial jet crossing the US. Weapons targeting instructions from an aircraft carrier in the Indian Ocean. Grocery shopping lists from hundreds of spouses waiting at home in New York and New Jersey. Vanessa, not normally an overly sentimental person, found the idea sad, in its way. The best thing to do would be to put *Voyager* out of its misery.

She rolled her desk chair across the floor to her shelf of research books "on loan" from JPL. Her fingers ran over the titles until she found the one that included a complete description of the command language for *Voyager.* She flipped to the back of the tome and found the page she needed—"Shutdown Procedures". She had already turned off most of the equipment on the craft. To put *Voyager* to sleep once and for all required she send five more strings of simple, binary pulses. That would shut down the CRS, turn off the receiver, and allow the RTGs with their lumps of radioactive material to slowly decay, unused and unbothered, until the whole ship was nothing more than a lifeless collection of metal and plastic, hurtling through the dark.

She keyed in the sequences and sent them into space. In about twenty hours, *Voyager* would receive its last command.

Saddened that a chapter of her life had come to such an anticlimactic end, Vanessa shut down her tablet and went to bed.

Phone ringing. Loud. What?

Vanessa rolled over, fighting her blankets for control of the bed, and grabbed her cell off the bedside table.

"Huh?" she said into the phone.

"What is *Voyager* doing?" Shao yelled into the phone.

Somehow JPL found out she had shut down the probe and they were mad at her. Vanessa's built-in humility before authority kicked in.

"Sorry. I didn't think there was any point in continuing..."

"Make it stop. They're all going nuts."

Make what stop? Who's going nuts? Vanessa swam up out of the remnants of her deep sleep, confused. JPL had long since given up on *Voyager*. They had given her the codes and the frequencies and the research materials willingly. It was that much less they'd have to compost.

"Shao, use small words."

"*Voyager* is blinding us!"

Vanessa pulled on a sweatshirt and jeans. At 2:30 in the morning, she didn't much care what she looked like. She tied her overlong red hair into a ponytail with a rubber band in the car while sitting at a red light. She caught sight of her face in her rear-view mirror and was suitably horrified, but she certainly didn't have time for makeup. With no traffic to speak of, she made it to her lab in record time.

Shao paced the floor of the white, fluorescent room, phone hanging over his ear, shouting. He looked at her and pointed to one of the monitors.

"No, the expert just got here… No, I said she just *got* here!"

Vanessa rolled a chair across the tile floor to the computer station and sat. An amateur's vision of astronomy involved pretty pictures of the Crab Nebula or the galaxy of Andromeda. Very little of their work involved visible light, so visual representations from the telescopes were often confusing, or worse, misleading to the untrained eye. This screen showed a map of a tiny sector of the northern sky, a sector with which Vanessa was very familiar. These were the stars toward which *Voyager* had sailed for decades.

On a background of white, little pinpricks of color indicated sources of infrared, ultraviolet, x-rays, any and every flavor of EM radiation. Most were stars. Some were more exotic beasts, like pulsars or black holes or distant quasars. Any sector of the sky would look similar.

A dirty smear, like a bruise, filled the middle third of the screen. Streaks of yellow and brown and purple, in a vague starburst pattern. If Vanessa read the screen correctly, the sheer power of these sources dwarfed anything else in the sky, with the exception of the Sun or the Moon.

"I don't get it," she admitted. "It's like someone is shining a flashlight right into the telescope."

"I'll call you back," Shao said, then tapped the phone to hang up. Shao Miller was a study in contrasts. A blond Asian. A pragmatic scientist. A humble genius. Vanessa considered herself lucky—and cursed—to work in the same lab with him.

"Well, either *Voyager* somehow exploded in a nova-sized, nuclear fireball, or we're looking at the end of the universe." He leaned over Vanessa, poking at the screen with a long forefinger. "I found this three hours ago, when the feed from OT14 started to wobble."

"Wobble?"

"Interference, from this. Problem is… it's growing."

"*Growing?*"

Shao pulled up a series of smaller images in little windows around the live feed. "Midnight. Midnight-thirty. One. One-thirty…" Each image showed the same sector of night sky, but the bizarre radio source grew slightly larger, frame by frame.

"It's got to be an object, a meteor or something, heading for Earth," Vanessa said.

"Nope. Off-axis confirms these signals are light-years away."

"How far?"

Shao frowned. "Just figured this part out a couple of minutes ago. Maybe you can confirm for me?" His phone rang. He reached up to his ear and shut it off. "Not all of... this... is from the same place."

"I don't follow," Vanessa admitted.

Shao cleared the screen and brought up two images, side by side.

"This is the... I'm gonna call it a cloud. This is the cloud from OT5."

Vanessa looked up at a clock to check the time. "Somewhere over the Pacific."

"Right. And this is from OT23, on station above Europe. If I do an off-axis plot..." He brought up a third image.

"Dear God," Vanessa murmured.

The whole point of off-axis was to use the parallax of widely spaced telescopes to determine the distance of an object. It was the same concept behind depth perception in human vision. The left eye and right eye could see the world from just slightly different angles. The differences between the images tell a person's brain how far away things are. The differences between the images of orbiting telescopes on either side of the Earth can tell how far away stars and galaxies are.

On the edges of the screen, outside the "cloud", individual stars were labeled with little numbers, showing their distance from Earth. 14 light years. 135 light years. One galaxy in the sample pushed the limits of the method they were using, and was simply labeled with an infinity symbol.

The cloud itself was carpeted with numbers, thousands of them. She saw numbers as low as 5 and as high as 3,300. This cloud wasn't an explosion or a single object flying through space. This was a collection of radio waves from sources scattered through the Orion spiral arm of the Milky Way galaxy.

"Okay... Is it a problem with the array? The data looks like garbage," she said.

Shao pulled up a mail program and opened a message. "We got this from Green Bank ten minutes ago." Green Bank was a medium-sized, land-based radio telescope in West Virginia. Green Bank's image looked identical to the ones from JPL's orbital telescopes. It wasn't a hardware or software problem. It was *real.*

"I don't even know where to begin," Shao admitted. "But that..." He pointed to the center of the cloud. "...is where *Voyager* is right now, isn't it?"

Vanessa nodded.

"So this can't be a coincidence! It must have something to do with your probe!"

"How? I don't... Here. Can we focus the image *right here?* In the exact center. What are we getting from there?"

Shao moved to his own console and grabbed his mouse, clicking and dragging furiously. The image blanked to white except for a very small, mostly yellow dot.

"Fifteen megahertz, give or take, mean distance of ninety-six light years," Shao said.

"What is it?" she asked.

"What do you mean?"

Vanessa reached across and took control of the mouse. She dragged the incoming radio waves over to a graphing tool. They were frequency modulated... kind of like FM radio.

She looked at it, wondering. It didn't seem possible that... No. Be rational. The graph looked impossibly chaotic. It could be anything...

Screw it. She transferred the feed to an audio program.

High-pitched, screeching white noise poured out of the speakers.

"Vanessa!"

She turned down the volume. "Narrow it. Give me a band width of a hundred kilohertz." The graph shrunk in width, the highest peaks and lowest valleys gone. The sound loosened up a bit, but still seemed entirely random. Vanessa twiddled with the equalization controls on the player. She shifted the pitch down a couple of octaves. Now, instead of nails on a blackboard, it sounded like coarse sandpaper running over wood.

"I'm still getting too much stuff. You said the mean distance of the signals is ninety-six light years."

"Yeah."

"What's the range?"

"Uh…" Shao sifted through some screens. "Between about five and about 2,400."

"Can you… Can you limit the feed to just signals coming from a small range? Maybe… between ninety and one-ten?"

"Never tried that before… Gimme a second."

While Shao worked, Vanessa flipped over to the live feed of the entire cloud. It had grown a bit just while they'd been talking. She took a series of the pictures and measured the width of the phenomenon. It was growing at about a half of a percent of a degree every hour. In four days, the cloud would be larger than the Sun in the sky, though it would never be visible to the human eye, of course. These signals were mostly in the radio frequencies, not visible light. She frowned, then redid her calculations. Impossible.

"It's growing too fast."

"What?" Shao said.

"Nothing."

She took a stylus and did the calculation by hand on an old tablet. If the phenomenon was growing at that rate, it literally *couldn't* be very far away. The speed of light said so. At a distance of a hundred light years, this thing would be expanding… about seventy-five times the speed of light. Impossible. So, whatever was causing the cloud to grow was closer than that. How close? That was the question.

"Got it," Shao said. He clicked. The sandpaper sound reduced to a low whisper. Vanessa had to increase the volume on the player just to hear it. A chill ran up her spine like she'd never felt before in her life. She shared a look with Shao, making sure he heard the same thing she had heard.

A conversation. They were listening in on a conversation between two people, on an unused radio band, from somewhere a hundred light years away from Earth. They couldn't understand the language, of course, but it was clearly voices. Alien voices.

Vanessa looked again at the live feed of the cloud with all its overlapping splotches of color. Thousands of frequencies. Millions of conversations. And the cloud continued to expand at a ridiculous rate.

"Well then," she said.

After a beat, they both broke into hysterical laughter.

Forty hours after Vanessa sent her signal to shut *Voyager* down, a super-cooled ball of liquid hydrogen streaked across the skies of southern California. The object was too small to be tracked by civilian or military radar—it measured only a centimeter in width. Because of its temperature, only a fraction of a degree above absolute zero, it lost very little mass slicing through Earth's atmosphere. The ball slowed over the town of Pasadena and headed straight and sure for the home of Vanessa Hargrove.

Vanessa's next door neighbor, Margie Dupont, watched from her porch, dumbfounded, as a ghostly, transparent figure of a man, faintly glowing blue, appeared at Vanessa's front door. The man knocked. He wasn't much of a ghost if he could knock on a door like that.

There was no answer from within Vanessa's home. The man's faint, ill-defined head turned to Margie. When he spoke, his lips did not quite match the sound of his speech.

"Where is the owner of this house?"

Any other time, Margie would have given someone asking a question like that a sizeable piece of her mind. She would have said, "I don't know you, and I don't know your business, so you better just move along or I'll call 911 on your ass!" But Margie had little experience dealing with ghostly blue figures who could knock on doors.

"I... uh..." she stammered. The figure started walking toward her. Margie snapped, the words pouring out of her. "She's gone! She's gone to the White House."

"In Washington, District of Columbia?" the ghost asked. Margie nodded, hating herself for cracking under pressure like that.

The ghost collapsed in on himself, until he was just a small speck of blue, hanging in the air over Margie's lawn. Then, with a whizzing sound, it was gone.

Vanessa thought she had fallen into some science fiction movie. Two days ago she was an unknown researcher in the backwaters of astronomy, and today, she was leading a briefing at the White House! She barely had time enough to pack her one decent business outfit. Her hair was a disaster, lying on her head like a tied off mop. Thankfully, Shao was at her side, providing much needed support.

Ranged around the decadent, glossy conference table were the Secretary of Homeland Security, the Secretary of Defense, the National Security Advisor, the President's Science Advisor, the Secretary of State.

And the President of the United States himself, of course.

Vanessa finished her nickel tour of the *Voyager* program and moved into the new material.

"Clearly, the *Voyager 1* probe has caused some significant event out at the farthest edge of our solar system. Since *Voyager's* nuclear power source is nearly depleted, the only energy she has to impart is kinetic energy."

"Energy of motion," the President offered.

"Yes, sir. The probe is—or was—traveling a little under a quarter of a million miles per hour. To put that into perspective, the Moon is about a quarter of a million miles from Earth. Imagine traveling from the Earth to the Moon in an hour."

The Science Advisor piped up: "So, what did *Voyager* hit?"

Vanessa took a deep breath. "She hit the heliopause." Dumbfounded stares answered that statement. "Our sun sends out more than light and heat as it burns. It also sheds radiation we call solar wind. Most of the solar wind is blocked from the Earth's surface by our atmosphere, but it can exert a not insignificant force. In fact, with Mylar sails, we could build craft that would—" Shao nudged her. She reigned in her flight of technological fancy for the moment.

"Anyway. The solar wind blows off the Sun in a very similar way to normal, atmospheric winds. Out in the interstellar wastes, there are also tides of radiation that we sometimes describe with the catchall phrase *cosmic rays*. These are the remains of supernovae, x-rays from black holes, as well as the solar winds of other stars.

"The heliopause is the place where the solar wind has expended so much of its force fighting against the cosmic rays that equilibrium is reached." She held her hands out in a spherical shape.

"Like a soap bubble," the President suggested.

"Exactly, Mr. President, except that the heliopause has never been considered a physical object. It's merely a term for a theoretical location in space, much like the equator on Earth."

She brought up a graphic on the screen behind her. It showed a tiny Solar System, surrounded by a vaguely teardrop shaped bubble. "Based on the evidence of the anomalous radio signals and the timing with *Voyager*'s position in space, we believe that, at the theoretical position of the heliopause, an *actual* barrier has been sitting for at least recent human history." On the screen, a hole ripped into the topside of the virtual heliopause. "*Voyager* tore a hole through this boundary, here, causing the barrier to unravel at an extraordinary speed."

The Secretary of Defense perked up at that. "How fast?"

"A million miles an hour." She received a few smirks at the use of that phrase. "It's actually 1.17 million miles per hour. We have to assume the barrier is rather lightweight. It was, perhaps, held in place entirely by the competing forces of the solar wind from inside, and the pressure of the interstellar medium from the outside. A break this size might be enough to destroy the barrier completely."

"And this... barrier..." the President said, "has been shielding us from these alien radio signals."

"Yes, sir," Vanessa said. "Incredible as it may seem, the barrier can let natural light of any frequency through, but it completely filters out artificial sources of radiation. That's why the sky seems normal—at least, as we define normal—everywhere else. But through this hole, where the barrier has peeled away, we are receiving an astounding number of signals that are clearly the work of extraterrestrials."

"This barrier could not be a natural occurrence. It was designed; it was built. That implies intelligence," the Homeland Secretary said.

"Significant intelligence. Transcendent intelligence," Vanessa said. Shao tugged on her sleeve, indicating again that she tone down the rhetoric.

"How long will it take for the entire barrier to fall?" the President asked.

"Assuming the rate of breakdown remains constant, about eight years."

"Eight years?"

"The heliopause is very large, Mr. President."

If this had been a movie, this would have been the scene in which the valiant scientist makes a case for benevolent aliens, for sending messages of greeting, for throwing off the yoke of militaristic thinking. Then the closed-minded government functionaries would have responded with fear, assuming the worst, precipitating a significant tragedy, which only the valiant scientist could avert.

It seemed that everyone here had already seen that movie. Like any group of competent world leaders, the men and women in the room took steps to ensure that they prepared for *every* contingency. Homeland Security would raise the alert level for the nation. The State Department would send out feelers to other world governments to take their temperatures, and to notify those few who had not yet learned of the phenomenon. The Defense Department would, in consultation with NATO, make ready for defense against an off world invasion—a scenario that had, amazingly, been written up decades ago, just in case. And the Science Advisor would work with State to fashion a message to send out to the stars: a hello of sorts. If the barrier had worked both ways, and all of Earth's television and radio broadcasts of the last hundred years never left the vicinity of the planet, maybe humanity could make a good first impression after all.

A nondescript man in a black suit entered and spoke a few words into the President's ear.

"Ladies and gentlemen," the President said, standing. Everyone stood with him. "We are going to adjourn to the Situation Room in the basement." Eyes flitted back and forth, between the powerful and the secondary, like Vanessa. Only the President and the Secret Service agent seemed to know what was happening. The entire roomful of people marched through the immaculate halls of the West Wing and down a stairwell to the dark and somewhat dingy confines of the Situation Room, escorted all the way by stone-faced agents of the Secret Service.

A heavy door closed behind them with a *thud* that Vanessa in particular found troubling.

Half the people in the room continued to lay their plans for dealing with this crisis. The other half muttered about the strange way they had been shuffled into perhaps the most secure room on the planet. The President stood in a corner whispering with quiet men in uniforms and dark suits.

Vanessa turned to Shao. "Is this normal?"

"I've only been to the White House once before," he said. "They sure didn't bring me down *here.*"

The tension in the room continued to mount. Any pretense at working fell away. The President came out of the corner to address the twenty-some people standing around a more lackluster conference table than the one upstairs.

"There's been a breach of security. An intruder has infiltrated the West Wing. It appears to be headed to our location."

"It?" the Secretary of State asked.

"What sort of weapons is it using?" the Secretary of Homeland Security asked.

"None. The entity seems…" The President was at a loss for words.

A loud *boom* sounded at the entrance to the Situation Room. Everyone near that end of the table—including Vanessa—scurried away. *Boom.* Vanessa heard the Secret Service agents chattering to each other over their radio feeds. Their colleagues must have been out in the hall, watching the attack. Why didn't they stop it? She heard the muffled stutter of automatic gunfire on the other side of the door.

Boom. Whatever the agents outside were doing, it made no difference to the invader. Previously hidden weapons came out of dark jackets. The President's bodyguards pushed him to the back of the room.

Boom-crack. This time, the heavy metal door gave way just a bit.

Silence.

Had the agents out in the hall finally finished the intruder off? Had it given up?

A pale blue mist slipped through the newly created fissure in the heavy door. Voices shouted for everyone to hold their breath. It was a gas attack. They all crowded farther back into the room. Vanessa, holding her hand over her mouth like everyone else, watched as the pale blue mist, the color of a natural gas flame, slowly took shape at the far end of the room. The mist coalesced into the form of a human. The figure looked like a low-quality CG image of a man. No coloring, no shading. Indistinct features. When the man spoke, his voice was strong and steady. It carried no accent, in that it sounded like someone from mid-America. It also carried no hint of malice.

"Who sent the signal?" it asked.

The Secretary of State, clearly believing her role as spokesperson for the United States extended to aliens, stepped forward.

"We have many people, sending many signals all the time. We did not know until recently there were any other intelligent beings in the universe."

The blue man considered this. "Who sent the final signal?"

Final was a word that carried too many negative connotations for those in the room. Fearful mutterings rose. The Secretary soldiered on. "Can you describe the signal you're referring to?"

The man began to beep. The beeps were simple tones in a seemingly random rhythm. It took him about fifteen seconds to finish relaying the message.

"It will take some time for our experts to determine where—"

"I sent that," Vanessa said. The looks on everyone else's faces were priceless; Vanessa wished she had a camera. "That was the shut down sequence for *Voyager*. The final signal. I sent it two nights ago."

The blue man turned to Vanessa, everyone else in the room now forgotten. "You must answer the question."

"The... question?"

"Do you wish the barrier restored?"

Slowly, a smile sneaked across Vanessa's features. She understood now. The heliopause barrier was not designed to keep humanity in the dark. It was designed for *protection*. There had to be a thousand, ten thousand, maybe a million different civilizations out there in the galaxy, and nearly every one of them was far more advanced than humanity. The barrier had been placed around the Solar System in an effort to let humanity evolve and grow. When they had the ability—and the desire—to venture far enough from their home to break the barrier, they were given the opportunity to join the galactic civilization... or not.

It was the answer to the age-old question, sometimes attributed to Enrico Fermi: "Where are they?" If intelligence was common, or even just rare, then the galaxy had to be littered with aliens, sending messages, al-

tering the luminosity of their stars, leaving behind footprints of their passage, footprints made of light—radio transmissions.

Some assumed the darkness of the heavens meant that humanity was
unique. Life is precious, these people would say, intelligence more precious still. The only interstellar civilization will be ours.

Others, unwilling to accept the uniqueness of man, posited elaborate
theories for why other intelligences remained so silent: point-to-point communication schemes, societies driven underground, alien cultures approaching technological singularity and winking out of normal existence
into an alternate state of being.

The truth was far simpler. They weren't missing and they weren't silent. They were out there all the time, loud and obvious, just as they
should have been. We simply couldn't hear them. They were hidden from
us, patiently waiting for *us* to make contact with *them*.

And now, humans had broken the barrier themselves, though by accident. Accidents of this type had to be common in the galaxy. If humanity wasn't yet ready to expand their understanding of the universe to this
extent, they could decide to remain hidden. Theoretically, they could lock
themselves away and *never* talk to another extraterrestrial again.

How many civilizations might have taken that path? How many bar-
riers remained in place around shy solar systems, their inhabitants living
quiet, bucolic, insular lives?

And how many more had taken the plunge, had allowed themselves
to be part of something *greater*?

"But…" Vanessa said, suddenly daunted by the scale of the decision.
"You don't want to talk to me."

"You sent the message," the blue man said again. "You controlled the
spacecraft."

"Well… I suppose that's true."

The others standing behind Vanessa came to life again, realizing the
importance of the conversation. The President came forward to talk to
the blue figure.

"I'm sure you understand," he intoned, "that we have a hierarchical
structure to our society. Miss Hargrove is a member of my team."

"I am?" Vanessa asked.

"JPL is a government entity," he said, still smiling for the blue man.

"Not really," Vanessa persisted, momentarily forgetting she was contradicting the President of the United States. "It's funded by—"

"Vanessa," Shao warned.

The blue man raised one ghostly hand and pointed at Vanessa. "She will answer."

Silence dropped, except for the continuing, muffled sounds of desperate military personnel still trying to break into the Situation Room through the non-functional door. Vanessa turned to the others in the room. She almost asked for a show of hands. She almost asked for each person's best pitch. Should the barrier be replaced or allowed to fall? In twenty-five words or less, please. Most of the faces looking at her seemed to be pleading with their eyes.

It's too much. It's too fast. We can't handle it.

Vanessa wasn't naïve enough to imagine that the galaxy was a utopian wonderland filled with benevolent creatures with uniformly pure motives. There had to be danger out there. But there was also some sense of order. If what she understood about the barrier was true, someone had put it there, specifically to shield the Earth from the rest of the galaxy until such a time that they were ready—or at least *possibly* ready—to interact with other civilizations. And more, the rest of the galaxy had *conformed* to this order. Maybe Earth was too backward to offer anything of value to these advanced societies. Maybe most of them didn't even know Earth *existed* until today. Vanessa imagined that if the forces at work in the galaxy could be capable of such a compassionate act as protecting the Earth from intrusion for a few thousand years, then the dangers they would face would be manageable.

It's too much. It's too fast. We can't handle it.

Vanessa had more faith in humanity than that. She turned back to the visitor.

"Let the barrier fall," she said to the blue figure.

The man nodded once, then dissipated in a flash of super-cooled air that blew across Vanessa like an ocean breeze.

Snake Oil

> *How unsound and insincere is*
> *he who says, I have determined to*
> *deal with thee in a fair way!—*
> *What art thou doing, man? There*
> *is no occasion to give this notice. It*
> *will soon show itself by acts.*
> *—Meditations, XI, 15*

The ship detected the telltale quicklight beacon of a collapsing co-coon. She calculated the distance to the emerging system and plotted a best-fit, meta-G trajectory, taking into account local variations in the galactic gravity fields. The ship knew that time was critical in such a trip. Arrival more than thirty million ticks after the breach of the cocoon would be a waste of her fuel. The sooner the better was the key for such a visit. This newly revealed star, shining brightly with fresh radio waves baking off the third planet, lay less than a third of a trillion d's along this arm of the galaxy. A single pulse from the ship's drive would put them inside the system's comet cloud in almost no time.

After activating her appropriate life support functions, the ship turned her attention away from navigation and into her interior, to her captain's sleep chamber. With a single command, she began the arousal process. Her captain's lids fluttered, opening to reveal bright, red eyes.

News of the torrent of strange signals raining down on the world through a hole in the sky could not be hidden from the bulk of humanity for long. Many drivers searching their radio dials for traffic updates or Top 40 music found a continuous squeal of horrendous noise from one end of the AM and FM bands to the other. Those with memberships to one of a dozen satellite radio providers were not immune; they lost con-nectivity to their digital channels entirely.

The zone of noticeable effect was small in those early days, passing over the planet like the umbra of an eclipse. Still, millions knew something was happening on a grand scale in the heavens. It impacted millions of cell phones, thousands of wireless internet coverage areas, a handful of televisions not attached to a cable provider and still receiving broadcasts on the old frequencies. Some significant percent of these people had the knowledge and wherewithal to seek out the pertinent information on the internet. E-mails and text messages and IMs and even the occasional face-to-face conversation did the trick. The fact—that Earth was about to be abruptly introduced to the much larger society of the galaxy—filtered out of government research facilities and universities to people all over the globe. Within four days much of the world knew the facts, if not the truth, of the situation. Facts are always easier to find than truth, anyway.

Bernie Lefkowicz, on the other hand, received both the facts *and* the truth in a very different way.

Bernie was, not to put too fine a point on it, a loser. At the age of forty-one years, he had no job, no wife, no kids, no prospects, no nothing. He had a doting mother with whom he had lived for all of those forty-one years and he had a mountain of debt that would have given the US Treasury Department a case of the shivers.

Mrs. Lefkowicz's home was in the middle of Omaha: a tired old home on a tired old street in a tired old city. Doris Lefkowicz had only the one son, the light of her life. She, a diminutive woman with stark white hair and an ungainly walk due to a childhood bout with scoliosis, had only the fondest hopes for Bernie. At least out loud. Deep down in the darkest, most selfish part of her otherwise charitable mother's heart, she was glad that Bernie still lived at home. He was her baby, and now that Mr. Lefkowicz had left this world—God rest his soul—Bernie was all she had.

Bernie was a shambling tower of a man—not strictly obese, just very, very large. He stood six-foot-seven, sported broad shoulders, and carried his three hundred fifty pounds in an uneasy combination of muscle and fat that had, through his thirties, shifted to a higher fat ratio than his historical norm. As he sailed the waters of his forties, that ratio was shifting again, since his weight was dropping, for reasons that had nothing to do with exercise or diet. Thankfully for the dozens of people he interacted with each day—on the bus, at the hospital, at the drugstore—he was also a kindly sort. Bernie had very rarely in his life lost his temper to rage.

After attempting a college education in his early twenties, Bernie was left with no degree and a truckload of credit card debt. This was not particularly unusual for children of his generation—or any other generation familiar with credit cards, for that matter. Bernie picked away at the debt for years while toiling in a series of uninspiring jobs ranging from barista at Starbucks to meter reader for the Omaha Gas Company. Strangely, despite diligently sending in the minimum required payments to Visa every month, Bernie's debt continued to grow.

It wasn't as if he lived an extravagant lifestyle. He never paid rent. Though he ate large amounts of food, it was rarely of high quality. He splurged on the occasional skin mag, cleverly hidden from his mother under the floorboards of his childhood room. But the debt still grew.

Bernie's overall situation may have begun under the too-sheltering wing of his mother, and may have been exacerbated by a personality heavy on love of leisure and light on ambition, but Bernie's *present* situation was, in the final analysis, no one's fault. Bernie had cancer. Pancreatic cancer, to be precise. Adenocarcinoma, to be ruthlessly precise.

The doctors were nearly as ruthless as the disease itself. An unresectable tumor—as Bernie's had become—called for chemotherapy and/or radiation. Recent advances in both of these lines of treatment made the doctors even more aggressive about attacking Bernie's cancer fast and hard. Bernie's mom invariably agreed with the treatment suggestions. They were nearly as unpleasant as they were expensive, but Bernie had to agree that if they saved his life, so much the better.

Lackluster medical coverage from his last job—as an e-mail mass marketing clerk—combined poorly with experimental cancer treatments. Soon enough, Mrs. Lefkowicz's savings were gone and their family worth had taken on the properties of a black hole, invisibly sucking everything good into a vortex of nothingness.

Were Bernie more of a man of action, he might have simply killed himself and saved his mother the trouble of trying to maintain his ever-worsening life. Instead, he crashed into an alien.

Bernie's car was a decade-old Chevy, which he kept running mostly on hope. The drive from his mother's home to the drug store was one of the few routes he took on a regular basis. On this day, Monday, April 26, Bernie drove his off-purple car down Third. He had the sun visor down, since it was a bright spring day. He did not see the bizarre flash of black streaking down from the sky to land directly in his path. The car bounced once, rattling Bernie's teeth in his head. He slammed on the brakes, the screech of metal on metal reminding him he needed new brake pads.

In the rear view mirror, he saw no indication of what he hit. He checked the side views as well. Just an empty street on a lazy weekday mid-morning. He allowed himself a moment for his heart to calm before putting the car back into drive. Movement in the rear view mirror caused his gaze to shift.

The first reaction his already fevered mind brought forward was that a werewolf was climbing onto his car. He saw fur and fangs and beady red eyes. Those details said *werewolf* to Bernie. But the creature had *hands*, not clawed paws. It stood tall, tall as a man. It was also quite slender, narrower in the torso than even his saintly little mother.

Bernie struggled to fend off a fainting spell as the midnight-black… thing… shook off the trauma of its collision with the Chevy. The thing used strangely human hands to dust off its shiny fur. Its blood-red eyes locked with Bernie's in the mirror. Bernie nearly had a heart attack.

The furry man-thing, which Bernie now saw wore a dark girdle of a sort around its narrow, straight waist, slunk around the back of his car, toward the driver's door. The idea of it as a sort of wolf-man vanished with the sinuous nature of its movement. Now it looked like nothing other than a huge, man-sized snake. A black, furry, girdled snake. With arms. As it reached Bernie's window, which was open to let in the breeze, it curled down to bring its wide mouth, ringed with yellowish gray teeth, to Bernie's level.

"No hard feelings, mate," the snake said, offering a horrifyingly toothy smile.

Bernie promptly fainted.

When Bernie came to, he lay on a park bench, less than a block from the place on the street where he encountered the man-snake. He sat up with a start. He saw that his car was carefully parked by the side of the road. He checked his own body for any snake-ish molestations that might have occurred. Everything seemed to be fine. He wondered if he might have had some sort of chemotherapy-induced hallucination. He should ask Dr. Srinivasan about that at his next...

Bernie's head swiveled to the right with horror-movie slowness. Coiled on the grass in a circle the size of a small Jacuzzi was the furry, black man-snake. Its head rose gracefully from the center of the coil and it held out its hands in a gesture of peace.

"Everything is jake, mate," the snake said.

"Sssss..." Bernie tried to say *snake*, but couldn't seem to find any vowels to add to the sibilant. The snake squinted its eyes and frowned.

"You speak English, right?" it asked. Bernie found the courage to nod. "Not a mute or something, are you then?" Bernie shook his head. He had the barest realization that the monster spoke with an accent, like it was from England or someplace.

The snake lifted its body to a fuller height, leaving only a yard or so of its coiled body on the lawn. It smiled again, though not so toothily as before. "I would like to introduce myself, but I'm afraid I do not have a name that you would find convenient to pronounce. I have learned that it is best for a new species to assign me a name. What would you like to call me?"

Bernie sat still, mouth open, panting like a goldfish dropped from its bowl. That image, of a poor little fish struggling and thrashing on the title floor of a kitchen, inevitably brought to mind a cat, a black cat, carefully pawing its way over to the helpless and tasty morsel. The man-snake did slightly resemble a cat, around its eyes and its tightly pinched nose. Black cat. A big, talking, black cat.

"Sylvester," Bernie said.

"Sylvester," the snake repeated. "Sylvesssster," it said again, playing up the sibilant. It swayed a bit, cobra-like, as it did so. Then it stopped and lowered closer to Brian's level. "Sorry about that, mate. I like it. I am, for Earth's purposes, Sylvester."

Bernie swallowed. Propriety, a virtue his mother had taught him well, indicated he introduce himself now. "My name is—"

"Your name is Bernard Lefkowicz, my good man. I know you only too well!"

On the drive back home, Sylvester sat in the passenger seat next to Bernie. His body was curled in three layers of tight coils. Only a tiny bit of his tail draped off the seat toward the dingy floor mat. He explained, in his remarkably erudite way, that Earth was no longer shaded from the view of everyone else in the galaxy. Bernie was understandably shocked.

"You hadn't heard?" Sylvester asked. Bernie shook his head. "Note to self: communication protocols," the snake muttered.

"How do you know me?" Bernie asked. For an alien to seek him out on a planet of several billion people seemed… unlikely. There was nothing Bernie could offer to a… person who could travel between the stars in a spaceship.

"I know you because I have what you need. In fact, I have what *many* need, but you need it more than most, Bernard."

"You can call me Bernie," he said, offering the snake a tentative smile. Sylvester returned the smile in kind. Bernie's smile wilted at the sight of those teeth. "And Sylvester? I should talk to Ma before you meet her. Okay?"

Bernie pulled the car into his driveway and hopped out, slamming the car door in his haste. He watched, revolted and fascinated, as Sylvester followed him right through the open driver's side window and onto the lawn.

"Wait here. Please."

Sylvester nodded. Bernie ran into the house.

"There's no need to run indoors, Bernie," Ma called from the kitchen. Bernie instinctively slowed his pace as he moved through the front hall into the kitchen, where he knew Ma would be preparing lunch. They usually had sandwiches, and today she was making up tuna melts with American cheese. Bernie's stomach did a queasy flip. His last chemo session was only two days ago. Ma was supremely confident that giving Bernie his old favorites was the best way to speed his recovery. Bernie— or at least Bernie's stomach—didn't always agree.

"Ma, I met someone." That announcement made Mrs. Lefkowicz's head twist around with comical speed. She nearly dropped the bowl of tuna and mayonnaise to the floor.

"A girl?" she asked. To Mrs. Lefkowicz, a female friend of her son would never be a *woman*, merely a *girl*. He was her *boy*, after all, regardless of his age.

"No. He's... He's..." Bernie searched for the words to explain Sylvester. He watched his mother toy with the frightening idea that her only son might be *gay*. Bernie wanted to head that line of thinking off quickly. "Something has happened. It's... The scientists have found something."

"What are you prattling about, Bernie?" She returned to her cooking, spooning almonds and carrots into the bowl the way Bernie liked.

"It's aliens. There are aliens out there. Lots of them. Millions. The scientists found them."

As a fan of *Star Trek* and *Stargate* and *Star Wars*—in fact, anything with "Star" in the title—Bernie's conversations often took on a geeky cast. Mrs. Lefkowicz knew this only too well, and smiled serenely as Bernie sputtered.

"I'm sure there are, Bernie. You want milk with lunch? Or Tang? I have a new batch cooling in the fridge... right..." Ma trailed off, her hands dipping to the point that more almonds dropped into the tuna than any self-respecting mother should allow. Bernie turned to see that Sylvester had decided waiting on the lawn wasn't the best use of his time.

"Mrs. Lefkowicz, allow me to introduce myself." Sylvester slithered around Bernie toward her, his furry body making a soft rustling sound on the linoleum. He was kind enough to stop on this side of the kitchen table, rather than invading Ma's personal space the way he had Bernie's. Sylvester, it seemed, learned from his mistakes. "I am a visitor to your world. I would be delighted if you would call me Sylvester."

He offered a hand for Mrs. Lefkowicz to shake.

Doris Lefkowicz had lived through tough times. She'd watched JFK's funeral on TV. She'd seen endless reports on the Vietnam War. The whole miserable Cold War, from beginning to end. Oklahoma City. 9/11. Boise. She'd buried her husband and carried her son through his terrible, terrible illness. She'd borne it all with a stoic, Midwestern, Protestant calm. And if it was her fate to live through an alien invasion, for what could this creature be, but an alien, as her Bernie had explained, she would weather that just as she had weathered everything else.

She shook the alien's hand and said, "Do you like tuna, Mr. Sylvester?"

It took both Bernie's and Sylvester's best efforts—as they sat around the kitchen table and ate tuna melts—to explain to Doris that, in fact, there was no invasion. Sylvester was simply the first of what would be many visitors from elsewhere to come to Earth. When that realization settled in, Doris's skepticism reared up.

"Why are you here?"

"Why, you ask?" Sylvester cooed, bobbing his head in a friendly way. "Because I hope to bring an end to young Bernard's suffering."

A surge of hope filled Doris's heart, followed by a crash of logic.

"In exchange for what?" she asked icily.

"Nothing at all."

Doris squinted at the snake. Though she was the second most experienced person on the planet with the snake's species—Bernie being the first—her expectation of reading his truthfulness was low indeed. She could not imagine what sort of tells a creature such as Sylvester might have. On the other hand, she knew a con man when she saw one, in any form.

"I don't believe you."

Bernie gasped at his mother's audacity. The snake, however, smiled. It would have seemed a friendly smile, if not for the frightening nature of his teeth.

"You have caught me in a half-truth, Mrs. Lefkowicz. I expect no *monetary* payment for this service."

"But you do expect something from us."

"From Bernard, in particular."

"Me?" Bernie sat up a little straighter in his chair.

"You're not taking Bernie away from me!" A fierce, animalistic mother's protectiveness came from Doris in a way that was almost scarier than Sylvester's smile. He waved off her concerns with his jet black hands.

"I will now be completely honest with you both. Is that alright?"

Bernie nodded. Doris thought through the request for a moment before agreeing as well.

"I plan to cure Bernard's cancer. The cure is not only free, it is painless and entirely without risk. In fact, it is also quite instantaneous. The only thing I ask in return is your word that you will tell everyone you know that I have done this."

Doris frowned, nodding in understanding. "You'll give it to *us* for free, but others will have to pay huge amounts of money!"

"That is not true. I will charge others for this cure, yes, but only what they can afford, I assure you." Sylvester swayed a bit from side to side.

"How do we know?" Bernie asked. Doris favored him with a bright, proud smile for his question.

"Because, Bernard, were I to bring the second person I cure to the brink of bankruptcy, where would the third customer come from? My standard rate is one quarter of the household's yearly income. This fee is, of course, waived for you." He smiled again, keeping his teeth nearly hidden this time.

Emboldened by his first question, Bernie pressed Sylvester further. "How can you possibly have a cure for cancer? You only heard about us four days ago."

"I learned about the opening of a new cocoon four days ago; I didn't receive the Central Authority memo until your leader agreed to leave the barrier down, which was two days ago."

"You found a cure for our worst disease in only two days?" Bernie asked, half suspicious, half filled with wonder.

"Nearly all life in the galaxy is cellular. Unchecked cellular growth is a common enough malady for all such species, mine included." Sylvester reached one hand around to a section of his back, which appeared to open like a pocket. Out of this he pulled a small, stoppered vial filled with clear liquid. He set the vial down on the table with a tiny *clink*. "This is—how shall I translate it?—a cellular calming agent. With the information in the memo, I was easily able to shift the chemical nature of the agent to fit Earth biochemistry. I will sell this agent—at the entirely reasonable rate that I mentioned earlier—to as many people as I can find with terminal illnesses of the appropriate type."

"Why not just sell it once to a pharmaceutical company?" Bernie asked. Sylvester shivered with what Bernie assumed was surprise.

"And wait for years while they test it and test it and test it again? It is *safe*. I have used this agent, only slightly modified, on a dozen worlds, on millions of individuals, with nary a single complication."

"It can't be that simple," Doris said.

"Mrs. Lefkowicz, very little about the next few years will be simple for Earth, I assure you. This, however, is an exception. I urge you to let your son take the agent. He will be cured, and likely become a celebrity in the bargain. I will make my tidy and entirely well deserved fortune. More importantly, your entire race will be better off. What can I say to allay your fears?"

Doris pursed her lips, taking her measure of the alien, and sending one last look at her beloved son. She reached for the vial. Before Bernie could so much as shout her name, she pulled off the stopper and swallowed the liquid.

"There! I'll be the one to die, not my dear Bernie."

"Ma!"

"It's alright, son. I've had a good life. I only wished I could have been here for you longer."

Bernie and his mother shared a long look, both thinking it would be their last. After a time, they realized that nothing had happened. Doris looked at Sylvester.

"You don't have cancer, Mrs. Lefkowicz. The agent will do nothing to you." He reached around to his back pocket and pulled out another, identical vial. This time he handed it directly to Bernie. "Your turn, Bernard."

Bernie, with a quick, almost guilty look at his mother, downed the oily liquid. It didn't taste bad. In fact, it didn't taste like anything at all. He waited for some kind of bizarre sensation: burning or tingling or intense cold. There was nothing. After a few moments he said as much to Sylvester.

"The agent has stopped the cancer from further growth. I'm afraid you still have existing tumors in your body, but they are now all entirely benign. You will need to consult a doctor to determine if and when they should be removed."

Sylvester slithered off the kitchen chair and moved toward the front door.

"Wait!" Bernie called. "That's it?"

Sylvester's head swiveled to face Bernie. "Was there something else you needed?"

"I…"

"Tell everyone. Remember."

"I will."

And Sylvester left, thoughtfully closing the front door behind him.

Bernie and his mother rose from their seats and came together in a joyous hug. They would visit Dr. Srinivasan later that day, and he would test Bernie seemingly endlessly to confirm that, yes, the tumors in his pancreas had stopped dead in their tracks. He would, in fact, assure Bernie that surgery would not be required, though he would beg Bernie to consent to one anyway, for the research value the now-benign tumors would provide. Bernie would politely decline.

In this moment, however, both mother and son knew in their hearts that the snake had told them the truth, that Bernie was cured. Doris could think of nothing but joy and thankfulness to God that such a strange angel had come to their home.

Bernie could think of nothing but how to turn this story into a way to meet girls.

Youngblood

How ridiculous and what a stranger he is who is surprised at anything which happens in life.
—*Meditations, XII, 13*

The best thing about the Lockheed-Hyundai G-11 orbit vehicle was that it worked in the atmosphere at any speed up to and including the hypersonic just as well as it worked in the near-vacuum of space. Wherever you were, you knew what you were getting. The worst thing about the G-11 was that it did neither of these things with any flash or style. It was a workhorse, pure and simple.

This flight, on Monday morning, April 26, 2021, was Captain Terry Youngblood's first ground-to-orbit test of the new machine.

Four weeks ago, Terry began the live test phase for the G-11 project. He performed one station-to-orbit run, putting a space-ready version of the craft through its paces in a sequence of five circuits around the planet.

Three weeks ago he flew two air-to-ground tests, riding in the belly of a C-191 Airlifter up into the stratosphere before being ejected from the monstrous plane like a newly birthed whale calf. The landings at the ends of these tests were marked by neither accident nor poetry, as far as Terry was concerned.

A week ago he'd completed a single air-to-orbit test, taking the G-11 from out of the Airlifter and flying up into orbit, parking the machine next to the other G-11 prototype, which was still docked at the ISS-2 station from the earlier test. This wasn't Terry's first time into space... but it was his first time flying up there *solo*. The only downside was a cramped and bumpy ride back down to Earth in one of the Orion return stages.

This morning, rested and recovered from last week's unpleasant return to the ground, he took off from the runway at the test facility outside of Saugus in a third G-11. For this test—ground-to-orbit—Terry flew the craft under its own power through the various layers of the atmosphere and into the somewhat empty reaches of low Earth orbit, or LEO as the techies liked to call it, their fondness for acronyms knowing no bounds.

"Masie, Pacifica. *We show you on nominal trajectory.*"

Pacifica was the handle of the newer of the two International Space Stations. *Masie*, unfortunately, was the nickname of this third G-11. The other prototypes he had flown were named *Jeanette* and *Beulla*; he supposed *Masie* wasn't too bad a handle compared to *Beulla*.

"*Pacifica, Masie.* I read you five by five."

While the G-11 wasn't as smooth a performer as the F-35s he'd flown for the Air Force over the past couple of years, it did make the transition from aeronautical to space vehicle without a hitch. *Masie's* attitude thrusters subtly came on line, providing a steadily increasing, stabilizing force as the airfoils became less effective in the high, sparse atmosphere. More importantly to Terry, the controls didn't shift into some archaic NASA configuration once he hit orbit. The designers of this craft had a clear sense of how a pilot thought, and set up the cockpit accordingly. He imagined that a few decades of video game culture might have also had something to do with that.

Terry brought the G-11 higher, pushing her into a faster orbital path as *Pacifica* passed above him. He caught just a glimpse of the awkwardly put-together station a few miles up. Dozens of blocky, mismatched modules were strung together like a necklace a four-year-old might make in preschool art class. The station managers were just as proud as that four-year-old, and the bigwigs on Earth praised it just like that kid's doting parent. Terry thought its jutting corners and awkward angles made docking a chore. Also, it was butt ugly.

Below, the wide, smooth expanse of the Pacific Ocean told him he had almost completed a single circuit of the Earth. Three more trips around the globe and this test flight would be complete, followed by a meticulous docking with *Pacifica*, followed by yet another head-rattling Orion transit back home. *Masie* wasn't configured for a return into the atmosphere. The ground-to-orbit-to-ground test wasn't scheduled to happen for a couple weeks yet.

The G-11 was the next phase in human space development: a true *shuttle* from the Earth's surface to LEO. For all the grand beauty of the

STS program from the last century, that monster took off like a rocket from a launch pad, a controlled explosion of fuel that literally shoved the Space Shuttle up to the lip of the Earth's gravity well. It was a necessary step, but it was expensive and dangerous and had survived well past its design life. The current Orion program was a step even *further* backward, into the quaint Apollo age of capsules and descent stages.

What *Masie* could do was far more elegant. She left the ground like any other plane, gently exiting the atmosphere, then docked with stations in space. A G-11 could carry twenty passengers, or a similar mass and volume of supplies. Its liquid hydrogen fuel was potent enough to make the round trip journey with no help from outboard tanks or station refueling. This craft was Earth's next step if they ever planned to go to the stars.

The stars were on *everybody's* minds now, what with the phenomenon the blogs were calling "the hole in the sky". Terry got an earful about it just after his Orion landing last week. Seems someone punched a hole in some barrier that had kept Earth safe from all the other civilizations out there. The news had caused a ruckus, alright. Terry ignored it, for the most part. So there were ETs out there after all. Good for them. Any decent scientist knew that the speed of light was too slow to allow any of them to visit Earth for a few dozen years at least. Terry kept tightly focused on the G-11 project; little else impacted him.

A bright flash in the sky ahead and below caught Terry's attention. He put the G-11 into a roll, filling his canopy with the Earth, to get a better view. A streak of burning atmosphere showed the path of a meteor. Terry noted that some trick of the light made it look like the meteor was slowing down. He oriented himself with respect to the ground to get a sense of where the chunk of rock might land, if it survived the descent at all: smack-dab in the middle of North America, maybe in the Dakotas.

A warning bell rang in Terry's ear. His training on the craft was still so fresh in his mind he knew the meaning of that warning without having to read the label on the corresponding light that was blinking away on his control panel. It was a proximity alarm. He brought up a scanning program on his small OLED computer screen to look at the radar signature of whatever piece of debris had triggered the alarm. On the screen, a field of sky blue represented his local parcel of space—a singularly inappropriate color choice from the L-H designers. The blue was marred by only a bare speck of yellow. Whatever the radar had found, it appeared to be very small. Which didn't make sense, since the collision detection protocols were designed to ignore anything with a mass too small to significantly impact the G-11. Random bits of space junk—snips of wire left behind by an untidy satellite repairman, a stray glove from an old STS flight, an ancient bolt out of a Gemini craft—would bounce off of *Masie*'s sturdy hull without leaving a scratch.

As a last resort, Terry looked out of his canopy. He hadn't expected to see anything, and he wasn't surprised. He saw the bright Earth below and the black, star-speckled sky above. That was it.

"*Pacifica, Masie.* I've got a proximity warning here, but I think it might be a glitch. Can you verify?"

"Masie, Pacifica. *Hold please.*"

Terry continued to work through his test plans, monitoring *Masie*'s progress on the flight. He allowed the alarm bell to ring so he wouldn't forget about the "danger".

He started singing softly to himself: "Older now but not much wiser for your miles... your misspent life spread out for your review..." He caught himself and stopped. That old song had gotten stuck in his head when a remake hit the radio last month.

Even after he stopped, Terry seemed to still hear the tune playing, echoing in his head the way songs do. He silently cursed the band and that killer hook, and kept on with his system checks.

"*...matter of no substance and too little style... cut adrift from a past you never knew, nothing new...*"

Wait a minute. That wasn't just his mind replaying the song. That *was* the song. And not a remake either. That was the original, back from... Wow. That was from back in the 1990s! Terry was about to call *Pacifica* and congratulate them on a well-executed—and entirely uncharacteristic—prank. They called him first.

"Masie, Pacifica. *Please keep this channel clear.*"

"But I didn't—" He tried to claim ignorance of where the music was coming from when the *Pacifica* comm officer rode over both him and the still playing music.

"*We have confirmation of a radar signature at eleven-point-three klicks from your current position, relative speed zero.*"

Relative speed zero? There was a piece of space garbage in *exactly* his orbit, just a few kilometers away? That didn't seem likely.

"*...Now you're in the wrong place at the perfect time... complications anything but kind...*"

"Masie, Pacifica. *This channel is for official communi—*"

The music dropped out and another voice entered the conversation. "*Is Masie your name, or the name of your vessel? Or both?*"

That new voice, loud enough to drown out any other chatter on the frequency, was *not* from *Pacifica*. Terry knew all the radio operators on the station. Only one was a woman, and she had a thick Romanian accent. This voice was that of a lilting, younger woman, with a bit of English in her tone.

"Identify yourself," Terry said.

"*I have no local designation as yet. I am the craft now directly ahead of you in your orbit of Earth.*"

In an instant Terry switched from laid-back test pilot to efficient, logical warrior. He knew from textbooks that the current tensions between the US and China were nothing nearly as bad as the Cold War with the Soviets back in the Twentieth. Terry hadn't even been born when the Germans gleefully tore down the Berlin Wall and put an end to all that foolishness. Still, the Chinese weren't to be taken lightly. If he was in contact with a Chinese spy ship, the next few moments would be critical.

Something about the way the woman spoke—perhaps it was that British precision to her pronunciation—made Terry think she wasn't Chinese. Indian, maybe? India had a limited space program, as did the Japanese. Of course, she might be European as well. Terry's head was stuffed full of possible scenarios to explain this situation, and yet, he never expected to hear what came through his headset next.

"*I am, I believe, the first ship to visit your planet from outside this system.*"

"Masie, Pacifica. *This is not amusing. Please limit your—*"

"Hold your water, *Pacifica!*" Terry wasn't sure, but he could have sworn he heard a chuckle on the band from the mystery ship. "Unidentified craft, I'm having a hard time believing you're on an alien ship."

"*I understand. Wait a moment.*"

Terry waited. He wasn't used to being idle in space, but this was an unusual situation, to say the least. If this was a hoax, maybe perpetrated by one of those space tourism companies, it was an elaborate hoax, and one that would have their launch privileges yanked in a heartbeat.

"Masie, Pacifica! *Collision imminent!*" The tone of panic used by the radio operator on *Pacifica* alerted Terry more effectively than the actual words. He checked his own radar. The point source wasn't eleven klicks away anymore. It was *five.* Then three. He looked out of his canopy but saw nothing at all rushing toward him.

"Preparing emergency burn!" Terry announced, flipping the appropriate switches and turning the needed dials to push the G-11 into a higher, hopefully safer orbit.

"*That is not necessary,*" the interloper said in her calm, soothing voice. "*Can you not see me?*"

Terry verified that the anomaly—still only a tiny point on his radar—was holding at a little under seven hundred meters away. He scoured the sky, but he saw nothing. If this "alien" ship was so tiny that he couldn't even see it from...

His eye was drawn to the ethereal blue glow of the atmosphere on the edge of the gigantic disc of the Earth. Part of that glow was eclipsed by a sliver of pure, slightly curved blackness. His eyes extrapolated what that tiny slice of black would look like when extended to a full circle, much the same way the eye automatically fills a crescent moon with the rest of its shape.

This was no tiny ship. Now he noticed that there were stars missing from the sky, occulted in a very wide disc.

"I see you... sort of."

This time the laugh from the voice was unmistakable. "*My apologies! I misread the memo. I will adjust.*"

Inside the phantom black disc, a lurid, deep purple orb emerged, sliding up out of the ultra-violet into a frequency visible to Terry. Based on his distance and the apparent size of the object, it looked to be about fifty meters in diameter, a fair bit larger than an STS orbiter, mammoth compared to a G-11. What's more, it was a perfect sphere, its surface so smooth and featureless it looked like a computer simulation rather than a physical object.

"*Is this better?*"

"Yeah. Much better." Terry could hear fevered mutterings from several voices on *Pacifica* who could see the alien ship from their higher vantage point. "So... you're from outer space?"

"*Yes, I am. I was alerted to the opening of your cocoon recently. My captain is currently on the surface.*"

"Your captain? Who are you?"

"*I am the ship. As I understand it, your culture has not yet developed non-biological intelligence. Am I correct?*"

Terry felt his extremities go cold. Beyond the very real concern that he—and perhaps his entire race—might be in terrible danger, the sheer concept of talking to a thinking, alien ship affected him so deeply he had a physical reaction to the idea. Being a pilot—and a damn good one at that—was such a basic part of his psyche that he couldn't quite grasp a ship that was its own entity, requiring no direction from a person.

This was a first contact—or maybe second, if the ship was correct about her captain being down on the planet below. He needed to proceed carefully.

"My name is Captain Terry Youngblood, United States Air Force. And you are?"

"*As I said, I have no local designation. Please allow me to... I believe an appropriate name for me would be* Cat Carrier."

Cat Carrier? Terry wasn't sure he wanted to meet the captain of this vessel.

"Okay... You know, my daddy always said, 'Ceremony is for priests and the justice of the peace.' You mind if I call you *Carrier* for short?"

"*Certainly.*"

"What is it you want?"

"*My captain is an entrepreneur. He wishes to transact business with your race.*"

The first alien to visit Earth is a door-to-door salesman? Terry laughed aloud.

"*Did I say something amusing?*"

"No. Well, yes." Terry's discomfort with the sentient ship was falling away rapidly. Amazingly, he was warming to *Carrier.* "That's what your captain wants. What do *you* want?"

Silence on the radio worried Terry. Had he broken some galactic ta-boo by asking a ship about her desires? She certainly hadn't left his local space. She still hung there, less than a kilometer away, looking like God's own raspberry gobstopper.

"*Carrier?* Are you still there?"

"*Yes. I am quite taken aback by your question, Captain. My owner and I have visited several new worlds such as yours, and I have never been addressed in this manner.*"

"I'm sorry if I—"

"*Please! Do not apologize. It is a remarkable thing that you would ask after my thoughts. Other cultures are either inured to the concept of sentient space vessels, and disregard me as a vassal of my captain, or they are unable to grasp the concept and look at me with awestruck horror.*"

"Like Goldilocks said, we're just right."

The cascade of delicate laughter that flowed from the radio made Terry smile. That did it. He liked *Carrier.*

"So," he continued, "you think there's hope for us?"

"*Without a doubt, Captain.*"

Keira Desai

> *If a thing is difficult to be ac-*
> *complished by thyself, do not think*
> *that it is impossible for man: but if*
> *anything is possible for man and*
> *conformable to his nature, think*
> *that this can be attained by thyself*
> *too.*
> —*Meditations, VI, 19*

Keira gathered the forms from her desk, pondering large thoughts. Humans spend their lives skirting the shoals of paradox. The dichotomies of their existence, whether psychological, spiritual or even financial, form the basis of their psychology. The tension of opposites informs every deci-sion a person makes, from the tiniest choices (Bread or rice for dinner?) to the largest (Shall I marry this man?). Rare is the action that requires no sacrifice, however tiny. Such thoughts were appropriate at a time like this, she thought, scanning the forms which required only a single signa-ture for completion.

Keira Desai was special, not in that her life was not driven by the same tensions as others, for it was. She differed from many because she recognized these forces at work. She differed from most because, rather than ignoring or rejecting them, she embraced them. For example, she would miss this place, this university with its rituals and its sense of scholarly tradition. She would *not* miss the cramped carrel she had been assigned in a dusty corner of the Engineering Library.

As a child of a Hindu father and a Christian mother, the dichotomy of her religious background was strikingly obvious. Among her classmates and students were many who adhered to faith as a drowning woman would to a life preserver. She, instead, bypassed the situation by paying polite lip service to both her parents' faiths, while embracing neither. She understood this was not a solution, merely a way to ignore a source of tension and spend her emotional capital elsewhere.

Demographically, she was on the cusp of another divide, this based on the accident of her birth. She was born on December 31, 1999, the last day of the second millennium, at least according to the most commonly accepted definition of the term, if not the most accurate. As one of the very last women on the planet to be born into the Twentieth Century, she held a strange position as being a bridge from the past to the future. All the undergraduates swarming across the campus around her were, according to this wisdom, of a different breed than their older, stately professors. Keira found such sophistry a waste of time, but she acknowledged that the *culture* seemed to find it very important. Those born *before* the millennium were thought of as different than those born *after.* She fervently hoped such distinctions would fade, as the new century ripened. In all likelihood, the breaking of the barrier in the sky would likely become more of a turning point than an arbitrary mathematical curiosity of the Gregorian Calendar.

On a day-to-day basis, Keira faced cultural tension between her traditional native land of India and the dominant exporter of culture to the world, the United States. How many of the students filing through the halls of the engineering building wore saris? How many wore jeans?

She loved both lands with all her heart. India, the nation of her birth, and of her parents, and her parents' parents, held treasures that a lifetime of study could not fully encompass. Within a short ride from her apartment in Bengalūru were the beauties of the Lal Bagh, the grandeur of several well-known Gopurams, and the simplicity of handcrafted samosa in any of a hundred local eateries.

On the other hand, Keira relished much about America, particularly its music. Her vast collection—spanning jazz, blues and rock—had spilled over from one music player to three; she considered buying a fourth. A long-planned visit to New York in August of last year had not disappointed. The thrilling sounds of that most American of cities still rang in her ears all these months later.

As a prodigy of sorts in the field of materials engineering, Keira's most troublesome internal struggle was that between research and application. Her career as a graduate student at UVCE put heavy emphasis on the research side of that balance. Her desire to use that technical knowledge for the construction of vessels that would take wondrous journeys to the stars pulled her away from the ivory tower mindset of most of her professors. She believed—perhaps to her detriment as a student of engineering—that the true path of design should embrace both of these extremes, not simply one or the other. Research without application was cold, emotionless, dead. Application without research was ineffable, impractical, unworkable. When brought together, they could do anything.

However, the struggle that loomed largest in her life today, May 3, 2021, was altogether more pedestrian. She had to decide whether to continue her graduate work, eventually completing an advanced degree, or to escape from scholastic life into the world of corporate research and development. All things being equal, the choice would have been a simple one for Keira, who had always seen herself as a teacher to others. After *Voyager* tore a hole in the sky to reveal a complex and amazing universe of possibilities beyond her stellar doorstep, all things were definitely no longer equal. This was why she entered Dr. Nadimpali's office today, unsigned form in hand.

Keira confronted her advisor, a gentleman in his sixties with an overlarge belly and a somewhat jowly face. Though the man was seated, and Keira stood a considerable one hundred seventy-five centimeters tall before him, she felt an annoying metaphorical sensation of looking *up* to him. Dr. Nadimpali had that effect on students.

"You, of course, must make the choice. I cannot make it for you," he said. Despite the professor's bland words, Keira heard his statement thus: "*For you to choose a career of application rather than one of scholastic pursuit would be an affront to me.*"

"Do you think the work is beyond me?" Keira asked, bold as always.

Dr. Nadimpali peered over his circular spectacles at the sheet on his desk. It detailed the duties of an Associate Research Assistant, the position Keira had been offered by Maccha-Yantra Consortium. "You would no doubt excel." Translation: "*These duties are beneath you.*"

"May I ask your thinking?" Keira asked. If Dr. Nadimpali had an argument that didn't rely on his pedantic reverence for the University and its associated lifestyle of introspective thought and automatic revulsion of matters economic in nature, she wished to hear it.

The professor shifted his bulk uneasily in the creaky old leather chair. His pudgy fingers restlessly tapped the spotless blotter on his immaculate desk. Dr. Nadimpali found direct questions such as this trouble-some. He preferred to offer his opinions unasked, when it was possible to frame his thoughts as evanescent possibilities, rather than cold hard facts; it made retracting incorrect statements afterward much easier.

"I will be frank with you, Keira."

She forced herself not to smile at his inadvertent admission that he had not, until now, been honest with her.

"The world of private commerce is a very different one from university life. Your advancement will not be governed by your abilities as an engineer, but by your ability to successfully navigate the dangerous waters of interpersonal politics."

Keira's previous amusement suddenly skirted very close to anger.

"You believe I would not excel in such things?"

The professor leaned forward to underline his next statement. "I believe your technical skills are exceptional." Unsaid: "*Your personality is not so exceptional.*"

The young woman planted her hands firmly on the outer edge of the heavy, ancient desk and leaned to within a few centimeters of her advisor. She chose to end this ridiculous sparring session with the man and cut directly to the core of her desire to leave and join MYC. "Who will build the first ship to travel to the stars?" she asked, with only a ghost of a smile playing about her lips. "You? Or me?"

Dr. Nadimpali realized that one answer would be an invalidation of decades of devotion to his academic career and to his employer, UVCE. The other, however, would be a bald-faced lie. Neither sat well on his tongue, so he leaned back in his chair, silent.

This somewhat grim victory over her mentor did not please Keira, but neither was she displeased. She slid the final form across the desk toward Dr. Nadimpali. He sighed and pulled a pen from an ornate holder near the phone, signing his name to convey his agreement with Keira's decision to take an indeterminate leave of absence from her studies at UVCE.

Her mission accomplished, Keira saw no reason for further acrimony. She offered the professor a wide, sincere smile.

"Thank you."

Early Warning

> *...if thou shouldst suddenly be raised up above the earth, and shouldst look down on human things, and observe the variety of them how great it is, and at the same time also shouldst see at a glance how great is the number of beings who dwell all around in the air and the ether, consider that as often as thou shouldst be raised up, thou wouldst see the same things, sameness of form and shortness of duration.*
>
> *—Meditations, XII, 24*

Terry checked his watch, nervous in a way he hadn't been on his first solo flight, or on his first day of basic training, or on his one brief but memorable combat mission over Srinagar City. Not liking what his watch told him, he pressed harder on the gas pedal and strove to find a path through the clogged Washington traffic. He'd hoped that today, being a Sunday, the traffic wouldn't have been so thick. No such luck. I-395 was a parking lot.

He wasn't late for his meeting, at least not yet. But he was cutting things far too close. And this wasn't the kind of meeting you want to be late for.

There it was!

Exit 10A: Boundary Channel Drive/Pentagon North Parking.

He swerved across three lanes and snuck his pick-up onto the ramp just a foot or so in front of a big, black Escalade.

Terry hoped nobody particularly important was in the SUV he just cut off.

He had no idea what to expect from this meeting. That was how they did things in the military, and he'd gotten used to it. But he never liked it. Terry was a pilot. He liked to see what was coming. Rushing through the hallowed—and somewhat stuffy—halls of the Pentagon felt to Terry like flying blind into a cloud bank. Who knew what he might crash into? The only bearing Terry had was the name on the office door where he was headed: General Alexander Woodley, Chief of Staff of the United States Air Force.

True to its legendary status as an efficiently laid out office building, Terry found his target only six minutes after entering the building's north entrance. General Woodley's office was as fancy as his title suggested it might be: everything dark wood and leather and gold inlay. Terry gave his name to the young woman in the anteroom. He saw that this starched, stiff little woman outranked him; she was a major. Rather than announce his arrival with a phone call or a knock on the door, she typed something into her tablet. Apparently, intercoms were too old fashioned for this new, modern Air Force.

"You can go in now, Captain," she said.

Terry pulled open the door and entered the General's office. His eyes tried to adjust to the sunlight coming in through expansive windows at the back of the room, which threw the figures before him into shadow. He knew to address General Woodley first. The problem was he didn't know which dark figure was the General. Terry entered hat in hand, so saluting was not appropriate. Without any better plan, he stepped forward into the room, standing at attention.

"Welcome, Captain," the man standing behind the desk said. Now that he could see a little better, Terry recognized this as General Woodley from his long, lean face and unusually soft eyes. The man had done a little press over the years, though nothing like the number of conferences done by the Chairman.

"Thank you, sir," Terry said.

"I'm sure you know General McGaw," Woodley said, gesturing toward the man to Terry's left. Terry gasped as he turned to address General Reginald McGaw, a stocky, bald man with a hard, round face that, during all of those press conferences, always reminded Terry of Popeye.

He could almost see the corncob pipe sticking out of the man's mouth. "Chairman," Terry said breathlessly to the Chairman of the Joint Chiefs.

"Good to meet you, Captain." McGaw stretched his hand to Terry, who shook it manfully. Manfully was the only way to shake when offered such a firm grip, other than wincing with pain and staggering to the ground. Terry came dangerously close to doing just that before McGaw released his hand.

Woodley continued with the introductions. "This is General Brown."

Terry turned to his right to see a slim, no-nonsense sort of woman with short, brunette curls, wearing a pair of dark-framed glasses. Carol Brown was the Commander of AFSPC.

"Captain," she said, offering Terry a less bone-crushing handshake. Terry began to understand why he was here. If Space Command was involved, it probably had something to do with his run in with *Cat Carrier*. Brown's team handled pretty much anything the military did that went on above the atmosphere, whether it was related to satellites, intercontinental ballistic missiles, the Space Shuttle, or the G-11 program. It was also somewhat heartening to meet a slightly less important person, though she still wore four stars on that uniform of hers.

"And, of course, this is Wilky," General Woodley said, causing Terry's mouth to dry up again. Standing unobtrusively to the side was a slip of a man, dark red hair going unflatteringly bald from the top down, his eyes wide-spaced on his ugly face, his civilian suit terribly out of place in a room with so many uniforms.

The man leaned forward and said, in a voice so low that it was hard to hear, "Captain."

Terry shook the hand of the Secretary of Defense and answered, "Mr. Secretary." He then took a quick look around the room to make sure no one else was waiting in the wings, like the President, or maybe Pope Marcellus III.

General Woodley led them all over to a conference table that dominated one side of the expansive office. Terry carefully waited for all these high-ranking officials to sit before taking his own seat between General Brown and Secretary Wilkinson. He suppressed a nervous urge to run his hands back and forth across the mirror-smooth surface of the table.

Despite his stature, his quiet manner, and his lack of uniform, Adam Wilkinson immediately took over the meeting, turning to Terry in a friendly way.

"Captain Youngblood, I've read your report on your encounter with the alien craft in April."

"Yes, sir."

Wilky smiled, leaning in a little more. His tone was almost conspira-torial. "Very formal stuff, wouldn't you say?"

"Sir?"

Brown came to Terry's defense. "The Captain's report adhered to Air Force protocol, Mr. Secretary."

Wilky waved a hand to assure General Brown there was no offense intended. "I hoped to get a bit more of the human perspective directly from the Captain. His impressions, his feelings." Wilky addressed Terry again. "You were part of the third encounter with an alien intelligence in history."

"The second," McGaw argued.

"I don't agree, General," Wilky countered.

Terry watched, fascinated, as an argument—albeit a very *carefully* argued one—broke out between the three generals and Secretary Wilkin-son. Terry knew about the visitation at the White House by a blue, glow-ing alien apparition. That was just too bizarre and important an event to stay secret for long. The four bigwigs discussed briefly whether that blue gent was a real alien, or just some kind of interactive recording. Terry had an impulse to knock these high-ranking heads together. Whatever that blue guy was, it wasn't relevant to this meeting. Finally, the four of them agreed to disagree on the issue of the blue man, and returned to the task at hand.

Now Woodley took over: "Not counting the White House visitor, there have been at least three alien incursions in cislunar space since the *Voyager* incident."

"Three?" Terry asked, eyes wide. He'd only known about the one: *Cat Carrier.*

"The first was *Cat Carrier*. This was the second." Woodley handed copies of a photograph to each of them. From the awkward angle and poor framing, Terry suspected this was something shot with a cell phone.

It showed a sky at either sunrise or sunset, with a dark shape flying past. If not for the fact that the thing was partly *behind* the Memorial Arch, and therefore quite large, he'd have passed it off as a bird.

"This craft was seen by two hundred thirty people in St. Louis last week. It never appeared on any military or civilian radars."

"Joy rider," Terry said, forgetting for the moment that in this room he was to be seen and not heard.

Woodley took the outburst in stride, saying, "That's our assessment. This next one is a bit more ominous." The next round of pictures were of a much higher quality. They showed a black, vaguely star-shaped object hovering in the noon sky over a plowed field. Terry could easily imagine that thing whizzing around the screen in some sci-fi TV series.

"How big is it?" Terry asked. Woodley turned to Brown.

"We estimate it to be between thirty-five and fifty meters across, based on the size of the shadow. It didn't bounce radar, so we were never quite sure how high above the ground it was. It left the area before we could scramble fighters."

"Where was this?" Terry asked.

"Kincaid, Nebraska," she said. Terry shrugged, looking around the table at some very somber faces.

Wilky filled him in: "Kincaid is, at present, the location of the single highest concentration of nuclear armaments on the planet." Terry felt a shiver up and down his back. Missile silos, ICBMs, almost forgotten by the public so long after the end of the Cold War, but nonetheless jealously guarded and carefully maintained by the US as a last line of defense against total annihilation. The crew of this ship—if it even had a crew—didn't happen upon Kincaid by accident. They sought the place out, and found it with no problem at all. This was bad.

"And those are just the ones we know about," McGaw added in a gruff, displeased voice. To be fair, he always sounded gruff and displeased, further enhancing his similarity to Popeye.

The *Voyager* incident had answered the question, once and for all, of why the skies seemed so quiet. Now that they weren't anymore, thousands of people were studying the rain of overlapping alien radio transmissions right now, trying to get a clearer picture of what was going on out there in the galaxy. That angle was important, sure, but not the immediate concern of the Pentagon. For them, the arrival of actual ships and aliens was more important than radio signals. The barn door was open and anyone from anywhere could just zip down to Earth and take a peek. Maybe that's not all they'd take, either.

"Captain," Wilky said, "we're very concerned about our inability to monitor traffic into our solar system. The President has asked me to head up a commission to investigate the possibility of creating an early warning system to watch local space."

"I see, sir." Terry understood the idea perfectly. Like the advent of radar in the middle of WWII, some new technology was needed to keep up with the changing tactical realities of the post-*Voyager* world. He still wasn't sure why they were talking to *him*, though. He decided to take a shot at finding out. "What can I do to help, sir?"

General Woodley paused a moment, then reached down below the desk and pulled up a locked Halliburton. He set the heavy briefcase on the table, and fitted a key in the case's lock. He opened it and pulled out a red-banded folder. He passed a new set of pictures around the table.

Terry almost laughed. The creature in the picture looked like something from a kid's puppet show. It was all black, with a flat, cat-like face and red eyes. Its furry body, shaped somewhat like a snake, further added to the illusion that it was a puppet.

"This is the captain of *Cat Carrier*."

Terry chuckled.

"He calls himself Sylvester."

"You're kidding!" Terry spouted. No one around the table laughed or even smiled. "You're not kidding."

"We know very little about him, except that he's based in Chicago, making a small fortune."

"Doing what?" Terry asked.

"Curing cancer." At Terry's open-mouthed stare, Wilky took over.

"Two hundred seventy-four patients at last count. We brought the first thirty-five to Washington to verify their status and quarantine for possible extraterrestrial infection. Every one of their tumors had been rendered completely benign. None showed any signs of infestation, genetic modification, psychological tampering. Nothing. They were clean. We're continuing spot checks, just to be sure."

"This… Sylvester… is curing cancer, one person at a time?"

"Young, old, rich, poor. It doesn't seem to matter to him. He charges high fees, to be sure, but nothing exorbitant. We have him under constant surveillance. We know he's been approached by GlaxoSmithKline and Merck."

"We believe," Brown added, "that Pfizer has been in contact as well, though we have no hard evidence."

Woodley continued: "To date, Sylvester has turned down all offers to franchise his treatment. He's seeing thirty new patients a day at this point. He has a six-month waiting list."

Terry looked again at the picture. He realized that this photograph didn't look like something captured during a covert op. It looked like a headshot, something you'd get done at Sears. He now noticed the fake meadow background behind the alien. Keeping this publicity still—what else could it be?—in a locked briefcase seemed like overkill.

"You want me to approach this guy for help with the early warning system?" Terry asked.

Wilky answered with a smile. "Captain, he approached us."

After his last, unexpectedly eventful G-11 flight, Terry had been in the loving embrace of Military Intelligence for quite some while, during which he was debriefed and poked and prodded six ways from Sunday. He'd had precious little time out in the world since.

Now he was back in the world. His C37 flight had originated in the controlled environment of Andrews AFB, but ended at O'Hare Airport in Chicago. During the brief walk through the terminal, Terry saw that the *Voyager* incident had a greater impact on John and Jane Doe than he had expected it might. For one thing, the airport was nearly empty. Family summer vacations, weekend getaways, business travel. All of it was severely cut back. He figured the USAF should have saved the taxpayers a couple of bucks by flying him on a civilian flight. The airlines must have been almost giving away their tickets.

Then there were the magazines and papers. Terry paused in a B. Dalton to scan the headlines. It had been plenty long enough for the weeklies like *Time* and *Newsweek* to weigh in. He saw three variations on the old sci-fi trope "We Are Not Alone". The *Sun-Times* newspaper, which had probably been dealing with the situation on the front page every day for weeks, was today featuring a story titled "Mayor Welcomes Alien Investment". Terry laughed, wondering what an alien might have to invest.

The overall tone was optimistic. Terry wasn't sure if that was good or bad. Having seven billion people panicking would have been a problem, that was for sure. But there was danger, too; he just knew it. For every cancer-curing alien out there, there was at least one nuclear-bomb-snooping one. And then there were the other trillion or so that they had no idea what to expect from.

He did run across one scare-mongering magazine cover. Strangely, it was *PC Magazine*: "The End of Technology?" It seemed like an odd conclusion to draw. He pulled the mag from the rack and flipped through it. The basic idea was that alien technology would be so advanced it would swamp us poor humans and we'd be at the mercy of minds beyond our own. The author likened it to Captain Cook arriving at Hawaii and mystifying the natives back in the 1700s to the point where he was revered as a god. Terry noticed that the author abandoned the metaphor before the grim end of the story: the Hawaiians killed Cook during his third visit to the islands.

Just down the mall from the bookstore, Terry ran into a blast from the past: a Hare Krishna. He'd never actually seen one except in movies, but there the guy was, head shaved, wearing an orange robe, handing out updated flyers that incorporated aliens into the Krishna religious package. Since crowds were thin, Terry took pity on the guy and accepted one of the leaflets, handing him a buck.

Terry left the secure area of the terminal and came out into baggage claim. He had only a slim briefcase for this trip. He was scheduled to fly back to Andrews at 4 PM. Since air traffic was so light, the lobby was pretty empty; he found his driver with no problem. The guy looked like a linebacker, wearing a severe black suit and a fiery red tie. He held a card that read "Cpt. Yungblud". Terry had seen some crazy spellings of his name, but never one this bad.

"I'm Captain Youngblood," he said to the lug of a man.

"Over this way," the man answered, and walked off without a look back. The guy's intense accent told Terry that he really was in Chicago now.

The sense that Terry was headed for a visit with Vito Corleone didn't end with the goon of a driver, or with the limo's satellite TV hookup and stocked bar. The overlong car pulled up at a swanky hotel that Terry had never heard of: The Gilded Swan. The massive doorman guarding the entrance could have been the driver's twin brother.

Inside, the place was precisely the glitzy sort of nonsense that Al Capone must have loved back in his day. Dark, intricate carpet. Puffy leather chairs. Marble fountain in the center of the lobby. Wide, sweeping staircase to the second floor. A reed of a man in a tuxedo approached Terry instantly.

"Captain Youngblood. The gentleman upstairs has been notified of your arrival. If you'll come with me?"

The concierge led Terry to a vintage elevator. The thin man closed the door manually, and pushed up on a huge, theatric switch to put the car into motion. The concierge tried to make small talk, about the weather, about sports, about the hotly contested Mayoral election. Terry grunted noncommittally enough that the concierge finally took the hint. They rose to the thirteenth floor—labeled "14", of course—without further conversation.

Terry considered asking this man if he had no other duties. What with the downturn in travel, it was always possible that he didn't, that the Gilded Swan Hotel was home to exactly one visitor: *the gentleman upstairs*.

The fourteenth floor, the highest in the building, was designed as a single, huge penthouse suite. The concierge pulled open the elevator door to reveal a Victorian Era sitting room. Wingback chairs, stained glass shades atop ornate lamps, a bearskin rug nestled up against a fireplace, complete with roaring fire, despite the summer heat outside. Terry even spotted what he thought might have been a fainting couch.

With a distinctly unsophisticated clatter of metal against metal, the concierge pulled shut the elevator door and took the car back down. Terry was left alone and somewhat bewildered in the precious room.

"I have learned that people are often unprepared for my form." Terry heard the voice coming from several directions at once. This disgustingly old-world room was wired for sound. "I have, therefore, taken to introducing myself thus to newcomers." The voice—Terry assumed it must be Sylvester—had an accent, a strange combination of English and Australian. Considering the preponderance of American radio and television signals sent out into the aether over the last century or so, the affectation seemed odd. Maybe Sylvester chose the accent to seem more astute and trustworthy to an average American? Maybe he just liked sounding like the newest 007 from the movies.

"My daddy always said, 'Don't trust a man if he won't look you in the eye.' I'd like to talk to you face to face, if you don't mind."

"Brilliant!"

A pair of double doors opposite the elevator opened to reveal Sylvester, much as the publicity still had shown him. Terry hadn't expected to see two arms with human-looking hands sprouting from the creature's snake-like body. Sylvester slithered over to Terry, modulating his height to look at him eye-to-eye. With a barely restrained gulp, Terry shook Sylvester's outstretched right hand. The alien's dry, velvety skin was just a few degrees warmer than comfortable for Terry.

The alien turned and led Terry into a more brightly appointed sitting room that had a nice view of the city. If Terry had expected to see the apparatus of hospital care—which he hadn't, really—he would have been disappointed. The room seemed nothing more than a nice place to have a cup of tea. In fact, the pot and cups were already waiting at a table. They sat.

"I expected to see cancer patients in line," Terry said as Sylvester poured the tea.

"I took the day off for our meeting. No need for us to be distracted, what?" Terry watched, fascinated, as Sylvester sipped at the tea with his fanged mouth. "Do drink up. It's quite good."

"Ah." Terry dutifully sipped at the tea. "Very good," he said.

"So, Captain, my ship has excellent things to say about you."

"She does?" Terry smiled, then thought how ridiculous it was to be pleased that a sentient spaceship liked him. "She was very cordial to me."

"Cordial! She'll like that!" The snake laughed, an unsettling collection of snorts and hisses that reminded Terry—despite the disarming accent and the tea—that this thing was from another part of the galaxy entirely. "Now, to business. I would like to offer the Earth a detection system for installation around your solar system."

"That's what my bosses told me. If you could be a little more specific, I'd appreciate it."

Sylvester slid off the chair and clasped his hands together in a very human way. "Why not skip the tell and move on directly to the show?" Sylvester slithered off to the north side of the room, to a swinging door that looked like the entry to a kitchen. Terry set the cup and saucer down on the table with a small rattle of china and hustled after the surprisingly fast alien. Sylvester led Terry through the well-appointed kitchen and up a narrow flight of servants' stairs to the roof of the building.

The roof of a fourteen-story—or, really, thirteen-story—building in Chicago doesn't offer the most panoramic of views, but Terry enjoyed seeing the city rising around him even if his sight lines were restricted. From here, he couldn't see Lake Michigan or the river. The Sears Tower was mostly hidden as well.

Terry wasn't a total sci-fi nut like some of the other pilots in the Air Force, but he knew a little about it. He expected Sylvester to wow him with some snazzy holographic light show, explaining the warning system's operation. The only thing on the roof, however, was a ten-foot-wide clear plastic ball on a little platform. Sylvester led Terry to the ball and slipped up onto the platform.

"After you," Sylvester said, gesturing to an opening in the side of the ball.

Afterward, Terry felt like a total idiot for not seeing what was about to happen. He was still imagining that the ball was some kind of wraparound computer screen. The fact that the whole contraption was on the roof made no impression on him.

He didn't even bother to wonder at how the bottom of the plastic ball seemed to be just an inch or two *above* the concrete platform.

Sylvester followed Terry into the ball. Since there was no flat surface to stand on, and no chairs, Terry took a seat, cross-legged, in the center of the thing. Sylvester, seemingly at the mercy of gravity and lack of friction just like Terry, wrapped his body *around* Terry. The feel of his too-slick fur was less disconcerting than the *heat* coming out of his body.

"Is this really necessary?" Terry asked.

"You'll be more comfortable in a moment."

Sylvester reached one of his black hands up to the side of the ball to an almost invisible set of buttons. With a single finger, he pressed the button in the lower right corner.

The building disappeared. Terry jumped to his feet in alarm.

"Do sit down, Captain."

Terry didn't sit down. He remained standing, bracing his hands against the top of the bubble, desperately looking around for some explanation. Looking down, past the coiled bulk of the alien, he saw that the building hadn't disappeared; it was just far, far below them. Any concerns about the limited view were gone now. He could see every bit of Chicago, including the *roof* of the Sears Tower. Even as he made out that landmark, he lost it again in the clutter of the entire metropolitan area. Now he couldn't find Chicago at all except as a slightly gray smudge on the edge of Lake Michigan.

As a pilot, Terry wasn't one to fall prey to vertigo. What was more disconcerting than the height they'd reached in just seconds was the fact that he hadn't felt any sense of physical motion.

"This is a simulation," Terry said, still stubbornly refusing to believe what his eyes told him.

"Certainly not! I had thought that if anyone would appreciate my orbit bubbles it would be someone of your breadth of experience with travel into space, my dear Captain."

In only the time it took for that short exchange, Terry finally felt a change to his equilibrium that only space travel—or an extremely ambitious simulation—could conjure; he felt weightless. His body floated up off the ball's curved floor. Thankfully, Sylvester continued to hug the "bottom" of the ball. Terry was no longer nestled in the alien's creepy embrace.

How high up were they? The bubble continued to rise at a significant clip, so it was hard to estimate. Terry figured they were at least a hundred miles up, maybe as much as five hundred. The sky was noticeably dark and the Earth below curved away in all directions. He could see the terminator of dawn rolling across the Pacific Ocean in the distance.

Looking up, Terry saw that *Cat Carrier* remembered his human optical limitations. The ship, which they approached at ballistic velocity, was still that unearthly purple color. Again with no sense of negative acceleration, the bubble slowed and came to a stop next to the purple ship. The two dissimilar spheres attached and an opening appeared between them. Terry felt only a slight shift in air pressure when the connecting walls disappeared. After a questioning look to Sylvester, he floated through the portal into *Cat Carrier*.

"It's good to see you again, Captain Youngblood," *Cat Carrier* said in that smooth voice of hers.

"You, too," Terry said. He pulled himself along a narrow tube toward an open space inside the ship.

The ship's control room wasn't pure technology like *Star Trek*, with harsh metal and plastic angles everywhere. Neither was it disgustingly organic like something from an *Alien* movie, looking like it was grown from a diseased fungal bloom. To Terry, the room looked like a compromise between the two. There were a few hard, flat surfaces strewn about the area: below, above, to the sides: screens showing schematics and data, presumably about the ship's operations, for Sylvester's benefit. The room showed no preferential direction as "down". All of the walls were gently curved, bowing out toward the six exits. It didn't *quite* feel like being inside the stomach of a whale.

Unfortunately, every surface—the walls, the exits, the screens themselves—was brilliant red, the color of arterial blood. Even though the light in the room was not bright, he found himself squinting against the oppressive sameness of that color.

Sylvester followed Terry into the room. Now he understood the alien's comfort in weightlessness. Sylvester, who had seemed akin to an oversized snake in Earth's gravity, showed a significantly more graceful side here in space. He swam through the air effortlessly, now resembling an eel in an aquarium tank. His "fur" was, in actuality, a complex system of cilia that allowed him to travel in any direction, twist on a dime, even double back on himself. The thing could have tied himself in a knot if he wanted to.

"I hope you've got a way to get me back down when we're done here."

"Sylvester," the ship said in a scolding tone. Sylvester answered with a feral grin. "You're quite safe, Captain," *Cat Carrier* said soothingly. "The orbit bubbles work both ways."

"Ah."

"I shall return in a moment," Sylvester said. Terry watched, wordlessly, as the snake disappeared down another tube-like corridor.

"I hope I didn't cause you any trouble at our last meeting," the ship said.

"No trouble at all," Terry lied. The debriefing process had been painstaking and grueling. But he considered it a worthwhile trade-off for the opportunity. "So, where are you from?" It seemed odd to make small talk in a situation like this, but with his host gone, Terry didn't know what else to do.

"Sylvester comes from a system about… eighteen thousand light years away. I was built elsewhere, some thirty-four thousand light years from Earth."

"What is the name of your home world?"

Carrier laughed. "I would tell you if I could. I originated on a world with no atmosphere. Its name is not a word as you know it, but a series of colors. Here, I'll show you." The screens around Terry changed to a muddy mustard color. As he watched, the screens seemed to shift very slightly from one minute shade to another. "Did you see that?" she asked.

"Just barely."

"There were seventeen syllables in that color sequence. I suppose we should be thankful your eyes could register their colors at all."

Sylvester reappeared, sliding back into the central room with a small, metal box in his hands.

"Captain Youngblood is curious about our home worlds."

"Is he?" Sylvester said. "I haven't been home in a couple billion ticks."

"Ticks?"

"A tick is about a half a second in Earth time," *Carrier* explained. "You'll learn the CA metrics soon enough." Terry had enough trouble with the metric system the Europeans used. He still thought in inches and miles. Now he'd have to learn a whole new set of measurements?

"Well, here it is," Sylvester said. He swept past Terry to set the box on one wall. Some force kept the box attached to the blood-red surface, which Terry now saw had a fuzzy sort of texture. Maybe it was as simple as Velcro.

"It's in that box?"

"It *is* the box."

Terry kicked off from where he had waited against the wall, and floated over to the box. It looked like a simple container, made of metal, maybe steel or platinum. He couldn't see a lid, though.

"What does it do?"

Terry hadn't gotten used to Sylvester's toothy grins. The snake angled over to the box and picked it up again. He went back out the corridor through which they had come. Terry followed. He and Sylvester re-entered the orbit bubble. But something was wrong.

"Where's the Earth?" Terry asked with a voice just a bit too high-pitched.

"Over that way," Sylvester said, pointing vaguely into the star field. One star was slightly brighter than all the others.

"That's our sun?"

"It's nothing special, of course, but a nice star all the same. The flarers always make my head ache." Sylvester fiddled with the array of almost-invisible buttons. A square section of the bubble where he'd set down the box went blue, then disappeared altogether. Terry tensed, expecting the air to rush out of the bubble, but, of course, not really expecting that to happen at all. The box drifted outside, then the square went blue again and the bubble's uniform, transparent shape was restored.

"You don't like to give a guy any warning about this stuff, do you?"

Another one of those feline grins. "Watch."

The box vented a little bit of gas, something white that dissipated almost instantly. It moved away from the bubble, from *Cat Carrier*, toward a black, rocky asteroid just a short distance away. The box landed gracefully on the asteroid. Terry waited for the thing to sprout wings or catch fire or... he didn't know what.

"Okay. What's it for?"

"That's your sensor net."

"That? It's not doing anything."

"Yes, it is." Sylvester pointed. Looking back, Terry noticed that the box was the wrong shape. It was almost twice as wide as it had been before. Then, like some amoeba under a microscope, the thing split in two. The box to the right let loose a puff of that thin, white gas, and it leapt up off the rock.

"It made a copy of itself?" Terry asked, astounded. He watched as the new box flew past *Cat Carrier* into the black unknown. "Where's it going?"

"To the nearest comet."

Comet? Terry looked back at the dark rock and realized what it was. A comet, or at least it would become a comet if it ever fell back toward the sun. They weren't simply far from Earth. They were *very* far from Earth. This was the Oort cloud, a huge collection of ashy snowballs orbiting the sun at a ridiculous distance. Occasionally some star would veer a little too close and a hailstorm of the things would fly toward the sun. This was where Halley's Comet had come from, along with all the other, less famous ones.

"How far out are we?"

"Six billion d's... neighborhood of eighty thousand AU."

Terry felt a thrill at that figure. He had traveled farther from Earth than any other person in history, a good chunk of the distance to the nearest stars. He'd have to ask *Cat Carrier* to take some snapshots, so he could prove it when he got back home.

"Wait a minute. This is where comets come from, right?"

"Of course."

"Why didn't these comets tear a hole in the heliopause barrier before now?"

"The cocoon is smarter than you think," Sylvester said. Terry still found the use of the word *cocoon* annoying, as if humanity were little more than a struggling tadpole in a pond. "It allowed comets to pass through, just as it allowed the natural radiance of the stars to shine down on your planet. In addition, it monitored your radio signals and compiled a brief memo on your civilization. This memo allows visitors to prepare for the unique qualities of Earth."

"We're unique, then?"

"Technically."

The alien spread his little arms wide, gesturing to include the nearby comet. "So, what do you think?"

"About what?"

"Your early warning detection grid!"

"I don't understand."

"Captain, those little boxes will continue to multiply and seek out new comets until your entire Oort cloud is completely covered. Each box represents a single node of what will soon be a network of over a hundred million sensors, each of which can detect almost any ship within a thousand astronomical units, which is more than adequate to tell you who's coming to dinner."

Terry looked back toward the diminishing child sensor box, but it was already beyond his view. The mother, sitting on the comet surface, was already birthing another one. This time, the new box flew in the direction Terry thought of as "up".

"This is it? You've already set up the network?"

"Started it, yes. We should seed more locations to ensure expansion will go as fast as practicable."

"I thought… I thought I was coming to negotiate the cost?"

"I haven't told you how to connect to the network yet, now have I?"

"And I suppose if we don't meet your cost, you'll hand off the controls to some unsavory alien race?"

Sylvester laughed again, the grating sound bouncing around the bubble like dried beans in a jar. "Who'd want it? Really, Captain, you Humans aren't such a bad bunch, but I don't imagine there'll be too many people who would fight over your little corner of the galaxy."

Terry's wounded pride fought with a sense of relief at the thought. Sure, almost anyone with technology like Sylvester's could conquer them… but why would they? What could Earth have that wasn't available just about anywhere else?

But then why had the strange bird-ship flown over St. Louis? Why had the dark star-ship hovered over Kincaid? Why had Sylvester and *Cat Carrier* come, for that matter?

"What do you want?" Terry asked the question with respect to the sensor network, but his real, underlying question was deeper. What did Sylvester want from Earth? The money he made from his cancer treatments would not be useful elsewhere in the galaxy. It only held value on Earth.

"One little thing," Sylvester whispered. "I want…"

Terry waited, worried for what might come next.

"…launch authority."

"Launch authority."

"Yes. I require unlimited, indefinite authority to launch vehicles from Earth into space."

Terry stared at the black alien, looking into his red eyes for some sign of subterfuge. Was Sylvester playing Terry for a fool?

"That's all? Launch authority?"

"Yes."

"That doesn't seem like… very much."

The alien waved a hand out to the rocky comet, where the mother box was splitting in two once more. Terry thought this was the third child, but there might have been another that he missed.

"I didn't do very much."

There had to be a trick, something Terry wasn't seeing.

"You said we're eighty thousand AU out from Earth."

"Give or take."

"That's, what, about a light year?"

Sylvester looked off in the distance, doing some mental arithmetic. "A bit over, yes."

"So, we'll only get the signals from these boxes after a year? What good will that do us?"

"Not a bit, if they sent their signals via the electromagnetic spectrum, which they don't. Captain, you're looking for a reason to be wary when I have given you no cause to doubt me. I'll provide you with the means to monitor this network in real-time. I'll give you a guarantee against failure. Networks of this kind routinely work for a trillion ticks or more without need of maintenance. This is solid, proven technology."

"But… If this system is so great, then why are you giving it to us for so little?"

"You say it's little now." Sylvester slithered closer to Terry, speaking in a low, conspiratorial tone. Terry fought an urge to back away, which would have been difficult in zero-g anyway. At least Sylvester's breath didn't smell bad. "I've visited many newly hatched systems that put severe restrictions on exports from their worlds."

"Exports? What do you plan to export?"

"Shall I be perfectly honest with you, Captain?"

Terry almost said no. He could imagine altogether too easily that furry, snaky body wrapping around him and Sylvester's fangs clamping onto his neck to suck out every last drop of his blood.

"What do I plan to export?" Sylvester's eyes rolled in a human sort of gesture to indicate he was pondering the question. "I don't yet know."

Love Songs

> *Everything which is in any way beautiful is beautiful in itself, and terminates in itself, not having praise as part of itself. Neither worse then nor better is a thing made by being praised.*
> —*Meditations, IV, 20*

After nearly a year and a half of long hours and difficult toil, Keira took her first vacation from her job at MYC. The research she had done these past sixteen months was beyond anything her wildest dreams might have suggested to her. Each week another exultant e-mail would flash onto her tablet screen, indicating the start of a new project. Batteries the size of a credit card that could start a car. Crystals strong as steel and transparent as air. Just last week the space division had gotten hold of something they called an *orbit bubble*. That machine alone looked to be worthy of a year's time of fifty of their best minds.

MYC had grown like a bacterial culture in that first year. Keira's employee number was 29. There were now over twelve thousand associates in the Consortium, and still it grew. Ten months ago her superiors had promoted her to Researcher, a bland sort of title for a grand sort of job. She no longer had to wade through endless screens of data or wait, eyes drooping from lack of sleep, for the mainframe to free up so she could push through her supervisor's latest modeling software run. Now she *managed* the research for a project. And what a project it was!

Carbon-aluminum they called it, a term Keira found somewhat lacking in poetry. She had petitioned for a name that would be easier on the tongue, such as *steeluminum*, but the project was already underway before she took over as Researcher. She had been saddled with the name carbon-aluminum, and it had stuck. The idea had come from a random bit of alien radio, one of the very few transmissions that had been translated since the *Voyager* incident. The snippet had, once it was rendered into

English, been a simple chemical formula, a previously unimagined way of merging carbon with aluminum to generate an alloy to rival steel in its manifold uses. A friend of a friend of a friend had e-mailed the translated formula to someone in MYC, not knowing the extraordinary value of the little string of symbols.

The idea had, in those early days, taken the Consortium by storm. It took nearly five months to work out how such a chemical miracle might be achieved, but achieve it they did. Now, Keira and her team had two goals. The first, and perhaps simplest, was to test the limits of carbon-aluminum. They needed to chart its density, tensile strength, ductility: anything and everything about a new alloy that needs to be tested before it makes its way into full production for use in the real world. The possibilities sent the mind spinning. There were precious few uses of traditional ferrous steel that might not also be achieved with carbon-aluminum, at a fraction of the weight, the foremost of which, in Keira's mind, being the construction of vessels for space flight.

The second, more critical task was to streamline the production process. At present, creation of carbon-aluminum was rather expensive and inordinately time-consuming. It required high temperatures and high pressures and a carefully constructed cocktail of bizarre chemicals that weren't commonly found in a high school science lab.

The project didn't have the exotic cachet of something like the orbit bubble, but Keira coveted the task nonetheless. Such things were the substance of her dreams.

However, even when pursuing one's dream, tireless labor takes its toll. Keira finally agreed to take a short vacation. She slept through the entire flight from Mumbai to Bengalūru, her childhood home.

Home was home. Keira's mother yelped with joy when she saw her wayward daughter on the front steps. She was quite proud of her over-tall, lanky daughter, though she had made it clear enough that a son-in-law, a grandchild or two, and a house down the block would make her prouder still. Keira's father, on the other hand, pressed her for details of the project. He had been in the business of making locomotives before his retirement, and watched the progress of Maccha-Yantra with great interest.

Dinner the first evening she was home was a grand affair. Keira's three older sisters came in to help their mother with the meal. All three were formed in the image of their mother—somewhat plump, somewhat diminutive. They each brought along their own children, filling the house with the sounds of laughter and playful argument. The three brothers-in-law trooped into the den to talk manly talk with their father-in-law. Keira spent the afternoon with her nieces and nephews, a bright-eyed bunch of kids that ranged from eight months to nine-and-three-quarters years. To these children, Keira was a wonder: a single woman living far away, doing important work. That she was tall added to her aura of unfathomable mystery.

Keira supposed that before the week was out she would be itching to get back to her project and all its complex and fascinating twists and turns. For now, though, for this evening, she simply relaxed and enjoyed the raucous sounds of children and the smell of a meal she knew would sate her completely.

Keira's mother waited forty-eight hours before setting her one remaining unattached daughter up on a blind date. For every excuse Keira could propose to avoid the excursion, her mother offered two more reasons to do it. Finally, with the promise of a visit to a local jazz club as part of the date, Keira relented.

Tommy was not the sort of man Keira would have pursued. He was just exactly her height; she believed a man should be taller, though, admittedly, taller men were rare in her experience. He wore traditional Indian garb; she gravitated to men with more modern—read *Western*—tastes. However, after only a few moments of conversation, she understood what her mother had seen in this man. He was brilliant; he was charming. That he enjoyed listening to jazz was icing on the cake.

The name of the club they went to after dinner was *Freddie's*. Keira had been here on a half-dozen occasions with friends during her time at university. The place was a black-painted box of a room with a slightly elevated stage at one end and a bar at the other. In New York, Keira had visited a number of jazz lounges with tables and chairs and expensive martinis on the menu. *Freddie's* wasn't like that. In fact, *Freddie's* didn't always play host to jazz acts. Rock and blues bands frequently took the stage as well.

Tonight the act was a singer, a woman named Elena Sabharwal. Keira had watched this woman perform once before, and found her to be talented, though nothing particularly special. Apparently, her popularity had grown since then, because *Freddie's* was packed. When they entered, Tommy was the first to notice what was different about the crowd.

"They're…" He couldn't say it. Keira could.

"Aliens."

Most of the people in the room were human, of course, but enough were from elsewhere that it was quite noticeable. Keira estimated one in four of the patrons were not of Earth. Her job gave her more interactions with aliens than Tommy's, so her reaction wasn't one of fear, more of curiosity. Why were there so many of them here, tonight?

Only a handful of alien races had made themselves known to Earth so far. The most gregarious of them, the Blues, were here at *Freddie's* in force. They were the most obvious aliens in the room, because the shortest of them still stood a good ten centimeters taller than the humans. Keira counted thirty of them, spread around the room. Their rail-thin bodies had skin similar to humans—save for the sky-blue color. With three double-jointed legs and three double-jointed arms, they found humanity's fascination with *left* and *right* somewhat puzzling. Further, since each Blue sported three eyes, spaced evenly around their pencil-eraser of a head, they tended to pity humans and their meager 180° vision.

"Why are they here?" Tommy asked, the fear in his voice quite obvious.

"For the music," Keira answered. She assumed Tommy wasn't asking the larger question: why did the Blues come to Earth so quickly, and in such numbers? Such was the topic of many lunchtime discussions back at the Consortium. The Blues seemed entirely too nice to be an invading force. They were too fascinated with humanity to be exporters of ideology or culture. The only thing they sought, it seemed, was new experience.

Though the Blues were the most populous non-human species in *Freddie's* this evening, Keira also caught sight of a pair of Trees. That race, Keira knew from one who had visited the MYC offices, were travelers by nature. Earth was merely the latest world their ship had found. They arrived two months ago and stayed to sample the culture. Each Tree was thicker at the base than even an obese human, with a sticky pseudopod that moved it, slowly, from place to place. The trunk of a Tree rose to about waist level, then began to branch. A mature Tree would have about thirty branches, each of which served some purpose—manipulator, intake for food and water, expulsion of waste, various kinds of sensors. At first glance, though, all of the branches looked identical to a human unfamiliar with the race. When one branch would swivel towards a person and begin to emit speech, the reaction was often either hilarity or a swooning faint. Keira was not surprised that the two Trees in the room—one a stark white, the other a faded yellow—chose to keep close together.

She caught glimpses of a few other species that she had no familiarity with: a lime-green fellow who looked for all the world like a living skeleton, a large creature that looked like a cross between an upside down jellyfish and a gargantuan lily blossom, a black, snaky beast with a cat's face and beady red eyes. Keira wondered, not for the first time, if sentient life was routinely molded in an upright configuration, or if she had only run across species of that type since they were the ones most comfortable in Earth's air pressure and gravity. As humanity learned more about what—and who—was out there, she imagined those questions would be answered by others.

Elena Sabharwal took to the stage along with a young man carrying a double bass, a woman of middle years who sat at the baby grand piano, and an elderly gent—this man a European of some type—who sat behind the drum set. Polite applause—all of it from the humans in the crowd—greeted the quartet of performers. Elena murmured a quiet "thank you" into the mic while the others prepared their instruments for the show.

Sabharwal was, Keira had to admit, a pretty little thing. She stood about 160, with a slim body and slimmer arms and legs. Keira supposed it was a trick of the light or makeup or simply her size, but her dark eyes looked enormous. She wore a simple black dress, much like any torch singer in New York would have worn. Keira guessed her age to be twenty-one. When she had hit the local music scene two years earlier, she hadn't quite been hailed as a prodigy, but her youthfulness definitely added to her appeal.

Keira glanced back to Tommy to gauge his reaction to the singer. He watched the girl speak in soft tones to her band, but without any sort of lust in his eyes. She smiled to herself.

"What?" Tommy asked.

"Nothing."

The thub-thubbing of the bass, the arrhythmic tapping of the drums, and the freeform plinking of the piano all stopped. Elena Sabharwal once again came to the mic, this time with a more focused presence, pulling in the crowd with a simple but forceful, "Good evening." Keira noticed that several of the Blues responded in kind, causing a polite titter of laughter from the humans in the crowd.

"Thank you all for coming. I'd like to give a special welcome to our guests from out of town." That caused more laughter, followed by a round of applause. None of the aliens joined in. She sensed the confusion in the Blues particularly, since their wrap-around faces showed emotions in a way that seemed a vague approximation of human.

A nearby Blue slipped in between Keira and Tommy. She knew from experience that they had difficulty with the concept of personal space. Tommy backed away quickly.

"I offer no offense. Query."

"Yes?" Keira asked.

"Is Miss Sabharwal mocking?"

"No. She was quite sincere. The applause was in agreement."

"Gratitude." The Blue did an elegant down-and-up curtsy on its three multi-jointed legs.

"You're welcome."

Tommy returned to Keira's side after the alien retreated. He seemed a bit shell shocked. Keira responded with a smile and hooked her arm around his. That took the curse off the awkward moment.

The first song began. Keira was pleased to note that this was a song she was familiar with: *River Bank.* It was a down tempo number. The percussionist used a brush on his snare punctuated with a few taps on a cymbal. The bass player laid down a foundation of four mildly syncopated notes. The pianist filled in with soft chords, complex resonances that sometimes complimented the bass line, and sometimes fought against it like a friendly rival.

Over it all came Elena Sabharwal's honey-dipped voice, not throaty enough to be a rocker, not sweet enough for opera. Her vocal talents were perfectly tuned to the format of a ballad such as *River Bank*.

I flow so slow down the river
Away from you, away from you
From long ago your words echo
All along the river

Keira found herself falling under the spell of the song and squeezed Tommy's arm in response. She supposed Tommy was less interested in the song than the feel of her skin on his, but at this moment, she decided not to worry about the sexual politics of a first date. She floated down the river with Sabharwal.

A soft rain falls on the river
Down on me, down on me
Gray clouds weep, gray clouds weep
All along the river

Sabharwal had improved markedly since the last time Keira had seen her perform. Two years ago, she had seemed a talented child aping the emotional turmoil of her elders in her performance. Now, either her talent for emulation had vastly improved, or her depth of experience had increased. She seemed not to be telling the story of a woman suffering from the pain of a bad break up; she seemed to be that woman. The wrenching way she sang the call back line "*all along the river*" brought a tear to Keira's eye.

You're on the bank of the river
So near so close, so near so close
Your heart calls, my heart falls
All along the river

A strange sound, something like a bird chirping, broke Keira from her musical reverie. She looked around. No one else, it seemed, had noticed the sound. It came again, quite obviously from the Blue she had spoken with earlier. The alien had two of his three eyes riveted on the stage, giving Sabharwal attention unlike any Keira had ever seen a Blue give. His nearly inaudible chirps seemed to be a reaction to the song.

In a brief silence just before Sabharwal went into her gut wrenching final verse, Keira heard more of the chirping from elsewhere in the crowd. All the Blues' gazes were fixed on the stage with something like religious fervor. Keira shivered. Tommy felt it, too, and put an arm around her shoulders. Keira appreciated that, nestling closer to him as Sabharwal finished the song, her vocalizations taking the deceptively simple melody into a new, complex, and darkly enchanting place.

> *My life is bound to the river*
> *No more to roam, no more to roam*
> *You're on the beach, my hand can't reach*
> *All along the river*

The combo finished out the song as Sabharwal held that last, haunting note for an eternity. The crowd, with a sort of collective telepathy that a perfect performance grants, broke into simultaneous applause at the ideal moment, just as the final note began to fade. The applause was energetic and sincere. Keira almost regretted the loss of Tommy's arm around her shoulders.

Few of the aliens in the room applauded, largely because, without human-style hands, they simply couldn't. Keira scanned the room. The Blues were still in a sort of fugue. The Trees were waving as if in a heavy breeze. The other aliens seemed just as pleased by the performance, though Keira could only assume, not being familiar with their cultures.

"Wow," Tommy said into her ear.

"Yeah." Keira felt there were quite a few reasons to say "wow" just then.

The balance of the concert went much as the first song. Sabharwal impressed the humans, but she brought all the aliens to something like a worshipful state. Before the show was complete, the Blues' chirping was loud enough for all to hear. Eventually the Blues—who held courtesy as a very high ideal—learned to save their chirps for the end of the song, serving as their form of applause.

As for Keira and Tommy, they grew closer still as the concert continued, arms entwined, swaying slightly. Tommy snuck two kisses at opportune moments, moments that Keira found quite acceptable.

Sabharwal finished her set and thanked the audience, who rewarded her with enthusiastic applause—and chirps. As the crowd filed out of the club, Keira asked Tommy to wait so she could take a run to the restroom.

Keira finished her business in one of the stalls. As she came out, she found herself face to face with another Blue. She suspected this might have been the same Blue she had talked to earlier, but her talent for recognizing individuals of this species was still limited.

"I offer no offense. Query."

"Yes?" Keira responded.

"This is the waste disposal room?"

"One of them. Yes." Keira held open the stall door. The Blue did a small curtsy, then ambled into the stall. Bald-faced curiosity kept Keira in the room, washing her hands far more thoroughly than necessary. She wanted to hear what a Blue defecating sounded like.

Sadly, the creature made no noise save for the familiar sound of a toilet flushing. As the Blue came out, Keira went to the towel dispenser to dry her hands. The Blue was about to leave, when Keira spoke on an impulse.

"I offer no offense," she said, copying their form for questions. "Query."

The blue stopped. Its anatomy did not require it to turn around. It simply addressed Keira with the eyes that currently faced in her direction.

"You may query."

"Did you like the music?"

The Blue responded by sagging slightly on its legs, nothing so graceful as a curtsy. It seemed to have a deep emotional reaction to the simple question.

"This performance altered me."

"It altered you? In what way?"

"Your species is…" The Blue paused, like so many other aliens Keira had met, seeking out the right word in the maze that is the English language. "…profligate with artistic talent."

Keira grinned, suspecting that the Blue wouldn't see that as the mildly accusatory gesture it was. "I see. Again, no offense, but I didn't think she was *that* good."

The Blue took three steps forward, coming within centimeters of Keira. She fought an instinctive urge to step back; she was close enough to see that the Blue's skin was only superficially human. It was, in fact, covered with miniscule scales, rather than a smooth surface.

"The melody of the song. The counterpoint of the pianoforte. The additional counterpoint of the bass viol. The accentuation of the percussive suite. The constant variation of all of these components. The words of the song. The meaning of the words of the song. The alternate meaning of the words of the song. The voice of the singer. The emotions evident in the voice of the singer. The synchronicity of the emotion and the voice of the singer with the multiple meanings of the words of the song. The accompanying impact on the listener who may or may not have experienced a similar—"

Keira held up a hand, politely suggesting that the Blue need not continue.

"They're good songs, and she does them well," Keira admitted.

"Miss Sabharwal and her accompanists are masters. In the first of the cycle, the song known as *River Bank*, all of these many layers are achieved in only…" The Blue paused to translate into Earth terms. "…greater than four and less than five minutes. No expression native to my culture is so dense with artistry."

"I see." Keira felt silent pride that Earth had this one thing—perhaps the only one—that the far more advanced Blues did not. "I'm glad you enjoyed the show."

"Gratitude," the alien answered, then slipped out of the restroom.

Tommy took Keira home and they said their goodbyes under what Keira assumed were the watchful eyes of her entire family. Tommy seemed tentative about the goodnight kiss, since he seemed to understand

Keira's family and their obsession as well as she. Keira solved the problem by kissing him first.

As she entered her parents' house and fended off endless questions about their evening, Keira considered calling MYC and asking for an extension of her vacation.

Tommy called the next day, inviting Keira to lunch, an offer that seemed slightly presumptuous. Keira agreed immediately. Lunch went well, offering them a much better opportunity to talk. Tommy taught secondary school. He was, in fact, teaching at the school Keira had attended not too many years ago. He seemed fascinated by her work with Maccha-Yantra, but not awestruck, which she found to be a nice combination.

It seemed his family was almost as worried about his bachelorhood as Keira's was about her spinsterhood. They shared a self-mocking laugh about that, even as they warily eyed each other for signs of interest in a long term relationship. Keira couldn't be sure what Tommy saw in her. For her part, she spied a possibility for something when she looked at him.

Keira never had much use for newspapers. She found them cumbersome, dirty, and pointless considering the availability of the internet. Her father had other ideas, and routinely read his *Rajasthan Patrika* each morning. On Wednesday, he called to her from his breakfast table.

"Keira!"

She dutifully responded to his summons.

"Yes?"

"What is going on with your aliens?" Ever since she took the job with the Consortium, Father insisted on referring to all extra-terrestrial intelligences as "her aliens". She found this tic of his outwardly annoying and secretly adorable. He wafted the paper at her, folded back to the second page of the Local section. She scanned the article and glanced at one pixilated image of a crowd of Blues on a street corner.

Bengalūru had become a magnet for alien visitors. The reporter claimed that more than a thousand Blues were encamped in the city. At least forty Trees were also staying in town, a claim that stunned Keira; she hadn't thought there were that many Trees on Earth. The story went on to enumerate a dozen other species, several of which Keira did not recognize, who were visiting Bengalūru.

"Why are they here?" Keira asked.

"That's what I'm asking you," her father insisted. "It's nothing to do with you, is it?"

Keira smiled at her father. "No, it's nothing to do with me."

He squinted at her, then nodded. She had not yet been able to convince him that she wasn't part of some grand government secret agency. How else, he claimed, could MYC get access to so many alien technologies? Keira had explained that some were intuited from unguarded radio transmissions, while most had been freely given to Earth by visitors. Nothing they'd learned yet indicated any alien culture saw Earth as a threat. An interstellar tourist's easiest currency of exchange was information, and MYC had the resources to pay well for such information.

"There's something about Bengalūru the aliens like," Father said with a final grunt.

Keira's fondness for Tommy continued to war with her duty to her job at MYC. Duty won the contest by a hair. Tommy took the setback in stride, vowing to visit her in Mumbai at the very next school break. Keira claimed she would keep him to his vow. To celebrate their final night together before her flight home, Tommy planned to take her to a new, trendy restaurant downtown.

He picked her up at six o'clock. Keira's mother and two of her sisters were there standing in the front hall to see them off. Her father had just switched on the television as they stepped out of the house. After watching only a few moments of the coverage, he jumped up from his chair to warn them not to go, but they had already left.

The traffic in central Bengalūru was always a chore, but it seemed particularly difficult this evening. Tommy was still nearly a mile from the restaurant when he gave up and pulled his two-seater into the nearest parking lot.

"I'm sorry about this. There must be a bad accident up there."

"I wore my walking shoes," Keira joked.

They strolled, arm in arm, along the sidewalk, past traffic that no longer moved at all. An orchestra of car horns accompanied their journey down the street. Most of the drivers confined their frustration to honking, though some did lean out of car windows into the pleasant October evening to shout incoherently at the drivers directly in front of them. Keira and Tommy chuckled at their pointless rage.

The first intersection they came to was gridlocked. Keira had heard of actual gridlock, wherein the cars at an intersection were jammed in such a way that they literally could not move. Neither she nor Tommy had ever seen such a thing in practice. The drivers whose vehicles blocked the intersection seemed angrier than everyone else, though they were actually to blame for the problem.

"What are they afraid of?" Tommy asked, his hand momentarily squeezing Keira's arm.

"Afraid? They're angry."

"They're angry *because* they're afraid. Can't you hear it?"

Keira listened more carefully to the tones of the shouting motorists. They did seem to carry a whiff of apprehension. But apprehension of what?

Tommy and Keira jigged to the right nearly half a block before they found a break in the glacier of cars wide enough to slip through. Their restaurant was still four blocks away. Keira wondered if the place would even be open. How could patrons get there, in this kind of traffic?

As they approached the next block, Keira noticed the signs in the shop windows. Antique shops, furniture shops, music shops, book shops. All of them were closed, shuttered, dark. She imagined some might normally have been closed this early in the evening, but not all of them.

"What's going on?"

At the next intersection, the locked-in drivers were more obviously frightened, though the source of their fear remained a mystery. An echo of sirens in the distance came to their ears. A police patrol helicopter *fwupped* its way over their heads, flying low enough to cause a swirl of trash to blow up around them.

"Tommy…"

"We should get back to the car."

Keira was about to agree when she noticed one man, a forty-something gent in a white shirt, sweater vest and slacks, standing on his sedan. His gaze was fixed to the north, toward the restaurant that Keira now had no interest in visiting. The man shouted something incomprehensible, then turned to the rest of the people in the crowd.

"They're coming! They're coming!"

This warning seemed to mean something to the drivers of the stuck vehicles. Many began to shout. Others simply opened their doors and began to run to the south.

"We should go!" Tommy warned.

A few people started climbing over the gridlocked cars, rushing down the sidewalk past Tommy and Keira. Keira tried to ask one or two what was happening, but they were too panicked to answer. The flow of people increased. The sounds of car hoods and boots being stomped on and dented competed with the crunch of glass breaking and the pounding of feet.

Keira lost contact with Tommy as a panicked, heavy woman slammed into him. Keira tried to elbow her way through the throng, but was batted away by waving, flapping arms. Keira turned and went the other way, toward the row of stopped cars. She opened the door of the first one she found and ducked inside. She rolled down the window and called to Tommy. If he answered, she couldn't hear him over the shouts of the frightened masses.

The keys were still in the car. She had no hope of driving it out of this madness, but she did hope to find out what was happening. She turned the key far enough to activate the electrics. The driver hadn't bothered to turn off his or her radio before abandoning the car. The dial was tuned to a station Keira knew specialized in dance music. There was no music playing just now. She rolled up the window to listen.

"...the thirteen hundred block of Brigade Road. The city has called for aid from the Karnataka government to quell the disturbance. All persons are advised to remain in their homes until the city sounds an all clear. Do not panic and do not approach the—"

A hand pounded on the window next to Keira's head. She shrieked. It was Tommy, barely holding his own as the crowd continued to rush past him. Keira pushed open the door and climbed into the passenger seat over the gear shift. Tommy climbed in and closed the door again.

"Whose car is this?" he asked.

"I don't know. Be quiet."

"...*reports, but the center of the disturbance is at the Malleswaram Circle. Authorities assure us that the situation is well in hand.*"

"Well in hand *my ass*!" Tommy shouted. Keira laughed.

"Wait," she said. "*Freddie's* is in Malleswaram Circle!"

"I think you're right."

"All of this started at *Freddie's*?" Keira couldn't imagine it.

The flow of escapees, if that's what they were, dropped to a trickle. For a moment, the intersection was empty. Keira gestured for Tommy to get out of the sedan. She followed him.

The sounds of the crowd's retreat were obvious to the south. Slowly, another sound came to Keira's attention, coming from the north. At first she thought it was birds, thousands of birds. She put one booted foot onto the tire of the sedan and pulled herself onto the hood of the car.

"Keira!"

Down the street, more than a block away, she saw the source of the chirping. A herd of Blues rushed toward them. Keira felt a momentary giddy lightheadedness, as if all of reality had taken a ninety degree turn directly into the unknown. *Invasion.* That was the first thought in her fevered mind. The end of humanity was upon them. How foolish they had been! How trusting! How...

Another sound came from behind the Blue herd, a darker, heavier sound. One which was all too familiar. The sound of a rampaging mob of people. Humans.

Keira climbed up the windshield and onto the roof of the car.

"Get down!" Tommy yelled. "We have to get out of here!"

"It's humans! We're the ones rioting!"

Behind the bobbing, scurrying Blues came a horde of angry people, some carrying makeshift weapons: umbrellas, cricket bats, canes, fire extinguishers. She jumped when a shot rang out. She could see a puff of smoke from somewhere in the human mob, but she couldn't quite determine who held the firearm. Thankfully, the sound was not repeated.

"Here they come!" Keira called out. The Blues were climbing in their alien, vaguely crablike way over the cars in the intersection. Keira noted with a queasy feeling the number of wounds the Blues had incurred. Some had limbs that were clearly broken. A few sported greenish splotches on their skin that might have been bruises. Many leaked a golden fluid that had to be their version of blood.

Tommy looked up to Keira, frightened. She reached down and offered him a hand. With her help, he climbed onto the car with her. The fleetest of the Blues galloped down the sidewalk faster than any human could run. The mass of them came next, many limping, some helping their injured comrades along. At the rear of the pack came those more severely injured. One stumbled and collapsed to the sidewalk directly opposite their automotive refuge.

The mob of people hadn't yet reached the intersection, but they would arrive in seconds.

"Get him!" Keira ordered.

"What?"

Keira jumped down off the car's roof. She opened the back door of the car and grabbed the Blue. The injured alien wheezed through two undamaged nostrils. Its third was caked with dried, yellow blood.

"Come on," she urged the Blue, lifting his rail-like body from the sidewalk. Tommy came down to help, his eyes shifting constantly to the north. The Blue chirped with pain, but used its two good legs to help propel itself into the car. Keira went in first. After making sure the creature had no appendages still outside, Tommy slammed the door shut, then climbed into the front seat and locked the car.

The bloodthirsty crowd roared past, too intent on the goal right before their eyes to notice one straggler locked away in a car.

"Are you mad?" Tommy asked.

"You want him to die?" Keira shot back.

"I don't want *you* to die!"

The Blue made a snittering sound which Keira took to be a cough. With some difficulty, the alien spoke. "I offer no offense. Query."

"Are you alright? Can I help you?" Keira asked.

"Gratitude. Are you skilled in *b-b-b-b* healing?" The Blue was in such distress, it had reverted to its own language briefly, which to Keira sounded like a poorly played tuba with a stutter.

"I know human first aid," Keira said. Hanging in the back of the sedan were hangers of plastic-covered, laundered shirts. She ripped off the plastic and pulled a white, starched shirt from a hanger. She wrapped one sleeve around the Blue's midsection, where its most significant wound was bleeding onto the upholstery.

The Blue chirped again in pain, then carefully said, "Gratitude."

"What happened?" Tommy asked the Blue. The creature shrank from his passionate question.

Keira leaned in and spoke calmly to the alien. "He means no offense."

"There were many. Too many, perhaps. We are new. Humans became afraid, became hostile."

"Many what?" Keira asked.

"Visitors. Too many of... Blues. Others. Many."

"There was a crowd of aliens?" Tommy asked. "Where?"

"The place of music."

Freddie's.

"Why?" Keira asked.

The Blue's two closest eyes widened. "To witness Miss Sabharwal. Profligate artistry. Many have come."

"Just for her?"

"Many have come. Most have come."

"Most?"

"Seven ninths. Perhaps eight ninths."

"Eight ninths of what?"

"Of... Blues."

Keira shared a worried look with Tommy. If she understood the alien, eighty-nine percent of all the Blues on the planet were in Bengalūru this evening, just to see Elena Sabharwal perform at *Freddie's.* The newspaper, the *Patrika,* had sorely underestimated the number of aliens in the city.

Now the whole scene played out in Keira's imagination. Thousands of Blues, polite though they were, would panic humans unfamiliar with alien cultures. Something small might have sparked the riot: a misunder-

stood word, one Blue who invaded the personal space of the wrong human, a confusing altercation between two alien races that frightened the
nearby humans. Anything.

This herd of Blues that had just scampered past numbered only fifty
or so. There were still thousands more out there. Were they all running?
Were they hiding?

Were they fighting back?

"Why didn't you just buy a memory slip of her latest album?"
Tommy asked.

"Such holds no value," the Blue answered.

"You could buy a player, speakers, whatever. You didn't need to all
descend on the poor girl," Tommy argued. Keira hadn't thought what
kind of effect this might have had on Elena Sabharwal herself. She'd developed into a good approximation of a worldly woman, but no twenty-
one-year-old should have to shoulder the burden of causing a city-wide
riot.

"Such holds no value," the Blue said again. "Secondary performance.
Only primary performance holds value."

Keira took a deep breath. She didn't want to yell at this poor being,
who had been so poorly treated by humanity, but the thing needed to understand what had caused the riot.

"I offer no offense, but you have to understand that humans only
learned about other species very recently. We're not used to having large
groups of visitors nearby. It's going to take us some time to get used to
having aliens in our midst. Do you understand?"

The Blue approximated a curtsy, though poorly, given its one broken
leg and the confines of the car.

It spoke softly: "We offer no offense."

Quiet Time

> *Time is like a river made up of the events which happen, and a violent stream; for as soon as a thing has been seen, it is carried away, and another comes in its place, and this will be carried away too.*
>
> —*Meditations, IV, 43*

Most of the worlds that generate life have a healthy proportion of ocean on their surfaces. Life rarely expands quickly or creatively in a very dry environment. Though, species which live their lives *entirely* under the sea are also rare in the scheme of things around the galaxy. Sylvester suspected that wasn't because aquatic creatures aren't intelligent, but that it is a particularly difficult engineering challenge to fly a space ship filled with water out of a planet's gravity well. He imagined hundreds of undersea civilizations humming along within their unbroken cocoons, blithely uninterested in the sparkling night skies above their watery worlds.

Such a waste!

All of this meant that Sylvester had seen what dozens of cultures had done to modify the landscapes of their planets, to reclaim much needed land from the sea. It was a common enough practice, since population explosions are almost as ubiquitous in the galaxy as ocean dominated worlds.

But Earth? These Humans were rather strange creatures, for a variety of reasons. And here was one more. On any reasonable world, synthetic land would be the province of the poor, or a place for the dirtier industries, prisons, waste dumps, etc. The rich and powerful would remain on natural land, enjoying the soothing undulations of hills and the pleasant effects of the water table: streams and lakes and whatnot.

On Earth, landfills were some of the most expensive real estate on the planet! Elaborate islands designed for the elite to spend their vacation time. Extensions of seaside metropolises jam packed with towering condominium developments.

Take this island toward which Sylvester's Gulfstream now flew: Kansei Airport, serving the city of Osaka in the nation of Japan. It was one of the largest artificial islands on Earth, now one of the most lucrative transportation hubs in Asia. Ridiculous!

It had been about two ninths of a billion ticks since the opening of Earth's cocoon, and Humanity seemed to be handling the intrusion of the outside fairly well, the occasional riot notwithstanding. For example, aliens such as Sylvester could, with the appropriate government-sponsored identification card, fly to and from most nations of the world on the Humans' local transportation network. The United States and India had been the most welcoming, followed closely by the strangely fractured collection of tiny nations collectively known as Europe. The only major industrial power who remained standoffish towards the visitors was Japan.

No matter. Sylvester preferred his private jet to even the poshest of first class airline accommodations.

His visit to Japan—Sylvester expected it to be a short one—was sponsored by a man named Isao Murakami, the CEO of Ken-Ya Holdings, one of those vast and impersonal conglomerations of unrelated businesses for which Sylvester felt a true affinity. Murakami seemed ill-contented with his empire at any given moment, continually adding and subtracting, of course generating healthy profits with each round of restructuring. Sylvester was in much the same situation, as he continued to build and expand his contacts with Humans around the world. The cancer cure was merely the beginning, an easy way to earn Humanity's trust. Sooner or later his opportunity would come. He would be prepared. Until then, he would continue to take meetings—and hopefully make sales—with people like Murakami.

The limousine rolled to a stop at the airport entrance at precisely ten minutes before the hour. Isao nodded silently to himself, then bounded out of the vehicle without the slightest word for his driver. For Isao, arrival at his destination at the appropriate time—not early, not late—was merely a result of the driver doing his job. Workers at such a level do not live in a world of variations of success. For them, life is up/down, on/off, success/failure.

Isao, on the other hand, lived on a higher plane, a more difficult existence colored with shades of gray. Many of those fellow Japanese who Murakami considered peers—and that was a short list indeed—determined success by how many yen they earned in a year, or how many school girls they might bed before their aging peckers finally dried up. For Isao, life was about *efficiency*—not exactly an unusual desire for a Japanese. But he coveted efficiency like no one else he had ever met.

With the rending of the sky and the appearance of alien visitors on Earth, Murakami found opportunities exploding around him at a rate that challenged his ability to keep up. Alien translation services. Customizations to automobiles for alien drivers and passengers. Automated orbital docking facilities for visiting craft. Ken-Ya Holdings were involved in all of these ventures and dozens more. Had Murakami enough subordinates with true initiative, these projects might have numbered in the hundreds. Even in an industrious society like modern Japan, men with drive to match Isao's were few. Time itself was his most precious commodity. And so, the meeting with the Snake.

It stood to reason that more scientifically advanced races around the galaxy might have developed some of the truly baroque technologies that even in this day of wonders were still the province of writers of fiction here on Earth. After a few discreet inquiries to the right people, Murakami learned that this Sylvester might have the answer he had long hoped for.

The helmeted security guard at the airport entrance bowed deeply to Murakami as he held open the door. This new terminal was still under construction, a much needed addition to the capacity of the overworked airport. With his ties to government, Murakami arranged for the alien to fly to Kansei, on the condition that he never leave the unfinished terminal, and therefore never officially enter the nation of Japan.

A trio of dark suited men greeted Murakami within the deserted terminal, greeting him with deep bows. The eldest of the three addressed him. "Murakamisan."

Isao responded with a swift, dismissive bow of his own.

"This way, sir." Murakami followed the men through the wide corridors and high ceilings of the sparkling, new terminal. The Snake's jet had been parked at the nearest gate. The security door to the jetway remained closed, another helmeted guard waiting at the checkpoint like a statue. The eldest assistant nodded to the guard. The guard opened the door.

Murakami tensed, not wishing to reveal any distaste at the sight of the alien. It would be disrespectful to the visitor and indicate weakness on his part. Neither of these was acceptable. When the creature slithered through the doorway, Isao found himself surprised. The thing resembled a child's toy. Its beady red eyes were devilish, to be sure, and its yellow teeth—stretched wide in a carnivorous smile—carried a hint of menace. But the creature was also covered in soft fur. Isao could imagine his grandchildren cooing at the thing and asking for a tiny stuffed version as a birthday gift.

Sylvester slid directly to Murakami and offered him a gracious nod of his head. Without hips, it was hopeless for the thing to even attempt a proper bow.

"Murakamisan."

"Sylvestersan."

"I've heard you're fluent in English," the alien said, slipping into his preferred tongue so easily one might expect he'd been taught the language as a child.

"I am," Isao answered, fully aware of his accent. He had learned the brutish tongue for expediency's sake, not from any love of its harsh sounds or its imperfect, ever-shifting meanings.

The Snake—such was the name humanity had given this creature's species, as others of his kind had come to Earth in the past few months—gestured with one of his hands back to the jetway.

"I have sample cases still on my plane, if one of your men would be so kind?"

Murakami looked to the eldest assistant, who in turn looked to the youngest. The young man bowed and practically ran down the jetway. He returned, rolling two sturdy metal travel cases. The larger was wheeled and had a retractable handle. The smaller sat on top, lashed down with a length of elastic cable.

"I would have brought a woman of my own, an assistant to help with such things, as I'm sure you can imagine." Sylvester held up his hands in a show of defeat, underlining his physical limitations. "But, as you could only allow myself and my pilot..." He left the accusation unfinished, which was just as well.

Murakami gestured to the assistants and the guard. All four men hurried off to a far corner of the empty terminal, leaving Isao alone with the Snake. The silence spun out for a moment.

"Well, then. I'm not so familiar with your culture, Murakamisan. Is it time for us to make 'small talk', or get right to business, then?"

"You understand my request?"

The Snake pulled himself to a larger height, as if excited by the prospect of making a sale. "Why, yes. I believe you are looking for a time machine."

Murakami nodded. A man of lesser fortitude would have felt foolish making such a request. As it was, Murakami had no tangible reason to expect that anything would come of this meeting, but it was a worthy wager of his time and resources, if only the faintest hint of the possibility lay before him.

"I'll tell you, sir, that what I have here..." The alien patted the sample cases. "...are not run of the mill items. It's not strictly against the rules for me to bring them to you. Let's say it is *frowned upon*, if you get my meaning."

Isao waited.

"A buyer who wants the salesman to talk! What a refreshing change of scenery! I think I might like to spend more time in Japan."

Isao narrowed his eyes. The alien took the hint.

"Ah, well, then I'll get right to it. If you want to travel forward in time, you can't. I'm afraid that is, as far as the best minds in the galaxy can tell, impossible. The future hasn't happened, you see. Similarly, you can't travel backward in time. While the past has happened, it seems that the universe is rather strict about the concept of paradoxes. It simply doesn't allow them to happen. I hope you aren't too disappointed."

"Are you saying this meeting was a waste of my time?"

"No! Certainly not, chum. I mean, sir. No, no." Sylvester undid the hooks holding the elastic cord around the cases and opened the latch on the smaller. He pulled out an oblong silver device that looked uncomfortably like a dildo. The alien seemed unaware of the connotation of the shape to a human.

"I think the best word for this item would be an *accelerator*. I can't jump you forward in time, but I can accelerate your personal frame of reference." The alien twisted the bottom of the device. At that moment, Sylvester froze. His eyes stopped swiveling in their tiny sockets. His hands held the device motionlessly. Isao peered closer, noting that the hairs of his coat were also frozen, untouched by the breezes of the air conditioning in the terminal.

"Sylvestersan." Nothing. The alien remained still as a statue. "Sylvestersan!"

Four heads popped out from behind a wall fifty meters away, looking to see if their master required assistance. He waved them off.

If this was all the alien had to offer, Murakami was not interested. He could imagine lesser folk would jump at the idea of skipping effortlessly past the more tedious parts of their lives. Murakami's life was not tedious. Waiting for this Snake to snap out of his temporal trance, on the other hand, was more than tedious. It was unbearable.

Like a paused DVD returning to life, Sylvester was again reanimated. "I hope that wasn't too terrible for you. I set the accelerator for sixty seconds."

"It seemed longer." Isao said nothing else. The alien understood.

"I see you have no need of acceleration. Your time is quite valuable. I understand. Perhaps then you would be interested in *deceleration*."

Isao's eyes widened in interest. The snake slipped the smaller case to the floor and unlatched the larger one. Inside was a box about the size of a toaster. It was sided in silver metal, with a touch screen on one side. Sylvester lifted the thing out of the case and set it on a nearby waiting area chair. The device was heavy, indenting the bright orange foam of the chair's seat.

"What does it do?"

"Precisely the opposite of the accelerator. It slows down your personal temporal reference frame." The snake pressed a few icons on the screen. "Perhaps I should warn you this time." Sylvester added a toothy smile. Isao nodded his agreement. The Snake pressed one last icon.

Nothing happened.

"What do you think?" Sylvester asked.

"I do not understand," Isao said. The snake pointed at the top of Isao's head. He looked up, noticing something shading his view. He reached up and pulled off a helmet.

At the same moment, sounds of alarm came from the distance. Isao looked at the helmet in wonder.

"You slowed time, went to the security guard, took his helmet and placed it on my head."

"Got it in one! Now all of that took me..." Sylvester looked at the display on the box. "...twenty-three seconds. I don't get those twenty-three seconds for free. I have to pay it back."

"Pay it back?"

"Yes." He held up the accelerator. "So, please, allow me to reset my temporal frame. I'll be back with you in twenty-three seconds." Before Isao could argue, the Snake turned the base of the accelerator again and froze.

Since Isao knew that the Snake would be alive and talking again soon, the wait was more bearable this time. *This* is what Isao needed. He eyed the innocuous looking box with envy. The ability to pull free time out of thin air. Remarkable. Lost in his thoughts, he was startled when the Snake said.

"So, did you like it?"

"It is acceptable."

"I need to make something clear to you, Murakamisan. You really must reset your frame after every use. The consequences of not doing so..."

"What are the consequences?"

Sylvester scanned the area. One level above the airy departure lounge was a balcony leading to the baggage claim area at the airport exit. Sylvester grabbed the elastic cord and slithered toward a single flight escalator. Murakami followed. Sylvester examined the base of the escalator, finding the power switch.

"Time is always moving, relentlessly, in one direction. If you slow your personal frame, you are asking time to roll forward without you." The Snake took the metal hook at one end of the cord and placed it around the escalator's power switch. "When you do this, when you put a stake in time and anchor yourself to it, your original frame continues forward in time." The snake took the hook at the other end of the cord and slid it under the rubber hand rail of the escalator. He tested both ends to make sure they were secure. "The larger the distance between your personal frame and your original frame, the more strain you put on your connection to the space time continuum."

All of this sounded like so much nonsense to Murakami. The Snake turned on the escalator. The steps began their never-ending ascent, and the hand rail slid up, pulling the cord taut, then stretching it tighter and tighter.

"The universe is continually expanding, as I'm sure you already know. It is expanding in space... and in time. Time may seem to move at a constant rate over the course of your life, but that is only because of your continual appearance in your personal frame. Time itself expands every second of every day of every year. Such an expansion is irrelevant if you travel in sync with the flow of time..."

The end of the cord now extended halfway up the escalator. Isao could hear the nylon cord squeaking in protest. The hook slipped a centimeter against the hand rail, then caught again. The cord continued to stretch.

"Even if you take a few minutes, if you don't return it, the universe won't like it. If you take more than a few minutes, if you take a day, for example, the universe won't like it." Sylvester brandished the unfortunately shaped accelerator. "You must use this."

"Or what?"

As if in response, the cord reached its limit. Isao expected the hook embedded in the hand rail to give way, perhaps tearing a chunk out of the rubber. Instead, the hook at the lower end, attached to the power switch, let go with a loud snapping noise. The cord shot halfway up the escalator, lying limply on the paused steps. The cord had put so much stress on the power switch that the switch was flipped, and the escalator powered down.

"What does this mean?" Isao asked. "I do not believe that misuse of this device would stop time."

Sylvester laughed. "No, of course not. Misuse of this device may stop *you*, however."

"Kill me."

"I don't precisely know."

Isao growled. "You would play with me."

"I am not playing with you. I'm saying that I don't know. Those I have heard of who have abused this sort of technology have never been heard from again. They simply... disappeared. I cannot tell you what their fate was. I can only surmise that it was not a pleasant one."

"Your warnings are duly noted."

Sylvester slipped effortlessly up the stalled escalator stairs to retrieve his packing cord.

"Payment, then," Isao said.

"One billion yen," Sylvester said simply as he descended the steps. "I imagine that is pocket change for you."

This alien was canny, Isao noted. In one moment, Sylvester had challenged him to even attempt a negotiation, and at the same time, indicated that such negotiation would be beneath a man such as Isao Murakami. He allowed Sylvester to see one of his very rare smiles.

"We have a deal."

For the first few days after he purchased the decelerator, Isao followed the Snake's instructions diligently. His first use of the machine allowed him to collate a variety of papers that his subordinates had sorted improperly, but which he needed for a board meeting. With the press of a few icons on the machine's simple, square screen, Isao brought the entire universe to a halt around him. He spent five minutes searching out and ordering the necessary paperwork before his meeting began.

After the successful meeting, Isao made certain his secretary knew he was to be undisturbed, then he used the accelerator to give back the five minutes. He watched the clock on his desk as he performed the action. As promised, the minute hand of the dial clicked forward, though Isao did not note a single second of time passing.

There were limitations, of course. He had to limit his jumps to moments when he was in his office. He could not use the machine, for example, to drive across town if he was running late. Without the passage of time, his car could not start, its engine could not run.

In fact, interactions with any sort of electronic device were impossible. During a jump his tablet was frozen, his cell phone was incapable of making any calls, the elevator in his office building could not travel from floor to floor. Isao never prepared his own meals, preferring to have lunches delivered to his office and eating in restaurants at dinner. He could decelerate his way through a lunch in the privacy of his own office; he could only imagine the looks from the servers at a restaurant if his meal disappeared in an instant.

So, Isao focused on the minutia of his daily office grind, sneaking a minute here, or a quarter-hour there, dutifully paying back the stolen moments, usually at the end of the day, before his driver took him home.

Isao's wife, Maia, took notice of the change, complaining that Isao's long days were now longer, that he seemed busier than ever and running low on patience for his home, his family, and his life outside of work. Isao, in an uncharacteristic burst of rage, claimed that his work was his life. Maia responded by requesting that Isao not come home anymore.

The Murakamis had dealt with problems in their marriage before, but their combined duty to their children had kept their relationship limping along. Now, their youngest was away at university. Their relationship finally succumbed to years of slow degradation and shattered under this newfound pressure. Privately, Isao felt this to be a grim, unwished-for blessing.

Isao found one daily activity to be more inefficient than all others: sleep. Now, with the opportunity to spend his nights at the office, where he had the decelerator, he could use the device far more freely. He preferred to sleep while using the decelerator. With the universe paused all around him, he was surrounded by total, lovely silence. He could steal as much as seven hours of time in this way, and then pay it all back during the next day.

By following this new routine—decelerating through his nightly slumber—he had all of the day at his command. He judiciously chose the moments to pay back the stolen hours, between one meeting and the next conference call. During the rare cancelled appointment. Unfortunately, finding enough moments to pay back all that borrowed time was difficult. His days were too full, overfull. He simply could not pay it all back.

On his third day after leaving his wife, Isao left ninety-three minutes unpaid before using the decelerator a second time. He knew he had done this: he kept meticulous records of his forays into and out of the time stream. He remembered the Snake's warnings. He simply vowed to pay the time back the next day. And he did, painful as it was to throw away an hour and a half. The only answer? Sleep less. He shifted to a six hours per night schedule. After two days with no serious after effects, Isao chipped that down to five hours.

Two weeks went by. Isao was more productive than he'd ever been in his life, but the reduced sleep began taking its toll on him. He seemed more tired every morning, buoyed as much as possible by caffeine. He began to slip, leaving a few seconds of quiet time unaccounted for here, another minute there.

His debt of time to the universe mounted, slowly but steadily.

After three weeks of separation from Maia, Isao's sleep schedule had shifted drastically forward. He continued to work long past midnight, and deep into the next morning. He generally took his abbreviated sleep at about 5 AM. This morning, he woke not at the end of this decelerated cycle, but nearly an hour later, after the decelerator had shut off. It was bad enough that he had overslept, but he would have continued to sleep if not for the ringing phone.

"Mushi-mushi."

"Isao!" That was Maia. She was in tears. "It's Ken!"

Isao's fatigue blew away in a wind of adrenaline. Ken was their eldest, a man of thirty-five years, with three children of his own. Ken was the joy of Isao's life, or had been, before he found the decelerator. He had named his company after the boy.

"What is it?"

"He was hit by a truck!" Maia rattled off the name and room number of the hospital. Isao vowed to be there soon. He cleaned himself up and was out the door in moments.

His temporal debt now totaled six hours and thirty-two minutes.

Ken Murakami had been injured quite dramatically by a run-in with a delivery truck in Abeno-suji while on his way across the street to a department store. Both legs were broken, one in three places. Five ribs were cracked. His spine was wrenched, though his spinal cord seemed undamaged. The real problems were his abdominal injuries. The truck's bumper had slammed into Ken's belly, damaging his stomach, his liver, his spleen, and his small intestine. The initial round of surgery lasted fourteen hours.

Isao waited with Maia in a white, antiseptic family room. Ken's wife and children were there as well, sobbing quietly. Ken's two sisters had sent word that they would arrive the next morning from Tokyo. Isao and Maia spoke together in hushed tones for a while, then simply sat, arms about each other's shoulders, as they waited for Ken's surgery to end. They both slept fitfully.

At midnight, a nurse gently woke Isao, explaining that the doctor wished to speak with him. He roused Maia and the others. The doctor, a younger man than Isao had expected, entered the room and explained in simple words the devastating effects of the crash on Ken, and their efforts to save his life. The doctor was careful to maintain a cautious tone even as he announced the surgery was successful. Ken's wife and children cried out in joy. Maia grasped Isao's arm, and he patted her hand.

"Can we see him?" Isao asked.

"In a short while, Murakami-san," the doctor said.

A short while turned out to be another five hours. Maia suggested Isao go back to their home to wash up and change clothes. He shook his head.

"I will wait."

The sun came up on a new day as the family waited to see Ken. Maia noted how much this ordeal had taken its toll on her husband. Isao looked tired and broken. More than once she saw him shake, as if a spasm had coursed through his entire body.

"Isao?"

He shook his head. "It's nothing."

Ken's sisters arrived, each with their husbands. Neither had children yet, but Rumi was pregnant with her first. They had barely completed their teary greetings with the rest of the family when the nurse came to announce that Ken could receive visitors.

As a member of the respected Murakami family, Ken had received a large private room in the hospital and was attended by a team of nurses. The family trooped into the room silently, seeing Ken lying there, body broken and patched, his face pale, his eyes closed.

Isao moved to the bed first, laying a hand gently on his son's fore-head. Ken's eyes flipped open. Gasps came from everyone in the room, followed by excited greetings. The nurse shushed them, but only half-heartedly. Maia watched as Isao backed away from the bed to allow the women in the room to speak to Ken. Isao's body spasmed again, the pain clear on his face. She moved toward him.

"Isao, what's wrong?"

"I…" His body jerked again. To Maia's tired eyes, it almost seemed as if he was being *pulled*, by strings, up off of his feet. Her first thought was that he was having a stroke.

"I'm not—" he tried to say. It happened again. The movement was more violent this time. It wasn't Maia's imagination. Isao *lifted* from the ground by a couple of centimeters. She hurried to him, grabbing his arms.

"Maia! Don't!" Isao tried to bat away her hands. She held him tight. When his body was pulled upward again, she could feel him being dragged away from her. She also felt something like an electric shock through his touch.

"I'll get a doctor!"

The others in the room turned, realizing something was happening with their father.

Maia felt another spasm shudder through her husband, and he was *yanked* up and out of her hands. Before he could smash into the ceiling, his body winked out of existence. Maia and her daughters and grand-daughters screamed. Ken yelled for the doctor. Pandemonium filled the room. The nurse returned.

"What's wrong?" She ran to Ken, assuming the problem was with her patient.

"My husband!" Maia shouted. "He—"

Isao returned, standing once again right where he had been. His face was contorted by confusion and pain. Maia reached out for him. His hands felt warm, as if he had developed a fever in just the last minute.

"Where did you go?"

"Sir? Sir?" The nurse moved toward Isao, reaching for him, eyes wide at the spectacle of a man appearing out of nowhere.

Isao swatted all of their hands away.

"Wait for me!" he shouted.

Maia watched, fixated on Isao's haunted eyes, as he disappeared again. She couldn't be certain, because the thing happened so fast, but he seemed to *blur*, like a picture of a runner taken with film of the wrong speed.

And he was gone.

The doctor came and took the statements of all the witnesses to the strange occurrence. This was out of his depth, so he contacted the police. An inspector came to the hospital and questioned each of the members of the Murakami family and the nurse who had witnessed the phenomenon. Their stories were wild and unbelievable, but they largely matched. Powerful businessman Isao Murakami had been pulled out of existence by some strange, unseen force.

"What did he mean, 'Wait for me'?" the inspector asked.

Maia had no answer. She only knew that she would follow her husband's instruction.

The other members of the family rotated in and out of Ken's room for the rest of the day. Ken's three girls went back to school. Ken's sisters took their things to their parents' house for their stay in Osaka. Ken's wife left the room to get a bite of lunch.

Maia stayed, waiting, patiently.

"Mother, you should get some rest," Ken counseled.

"He told me to wait."

"You don't know how long that will be," Ken said, his tone making it clear he never expected his father to reappear. Ken-Ya Holdings had many projects in the works dealing with exotic alien technologies. Who knew what kind of craziness Father had gotten rolled up into?

"He told me to wait, and I shall wait," Maia said simply. She smiled, trying to put Ken at ease. He had a long recovery in front of him. "You should rest."

Ken agreed, drifting off after only a few moments.

The room was quiet. Only the steady sleep-breathing of her son told Maia that time hadn't simply come to a standstill. She was close to sleep herself.

A smell filled the room. It made Maia sit up straight, looking around. It smelled like... smoke. Who would light a fire inside a hospital? She jumped up and rushed to her son's bed, to make sure nothing was amiss.

Six hours and thirty-one minutes after Isao disappeared, a blast of roaring hot air rolled over Maia's back. Since she stood by the bed, her body inadvertently guarded Ken and his delicate wounds from the rush of superheated air. The hospital's fire alarm began to blare. She turned to find a flaming mannequin standing in the room. In a frightening moment of clarity, she knew—she *knew*—that this was Isao.

Isao screamed, seeming to be as surprised by what was happening as Maia was. He fell to the floor and rolled, trying to put out the flames that engulfed every inch of his body. Maia yanked the top blanket from Ken's bed and threw it on top of Isao to smother the flames. Ken awoke, shouting for help.

Two nurses arrived. The alarm warned them what to expect, so they each carried a fire extinguisher. They sprayed foam onto Isao. Between his thrashing, the blanket, and the foam, the flames finally went out, though the smell of burning clothing and flesh filled the room with a horrifying stench.

Maia knelt next to the red and black monster that was her husband. He moaned, unable to move more than a few inches. Maia burst into tears, in this terrible moment simply glad that Isao was still alive.

More people rushed into the room, a nurse and two doctors. They moved Maia brusquely out of the way, and tended to Isao, preparing him for transport out of the patient recovery area and into their burn ward.

Isao's debt was repaid.

Defense of the Realm

> *And it is enough to remember*
> *that law rules all.*
> —*Meditations, VII, 31*

A year ago, Terry Youngblood would have blanched whiter than snow at the thought of going to the White House for a meeting with the President. Now, such things were old hat. Of course, he still found the process nerve-wracking, but at least he had experience dealing with that particular brand of fear.

After being the first government agent to speak to an alien—a sentient spaceship, in fact—and after successfully brokering a deal with the enigmatic Sylvester for an early warning system in the Oort cloud, Terry had become the nation's official military expert in all things extraterrestrial. With this added visibility and responsibility came a promotion; he was now Major Youngblood. It also meant he hadn't flown in ten months. He missed the feel of a yoke in his hands, but he knew this work was important, important enough to make sacrifices.

Today was Sunday, July 23, 2023. The heliopause had broken a little over two years ago, and things were definitely taking a turn lately.

Immigration from off world was skyrocketing—no pun intended— around the globe, largely in the major metropolitan areas of Asia and Europe. Visits to the US were high, too, but tourist-friendly America seemed better prepared for an influx of unexpected visitors. The problem was that the aliens didn't seem to much care for the traditionally popular destinations. Only a sprinkling had visited London or Paris or Rome. They had grown fond of places that most Americans would have to check an atlas to locate: Bucharest, Dalian, Ulan Bataar, Gdansk, Bangalore. The single most visited city in the United States was Austin, Texas, for God's sake!

There were twenty-three thousand known visitors on the planet right now, representing nearly fifty distinct species. Estimates of the ac-

tual number of aliens on Earth were between double and triple that number.

The sectors of humanity who were most concerned about the visitors had quieted down after the first few months. Religious groups around the world—Hindu, Muslim, Christian—had warned their flocks that this was a precursor to whichever flavor of the End of Days they subscribed to. Economic doomsayers had warned of a dangerous destabilization of markets with an influx of "cheap goods". True, a few aliens had brought items for trade, but they were uniformly technological in nature, and brand new technologies at that. The investors who had shorted light sweet crude a year ago because they thought free energy was around the corner were paying for their mistake now.

While most of the visitors acted like civilized people—strange, often, but civilized—there were disturbances...

A tense standoff with local police in New York City led to a confused "hostage" situation. A race of colorful—and, to Terry, slightly disturbing—aliens who'd been dubbed Lilies had begun eating the trees in Central Park, something New York's Finest hadn't been too happy about. The eight-hour, highly televised confrontation finally ended without loss of life—of any species. The Lilies agreed to leave the city, and the State of New York offered them a buffet of their pick of trees in Old Croton Aqueduct State Park as an apology.

An incident in Mecca did not go nearly as well. It ended with the deaths of twenty-six Skeletons, a race that subsequently left Earth en masse. They had not yet returned.

A riot in Bangalore, which began at a jazz concert, ended with the deaths of fifteen Blues and five humans.

One alien—from a race nicknamed Rope Men—had been captured in Vladivostok and sentenced to life in prison for three counts of murder—of humans. A UN team had observed the trial and sentencing, reporting that, in their opinion, the Rope Man had been treated fairly. Thankfully, there were no significant repercussions from the alien community.

But when would these unfortunate, unrelated incidents evolve into larger altercations between humans and aliens? When would enough aliens descend on the planet to seriously derail humanity's ability to self-govern? When, in short, would the military be needed? These were the questions that kept Terry up at night, because it was his job, not only to answer them, but to ask them in the first place.

Terry dropped the lanyard with his security pass around his neck as he entered the White House. A college-age girl escorted him through the maze of hallways to a large conference room, which was slowly filling with suits and uniforms alike. Terry made his way carefully through the room to General Carol Brown. Her role as Commander of AFSPC had become vastly more important in the past two years. She managed the increased military presence in LEO, the feeds from the early warning system, and the still growing land-based team dedicated to Earth's safety from off world threats. Terry reported directly to her.

"General, what's up?" Terry indicated the crowd. His meetings with the President had, in the past, been smaller affairs.

Brown answered with a knowing tilt of her head. Terry followed the gesture with his eyes. A civilian woman with pale skin and auburn hair in a stylish bob was talking in soft tones with Victor Fremont, the President's very hands-on Chief of Staff.

"Who's she?" Terry asked. General Brown's look of surprise answered the question. Terry put two and two together. He hadn't met her yet, but he'd certainly heard of Vanessa Hargrove.

After her whirlwind visit to the White House in April of '21, Vanessa was the Flavor of the Month. She stayed in D.C. for four weeks, downloading every bit of knowledge about the *Voyager* program to people from NASA, from the military, from Congress, from the FBI. She was patient—at first. She knew that the debrief was a necessary evil. She bore up under the strain, confident that soon enough they would stop asking for *information* and start asking for *opinion*.

This, of course, never happened. One day she was telling her story for the fiftieth time to a team of shadowy NSA operatives, the next day she was handed a first class ticket back to Pasadena. Thanks for all the help, Ms. Hargrove. Keep in touch. Don't let the door smack you in the ass as you leave.

When she e-mailed Shao with the news that she was on her way home, Shao—whose interrogation ended after only three days—offered to plan and execute a huge celebration, to commemorate her return and her discovery. She told him not to bother. She used what she hoped was exactly the correct tone to make it clear that she felt a party wasn't necessary, but that she'd like one all the same. Shao read her tone perfectly, and celebrate they did, with much of JPL coming to the hastily prepared event. Shao went so far as to get a local baker to make a heliopause-shaped cake.

Vanessa enjoyed her moment, her fifteen minutes. She felt a little sad that it hadn't lasted longer, but, in the end, her name would be in the history books. It was she, after all, who ordered the barrier to fall.

A few days later, on Thursday, July 22, circumstances yanked Vanessa back into the spotlight. One of the very small perks of her celebrity was that she no longer had to work strange hours at JPL. She had a very reasonable, nine-to-five, Monday-to-Friday schedule now. And Vanessa did covet her weekends. On Saturdays, she would routinely sleep in as long as her mind and body would allow... which was usually until about 10:30. On a weekday, however, she was always up by six, sometimes to check the net, sometimes—but not often enough—to go for a run. On this day, a knock at her door woke her closer to five. She pulled on a robe and shuffled to the door, hoping it wasn't one of the occasional reporters looking for an interview—or worse, a picture. She peered through her front door's peep hole and saw nothing.

"Hello?"

"Vanessa Hargrove?" came a nasal voice.

"Yes?"

"Vanessa Hargrove?" the voice repeated exactly as before. Vanessa slipped into her tidy little living room—where she had a too-nice sofa and a couple of high-backed chairs that maybe five people had ever sat on—and looked out at the street. There were no cars parked nearby. Unfortunately, the angle from here didn't allow her to see who stood at her front door.

The knock sounded again. She went back to the door, made sure the chain was drawn, and cracked it open just enough to look out.

"What is—" She paused. There was no one standing on her porch. There was only a silvery sphere, floating at eye level. The sphere was just about the size of a human head, and to add to the creepiness, it had a single, ruby-red eye at its center, just about the size of a human eye. The sphere spun a few degrees, far enough for the eye to fix directly on her. "What are—" Her question was interrupted by a flash of light. Nearly blinded, she backed away from the door.

The device—whatever it was—spoke again. "Identity confirmed." Then there was a strange crinkly, metallic sound. Vanessa blinked, and caught just a glimpse of the metal sphere folding itself inside out and falling to the concrete porch with a plastic clatter. Vanessa rubbed her eyes, making sure her vision hadn't been permanently damaged, then looked out again. The sphere was gone, replaced by what looked like a three-ring binder. Slowly, she unchained the door and reached for the binder. The words on the cover made her shiver:

Central Authority
Rules of Conduct
(Earth Edition)

Down in the lower right-hand corner, in smaller type, were these words:

Presented to Earth Representative
Vanessa Hargrove

Vanessa realized that her fifteen minutes were not up just yet.

Victor Fremont brought the meeting to order, finally. Vanessa scrolled through her notes on her tablet. This was going to be a difficult meeting. The better prepared she was, the less painful it would be.

This was her first major interaction with the higher-ups at the Pentagon. She saw all manner of uniforms on the other side of the table. For better or worse, it was time to consult with the military.

Fremont just barely had control of the room when, as one, everyone at the table stood. The President strode into the room and sat at the end of the table. As always, the President avoided small talk and got right down to business.

"We have only two items on the agenda, ladies and gentlemen, but they are both crucial to National Security." Vanessa refrained from rolling her eyes. The time of "national" security was long since past. The sooner the people at this table realized that, the better. "I want to know," the President continued, "who leaked the Rules."

All eyes swiveled to Vanessa. Some were accusatory, others simply confused.

"Mr. President, I can explain that."

"Can you?" The President's tone was stern.

"Yes, sir. A reporter from the BBC interviewed a Blue in Liverpool two days ago, asking her a fairly straightforward question: is there a galactic version of the UN? The Blue answered that there was, and went on to offer everything she knew about CA—Central Authority, that is. The reporter contacted my office for verification of the story."

"And you gave it?" Fremont asked, aghast.

"No, of course not." Several of the people at the table likely didn't believe Vanessa. She had championed the idea of making the Rules of Conduct public knowledge since the day they had been dropped quite literally on her doorstep. She had argued that keeping them secret was the equivalent of keeping the Constitution secret. There were no security implications in revealing the Rules to the public, to our allies or enemies around the world, to the press, to anyone.

More cautious heads, however, prevailed, and the Rules were made Top Secret from then on. The only thing more incredible than that decision was the fact that the Rules had remained secret for two years. In Vanessa's view, keeping this information close to the vest had merely injured the President's relationship with the nation. If something as innocuous as this was being kept from them, what information of real importance was he sitting on?

Well, now the damage was done.

"My office has drafted a statement, explaining the nature of the Rules, and justifying the policy of secrecy." One of Vanessa's deputies—a stern-looking young man named Dale—walked around the long table, handing each person a copy of the statement. They had written into the statement many of the concerns of the Administration, and some other ideas of Vanessa's own, trying to make the whole thing sound like caution rather than paranoia. She saw heads nod as they scanned the two para-graphs. The conversation soon shifted into a political discussion of how this story would impact the party's chances for reelection in '24, the effect on the current legislative session, the spin machine of the web pundits, etc., etc. Vanessa tuned most of that out, returning to her notes for the second part of the meeting, which would make *this* discussion seem like a cakewalk.

"Excuse me." A youngish soldier at the far end of the table spoke up. He was blond and tan, handsome, with a bit of a southern drawl.

"Yes, Major…" Fremont prompted.

"Youngblood, sir. Can we see the Rules?"

Silence around the table.

"If they're gonna be on the web tomorrow anyway… Can we see a copy now?" he persisted.

Vanessa tried to hide a smirk. She remembered her first few days in D.C. as a power player. She had shown her innocence with questions like that, questions that seemed perfectly reasonable on their face, but opened a person up for ridicule and chastisement. She expected Fremont to lay into the boy. She was surprised when the President piped up.

"Son, we haven't officially declassified the document," the President said.

"I understand, sir. I just think that if these are the aliens' version of the Geneva Convention, our department needs to see them as soon as possible."

The silence got louder. The President was a kindly enough gent with the public, but behind closed doors he didn't take crap off anyone. This Youngblood looked like he was still in his twenties, and he was mouthing off to the Leader of the Free World! His superior, a woman Vanessa rec-ognized as General Brown, tried to calm the boy down. It didn't work.

"Look," Youngblood continued, "if the answer is no, that's fine. I'll look it up on BBC.com tomorrow morning. I just think you'd want us to work our plans off the original document, and not from some third-hand version that was translated by an alien that learned English last week."

This kid was about to get himself ejected from this meeting, and maybe from the US Armed Forces while he was at it. Vanessa decided to try to save him.

"Mr. President, in light of the nature of our second topic, perhaps Captain Youngblood—"

"Major!" he interrupted.

"Major, sorry. For what it's worth, I believe Major Youngblood is right. The Pentagon should be brought into the loop as soon as possible." Youngblood looked at Vanessa with a hilarious combination of peevishness and gratitude. The President, on the other hand, looked like a storm cloud ready to rain down on everyone in the room. Fremont stepped into the pause, taking control of the meeting once again.

"If we're done with the security discussion, I think we should move on to the newest communiqué from Central Authority. Ms. Hargrove?"

"Thank you, Mr. Fremont." They weren't really done with the first topic, but Vanessa wanted to get things moving, too. "I received a new message from CA two days ago, and this one is far more sensitive in nature. I would like to read it verbatim to the room, if that's alright, Mr. President."

He nodded, still steaming, but at least his focus was on the issue at hand. Vanessa queued up the document on her tablet and read:

"We have allowed your culture 129,140,163 ticks to absorb the difficult and surely revelatory knowledge that you are not alone in the cosmos. We have every hope that your society will become a valued member of the community of the galaxy. It is, however, with sore hearts that we must make our displeasure at certain of your current transgressions known. Insofar as perfect justice cannot in all expectation be achieved, those gross miscarriages of justice which, by any measure, must be ruled as heinous and predatory, cannot be allowed to continue in any civilized society. We refer in particular to those instances of genocide which, at this intermediate stage of your development, continue to occur in your system. We do not, as a benign and unbiased body, offer any judgment as to the relative merits of either party in these conflicts, only citing our displeasure at the machinations of death and suffering which your people have chosen to use on one other. Such activities, while repugnant in a cocooned society, are unacceptable in a culture on the brink of developing a galactic presence. It falls to this body, therefore, to place a requirement on your people to end all practice of genocide within the next 387,420,489 ticks, or else force may be used to prevent the deaths of innocents. We offer any help that we can provide to aid you in meeting our conditions."

Dale circled the table again with printed copies of the short but explosive ultimatum. Vanessa paused to allow it to sink in. She noticed several confused frowns. She wasn't surprised that this crowd might get stuck on minutia, so she explained.

"I realize these numbers seem arbitrary, but they are quite straightforward in base nine arithmetic, which is the standard for the galaxy. They're giving us a little over six years to clean up our act."

Adam Wilkinson, the diminutive Secretary of Defense, was the first to respond.

"We don't practice genocide," he said firmly.

"You need to be more careful with your pronouns, Mr. Secretary. 'We', to Central Authority, are humanity, not merely the United States of America. 'We', in their eyes, bear the responsibility of crimes carried out on our planet, to our people."

"That's ridiculous," Fremont said. "How can all of humanity be held responsible for the crimes of warlords in Africa?"

"Do you want the moral answer or the practical answer?" Vanessa said.

"Moral," the President snapped.

"We are the most powerful nation on Earth, Mr. President. We have used our power to save innocents before, and we will again. That we aren't using it now to save these particular innocents is, I would submit, a moral outrage."

"We can't hope to end a cycle of cultural rage that has gone on for millennia!" Fremont seethed.

"Don't be so quick to blame this all on Africans. The worst single genocidal event since World War Two was the Hutu and Tutsi conflict in Rwanda in the 1990s. Hutus and Tutsis weren't some sort of ancient tribes. They were racial divisions, based on skin color, concocted by Belgian conquerors in the early Twentieth Century."

"You expect us to pay for the crimes of Europe?" Fremont asked.

"We involved ourselves in the affairs of Europe in 1918. We did so again in 1941. The Middle East in 2003. Kashmir in 2017. Why shouldn't we do it Africa in 2023?"

Vanessa noticed a subtle nod from Major Youngblood.

"Because it's an impossible goal." This gruff voice came from General Reginald McGaw, the Chairman of the Joint Chiefs.

"We attempt the impossible every day, General. Staving off illness and death. Educating our children. Rehabilitating our criminals. Preventing murders within our own borders. We have no hope of achieving these goals perfectly, but we strive for perfection nonetheless. When you led our forces into Kashmir, how many of our men did you plan to kill?"

"You're treading on dangerous ground, little lady," McGaw said, rising slightly from his chair.

"You misunderstand, General. I have nothing but respect for the job you did. It was a phenomenal success, greater than I or anyone at this table might have expected. But still, it was less that we *hoped* for. We hoped for perfection. If I read this statement right, CA hopes for perfection as well, but they are certainly not going to expect it."

"It sounds like they expect perfection to me," Fremont said.

"Bureaucratic rhetoric—that's my guess," Vanessa said.

"Ms. Hargrove," the President said, "you had two answers: moral and practical. What's the practical answer to why we can be held responsible for actions done by others a world away?"

"The practical answer, Mr. President, is that we simply don't have a choice. According to the Rules of Conduct, we won't be allowed a voice in Central Authority to even defend ourselves for several more years. What might other civilizations choose to do to us in that time?"

The Rules of Conduct were, in the final analysis, largely toothless. There were a small handful of taboo actions that the galaxy had collectively agreed to criminalize, and to punish those who committed them. CA frowned on sending stars supernova and the distribution of destructive von Neumann machines. Unfortunately for Earth, they had also outlawed genocide. There were no official protections for Earth should some crusading, do-gooding culture decide the galaxy was better off without humanity. The harsh truth, which Vanessa chose not to lay out on this particular table, was that humanity carried a heavy burden of proving that they were *worthy* of joining Central Authority. Such moral sophistry would devolve into pointless rhetoric in this room. Instead, Vanessa focused on the practicality of their situation.

"Sir, if you don't think that there are a hundred civilizations out there that could conquer or kill all of humanity in a long weekend, then you're fooling yourself." Vanessa realized she was acting almost as rashly as the young Major. She glanced at him, and noted his conspiratorial smile. "We, as Americans, have gotten very used to being at the top. We, as humans, need to get used to being way, *way* down at the bottom of a new pecking order. If we don't smile and nod when our betters tell us something, our life expectancy goes down drastically."

She held up her tablet to illustrate her next point.

"The Rules of Conduct make it clear that the galaxy is a civilized place. We will find allies out there. However, we cannot afford to make very many enemies. By ignoring this ultimatum, we would make an enemy of Central Authority, the most powerful force in the galaxy. That is something we simply cannot do."

Fifteen voices began speaking at once, each with their mutually contradictory opinions about what Vanessa had said, and what it all meant for the United States, for the world. The President rapped his hand on the table, not loudly, but firmly. The babble ceased.

"We have three goals ahead of us. Victor, you need to come up with a communication strategy to explain the Rules to the nation. And you need to start working on language to deal with this ultimatum from Central Authority, because we know that information will eventually get out."

Fremont threw a vicious glare at Vanessa. She ignored it. She decided that was a safe course of action because the President ignored Fremont's unspoken accusation as well. The President, instead, turned to General McGaw.

"General, we need to start working on plans to thwart any genocide which is occurring right now. Central Africa, Myanmar and Columbia should be our top priorities."

"Mr. President—" the old general began to protest. The President held up a hand to stop him, though respectfully.

"I know. The difficulties are enormous. All we can do is all we can do... Just make sure all we do is succeed." The President offered the Chairman a wry smile. McGaw's face changed from one frown to another, slightly softer frown. Perhaps that was as close as he ever came to a smile.

"And, the most inscrutable task I leave for you, Ms. Hargrove, to tackle with Major Youngblood. What are the most likely ways in which Earth might be attacked by extraterrestrials, and how can we defend ourselves?"

Vanessa very nearly balked at the assignment. Still, if McGaw didn't get any slack, what sort of chance did she have? She wanted for her opinions to matter in Washington? She just got her wish, and then some.

"Yes, sir."

Terry conferred briefly with General Brown then accompanied Ms. Hargrove back to her office. Since an advisor to the White House on extraterrestrial cultural matters hadn't been conceived of before the *Voyager* incident, no one had known where to put Vanessa Hargrove and her steadily growing department of bureaucrats. The best they could come up with was an ill-maintained suite of offices in the old Smithsonian Building—sometimes called the Castle—right on the Mall, within spitting distance of the WWII Memorial and the Reflecting Pool.

When Ms. Hargrove had cheekily suggested they walk from the White House to her office, Terry simply could not refuse. He had that much machismo on tap, even in this enlightened age.

"It'll give us a chance to talk," she said.

"Talking doesn't seem to be a problem for you," Terry ventured. She laughed at that.

"We both did some talking in there, didn't we?"

"And now we're paying for it."

They passed through the security gate and headed east on Pennsylvania. They had a walk of a couple of miles ahead of them, but the day wasn't too terribly hot, and there was a bit of a breeze.

"So," Terry said, "how are they going to attack us?"

"You don't beat around the bush, do you? I don't think we're going to be attacked. Unless we ignore the CA warning, that is."

"You're all sunbeams and rainbows, aren't you, Ms. Hargrove?"

"The problem with preparing for an attack from off world is that there is simply no way to do it. I could give you ten different ways we might be wiped out, and that's with technology I can imagine. Who knows what's out there that I can't?"

"Ten ways? Really?" He grinned at her. She took up the challenge.

"Number one. Genetically engineered virus that is programmed for maximum transmissibility but with no side effects. Then, after a predetermined number of generations, enough for it to work its way into every person on the planet, it self-mutates into a deadly form."

"Is that even possible?" Terry asked, the idea making his stomach turn. He didn't like germs, even of the run of the mill variety.

"We're on the verge of that kind of technology ourselves. You can bet there's someone out there who could cook that up in their garage." The idea made Terry's throat want to close up. "Number two. Self-replicating nanomachines that strip water into its constituent elements, oxygen and hydrogen. Drop a few of those in any ocean and within a few months, the planet can no longer support life. Tell me how we might defend against that."

Vanessa led Terry to the right, down 12th at the next intersection where they walked under the clock tower of the Old Post Office. Terry wondered what the guys who built that tower more than a hundred years ago would think about all of this. Maybe they'd handle it better. That was when H. G. Wells introduced the world to one of the first stories about alien invasion. Terry hoped things wouldn't go quite so poorly in real life as they did with those fictional Martians.

"A weapon like that, something that would destroy all water, would be too dangerous to the society that developed it," Terry argued. "They wouldn't risk it."

"The same could be said for nuclear weapons. Didn't stop us, did it? Of course, the better answer is that such a weapon is only dangerous to a society that needs water to survive. It seems like most do, but not all."

"Yeah, but—"

She didn't wait for Terry to comment. "Number three. They seed our sun with a load of hyper-massive atoms, causing a chain reaction that makes the sun go supernova."

"That's not even possible," Terry balked. Now she was just making stuff up that would seem implausible in a movie.

"It's not only possible, there's a specific prohibition against it in the Rules of Conduct. So, if someone did try that, they'd have to answer to CA. On the other hand, that wouldn't do us much good after the fact, now would it? Number four—"

"Okay, okay. I get it. So there's no point?"

"There is a point. We just have to make the higher ups understand that the goal isn't trying to save the US, or Washington, or even Earth. The point is trying to protect *humanity*."

"Humanity lives on Earth, Ms. Hargrove."

"That is a problem," she admitted.

Vanessa escorted Major Youngblood into her office, which was tidy if not very attractive. The best offices in the old SI building were rigorously fought over in battles that might even frighten the young Major. When she offered him a choice of coffee or tea, he picked tea.

"Not a coffee drinker? They might just drum you out of the military," she teased.

"It's been discussed," he said, sipping at the freshly brewed cup of oolong.

Vanessa's tablet connected automatically to the LCD projector installed in the ceiling of her office. The tablet's image lit up a white section of wall. She scrolled through a variety of programs, finding her stellar charting software. Once simply a tool for astronomers or a hobby for geeks writing novels of interstellar conquest, accurate maps of the heavens were now a mainstream industry, and Vanessa had access to the state of the art.

"This is our neighborhood." She used a stylus to highlight sections of the image. "Here is our star. This is Alpha Centauri, and Barnard's Star." As she ticked off the names of the nearby stars, she marked each with a ghostly halo, making the little cluster stand out in the field of two or three hundred pinpricks of light on the screen. She had five of them highlighted. "These are ours."

"Ours? For nothing?"

"For nothing."

"Huh. My daddy always said, 'After you check the horse's mouth, check his hindquarters.'"

Vanessa grinned. "The Rules of Conduct aren't all bad news, Major. The galaxy has systematized the ownership of real estate. There are few wars of conquest, mostly because they're almost impossible to win without using force that would annihilate your opponent, but also because there are a few simple rules for who owns which star systems. If a system has a planet which is sprouting life, it is cocooned, as ours was, and monitored. It is officially off limits."

"Everyone follows these rules?" the Major asked.

"Mostly. I haven't gotten access to any definitive histories of the galaxy yet, but it seems that infractions of that kind are rare. The reason is that the risk/reward ratio is just too scary. There are far more systems without indigenous life than with it. You might find some rare and precious resource in such a system, but the risk of having CA come down on you hard is also very real. It simply doesn't pencil out."

Vanessa noted Youngblood's confused reaction to that turn of phrase. It made her feel old, remembering using pencils for her math homework as a kid, instead of a tablet.

"The next rule is, if a system is not biogenic, it belongs to whichever CA member system it is closest to."

The Major laughed. "You're kidding."

"No, that's the rule. And it's a great incentive for systems like ours to join CA." She indicated the four other stars that were glowing on the screen. "We get four stars and all their planets and asteroids. For free. Not a bad deal."

"We can't even get *to* them."

"Oh, we'll get out there soon enough. Incidentally, there will be a problem with Wolf 359." She pointed to a red star that was a little less than eight light years away. "There's already a settlement on one world of that system."

"I thought it was ours?"

"Technically, it won't be ours until we send our first representative to Central Authority. This other race wagered that we'd never break out of our cocoon, in which case they'd have been able to keep Wolf 359. They lost that wager."

"And they'll just up and move?"

"That's where things get sticky. The Rules of Conduct are vague on this particular point. We need to begin diplomatic relations with the Pigs immediately."

"Pigs?"

"Sorry. The package that CA sent with the Rules included a few bits and pieces about the race that settled there, and they included a picture..." She rummaged through the files on her tablet. She brought up the one she was looking for.

Major Youngblood let out a yelp of surprise. She couldn't blame him. The alien in the picture wasn't the prettiest thing. It had a bulbous, tannish-gray body, with four stumpy legs. It carried the vestiges of its evolutionary history in two parallel ridges that ran down its broad back, angling at its rump toward a sprig of a tail. Its oval face added to the illusion of it being a variation of an Earth pig, with a blunt, wet, dark nose and two beady black eyes. Its round, toothy mouth was reminiscent of a moray eel, giving the creature an air of menace. She'd grown used to the image of the Pig. The Major hadn't yet.

"Would you mind...?" He waved at the image.

"Oh." Vanessa minimized the file viewer program. "Yeah, that's a Pig. The notes from CA say they're quite nice and will be more than willing to enter into negotiations."

"For them to leave?"

"Or not. The planet they've colonized wouldn't be ideal for human habitation anyway: low gravity, low atmospheric pressure, periodic flares from Wolf 359. We could always terraform, but we might get some very good concessions out of the Pigs if we agree to let them stay, either indefinitely, or on some kind of extended lease. There are intermediary firms we could hire who specialize in managing exactly this kind of relationship."

Major Youngblood squirmed in his chair. Vanessa knew he wasn't disturbed by the image of the Pig anymore. "What's on your mind?"

"It's you."

"Me?"

"I was right. You really are sunbeams and rainbows. Where are the dangers? There have to be dangers. If not from invasion, then what?"

"The dangers are from the unintended consequences."

Vanessa knew she was flying nearly blind, to use a metaphor that Youngblood would probably appreciate. Her advantage over the Major, and over most of the rest of the world for that matter, wasn't anything amazing. It was merely a razor thin edge of experience. She had been pondering the Rules of Conduct for two years. She'd gotten access to most of the smattering of deciphered transmissions that continued to rain down on the planet through the still-widening hole in the cocoon. She had spent a lot of time sorting through the possibilities and the pitfalls of interstellar war. Everything she had read made her think it wasn't very common.

If her scattershot knowledge of galactic history told her anything on the subject it was that invasion fleets more often than not mutated into enemies after reaching their destination, turning on their former masters. It was similar to the history of the formation of the United States. How does one group of people impose their will on another when travel between the two takes weeks or months? Britain was the preeminent power on the planet in 1776, and they couldn't do it. The expansion of colonialism in the 1800s was a technological achievement, not a function of imperial will. Fast travel connected disparate land masses, enabling continuing conflict and eventual submission. Slow travel necessitated a far different dynamic.

There was FTL travel out there, of course. A dozen different varieties of it, in fact. But there wasn't some magical instantaneous travel technology, at least none that Vanessa had learned of. She estimated that the first Earth starship to fly to CA headquarters near the center of the galaxy would take, at *best*, three months to make the outbound journey. And that's assuming Earth either developed or purchased the state of the art.

"What sort of unintended consequences?" Major Youngblood pressured.

"I think we can classify them as biological, technological, or cultural."

"Biological would be a virus, like you talked about before."

"It's very unlikely that any virus which evolved naturally on another world would find any purchase in our biome... but it's always a possibility."

"And technological makes sense. Someone brings a black-hole-making machine here and we're screwed." Terry squinted in thought. "What's a cultural danger?"

"Remember the massacre of the Skeletons in Mecca?"

That memory sobered the young Major considerably. It had been a terrible misstep in off world relations. And it hadn't done the tense relationship of the West with the Muslim world any good either. What was worse, it was merely the most widely known altercation between humans and aliens. There had been dozens, some large, some small. Vanessa heard about them all. Part of her job was to make them stop happening. Talk about an impossible goal.

"The other thing to remember, Major, is that these aliens—Snakes and Blues and Trees—these are the most open minded, curious, culturally sensitive races in the galaxy. They're the ones who seek out newly opened cocoons. We haven't met the..." Vanessa struggled for the correct word.

"We haven't met the assholes yet."

Vanessa laughed so loud she covered her mouth in embarrassment.

"Exactly," she agreed.

Training Materials

> *From Rusticus I received the
> impression that my character re-
> quired improvement and disci-
> pline...*
> —*Meditations, I, 7*

The first alien that Keira knew well enough to refer to by name was a Blue named Gainsborough. He had received the moniker from colleagues at UCS in the UK, where he had served as a guest lecturer for six months. Maccha-Yantra had learned of Gainsborough's engineering knowledge, and requested he join their research team. The Blue had politely agreed to the request, and now served as a special advisor to Keira on her carbon-aluminum project.

Gainsborough acclimated to the culture of Keira's team remarkably well. She suspected that the answer to every question they had about carbon-aluminum was somewhere inside his enigmatic Blue mind, but he—at some point, Gainsborough agreed to be addressed as a male—was astute enough to merely offer nudges, allowing the human team to learn. When Keira, in a closed-door meeting with the Blue one day, asked him point blank if that was the case, Gainsborough demurred, suggesting that the unique conditions on Earth made everything new for him, just as it was for everyone else.

Keira wondered at Gainsborough's ability to so carefully deny the truth without ever lying.

Keira's relationship with Tommy continued, nearly a year after their first meeting in Bengalūru. They continued to live hundreds of kilometers apart, but a combination of e-mails, chats, phone calls, and too-infrequent visits kept them on a track which Keira assumed might lead to that ring on her finger so coveted by her family.

On the occasion of the first anniversary of their first date, Tommy flew to Mumbai for a three-day weekend. Keira had the whole celebration planned: an intimate dinner the first night, a day of sightseeing on Saturday, followed by an evening with her research team, who all wanted to meet the oft-mentioned Tommy. Sunday would be down time, a chance for them to enjoy each other's company, simply sitting at home, or walk-ing to the nearest café for a cup of coffee. By the time Tommy flew out on Monday morning, he would have one more happy memory of Mumbai, and perhaps finally agree to relocate.

"Will the Blue be there?" Tommy asked during their quiet dinner on Friday night.

"You can't be jealous!" Keira announced.

"Keira…" Tommy continued to be more affected by memories of the riot last year than Keira. Keira's working relationships with aliens, Blues in particular, had rendered her more or less ambivalent toward them. Tommy represented the average Indian viewpoint, someone who had at most a passing acquaintance with aliens and whose experiences with them weren't always positive.

"Gainsborough isn't like other Blues. You'll see."

The dinner party on Saturday was at a casual restaurant a few blocks from the MYC offices, a regular spot that Keira's team frequented. Keira and Tommy were not the first to arrive. One trait Gainsborough did have in common with most other Blues: he was always early.

"Good evening! You must be Tommy." Gainsborough, towering over both the humans, offered Tommy the nearest of his three upper limbs for an approximation of a handshake. He also remained a respectful, human-friendly distance away.

"Hello," Tommy said, his voice a little shaky as he greeted the alien. "I've heard a lot about you."

"As have I. As have I." The hostess led the three of them to their table for the evening, which had already been prepared with one low-slung, canvas chair for Gainsborough. Keira noticed how close Tommy stayed to her. She couldn't be sure if he was protecting her… or himself. The waitress took their drink orders, beers for Keira and Tommy, a lem-onade for Gainsborough. Blues were notoriously fond of sweets. The waitress left them to their conversation.

"I would like to get your thoughts on a matter that Keira and I have discussed at length."

"I don't know much about engineering," Tommy admitted.

"Gainsborough, I don't think—" Keira tried to stop him.

The Blue waved his arms brusquely. "No, no. Romantic relationships. We know there is nothing universal about them. In fact, they are relatively rare in the galaxy."

"Are they?" Tommy asked, throwing Keira a wide-eyed glance. He didn't know that Gainsborough was well-versed enough in human interaction to understand the significance of this gesture. The Blue was, on the other hand, far too polite to say anything, and had too much equanimity to be offended.

"When we researched the figures, only about five to six percent of civilizations have the strong emotional attachments between reproductive pairs such as yours. The question, though, is whether this is simply a biological imperative which has been honed by millions of years of evolution, to accommodate the long developmental periods of your young, or if there is something deeper in the collective psyche of Humans that requires this sort of pair-bonding. Your thoughts?"

Gainsborough paused to take a long sip of his lemonade. Tommy looked shell shocked by the question.

"I hope I haven't offended you," Gainsborough added.

Keira jumped in. "It was quite a question for anyone to process." She put a hand on Tommy's arm, to take the edge off the tense moment. Keira had no intention of pressuring Tommy to move in together or get married. Her sole goal at this point was to get him to move to Mumbai.

"You haven't discussed the issue with him previously?" the Blue asked. "I would have thought it fit in perfectly with the question of your possible betrothal."

At that, Tommy choked on his beer. Keira handed him a napkin to clean up.

"What have you been saying to him?" Tommy said, his voice taking on that ridiculous tone which is low enough to indicate the question is private, but not low enough to actually prevent a third party from hearing it. Keira wondered how an alien could ever begin to navigate the social waters of humanity. She had trouble enough herself sometimes.

"I told him that we've been dating for a year, and I told him we haven't discussed marriage. I hope you don't mind."

"I must take the blame for this faux-pas, if, indeed, that's what this is. I often pressure Keira for these kinds of details, as I am endlessly intrigued by your species."

The rest of Keira's team began to arrive, and the conversation shifted to the much less controversial topics of what Tommy's interests were and how the happy couple were planning on spending the rest of their time together in the city. In Gainsborough's defense, Keira's human friends were almost as intensely curious as the Blue, though they certainly showed it in different ways. Tommy held up quite well under the onslaught. Were Keira the kind to grade Tommy on his performance in front of her friends, he would have received an A-. His only misstep was his instinctive distrust of Gainsborough. Still, she could forgive him that. The inquisitive Blue was, if anything, an acquired taste.

As the days and weeks went on, working with Gainsborough began to take on the nature of a university class. Keira would suggest a track for their research into the fabrication process for carbon-aluminum, and Gainsborough would thoughtfully appraise her choice. He clearly understood the correct path to take, but from either some unwritten nonintervention policy of the Blue civilization, or his basic standoffishness, he would not overtly comment on her choice. Even his occasional suggestions were often as not dead ends of their own, time-killing diversions that he must have looked upon as training tools.

Keira did not confront him directly on these matters. Their progress was rapid, even with their occasional setbacks. She chose not to see this as a conflict between herself and Gainsborough. Instead, she thought of it as a game.

When Gainsborough heard a new idea from Keira, sometimes his response was overwhelmingly optimistic, filled with superlatives. Keira had learned, with some difficulty, that this meant her idea was not a good one. She came to believe this wasn't because the Blue was being cruel, merely that he was not a very good liar, and felt the need to overcompensate when attempting to mislead Keira.

Gainsborough would, at other times, make a happy chirping noise. Keira came to the wary conclusion that this was his highest praise at a demonstrably good idea. Much like the Blues she had run across back at *Freddie's*, chirps seemed to come from the depths of the Blue soul, much like laughter or tears from a human.

Keira was most pleased when one of her ideas was met with hushed stillness from Gainsborough. As best as she could tell, that meant that her idea, whether good or bad, had nonetheless taken the alien by surprise. She felt a secret flush of achievement when that happened.

Gainsborough was no fool, of course. He soon tipped to the fact that Keira had decrypted his responses. So, he changed them, and the game began anew. True, part of her enjoyed the game, but she imagined that soon enough she would grow weary of it. She wanted to have a simple, straightforward conversation with him, just once.

In early April of '24, Keira's mother called with bad news.

"Your father is in the hospital. He's had a heart attack."

Keira's very rational mind told her that victims of heart attacks who didn't die immediately almost always recovered fully. It told her that her father was in good hands with his doctors, and his pension would cover the costs. Keira's mother was strong, and there were lots of family around to help.

Keira's gut, on the other hand, rolled like a tiny ship in a gale. She immediately booked a flight to Bengalūru for the next morning.

She was strong, while telling her supervisor at MYC that she would be taking some time off. She was strong while packing for the trip, while waiting for the flight, while sipping at the little plastic cup of water in her cramped coach class seat. After the flight took off, Keira pulled on her earphones and pushed the volume on her music player to the highest setting, cacophonous piano and bass improvisations competing with the pilot's announcements and the vibrations of the airplane's passage through the atmosphere. The less she thought—the less she fixated on her father's health—the better.

Tommy met her at the airport. The second she fell into Tommy's arms, she broke into sobs. In a way, it was a relief to finally cry.

"Stop making such a fuss, Jess," Keira's father said to his wife. Keira watched as her mother checked all of the items on his meal tray.

"I don't know what they're trying to do to you with this."

"Keira?" Madhu Desai implored his daughter to intervene. Keira could do little more than offer him a supportive grin. She knew not to interfere when her mother got into mothering mode. Help came from an unlikely source.

"Mrs. Desai, why don't we go out and get some decent food for your husband?"

Keira was so stunned by Tommy's thoughtful offer, she let out a little yip. She tried to cover with a cough. Jessica Desai saw through the ruse in an instant. Thankfully, she was smart enough to realize that Keira should have a quiet moment alone with her father.

"You're a good boy, Tommy. Let's go."

With all of that out of the way, Keira finally spoke to her father.

"How are you feeling?"

"Weak, tired, embarrassed."

"There's nothing to be embarrassed about!"

"You don't know what caused the heart attack," he said with a grin. Keira put the odds at fifty-fifty that he was referring to either a bowel movement or sex. Either way, she didn't care to hear the details.

"It sounds like you'll be fine."

He waved his hands to indicate he would be more than fine. "Enough about me," he said.

"Enough about you? You're the one in the hospital!"

"When is that young man going to propose?"

Keira felt the levity of the conversation escape like gas under pressure. "You'd have to ask him, Father."

"Don't be a fool, Kiki. He's ready. He's waiting for a sign from you that you'd say yes."

"You think I'd say no?"

"Tough to have a marriage across eight hundred kilometers."

"I don't think he's ready to move."

The look from her father was eloquence itself.

"You don't expect *me* to move?"

"Is that so much for a husband to ask of his wife?"

"There are schools in Mumbai. There is no Maccha-Yantra in Bengalūru." Keira felt the grit in her tone, regretting every word as it left her mouth. Her father did not deserve such attitude. Proving himself to be the best of fathers, he ignored the tone. He knew it wasn't aimed at him.

"The question isn't what is or isn't in Bengalūru. The question is, is there happiness in Mumbai?"

Keira stayed in town only two days, spending the time with her family and with Tommy. She was withdrawn, quiet, not her usual self. Everyone assumed she had been sobered by her father's condition. Only her father knew what was really on her mind.

She returned to MYC in much the same state of mind. Her team accepted the change of mood as natural, something to be expected when one's father had undergone something of such gravity. Amazingly, even Gainsborough sensed that his usual playful banter would not be appropriate, at least not yet. His conversations with Keira remained focused on the tasks at hand: sorting out the parameters for creation of carbonaluminum.

He remained, however, stubbornly vague with his advice. The team was currently looking for an alternative to the electric arc kiln they were currently using to fire the aluminum, since it was very energy inefficient. During one morning conference, Keira suggested a modification to the chemical bath they were using which might allow for processing at significantly lower temperatures. Gainsborough responded with a long, theatric sigh. For some reason, no one knew exactly what it was, least of all Keira herself, she exploded.

"Why can't you give me a straight goddamn answer just once?!"

The humans in the room were shocked into silence. Gainsborough retreated into his most basic, instinctive Blue behavior. He lowered himself on his three legs, closed all three eyes, and said so softly Keira almost couldn't hear him, "I did not mean to give offense."

An unspoken cue told all the others in the room to file out quietly, leaving Keira alone with Gainsborough. The Blue remained cowed by Keira's outburst. She, on the other hand, worked to calm herself, to control her breathing, to cool the hot flush she could feel on her cheeks, her ears, her neck. She was unaccustomed to rage.

"I'm sorry, Gainsborough."

"This was my misunderstanding," he said, still bowed, eyes still closed. Keira felt like the alien was her friend, but she didn't know quite how to comfort him. A Blue's angular, stick-like body did not invite gestures like hugs or pats on the back.

"I've had a tough few days. It's nothing to do with you. Really." Keira's tone got through to the Blue, and he opened his eyes warily. "I shouldn't have yelled."

"You need not apologize. I assumed that the carbon-aluminum project was an emotionally important project to you."

Keira paused, thinking she had misheard him. "You mean you assumed it *wasn't* important to me."

"I understand it is important, as are many things. I overestimated its *emotional* importance."

"Underestimated, you mean."

Now Gainsborough brought himself back to his full height. He wasn't being aggressive; he was fully engaged now in a conundrum of his own. He began to do a slow pirouette, completing a full spin in about thirty seconds. This was a Blue habit that Keira had gotten used to over the past few months, though it still tended to make her dizzy if she focused too closely on him.

"I admit to a great deal of confusion," he said. "My experience has taught me that goals of great emotional importance tend to be approached obliquely by Humans, as if you value the difficulty of attaining said goal."

"No, Gainsborough, no. I appreciate that there are reasons to hold back truly dangerous information from us, but I can't imagine our carbon-aluminum research is going to backfire and endanger Earth."

"Certainly not. It was, however, my conclusion that you preferred the more difficult path, so I obliged."

"What would have given you that idea?"

"Your interactions with Tommy."

"Tommy?" Keira's face felt hot again, though this time not from anger, but embarrassment. "That's different."

"How is it different?"

"That's personal. This is work."

"I thought carbon-aluminum was personally important to you as well."

"It is. That's not… Look, relationships are different from science."

"So, you make developing a relationship more difficult for yourself, while you prefer your scientific pursuits to follow straightforward lines? Am I correct in my conclusion?"

"Developing a relationship is more difficult. I'm not doing anything to complicate it." Even as she said it, Keira knew what Gainsborough would say in response. His inherent Blue sense of propriety did not stop his profound curiosity.

"You do not wish to move to Bengalūru. Tommy does not wish to move to Mumbai. Your betrothal is seemingly impossible, yet you continue to spar with him in the hopes of bypassing this essential discrepancy. What is there left in your relationship now but sheer gamesmanship?"

Keira had no words to respond to that.

Her phone call with Tommy that evening was possibly the worst twenty-two minutes of her life. She never wanted to hurt Tommy, but, in the end, that's precisely what she did. It was a necessary evil. What troubled her even more, though, was how easy it was to go back to work the next day and act as if nothing at all had happened.

Undocumented Immigration

> *Do not be whirled about, but*
> *in every movement have respect to*
> *justice, and on the occasion of*
> *every impression maintain the fac-*
> *ulty of comprehension.*
> —*Meditations, IV, 22*

Terry Youngblood's office was only a few yards from General Brown's inside the E-Ring of the Pentagon. Of course, he didn't have a view, or a conference table, or a couch. But it was prime real estate any-way, and he knew it. He sipped a cup of tea as he pored through a recent MI-5 report on suspicious alien activity in the north of England.

Terry had gotten frustrated over the years with the naming conven-tion for newly arrived alien races. Nobody thought twice now about names like Blues or Rope Men, but every time a new race's name came across his screen, he felt like he'd dropped further down Alice's rabbit hole. This new group, of which there were about fifty in Birmingham, England—God knew why they chose to go *there*—had been saddled with the name Vampires. Every new "official" race name was vetted by Vanessa's department. She must have taken the day off when this one came through.

Vampires were tallish, usually over six feet, and had pale, pink skin the color of a deathly ill person. Their overlong, down-sloping heads, nar-row shoulders, and veiny wings made them look more like pterodactyls to Terry, but nobody would be able to spell Pterodactyls, so Vampires it was.

The report dramatically illustrated—using classic British under-statement—MI-5's clear worry about this "infiltration" of "unknown ele-ments". Terry hadn't found any indication in the report of why exactly they were worried. Every contact with a Vampire had been pleasant, and none had tried to drink anyone's blood. At least, not yet.

Every intelligence service in the world, not just the British, seemed to be waiting for the other shoe to drop. How could all these aliens be visiting the Earth and there be so few incidents? If they knew what Terry knew, they'd be more worried still.

Terry was one of only eleven people with access to the Oort Cloud Detection System, or OCDS for short. Signals traveling from the little sensors—which were still multiplying, filling out their expansive detection lattice—came to Earth via something Sylvester had called quicklight. The transmissions weren't instantaneous, but they were significantly faster than run of the mill radio. The sensor count was just shy of one hundred thousand, after two and a half years of expansion. They only covered fifteen percent of the sky, but just that little bit told them more than they really wanted to know.

Earth was *popular.* At least fifty vessels a month were entering local space, from gargantuan Tree ships measuring ten kilometers in width, to pebble-sized artifacts that Terry could only guess were unmanned probes. He hoped they were unmanned. He didn't want to think about defending against aliens that measured microns in size. A healthy share of these craft registered with one of three orbiting entry platforms that humanity had been kind enough to prepare for visitors. The US constructed and manned the first, *Abraham Lincoln*, a mammoth workhorse of a station that put *Pacifica* to shame. Not to be outdone, the Chinese had put *Chien-Shu* into space six months ago, offering similar registration and emigration services. Europe had come late to the party last week with *Excalibur.* By mutual consent, the alien registration process was identical on all three stations, and papers allowing entry were standardized for just about every nation on Earth, even Japan, who held out the longest on the issue of alien visitation.

Terry knew, first hand, that technology able to defeat the OCDS was unremarkable. In fact, it was commonplace, to be found on the alien equivalents of luxury liners and family campers. From a handful of conversations with visiting pilots, Terry learned that keeping your ship "bright" was considered common courtesy, particularly when visiting a recently emerged system. Humans were already beggars to this feast, treated like wild-eyed savages being visited for the first time by the white man.

Using OCDS, the Pentagon estimated how many visitors to the Solar System were registering with one of the platforms, and how many were simply ignoring the process. The numbers of those following the rules ran around seventy-five to eighty percent. Ten ships were arriving each month that went unaccounted for, and that was only the ones picked up by the unfinished OCDS. Beyond that, it was anyone's guess.

Technically, it was Terry's guess. Based on a variety of reports, including data from the FBI, the CIA, and the traditional news media, he estimated that untracked visits to Earth couldn't be happening on a large scale, simply because there weren't enough problems occurring.

That thought made Terry grin. There were disturbances, everywhere, all the time now. Not all of the disturbances were bad, though. Just yesterday, a much heralded report out of Zaire indicated that some alien—from the terse press release, it seemed to be a Lily—had developed a vaccine for HIV, with a cure for AIDS possibly on the boards for the next few months. Africa and Asia were now *very* glad that the heliopause had been pierced.

Things weren't so rosy in the West. After a century of booms and busts—the most famous in 1929, the most recent in 2000—the US stock market had nearly perfected a variety of controls that ensured the market could simply not shift more than a couple percent in a single day. Downturns and upturns alike were forced to trickle through the market slowly. The European and Asian and South American markets had all taken similar measures. The sheer strangeness of the impact of the visitors swamped all the computer-controlled safeguards. Worse still, the impacts weren't uniform.

The opening of *Lincoln* Station created a boom in a variety of high tech areas that sustained a "bubble" until a roughly forced correction from the Federal Bank brought the market back to its senses. More recently, the Central Authority ultimatum on genocide had leaked, resulting in an overall dip in stock value unseen since 1987.

Speculators loved it. The rest of the investment community didn't. At all. The volume of shares traded had been steadily decreasing for the last five months. Slowly, ever so slowly, many of the big money concerns were shifting their capital away from the market and into either municipal bonds for communities that were favorites of the visitors, or else to venture capital arrangements with private firms specializing in catering to aliens or adapting their technologies to Earth.

Terry still feared the inevitable military showdown with some un-friendly visiting group, but for the time being, the direction from the White House and, therefore, the Pentagon as well, was to focus on con-taining the economic maelstrom. Terry was just glad no visitor had come to Earth with a machine that could spin gold from straw.

An IM popped up on Terry's screen. It wasn't from General Brown's assistant. It was from Brown herself, and when she said jump, he knew to ask how high.

"We have a visitor," General Brown said the instant Terry entered her office.

"We've got a lot of them."

"Not like this one. He's the first rep from Central Authority to grace our humble shores." She spun her screen around to show Terry the e-mail from *Lincoln*. Terry scanned it.

"I don't recognize the description of the guy. New race, I guess."

"Yeah, well, your girlfriend will be very excited." Terry simply sneered at the joke. Claiming that his relationship with Vanessa Hargrove was entirely professional tended to fall on deaf ears, particularly when those ears belonged to a woman.

Terry continued to read the e-mail. "He asked to see our... Exile Of-ficer?"

Brown nodded. "That's why they bumped this up to me."

"We've never exiled anyone off the *planet*."

"Something to look forward to," Brown said with a grin. "Hopefully this isn't some inspection of our progress on eliminating genocide."

Terry nodded agreement with that. It'd been more than six months since the ultimatum from Central Authority, telling Earth to clean up their act. Officially, the White House had been putting the diplomatic full court press on the governments of Columbia, Myanmar and Sudan. Unof-ficially, the first boots wouldn't be hitting the ground for another three months at the earliest.

"Just to be safe, I'll take along a copy of the last NIE, so they know we aren't stalling."

"Good idea." General Brown typed an instant message to her assistant. "Major Ruiz will have the document for you as you leave. You need to get to Andrews."

"When will he be there?"

Brown glanced at the clock on her wall. "If you shag ass right now you'll only be ten minutes late."

Major Terry Youngblood now rated a car and driver. He hated losing even *more* control over his movements, but he made use of the time in the car and gave Vanessa a call. She was in a meeting, so her tablet answered, allowing her to quietly text her responses back to him. The false voice the machine sent back to Terry's phone was clearly Vanessa, but such a soulless, antiseptic version that no one would ever be fooled. And it still didn't handle contractions very well. He figured the technology to really simulate another human's voice was about five years away. Or maybe next week, if the right alien landed tomorrow.

"How conciliatory should I be?"

"MORE THAN WITH ME. LESS THAN WITH PRES."

"Very funny."

"IM SERIOUS."

"Oh. Why's he even here?"

"WHY YOU THINK HES MALE?"

"Let's save the sociology discussion for later? I've got three minutes or so."

"COULD BE WELCOME VISIT. DONT WORRY."

"You wouldn't like to come out and help me?"

"NOT ON YOUR LIFE."

The description from the *Lincoln* staff said this visitor was short and furry, but didn't elaborate. Terry had worried that his initial reaction would be insulting. As he entered the visitor's lounge at Andrews, he didn't expect his reaction to be outright laughter.

"I am humorous in some way?" the alien said, looking down at his body. "Other Humans had similar reactions to my presence."

"I apologize. It's just…"

Terry knew instantly what the name for this race would be. The alien stood just under five feet tall, but might have weighed in at over two hundred fifty pounds. He seemed to come from a world with less gravity, since his steps had a lumbering quality to them. His round belly hung down somewhat, obscuring the tops of his stumpy legs. His arms were long, reaching nearly to the ground, giving him a slightly hominid look, but the rest of him evoked only one image.

"You look like a teddy bear," Terry explained. He offered the alien a hand to shake. The Teddy Bear had obviously been briefed on human customs, and returned the gesture. His hand was three fingered, with vestigial claws that put a human's fingernails to shame. His torso and upper arms were wrapped in something like gray bandages, his version of clothing. Everywhere else, his skin was covered in golden brown fur, and looked quite fluffy. His round head was even topped with perky little ears.

"That is a local variety of fauna?"

"It's a children's toy."

"I see. My name is Krd."

"Kird?" Terry said, trying to mimic the strange sound of the name.

The creature's black, bent mouth seemed already to be smiling, so Terry couldn't read if Kird had reacted well or poorly to the pronunciation. "That will do." Kird paused. "And you are?"

"Oh! Sorry. I'm Major Terry Youngblood, USAF. I'm the closest thing we have to an Exile Officer."

"I understand. These are still early days for your system."

"Well, we were around for a few thousand years before the cocoon broke."

Kird made an odd swishing gesture with his long arms which Terry took to be a brush off. "Yes, of course. It has come to my attention that a fugitive from one of my investigations has arrived on Earth. I am here to accompany her back to Central Authority for processing."

"Processing?"

The Bear's squinty black eyes betrayed nothing. Kird seemed unwilling to elaborate.

"Well, then. What can you tell me about this fugitive?"

"She is a Kzztzk, wanted in connection to a genocide on a colonial outpost of her home system. Her name is..." Kird seemed to smile. Or not. "Her name is quite elaborate and also immaterial." He moved to a coffee table and pulled a folder from a pocket of his outfit. Terry was a little surprised to see an alien using something as old fashioned as paper. Kird seemed to understand. "My tablet's screen does not generate images within your visual parameters." Kird flipped open the folder. Terry bent over to look. Amidst a sea of linguistic gibberish that looked a little like Tamil, Terry saw a photograph of the Kazizitizik. He recognized the race immediately.

"We call them Rope Men."

"She was jailed for murder," Kird explained. "The story figured prominently in your journalistic media. Otherwise, we would not have known she was here."

Terry sighed. "This may get complicated."

"She has not escaped?" Kird asked. Terry filed away the stretched look on the Bear's face for future reference. It must have indicated horror.

"No. It's just, she's in Russia."

"Is that far?"

"No. Well, yes, but that's not the problem. Russia and the US aren't on the best of terms lately." Terry underplayed the situation. The two one-time Cold War enemies weren't openly hostile, as they had been in the 1960s, but continuing strong arm tactics in Russia since the Putin era hadn't made them any friends in the US. The two countries' shared fear of China ensured their uneasy alliance, but that was about all they had in common. There were many ways that the breaking of the cocoon had made international cooperation more common. Still, some disputes died harder than others.

"Many newly hatched systems employ the use of nation states."

"I'll bet."

"This too shall pass."

And now Terry knew what a Teddy Bear's facial expression for condescension looked like.

Terry spent two hours on the phone with a dozen members of two governments. Finally, he was able to escort Kird onto a Boeing 818 jump plane. The twelve-seater was owned and operated by the Air Force, but used most often to shuttle State Department big wigs to far flung hot spots.

Terry was old enough to be duly impressed by a flight time from Andrews AFB to Vladivostok International Airport of only two hours. Kird remained diplomatic enough to not complain about the *length* of the trip. Instead, he seemed noticeably pleased by the accommodations. The seats were all First Class quality, and the steward—a young Lieutenant named Hawkins—offered them beverages. Kird was quite stupefied by the concept of sparkling water, and drank three bottles of Perrier before the end of the flight.

"It does seem to *sparkle* in one's mouth," Kird said with glee.

"I'm glad you like it. Kird, may I ask a question?"

"Certainly."

"I'm sure you realize that humans have two genders, and at least in English, our language tends to make us assign a gender to a person."

"I understand. You may refer to me as a male."

"That's fine. And you referred to the fugitive as a female?"

"I did. Many races have one, two, three, or more rarely, more genders, in the sense of a gender being a set of sexually relevant physiological differences between members of the same species. Two-gender systems, wherein the 'male' provides genetic material, and the 'female' gestates the newly formed offspring, are quite common, and so, your linguistic constraint is also quite familiar to us. Galactic etiquette suggests the use of male pronouns for providers of genetic material and female for those who give birth to young. It is ironic that you chose the name Rope Men for a race with but one gender: female."

Terry laughed. "Good to know. Since we're on the subject, can you tell me how many races there are out there? We've asked several visitors, and their estimates are all over the place."

"I am not surprised."

"You're not? Frankly, we were."

"Major, please tell me how many nation states there are on this planet."

"Uh… I think there are… about two hundred, give or take." Terry found himself embarrassed at his lack of knowledge about Earth geopolitics. Of course, he'd spent a lot of time recently focused on things *beyond* the Earth.

"You are a well informed, intelligent member of one of the eminent powers of this system, and you do not know the numbers of your own people, on this one planet. Why would tourists who happened upon your world know more about a galaxy as vast as ours?"

"I see your point. But I imagine *you* have better knowledge than your average space tourist."

"Your imagination is correct, but your question is somewhat more complex than you perhaps think."

Aren't they all? Terry thought.

"I will explain. There were, as of my last visit to Central Authority, 15,611 inhabited, uncocooned systems in our galaxy. These are controlled from 11,915 autonomous star systems."

"The difference being colonial outposts."

"Correct. In all, these inhabitants represent 9,604 distinct species."

Terry realized he'd been holding his breath. "None of the estimates we'd gotten were *near* that high."

"Few of these cultures have galaxy-wide impact. Most individuals know of the *b-b-b-b*, the race you have named Blues. Few know of Humans. I offer no offense."

Terry knew enough about Blue culture to realize Kird was aping their oft-used turn of phrase.

"I see that Teddy Bears have a sense of humor."

Kird's smile-that-wasn't-a-smile returned. He toyed with his latest bottle of Perrier. "Perhaps the bubbles have gone to my head."

Vladivostok lay sprawled over a crooked-finger of a peninsula that extended from the Asian mainland into the Sea of Japan. The city's history was littered with military importance—from the battlements built to defend Russia from the Japanese to the naval base that reached its greatest importance during the Cold War with the US. With all of that, the place never saw battle.

This was the farthest major Russian city from Moscow. It was also the closest to Beijing, Tokyo and the US. Vladivostok had developed a schizophrenic personality that perfectly matched its debilitatingly rapid growth. Terry could see the pollution that blanketed the city as a low-lying gray-brown haze, only broken by a few of the terrain's taller mountains.

The jump plane circled the naval base once, then descended for a landing on their tidy, no-frills airstrip. The plane's engines had barely begun powering down when Hawkins lowered the stairs and gestured for Terry and Kird to deplane.

The air was crisp, not surprising for a March day in Siberia. A contingent of police officers—all young, blond and imperious—waited patiently at the foot of the steps. The young man on the far left took a step forward and addressed Terry, his eye flitting nervously to Kird.

"You are Major Young?" he asked in a thick accent.

"It's Youngblood. Yes."

The policeman rechecked his clipboard and exchanged a few unintelligible words with the man on his left.

"Youngblood. Yes. This is good. Follow please."

They trooped across the concrete toward a sterile black box of a building with one door and no windows. The structure could easily have been fifty years old, a veritable relic of the Cold War. Terry felt almost giddy with excitement. He'd been born after the collapse of the Soviet Union, but the reverberations of that time still echoed through his childhood, in movies and TV shows and video games. It was almost like going back in time.

Whatever he might have expected of the interior of this formidable building, this wasn't it. Everything was light and friendly, old fashioned to be sure, beiges and tans and light grays. The colors of Terry's childhood. A dark man in an expensive, charcoal suit stood from a comfortable couch and approached.

"Major Youngblood. Anthony Garza, US State Department. I'm the local attaché."

They shook.

"Mr. Garza, this is Kird, Conduct Officer of Central Authority."

Garza's diplomatic training served him well. He neither cringed nor giggled as he shook hands with the Teddy Bear.

"You're here for Piotr?"

"Who?" Terry asked.

"This is the name the Kzztzk has taken locally?"

"He never gave us a name. The guards chose Piotr."

"She," Terry added.

Garza's answering nod and knowing look slipped out before he could put back on his mask of State Department sang-froid. Terry understood the reaction nonetheless. His was similar when he learned that the incarcerated Rope Man was a female.

Figures.

With growth, of course, came crime. Vladivostok hadn't been the safest of cities twenty years ago, a haven for the ascendant Russian mob. Now, with its population doubled and its total wealth tripled, the Russian mob was the least of Vladivostok's worries. Chinese, Korean, and Japanese gangs fought for the low-hanging fruit of drugs, gambling and prostitution. Russia responded by doubling the police force and building a high-tech, supermax prison on the northern outskirts of the city. Muravyov Prison claimed to be escape proof.

From the outside, Terry almost believed it. The walls must have been twenty feet high, and far too smooth to climb, topped with razor-wire, watched from several manned towers. Garza rode with Kird and Terry in the back of a roomy Hyundai SUV, driven by a State Department aide who attended Garza wordlessly. Judging from the traffic, for once Terry was glad he *wasn't* driving.

The SUV moved slowly past a series of three thick-barred gates, all of which retracted down into the ground to allow them to pass. Watching through the back window, when the gates popped back into position, it was fast. Terry wouldn't want to be in a car that got flipped—or more likely skewered—by one of those.

They parked in a shaded courtyard and climbed out of the Hyundai. The cadre of guards here didn't have the schoolboy looks of the city cops. These men were hard edged, older, scarier. That their outfits were distinctly reminiscent of Nazi uniforms added to their air of intimidation. A huge man with ash-dark hair and a graying beard approached the car. He wore a baggy, brown suit and scuffed shoes. The big man shook hands grandly with Garza. The two men exchanged ebullient greetings in Russian. Garza then introduced Terry, though the only word in the stream he recognized was "Youngblood".

"Major, this is Warden Kolovsky." Terry took the warden's massive hand and held the grip as long as he could.

"Good meet you," Kolovsky said in heavily accented English.

Another string of Russian words led to the introduction of Kird. Kolovsky's reaction was joyous, as he shouted, "Ewok!"

Kird turned to Garza. "I am not familiar with the warden's dialect. Was this a greeting?"

Garza and Terry shared a confused look. Neither was familiar with the word. Kolovsky rode over their bewilderment and greeted Kird as he had the others. Terry watched as the two engaged in a quick contest of strength, their handshake lasting far longer than customary. With a bit of a wince from Kolovsky and a strange squeak from Kird, it appeared they finished with a draw.

Attempting to fit in as best he could, Kird declared, "Ewok!" Kolovsky merely laughed and waved them all into the main building for tea and pastries.

With Garza acting as translator, Kolovsky explained that Piotr was their most troublesome prisoner. That she was their only alien incarceree was only part of the problem. Kird did not press for clarification of why she was such trouble, so Terry did not either. Kolovsky asked Kird a question, which Garza translated.

"Are you prepared to take possession of the prisoner?"

Kird nodded, a human affectation that he had picked up very quickly. He pulled a small metal rod from one of the pockets of his clothing. Terry couldn't imagine the thing—which was about the size of a flute, though black and featureless—would do much as a blunt instrument.

"Is it a stun rod?" he asked.

"Somewhat," Kird answered.

Kolovsky nodded, downed the last of his tea, and stood. He called one of the guards—a toad of a man named Zorov—to accompany them. The five of them left the headquarters building and crossed a lifeless stone courtyard that led into the maximum security wing of the prison.

Every movie Terry had ever seen about prison had the prisoners in open-face cells, with thick, wide-spaced bars, facing cavernous tiers of the prison. This prison was very different. Kolovsky gave them a high-spirited running commentary, which Garza translated.

This prison's design required every cell to face a blank wall, thus reducing the opportunity for communication between prisoners. Cell doors were thick, unbreakable, transparent plastic. Their cots, desks, chairs, sinks and toilets were made of the same material. No metal was allowed in a cell. Prisoners were allowed reading material, but only on specially made soft paper, somewhat like newsprint. In a pinch, the stuff could be pressed and compacted, and thus used as a weapon, but the paper completely disintegrated when it touched water. Shivs made of this stuff did not react well to sweaty palms. And in the case of a fight, the area would be drenched by sprinklers, thus destroying all the paper in the vicinity.

In years past, the inmates were kept in their cells for twenty-four hours every day. Through trial and error, though, the warden had learned that if the prisoners were given an hour of social time per day, and another hour of outdoor time each week, the number of attacks on guards was minimized. The frequency of suicides also dropped somewhat. This was considered an acceptable trade-off.

Piotr received none of these enticements to good behavior. She had attacked thirteen fellow prisoners, killing three, and had seriously injured two guards. Her cell door never opened. In addition, she was put at the end of a row, and the cell immediately to her right was kept empty. Human prisoners could not be heard outside their soundproofed cells, but Piotr had some kind of conduction ability that allowed her to talk directly through the thick concrete walls of her cell.

When they reached her wing, Kolovsky ordered three more of the guards to accompany them.

"Is this all really necessary?" Terry asked.

The chorus of *yes*es and *da*s that answered him revealed no doubt on the subject.

A few years ago, a remake of *The Silence of the Lambs* came out. Terry saw it, and thought it was pretty good, though most of the critics panned it as a pale imitation of the original, which was made back in the 1990s. So he streamed a copy of the Hopkins/Foster version. He found the pacing to be a little slow, but on the whole, he agreed that it was a great movie. He particularly enjoyed the scene where Jodie Foster slowly approaches Hopkins' cell. He flashed on that scene as they walked down the tier. Superficially, little here was the same. Pale concrete walls and floor instead of the dark stone of the movie set. Everything here was flooded with natural light from skylights installed high above, not wreathed in cinematic shadow. Instead of the taunting, disturbing words from other inmates calling out from their cells, here the only sounds were Kolovsky's words, echoed by Garza in a different tongue, and the click of their dozen shoes on the floor.

Then Terry remembered that in the movie, Hopkins had been behind a plastic wall, and he suppressed a shudder.

The last cell on the left. Terry crossed that final couple of feet and stopped, looking into the unadorned white box.

Nothing. No one. He looked to the others to gauge their reactions. The Rope Man had *escaped*!

Kolovsky read Terry's concern. "All good," he said calmly. He moved to the cell door and slid a panel back, opening a small porous section of the plastic. He spoke a few words into the cell.

Terry didn't understand. There was the cot—which he wasn't sure a Rope Man would even use. Rope Men were without a doubt the most *alien* of aliens.

Terry had seen video of the trial. Piotr stood about three feet high. She had four slender legs at a shallow angle leading up to a squarish base of bone that could be considered her waist. From there, more straight segments rose to a point. She held a superficial similarity to a Skeleton, but a Rope Man had nothing that could be called a head. She looked like the framework of a tent, without the nylon to cover the struts. The "bone" sections were muddy maroon color, while the "muscle" sections—which writhed over and around and between the bones—were a livid, blood red. And that's all she was. Bone and muscle, a freakish alien version of the Visible Man, just with no insides inside. Somehow the thing sensed her environment, could hear and see and speak. No other Rope Men had come to Earth, and this one didn't particularly want to be examined, so the mysteries behind her anatomy remained unexplored.

But where was she? At the sound of Kolovsky's voice, a whisper of movement underneath the cot drew Terry's eye. What he had taken for a pile of discarded rags in the shadow under the opaque white bedding came slowly to life. A knotted mass of red tissue squirmed into the light. The confused, seemingly random collection of sluggish, glistening ropes slowly gained definition, found their order. Or, more accurately, their order was revealed. Some of the ropes lengthened and thickened, growing tense and hard, uncomfortably like so many disembodied, engorged penises. Wrapped around and between these were the red muscular tissues. These pulled and pulsed and levered the bones into upright positions. The macabre yet fascinating symphony of biology and geometry finally came to a close with Piotr standing on three legs, with a triangular waist, and only three bones reaching up to the creature's pinnacle. She resembled less the army tent creature from the trial videos, and more a stylized kind of teepee.

"Where's her other leg?"

"Kzztzk can take many forms, alternating structural and muscular sections at will to better adapt to their environment."

Kolovsky explained that Piotr had shifted to this more compact shape while in prison, allowing her to gain more strength from the added muscle mass. He spoke again into the cell. The voice that came back spoke Russian, but it was certainly not human. Piotr's words had a grating, buzzy quality that made Terry guess she vibrated her bones to generate the sounds. He leaned closer to the plastic barrier, watching her. She used her muscles to rattle her top three bones together to generate the sound.

Terry had been unsettled by the pictures of the Pigs and been unnerved by the appearance of the Vampires. This, however, was the first time that a visitor had been so entirely alien that it threatened to unman him. He focused on the job at hand. He couldn't simply run away. Apart from being embarrassing, he was in a prison. There was nowhere to run to.

"Does she understand that Kird is here to take her away?" Terry asked.

After a few words through the cell grate, Kolovsky turned to Kird. Garza translated. "She's calling you The Wolf."

"Cute," Terry said. He received a number of confused glares at that comment. "We call her Piotr... Peter." Nothing. "Peter and the Wolf? She's got a sense of humor, I guess."

Kird's answering growl was less like a wolf, more like a bear. That detail comforted Terry for some reason. Not all aliens were beyond his understanding, nor his ability to cope with their differences.

"Open the cell," Kird ordered. Kolovsky seemed to understand before Garza translated. He called to the guard at the end of the tier. With an audible clank, the cell door unlocked, then slid to the side, revealing an opening which was half the width of the cell itself. Kird entered first, just barely fitting his bulk through the door. He was followed closely by Zorov. Kird raised the black weapon, showing it to Piotr. She responded remarkably fast.

Piotr lifted one leg high into the air. She unlatched one of the sideways oriented bones from her waist, creating a jointed limb of a sort. That limb then detached from the waist, creating a longer, three-boned limb attached to her tallest point. She whipped this around, something like a biological version of a nunchuck. The bony end of the improvised weapon struck Zorov hard in the face, knocking him to the ground. The extended limb whipped around further, encircling Kird's head. The far end reattached to the top of Piotr's teepee, thus trapping Kird in a deadly embrace. Another limb from her left side slammed into Kird's hand, forcing him to drop his baton weapon.

Confused shouts from the guards caused a rush into the room, pushing Garza and Terry in with the prisoner. The two unarmed humans retreated to a corner of the cell to stay out of the fray. One guard knelt to attend to Zorov, who appeared to have at least a broken nose, and possibly a concussion. The others descended on Piotr, attempting to pull the triangular noose of bone off of Kird's neck. The Teddy Bear seemed more angry than endangered, pummeling the sections of Piotr's body that he could reach. The yelling and struggling mass of humans and aliens flipped over onto the cot, which squealed in protest from the weight.

Terry saw Kird's black baton lying forgotten on the ground. He picked it up.

"How does it work?" he yelled at Kird.

Two more guards, these from the control room at the end of the tier, stuffed themselves into the room to pry at Piotr's hold on Kird. The creature had reformed herself yet again, with a pentagonal loop of bones encircling Kird's thick belly, constricting, crushing him.

"Do something!" Garza yelled. Terry agreed with the sentiment, but didn't know exactly what he could do. On a sudden impulse, he raised the baton like a cudgel and brought it crashing down on the nearest section of Piotr he could reach, one that lay flat on Kird's belly. A loud *zap* echoed in the small room, followed by the stink of ozone. The baton flew out of Terry's hand as he was tossed backward from the electrical shock that it created. Since Piotr, Kird and the guards were all in close contact, the burst of voltage arced through them all. The guards fell away and dropped to the ground, more impacted than Terry had been. The handle of the baton must have insulated him a little bit. Kird let loose a high pitched roar of pain and doubled over to protect his burned belly.

Piotr reacted most dramatically of all. The bone Terry had touched directly with the baton burst in a shower of familiar-looking crimson blood. The connected muscles tensed violently. If the forwardmost bone around Kird's belly hadn't shattered, that sudden constriction would likely have cut the Bear in half. As it was, the bulk of Piotr's body retracted like it was on springs, collapsing onto the cot. Fortunately, the triangle of bone around Kird's neck wasn't small enough to strangle him. It convulsed once, then slackened.

Terry reached down and, with some difficulty, pulled Kird from the bed. The remains of Piotr littered the cot like some sort of poorly executed autopsy.

"Is she dead?" Terry asked.

Kird grunted, then turned to survey the damage Terry had done to the prisoner.

"We must inventory the body."

"Inventory?"

"Separate sections can maintain viability without the whole."

Terry's mind stuttered briefly. *Silence of the Lambs.* Army tent, teepee. Maintain viability.

Kolovsky spoke into a radio. From his tone, Terry could tell he was calling an end to the raised alert level. In response, the alarms quieted. Terry hadn't even noticed they were sounding during the brief skirmish.

Terry grabbed Garza. "Tell him to raise the alarm again." Before Garza could ask why, Terry grabbed Kird. "Can you run?"

"Run?"

"This was a ruse. She's escaping."

Kird understood instantly and was out the door without another word. Terry followed. At the end of the tier, through a traditional barred door, they saw a dead guard lying on the floor.

"Open the door! Open the door!" Another guard poked his head out of a room at the far end of the hall and saw his fallen comrade. He rushed up and checked the man for a pulse. Terry continued to yell, but the guard didn't understand. Kolovsky came up behind them, puffing and blowing. His order was curt and not to be ignored. The guard rushed into the little control room for this tier and unlocked the door. Kird and Terry ran through.

The sirens kicked on again. Terry didn't know what kind of head start this Piotr offshoot had, but it couldn't have been much. She wouldn't have tried to slip out of the cell until after *all* the guards on the tier were called into her cell. She could go right past the other inmates' cells, since no one would be able to hear their shouts of warning through the soundproof cell doors.

Terry noted in passing that when forced to run, Kird shifted into a loping, simian gait which made use of his long arms as well as his legs, his vicious claws making click-clack noises on the concrete floor. So much for looking like a cute little teddy bear.

They reached an intersection of corridors.

"Which way is the nearest exit?" Kird asked. Terry quickly oriented himself with the outside and overlaid his best guess of the footprint of the prison. He pointed to the left and took off with Kird following.

They came upon another barred door, locked. Whatever portion of Piotr had escaped could easily have slipped right through these bars. Terry pounded on them in frustration. Kird pushed him aside and grasped two of the bars. He pulled, bending the steel fractionally, but enough. Clearly, Kird had been playing with Kolovsky earlier. He was *strong.*

Terry squirmed through the narrow opening, then looked back to see that there was no way Kird's stocky body would fit through.

The Teddy Bear handed over the baton. "Go!"

Terry ran. At the next junction, he caught sight of the diminutive Rope Man. Piotr had removed only three bones and a small collection of muscles for her escape attempt. Terry didn't know if she could regrow the rest of her body like some single-celled organism, or if this was really just a last ditch effort for some modicum of freedom. Whatever the case, he had to stop her.

With only three bones, Piotr's gait was ungainly. All three were jointed together at one point. With each step, the third limb would flip over to the front, giving her another "foot" to take the next step. She seemed to be pinwheeling her way down the corridor. She made good progress, but Terry was faster. He had all his limbs, after all.

Piotr sensed someone behind, and she stopped. She balanced on one limb. Terry watched in dumb fascination as she unlatched one of her tripod legs, changing her configuration into a single, sinewy structure that stood about four feet in height. Terry felt like he was facing off against a predator snake, a cobra or some such.

"You understand English?" he asked.

Piotr's buzz-saw answer seemed not to be Russian, but her own native tongue. In that moment, Terry wondered if a Rope Man could manifest teeth, if it was poisonous, if it even might have some sort of telekinetic or psychic powers that he could never hope to guard against. The best course of action would be to hold it here for the guards. They'd eventually get here.

The topmost bone leaned over to touch the ground. It looked like it was bowing to Terry. Then, in a decidedly non-snake-like maneuver, the creature was suddenly standing entirely upside down—as if such considerations mattered—and had halved the distance to Terry. He started to back up. It made sense. He could goad the thing into following him deeper into the prison.

Lightning quick, Piotr launched herself at Terry's neck, dark bone and livid red muscle stretching toward him. Without a moment's pause, Terry batted the thing out of the air with the baton. The shock was greater this time, throwing Terry off his feet. He fell backwards and cracked his skull on the hard floor. As much as he knew it would hurt like hell, he had to make sure he was safe. He lifted his head.

The only things left of Piotr were bits of gristly flesh and a pint of arterial-red blood splattered all over the corridor.

Terry followed his pounding head's command and he lay back down and closed his eyes.

So, he thought, that's *one* alien fugitive down.

How many more to go?

Junior

> ...*very little indeed is neces-*
> *sary for living a happy life.*
> —*Meditations, VII, 67*

At seven years of age, Quince had been living in a world filled with aliens for half his life. Some of the kids at school were collecting Visitor Trading Cards that featured elaborate paintings of various alien races on the front, and tidbits of information about their physiology and culture on the back. When Quince asked for a pack of the cards at the toy store, his dad told him that he wasn't going to spend good money on cardboard. Surreptitiously and methodically, Quince had been trading away the des-serts out of his sack lunches to friends to get some of the cards. He had fifteen so far, out of a total of fifty.

No, Quince never thought twice about the fact that there were other worlds out there with intelligent life. When he'd watch an old movie on TV and there'd be fake aliens, he'd laugh at how silly they looked, since he knew—from the cards—what *real* aliens looked like.

Even so, he'd seen only a few of them in person. Once or twice on the street when his dad took him into Seattle for a Mariners game. A Lily came to his school once for a special Alien Awareness Day. The thing was big and wavy and really pretty, like a drip of oil trapped mid-splash, with the sun shining off of it in a million colors. Quince and the other kids listened to the Lily make a big speech, which was okay. Then they got to ask questions.

"How old are you?"

"Do you have any brothers and sisters?"

"Can you swim?"

When Quince got his chance, he asked, "Do Lilies have pets?" The visitor said that, no, Lilies never kept animals as pets. They were allowed to roam free on their home planet. Quince politely thanked their guest for answering his question, but he was still somewhat sad.

Quince really wanted a pet. His dad, who had an answer for every-thing, it seemed, said that he wasn't going to spend good money on some-thing that would poop all over his house. Even after Quince's heartfelt and entirely sincere insistence that he would totally take care of a pet—he wanted a dog—his dad didn't budge. A half-hearted attempt to get his sister, Sarah, and his mom on his side of the issue didn't help either. His mom didn't want to have to wash a dog. Sarah just thought they were gross. What did she know? She was only five. And a girl.

Dad always took Quince and Sarah to school in the morning, and their mom always picked them up after school to bring them home. One Thursday afternoon, Quince was surprised to see his dad's Volvo parked in the driveway when they got home. Dad almost never came home early. There was another car parked there, too, a big black limo.

"Dad's got a meeting," Quince observed.

"What's that?" Sarah asked, kicking the back of Quince's seat as she did so.

"Quit it!" he yelled at her. "Dad's talking to someone from work."

"You both need to stay out of Daddy's study until his meeting is over," Mom warned.

"Okay," Quince lied.

Quince followed Sarah up the walkway and into the house. Sarah ran up the stairs to her room, little legs pounding on the carpet. Quince stopped at the first step, crouching to tie his shoelaces, which seemed to always come undone all by themselves. He tied slowly, carefully, waiting for his mom to go into the kitchen to put away the two bags of groceries she picked up at the store.

Quince crept across the hall to the door of his dad's study. The door was delightfully ajar and Quince peeked in. Dad was talking with a Snake.

"—the properties you're looking for," the Snake said. He sounded like he was from another country.

"Look, I'm not paying good money for this unless I know it'll help with the project."

Dad talked to the Snake just like he talked to Quince. That was funny.

"No worries, mate. There is no better species in the galaxy to study for electro-biochemical mass transference."

Quince didn't know what they were talking about. He was more interested in watching the Snake. The alien's back was to Quince, but he could see most of his furry body coiled on the chair. He held a small, metal box in his human-looking hands.

Dad stared at the Snake for a moment. Quince knew that stare. He used it on his kids when he thought they were being bad and lying about it.

"Okay." He pulled his checkbook out of the desk and wrote the Snake a check. The way he pursed his lips, Quince knew he was paying a lot of money for that box.

The Snake took the check, glanced at it to confirm the amount, and then slipped it into a pocket that seemed to be hidden in his clothes. "It's been a pleasure, Mr. Almeda." The Snake slithered out of the chair as Quince's dad got up from behind his desk. Quince scampered away from the door and ran up the steps far enough to hide from Dad's view.

The Snake left the study with Dad following. They said their good-byes at the front door and the Snake left. A couple of seconds later, Quince heard the limo drive away. Dad turned to go back into the study, but he was stopped by Mom's voice.

"Vance! Is your meeting over?"

"Yes. Just a second."

"I could use your help out here."

Quince recognized that tone just as well as his dad did. Ignoring that tone was perilous. Dad dutifully went down the hall to the kitchen. Quince saw his opportunity and flew down the steps—careful not to make any sound—and snuck into the study. The metal box was still on the desk. He undid the latch and flipped up the lid. The inside of the box was padded with dark gray foam. There were twenty little holes in the foam. Ten of the holes were empty, but the other ten had stoppered test tubes nestled in them. Quince gingerly pulled one of the test tubes out. Inside, floating in a little bit of water, was a small, gray seed. Or, at least, it *looked* like a seed.

"Elaine, you know I don't like beets." Dad's voice wafted in through the open door.

"It's the only vegetable I can get the kids to eat," Mom complained. Quince knew Dad would be back soon, but he wanted to get a closer look at the seed. He pulled off the stopper and dumped it out into his hand. The water splashed onto the floor, but the seed caught between two of his fingers. He held it between his thumb and forefinger. It was a little squishy, kind of like a Brussels sprout, but smaller.

Quince put the stopper back on the test tube, pushed the test tube back into the foam, closed the lid on the case, and swiped at the water with his shoe to spread it around and make it less noticeable on the wood floor.

"Can't I have a salad just once in a while?"

"You want me to spend good money on salad ingredients when you're the only one who—"

"Don't do that," Dad said. He sounded a little bit mad. Quince did *not* want to be in the study when he got back. He checked the hall and saw his dad was *right there*, turned around, still facing the kitchen. Quince opened the door and slipped carefully out into the hall.

His dad took that *exact moment* to turn around.

"Quince!"

"What?"

"Don't go into my study when I'm not there. You know better than that."

"I wasn't," Quince protested.

Dad waved a hand at Quince, the standard gesture he used to tell his kids he wanted them to go to their rooms. Quince obeyed, careful not to crush the seed in his hand as he ran upstairs.

Safely in his room, away from prying eyes, he opened his hand and looked again at the seed. He needed better light, so he took it over to the window to get a good look at it in the sunlight. Quince set the seed down on the windowsill. He got down on his knees to get close to it to see what it really looked like. In school once, his teacher showed the class a picture of a pig embryo when it was really small. It looked like a sea creature, but with closed eyes and with all its legs pulled in like it was sleeping. The seed looked a lot like that. Quince realized it wasn't a seed at all. It was an *animal!*

Then it moved. Not a lot, but a little. It shivered, squirmed, tilted over just a bit. Quentin watched with clear anticipation as one of the little creature's legs stretched out. Quentin gingerly brought one finger down to touch the waking creature.

"Quentin! Sarah! Dinner!"

"Not fair," Quince complained. He spoke softly to the little animal. "I'll be right back up, Junior."

He was, in fact, not right back up. Dinner was, as always, a long and boring affair. Quince generally ate as fast as he could and then spent the better part of an hour trying to convince his parents to excuse him from the table. Sarah had decided lately that mimicking Quince was the best fun possible, so she wolfed down her meal as well and pestered their parents just like Quince. The net effect of this was to have both Mom and Dad insist they stay at the table and act like a gentleman and a lady.

In a burst of brilliant clarity, Quince decided to start calling Sarah "Pigface". This had the first effect of making Sarah mad, then it made his parents mad, then Sarah complained, making his parents even *more* mad.

"Go to your room, young man!"

"Okay!" Quince said, and ran up the stairs. He made sure to shut his door so he could check on Junior with no interference from anyone. He went back to the windowsill... but Junior was *gone*! He checked the little trough where the screen slid back and forth. Nothing. He got down on hands and knees and looked on the floor under the window. The sun had dropped behind the houses across the street, so he had to turn on the lamp to get more light in the room.

"Where are you?" he whispered.

An answering clatter came from inside his closet. The light in there was already on—a bad habit that his father had little success breaking him of—but the door was almost closed. Quince went to the closet and slowly opened the door, peering at the floor. If Junior made it all the way over here, his new little legs must have been working pretty well.

Quince was not prepared for the surprise inside the closet. The clatter had been a huge tub of Legos tipping over and spilling everywhere. Standing in the middle of the sea of multi-colored blocks was Junior. At least, Quince had to assume it was Junior.

The little "seed" had been smaller than the fingernail on Quince's pinkie. This gray creature was as big as a football. It still looked a lot like a pig. Not a Pig, really, which was a scary kind of alien, but a regular Earth pig. It had a pudgy body and a round head. It even had a short snout like a pig, though at the end, instead of two nostrils, it had a funny bunch of dark, wet wrinkles. It had two black eyes, set wide on either side of its head. Its eyes were big compared to the size of its head, almost like a horse would have. Junior's legs were kind of like a pig's, thick and short. The ones in the front were larger, more muscular than the ones in the back... or the ones in the middle. With *six* legs, it was clearer than ever that Quince's pet was something from another planet.

Junior turned its head toward Quince and made a loud snort.

"Shh!" Quince whispered, pushing his way into the cluttered closet and closing the door behind him. He squatted down to get closer to Junior. "If my parents find you, they'll *kill* me!"

Junior sniffed at Quince. He took a couple of steps toward the boy, little hooves knocking aside the scattered Lego blocks. Quentin slowly, carefully lowered his right hand to the creature. The snout came up, smelling Quentin's hand somberly.

"I smell okay?"

Apparently, he did. Junior rubbed his wet nose against Quince's hand. Quince let him do it, even though his nose was kind of gross and snotty. With his other hand, he petted Junior across his back. His skin was soft, which made sense, since Junior was just a baby. He had some very fine hair as well, which Quince liked. It made Junior seem more like an Earth animal, like a really weird dog or something.

"You are so cool!" Quince concluded.

After an evening getting acquainted with his new pet, Quince finally had to get to bed. Tomorrow was a school day.

When he woke, Junior was already up and perched on the windowsill, butting his head against the glass. Outside, the sky was cloudy, and looked like it might rain. Quince hopped out of bed and lifted Junior to set him down on the floor.

"You can't go outside yet. I'll try to take you out this afternoon after school. Okay?"

Junior looked up at Quince with his wide, dark eyes. He looked like he understood, but with pets, did you ever really know? Quince planned out in his head how he would stuff Junior into his backpack after he got home and then go out for a walk. Maybe he'd take him down to the park. He hoped Junior would get along okay with the dogs in the park.

Dad's voice intruded on his planning. "Quince! Sarah! Up and at 'em!"

Quince set about getting ready for school.

They almost didn't have recess. Just like Quince had expected, it did rain most of the day. Thankfully, there was a short break, and the sun even came out briefly. All the grades in the school decided to take the opportunity to let the students out at the same time, so the playground was really crowded. Quince didn't mind. He pulled his best friend Barry off to the side of the playground to talk to him in private.

"I found a pet."

"A dog?" Barry asked. Barry had a profound desire to get a dog himself. He wanted a husky.

"No. It's an *alien* pet."

"No way!"

"I call him Junior. He grew really fast. He's about this big." Quince held out his hands.

"Can I see him?"

"Can you come over to play after school today?"

Barry's face fell. "I can't. We're going out to the mountains this weekend."

"You can see him when you get back."

"Cool."

The day dragged like no other in Quince's memory. He realized he hadn't fed Junior. The little guy had grown from seed-sized to where he was without eating anything. He *was* an alien. Maybe he didn't have to eat at all? That'd be weird, Quince concluded.

Back in class after lunch, Mr. Weiland showed them a PowerPoint of the Blues' home planet. The pictures looked like something out of a movie, with bizarre cityscapes and some natural rock formations that looked kind of like Earth, but with all wrong colors. This seemed like a perfect opportunity to do a little research.

"Mr. Weiland?" Quince asked, his hand politely raised.

"Yes, Quince?"

"Do all aliens eat?"

"Do all aliens eat what?"

"Do they all have to eat food?"

"I think they do."

"Oh. Okay."

Now Quince was a little worried. He glanced nervously at the clock on the back wall of the classroom. It was more than an *hour* until class let out. Junior was at home, probably starving, and he couldn't do anything to help him!

Quince prayed that his mother would be there to pick them up on time. She wasn't usually late, but it had happened a couple of times. Quince prayed that she wouldn't have some kind of errand to run on the way home. That was more common, but today, amazingly, luck was on Quince's side. Mom drove him and his sister straight home.

Quince hit the front door at a run.

"You want a snack?" his mom called after him.

"No, thanks!"

Quince entered his room, worried that he'd find Junior sick, or dying, or maybe even *dead*. He really didn't want Junior to die.

Junior wasn't dead. Junior was doing *great*. He had figured out how to pull open Quince's dresser drawers and had pulled out all of Quince's clothes. He had yanked all the blankets and sheets and pillows off Quince's bed. He had strewn not only Legos, but all the pieces from every board game Quince owned all over the floor. Checkers and Monopoly money and little white plastic organs from Operation were everywhere.

When Quince entered the room, Junior was nosing a glob of Silly Putty around the floor with his snotty nose. He looked up when Quince came in and gave him a friendly snort.

"Junior! What are you doing?" Quince closed the door and went over to pick up the animal. He seemed really heavy. Maybe that was just Quince's imagination. He also seemed to be *bigger*. He sat on the end of the bed and held Junior, who squirmed a little in his arms. He was bigger.

Not a lot, but definitely bigger than this morning. He couldn't fit Junior into his backpack now. It'd look like he was carrying Sarah in there.

"What are you eating?" Quince wondered. He went through the clothes that were strewn around. Nothing seemed to be missing. He must have been eating *something.*

"Wait here. I'll be right back." He set Junior down on the bed. Junior folded his six legs under him and sat.

Downstairs, Quince went into the kitchen and started to gather up things that Junior might like to eat. He got a fruit (some grapes) and a vegetable (a zucchini) and a bread (two slices of whole wheat) and a dairy (a hunk of blue cheese that Dad planned to put on salads).

"Quince, I thought you didn't want a snack," his mom called from the dining room, where she was working on her laptop.

"I'm just getting a drink," Quince said. Thinking that was a good idea, he got a bottle of water from the fridge. It was tough to carry all this stuff, using both arms and his chin to keep it from falling. But he didn't want to make two trips and maybe have to answer more questions from Mom. Back up to his room he went.

Junior was still waiting patiently on the bed. Quince sat next to him and methodically offered each of the foods to Junior. The alien sniffed each of them, seeming to like some, but not others. But he didn't try to eat any of them.

Quince was puzzled. He opened the bottle and was preparing to feed some of the water to Junior when he realized something that he should have seen all along—Junior didn't have a *mouth.* Under his snout, where a pig's mouth would be, was just smooth, solid flesh. He looked all over Junior's head. Nothing. Maybe there was a mouth hidden inside the nest of his wrinkly nose? He hoped not. Eating through there would be really sick.

"You're kind of weird, aren't you?"

Junior responded by jumping onto Quince's lap and pushing his forelegs onto Quince's chest. Quince laughed, rolling Junior off of him and tickling his belly. Junior *loved* that, squirming around and making a surprisingly low-pitched grumbling sound that had to be laughter.

"Quince!" That was Dad. He was home early again. Quince quieted Junior down, then went downstairs. Dad was in the living room with Sarah and Mom.

"So, what's the big surprise, Dad?" Mom asked.

He held up four tickets and handed one to Mom. Mom laughed. "You're kidding?"

"What?" Quince asked. He took his ticket from Dad. It was for something called the Chevrolet Cup. "What's that?" Quince asked.

"It's the hydroplane races. Out on Lake Washington. We've got a spot right on the I-90 bridge. We're gonna watch the speed boats from right there on the water!"

"Cool!" Quince shouted.

"Cool!" Sarah parroted.

"When is it?" Quince asked. Dad pointed back at the ticket. Quince read the date: Saturday, August tenth. "Tomorrow?"

So much for sneaking Junior out to the park on the weekend. Still, this was going to be *great*!

Quince spent the evening—after another interminable dinner—in his room playing with Junior. He knew Junior had to be just an animal. If he was an intelligent alien, like an Eel or a Vampire—two of Quince's favorites from his card collection—then that Snake wouldn't have sold the little baby Juniors to his dad. That'd be wrong.

And anyway, since Junior didn't have a mouth, how could he talk? Some aliens had strange ways of talking, like Rope Men and Skeletons, but Junior hadn't even tried to talk. Well, he was just a baby, though. Maybe he'd talk some later? That'd be really cool.

A knock at the door startled Quince. Junior snuffled. Quince shushed him, then led him into the closet.

"Yeah, Dad?" Dad opened the door and looked in.

"Quince, we're gonna… What happened to your room?" Dad looked at the devastation with wide eyes.

"Oh, yeah. I was looking for something."

"Not the floor, I guess. You need to pick this all up."

"I'm gonna."

"We're leaving at eight sharp tomorrow."

"Uh-huh."

"You still have that Mariners cap I got you?"

"Uh…" Quince cast his glance around the messy room. He saw the cap and pulled it out of a pile of underwear. "Yeah, I got it."

"You're gonna need it tomorrow. It's supposed to be sunny all day."

"Gotcha. Night, Dad."

Dad looked around the room again with a concerned frown. "Night."

Quince sighed with relief.

In the morning the family went through their normal getting out of the house routine. It was loud and frantic and confused. Sarah insisted on wearing two different colored shoes. Mom was horrified, but Dad finally asked her what the big deal was. They had to *go*.

Quince still hadn't figured out what Junior ate, so he snuck a box of cereal up to his room for him. Junior didn't even turn from the window. He had his nose pressed against the glass, leaving a gooey smear. Quince made a gagging noise, petted Junior once, and ran out of the room to join his family, who were already getting into the Volvo.

In his haste, Quince left the door to his bedroom open.

Redmond, Washington was a community of great wealth. Not *ostentatious* wealth, generally, but obvious nonetheless. Virgil Cho was edging his lawn as the Almedas trooped out to their brand new Volvo wagon, the mother with her Prada bag, the father with his Ray-Ban sunglasses, the two kids in colorful Gap Kids clothes. He waved and was waved to in return. He'd spoken briefly with Vance, the patriarch of the Almeda family, on a few occasions. Vance Almeda was nice enough, but he was one of those men whose every move is calculated to advance his career in some way. Redmond was a destination for Virgil, headed for retirement from a merchandising position at Microsoft. This place was just a pit stop for Vance Almeda.

The family drove off prepared for a day in the sun, probably something to do with Sea Fair. Virgil went to one of those parades back in '19 or '20. He was too old to deal with all the kids now. He preferred to spend his Saturdays on his lawn.

The Almedas never worked on their larger, more impressive garden. They hired people to come in to do it. When Virgil went to the dry cleaners and was helped by a kindly old Chinese gent, he felt a little pang of guilt that he was paying one of his countrymen to wash his jackets and ties. Did Vance feel the same when he paid his Latino gardeners? Proba- bly not. People so concerned with advancement didn't feel emotions like that.

Virgil's annoyance with the Almedas was aggravated—or perhaps even *caused*—by the fact that their house was so perfectly positioned for that garden of theirs. The *light* their front lawn got was stunning, at least on days like this when the sun was out. Their front room—which Virgil had never been invited to see, incidentally—featured wide, tall windows that let the sun stream in.

The edger buzzed angrily as Virgil overshot the end of his lawn and ran it up against the street curb. He cursed loudly and shut down the ma- chine. Enough woolgathering, he thought. He went back to the garage to get the hose and set up the sprinkler. Best to get the grass watered before the sun rose over his house and started to shine on *his* lawn.

When he opened the faucet on the side of his house, Virgil heard a scary rumbling sound. Were his pipes *that* bad? The house was only built in '08! He hurriedly turned the wheel back, shutting off the water flow, even before any of it made it as far as the end of the hose.

The sound remained. It grew in volume. Virgil went around to his front yard to see where the sound was coming from. It rose again, then fell, but didn't disappear entirely. He thought it was coming from the Almedas'... Strange.

There was someone moving around in their house. Virgil took a few steps across his dry grass. He couldn't really see into the Almedas' front room, but there was a shadow shifting across the glass. Who was that? The maid? He had seen the whole family leave just a few—

The rumble expanded into a full-fledged *roar.* The whole bank of windows on the front of their house exploded outward. A bull charged out of the house! Virgil instinctively backpedaled, tripping over the hose and landing on his ass. Through the trembling ground he felt the creature approach, its hooves audible on grass, and then quite loud clopping on the street between their houses.

Virgil raised his head, almost scared to look. The large animal snuffling in the street not ten feet away wasn't a bull. He had thought that because it was so much thicker in the front than the back. Its front legs were nearly as big around as Virgil's torso. Its gray skin reminded Virgil of an elephant. Its face was piggish.

That massive head twisted toward Virgil, the two huge, wide-set eyes stared at him. Virgil tried to crabwalk backwards. The creature took that as an invitation, and it rushed forward, covering ten feet in no time flat. Thick, dark hooves crushed into Virgil's lawn on either side of his head. The other *four* legs straddled his body. A wet, noisy nest of wavy flesh—the creature's nose?—lowered to Virgil's face. *Sniff. Sniff.*

"Please…" Virgil whimpered.

Whether it was his smell or his plaintive cry, something about Virgil was lacking, and the creature slowly backed away. It turned in a wide circle and went back out onto the lane. The nose came up to smell the air. It turned, faced west, and galloped away.

Virgil said a quick prayer of thanks that he hadn't been killed or eaten by the creature. Then he fainted.

Officer Andrea Slagle cruised around town in search of illegal parkers. A lot of her fellow officers on the Redmond Police Department tended to be lenient about that kind of thing. They told her they preferred to investigate *crime*. Screw that. Parking illegally *was* a crime. Not a destructive or sexy crime, no, but something she hated. People were a little too lax up here in the *North West*. Angela was from Texas, Houston in particular, and she was just bringing a little bit of her home's law abiding history to this breezy, touchy-feely place.

"*Slagle, where are you?*"

Angela tapped the mic at her lapel. "This is Bravo Six Zero. I'm traveling north on 148th Avenue. Over." She followed procedure, even when the dispatchers didn't.

"*Yeah, we got a call that there's a rhinoceros on Redmond Way, headed for Kirkland. Are you close to there?*"

"Roger." A rhinoceros? Must be some kid tripping. She'd keep an eye out for reckless drivers. If this kid was tripping and driving *and* talking to the police on a cell phone, he was about to win the Slagle trifecta.

She was only a couple of blocks from Redmond Way, in the middle of a quiet suburban neighborhood. When she pulled up to the intersection, the light was red, so she came to a full and complete stop. She peered to the right. She tapped her mic.

"Dispatch, this is Bravo Six Zero. I'm at Redmond Way. I don't…"

Her voice trailed away in a very unprofessional way.

"*Slagle? You there?*"

Two SUVs and a man on a motorcycle blew past Angela's squad car, going west. Traffic from the east came to an abrupt halt, with half a dozen vehicles doing very illegal u-turns in the middle of the intersection.

The creature running down Redmond Way didn't look like a rhinoceros to Angela. It looked like a dump truck. A *big* dump truck. This thing didn't really even fit into one lane. As it galloped past Angela, she felt the ground tremble. The beast had to shoulder aside a Mercedes that hadn't finished its impromptu u-turn quite fast enough. The car's air bags deployed as it flew five feet and crunched into a stalled Honda.

"Dispatch, I'm in pursuit!"

She flipped on her lights and sirens and peeled out onto the street, turning left from the right lane, following the wide swath of open street left by the passing animal.

"*In pursuit of what?*"

More cars ahead scrambled to get out of the way of the oncoming monster. From the rear, it looked a lot less dangerous, since its backside was smaller than its front, though still freakishly large. "It's an animal, six legs, at least ten feet tall." The beast's rounded back brushed up against a hanging traffic light as it moved through another intersection. "Make that twelve."

According to her speedometer, she—and the beast—were doing between forty and sixty miles per hour. This section of the street was marked by sweeping curves. She saw the creature's dark hooves skid a little on the turns, forcing it to slow down. It picked up speed again on the straightaways, sunlight filtering through the tall pines that lined the road, painting the beast's light gray hide in striped shadows.

"Approaching the 405 interchange. Please advise, have Kirkland police been notified?"

"*Yeah, we're working on that.*"

Angela muttered something *really* unprofessional under her breath.

At the 124th Ave intersection, the monster didn't simply brush against the traffic light. It bashed directly into it with its nose. Angela tried to remember if that light was hung at the same height as the one the creature had just nudged a few moments earlier. She couldn't be sure, but she *thought* it was. During that moment of reflection, the creature slowed down, shaking its head, as if annoyed by the collision with the signal lamp. Angela had to slam on her brakes, feeling giddy with the knowledge that she was about to collide with an alien monster under the bright, summer sun.

The creature started to move again, and Angela barely managed not to crash into its rear. As they passed from Redmond into Kirkland, the land began to slope down toward the lake. Now, with a wider street ahead of it, fewer trees to hedge it in, and gravity on its side, the beast edged up to nearly seventy mph.

Thankfully the motorists were giving the beast a wide berth. Angela pulled into the oncoming lane to look ahead at the busy intersection that was coming up just before the 405 overpass. There were a *lot* of cars stopped at the light. The creature was wide enough to fill *three* lanes. This was not going to be pretty.

Three lanes? Was the monster *growing* right before her eyes?

It seemed to understand that these obstacles needed to be removed from its path. Rather than simply trampling the cars—which would have meant instant death for most of their occupants—it lowered its snout near to the asphalt.

The closest car in the left lane, a Porsche—thankfully one with a hard top—took the brunt of the creature's blow. The little sports car flipped up on one side and bashed into the rear of a minivan, pushing the van into an ancient Ford. The abused Porsche was edged to the side to join a line of violently sidelined cars in the right lane. The truck in the turning lane on the far left tried to escape by pulling out into traffic and got sideswiped for its trouble.

The damaged minivan continued forward, butted roughly by the monster's huge snout. It was now locked in an awkward embrace with the Ford. Both cars—which looked less and less like vehicles each moment—launched like spinning ice dancers into the intersection and directly into the path of cross traffic, which was blithely unaware of the danger galloping down the hill.

Protesting squeals from abused tires and brake pads filled the intersection. When the beast caught up with the carnage he'd caused, he battered against all of it, sending a dozen more vehicles careening around like billiard balls.

She called in the scene to her dispatcher while trying to snake her way forward. Ahead, the beast reached the 405 overpass. It couldn't run under the bridge, since it was just a bit too tall. It bent into a crouch and began to crawl through. This gave Angela a chance to catch up. She had to slow down significantly to negotiate the aftermath of the multiple collisions. She cleared the mess just as the creature reached the far side of the overpass. Back on the open road, the chase continued.

"He's past the interchange and still traveling west."

"*Kirkland Police are on their way.*"

I know, Angela didn't say. She could see down 5th Avenue—the new name of this street on the west side of the highway. Three Kirkland squad cars, lights spinning and sirens blaring, sped toward them from the city center. The beast ignored them and continued west. When the creature ran past, the drivers of the three patrol cars panicked and each attempted to do high speed 180 degree turns to follow. Not one of them accomplished the maneuver. Angela glanced into her rear-view, hoping that they would pull out of their ridiculous, tire-smoking spins and join her in the chase.

For the first time, Angela wondered what she planned to do when she *reached* the beast. This wasn't a dog or a cat or even a stray deer. It was three lanes wide… no, check that. *Four* lanes wide.

"Dispatch, the thing is growing."

"*Growing? Growing what?*"

"I'm not talking about a beard! It's getting bigger. It's twice the size it was when I first saw it!"

"*Uh, yeah. Okay.*"

Angela growled into the mic in response. She wasn't the one who had called about a stray *rhinoceros* strolling through town.

Deeper into Kirkland, the traffic was thicker. The creature slowed a bit. It still knocked cars—and one *bus*—aside as it went, but it was down to a sedate forty mph. Then thirty.

"Dispatch, the thing is slowing down."

"*It's not* growing *as fast?*" She swore she heard laughter on the other end of the radio.

"It's slowing down. Moving slower."

In the heart of the Kirkland shopping district, the beast couldn't help but slow down. It barely fit on the street, taking up both directions of travel, crushing trees and signage on the narrow median with its low-hanging belly. Occasionally it brushed up against the shops with its flanks, leaving shattered glass and destroyed neon signs in its path. Following it now at just a little faster than jogging speed, Angela noted how smooth its skin looked. She saw a handful of scratches on its haunches from cars and trees it had scraped against on its journey, but no blood.

They reached the end of 5th. The creature made a sharp left, trotting down toward a small park with a boat dock on Lake Washington. The beast slowed to a walk as it approached the water. Now Angela had the chance to hear the terrified citizens screaming. Joggers and bicyclists and parents with strollers all hurried out of its path. Many people evacuated their cars in the middle of the street and ran. When the mammoth beast was within only steps of the lake, it came upon a row of stopped cars. Angela killed her siren and stopped her squad car. She hopped out and brandished her weapon.

"Freeze!" she yelled. The handful of onlookers brave enough to watch from the sidelines looked at her like she was crazy. In her defense, she didn't know if the creature knew English. It was an alien, after all.

The beast ignored her as it surveyed the obstacles. It chose a stylish BMW convertible that had its top down and stepped onto the car, strangely gingerly. The German automobile groaned and crunched in a final death rattle as the monster used it as a stepping stone. Free of the gridlock, the beast trundled forward to the edge of the water. Angela followed, stepping between two sedans to get over to the park.

The creature lowered its nose into the water and sniffed. Its head reared up and it sneezed out a great gout of lake water. It shook its head, as if it didn't like the taste. Angela, her pistol still out and unsafetied, approached. She tried a different take.

"Hey there, big guy?"

Now the beast turned around, massive hooves tearing up manhole sized chunks of earth. It took a single step forward and was upon her, standing over her like a three-story building made of gray flesh.

"Uh…" Her training fled. Really, what training did she have that could contend with *that*? "Uh…" she mumbled again.

As if bored by her, the creature did a strange little circular dance on its six legs, sniffing at the air. It didn't seem to like what it smelled. Then, it saw something to the southwest. It did a little hop, causing the ground to quake so roughly that Angela nearly lost her feet.

It took off to the south, following the lake shore road. Angela looked where the creature had. From a distance, she could see part of the 520 floating bridge. She activated her mic.

"Dispatch, it's heading for Seattle."

Vance applied sunscreen liberally to his head. Every time he'd said something to Elaine about getting plugs, she'd run her fingers over his scalp and said something about how sexy he was, ending the discussion, at least until the next time some young punk of a clerk confused him for Quince and Sarah's grandfather.

"When do they start?" Quince asked.

"I told you, it'll be a while."

The broad span of I-90 was shut down for the day. This served the dual purpose of avoiding gaper's block on the bridge during the races, and also allowing certain ticket holders a place to park and watch the action. Vance had thought he'd brought the family terribly early. As it turned out, he'd been part of the main rush as hundreds of vehicles were waved onto the bridge by uniformed attendants and shown to their parking spots. Everyone left their cars and wandered around the floating section of the bridge, enjoying the water, the sun, the cool breeze, and even just the novelty of strolling across the rough surface of an interstate freeway.

Vance kept a close watch on Sarah and especially Quince. Those two could generate more trouble than any five kids he'd ever met before. He tried to be a disciplinarian, but he knew in his heart that anything less from them would have disappointed him. He was like that when he was a kid, made trouble, caused his parents a certain amount of stress, and he'd turned out alright, hadn't he?

"Daddy!" Sarah called out. "Look!"

Vance turned to the south to see if the racers were doing a trial lap of the course. He couldn't see anything more than he'd seen when they first parked a couple of hours ago.

"No, Daddy!" Sarah yanked on his arm, pointing to the north. "Lookit!"

"Sarah, the race is gonna be over *here*."

"Vance..." Elaine said. That wasn't her admonishing tone, or her sexy tone. That was the tone she'd used when Sarah stopped breathing one horrifying night when she was seven months old. That was the tone she used when Quince stumbled into the house, white-faced and wide-eyed, one end of a croquet hoop plunged rudely into his thigh. Vance's blood went cold at the *tone*. He turned.

At first, it didn't make any sense. They were looking across Lake Washington at the 520 bridge. There was a truck on it.

"No *way!*" Quince shouted, his small binoculars glued to his eyes. Vance raised his own binoculars and looked closer.

That was no truck. It was far too *tall* to be a truck. For a few moments Vance simply watched, like a theatergoer enjoying a particularly nifty bit of special effects in a film. The *thing*, whatever it was, was so heavy that the entire bridge was bobbing in the lake. Vance had driven over that bridge a hundred times, sometimes in terrible downpours with gale winds blowing, and it had never felt like anything other than a solid span of concrete. Now, it was rolling with sinusoidal waves caused by the mammoth beast galloping down its length. He could see the water churning underneath, spilling out across the lake, rolling in concert with the motion of the bridge.

"Dad," Quince said.

The thing slowed a bit as it reached the middle of the bridge, where there were two slender walkways that allowed maintenance personnel to get from one side to the other without risking the always-busy roadway. The thing butted its head up against the first walkway, once, twice. On the third hit, the walkway shattered. The thing stepped forward a few feet and repeated the action on the second walkway. Then it started to run again.

"Dad!" Quince insisted.

The westernmost part of the bridge wasn't floating, but elevated, complete with a high ironwork structure over the lanes of traffic. The structure wasn't tall enough to admit the gray creature, though. The thing would have to batter it down. It didn't, though.

"It's going to jump," Vance muttered.

"Dad, I need to talk to you!"

The thing ran, hard and fast. The rolling, bobbing motion of the floating sections of the bridge caused a couple of them to crack, concrete and steel flying in the thing's terrifying wake. It reached the upslope section and put on even more speed.

"Wow…"

"Don't!" Quince shouted.

The thing reached the top of the upslope and instead of continuing forward, into the lattice of steel, jinked to the left and *leapt*. High and far, massive front legs reaching forward, smaller middle legs and smallest rear legs pinwheeling behind.

"He's not gonna make it," Quince warned.

"He's gonna make it," Vance said.

The thing smashed snout-first into a ten-story block of condos right on the water. For a moment, all they could see was smoke and dust and spray from where chunks of the building's face had sloughed off into the lake. Everyone on the I-90 bridge—not just Vance and his family— everyone watched in hushed anticipation.

The dust began to clear and a large, dark-snouted, gray head emerged from the rubble. It climbed out of the pile of shattered brickwork and concrete, shook off the dust, and trotted out of sight, into the city.

"Dad!"

Vance, finally, turned to look down at his son.

"I have to tell you something."

Marion Atwater had overcome a whole host of obstacles to become the mayor of Seattle. He was the first black mayor in the city's history, which even in this day and age was no small feat. He had come up, not through the ranks of lawyers or self-made entrepreneurs, but as a university professor at the Dub. Above all, he had done it with the lame-ass name "Marion".

It surprised him, when he started, how little time he got to actually spend in the city he governed. Visits to neighboring major cities, conferences, speeches, fact-finding missions. There were times he resembled all those virtual employees that infested the coffee shops and diners and parks all over town. Virtual Mayor Atwater. That's what he felt like most of the time.

But today, today was different. Sea Fair was an institution, one that pretty much every Seattleite bought into in one way or another. He couldn't *not* be in town this weekend. In fact, he was up in the city's most enduring landmark, so retro it was cool again, the Space Needle. Today he hosted a special luncheon. Half the observatory level was cordoned off for the influential and powerful members of Seattle's elite to have a nice meal, while looking out at the nearly cloudless and fantastically beautiful day.

As the host, Marion got to spend precious little time eating, instead wandering from table to table to shake hands and make small talk. He would never admit it in an interview or even to his aides, but this was a part of the job he actually liked. In a profession that was all about people-people, Marion Atwater had perfected the skill of small talk. More than one pundit commented on it, since no one expected an English Lit professor to be able to connect with anyone who hadn't written a scholarly treatise on the works of James Joyce.

As chance would have it, Marion was speaking with *the* man in the room when he was interrupted. The not-quite-retired billionaire was nearing seventy but still maintained a boyish nerd-charm, pulling Marion into a fascinating discussion of the challenges of marketing his company's software to the alien community.

"Mayor."

Marion frowned and turned to Linus Swindol, a short, heavyset, hirsute young man who was also Marion's chief assistant.

"Yes, Linus," he said, his eyes adding the addendum, *and this better be important.*

"I think we should talk in private," Linus added, his nervous glance at Gates not subtle in the least.

"I'll let you guys get back to work," Gates said. "We'll talk later." He shook Marion's hand and moved off to talk to his wife.

"What is it?" Marion snapped.

"Uh... there's a dinosaur loose in the city."

"You interrupted me for a *joke?*" Linus strengthened his bear-strength grip and pulled Marion away from the luncheon tables into a corner of the observatory level, away from the windows. On the wall, a series of illustrations compared the Needle to a number of other, much taller towers around the world.

"I've gotten calls from the police and fire departments of Seattle, Redmond and Kirkland. No one knows what it is, but it's big and it's alien and it just entered Seattle."

"From where?"

"The 520 bridge... or what's left of it."

"But they—"

Linus put up a hand. He tapped the phone it his ear. "Yeah... Yeah... Oh, God!"

"What?"

A tide of excited voices from the other side of the room distracted Marion for a second. His instinctive worry was that one of the kids at the party had ventured too close to the railing outside and spooked his mom. Marion wasn't really fond of heights. More shouts of alarm rose.

"Come on!" Linus shouted, physically pulling Marion out to the windows. They faced north-west, toward Capitol Hill.

"What are we...?" Marion didn't finish. He understood now. The dinosaur—what else could you call something *that* size—had just crested the hill. It dwarfed every other building in the vicinity, except for St. Mark's Cathedral a few blocks away. At this distance it wasn't very clear what kind of damage it was doing to buildings, streets, vehicles— *people*—but it had to be tremendous.

"Right... Right... Call me back." Linus ended his call.

"What can we tell them?" Marion whispered into his aide's ear as he eyed the crowd around them.

"Not much. We—" Linus took another call. Marion really wanted to snatch that thing out of his ear and throw it over the edge of the observation balcony.

Eyes turned to Marion. These weren't random people who had come in off the street to enjoy the view. These were the most powerful players in the city, individuals with nationwide—in some cases *global*—influence. They were watching a disaster unlike any in history unfold directly below them, with their mayor standing right next to them. Marion wondered if any politician had undergone scrutiny quite like this. He took a deep breath.

"Ladies and gentlemen, I am in contact with local law enforcement. At this point, we are monitoring the situation. When I know more, you will, too. Please, stay calm."

That seemed to mollify most of them. The colossus continued to crunch its way down the hill. Its most obvious victims were trees; the usually green hill now had a wide swath of gray-brown destruction sliding down from the ridge. When the creature got to the steep cut in the hill that fronted I-5, it paused, considering the situation. It walked north and then south, bits of the concrete retaining wall crumbling under its titanic feet.

"Mayor, we just got a call from a man who has information about the creature."

Marion moved back to Linus instantly.

"What is it? Where did it come from?"

"He claims…" Linus looked away, clearly still talking on the little phone. "He claims that it's his son's *pet*."

"Pet? That's a pet?"

The thing finally decided to jump down, immediately snarling traffic on the interstate in both directions. It blithely disregarded the cars—why not, since it had to be at least fifty feet tall and twice that in length.

"Get them here. Now!"

"They're locked in over on the I-90 bridge. Nothing's moving. Traffic's nearly at a standstill on that side of the city."

"We have helicopters, don't we?"

Quince felt guilty, because he'd stolen Junior from his dad, and that wasn't right. He was scared, because Junior was probably going to get killed. (He'd seen *Godzilla* for the first time just last month. The parallels weren't lost on even his seven-year-old mind.) But bubbling on top of all that was sheer *excitement*. He and his dad were riding in a *helicopter* from the bridge—where they left Mom and Sarah behind—over to the city. He kept an eye peeled for Junior.

"There he is!" Dad called out. Quince jumped out of his seat and climbed into the seat behind his dad.

"Quince!" Dad scolded.

"I'm buckling in." They were passing over Lake Union. Junior was right below them, looking even *bigger* than before! He was walking up to the lake shore, trampling a whole row of restaurants on the lake's edge. He dipped his snout into the water.

"He's thirsty," Quince said.

Junior pulled his head back up and sneezed out the water, sending the spray halfway across the lake.

"Guess he doesn't like it," Dad said.

The helicopter landed in a parking lot near the Space Needle. Quince had been up in there once, when he was little. The elevator operator took him and his dad and their police escort—a big guy named Dave—up to the restaurant. Quince remembered that the restaurant usually spins, but it was shut down for now. It was empty, except for a couple of tables where some people were talking and working on tablets. Quince and his dad went in and met the mayor, Mr. Atwater.

Quince told his story. He said he was sorry, but he didn't think Junior would hurt anyone. From the frowns of all the adults in the room, he guessed something bad had already happened. If Junior had killed someone, it must have been an accident. He was so big now, it would be easy for him to make a mistake like that.

The mayor turned to Dad.

"Well, Mr. Almeda?"

Dad leveled a glare at Quince. "Quince and I will be having a very long talk this evening." Quince felt his face get hot with shame.

"Laws have been broken," Mr. Atwater said. Dad looked at him, surprised.

"He's only seven years old."

"No, Mr. Almeda. *You're* the one I'm talking about."

"Me?"

"You imported a dangerous alien animal into my city."

For a second Dad looked scared and worried, even a little guilty. Then Quince watched as his father stood a little straighter and looked Mr. Atwater right in the eye.

"I didn't break any laws because there *are* no laws on this topic. I can't import something from Canada or Japan or New Zealand. I researched this, Mr. Mayor. There's nothing on the books in Seattle or in the state of Washington about *alien* importation. Tacoma has talked about it, but nobody wants to legislate the issue because they're all too worried about missing out on the next big thing. I brought in the creature—"

"Junior," Quince prompted.

"I brought in Junior for some bioelectric research we're doing at Microsoft. You can't tell me you wouldn't *want* us to find a breakthrough. It would mean money for the city."

The mayor looked angry. "Your boss is one floor up. You think he's going to be pleased at what you did?"

"Leon Zucker is here?"

"No, Mr. Almeda. I'm talking about Bill Gates."

"Oh... *Oh*..." Dad paused, looked down at Quince, then back at Mayor Atwater. "Tell him. I don't care. I made a mistake, I'll admit that. You pass the laws and we'll abide by them. Until then, you can't think I could have foreseen something like *this*."

"Look—"

"Sir!" A fat man, Mr. Swindol, called over from his tablet. The mayor wanted to keep arguing, but he had to stop to see what Mr. Swindol was looking at. Quince and his dad followed. They gathered around the small screen, which was showing a live newscast. Quince looked out the window. He could see the helicopter hovering below and he could see Junior's path in from Lake Union. The dual tracks of the monorail were broken where Junior had passed through. Quince couldn't get a view of what Junior was doing right now, though, since he was right below them. He turned back to the tablet to see what the news chopper saw.

Five hundred feet below, Junior lumbered up to the base of the Space Needle. His front hooves left holes in the valet driveway big enough to park a car in. He craned his head up to get a look at the tower above. He sniffed at the base, his snout brushing up against the gift shop, cracking several windows. Then he moved closer and started to rub his shoulder against the flared base of the tower.

"It's trying to knock us down!" Mr. Swindol shouted. They could feel the vibrations all the way up here.

"He's just scratching himself," Quince said. After a few moments Junior turned around and scratched his other side. "He's not a bad guy, Mr. Swindol. He's just an animal."

"What does it want?" Mr. Swindol asked. No one had an answer to that.

"How big is it now?" the mayor asked. Mr. Swindol made a call to somebody to find out.

The mayor turned to Dad. "We need your help."

"I understand," Dad said. "But I don't know what I can do."

"Where did you get it?"

"From Sylvester."

"The Cancer Snake?" the mayor asked.

"Yeah," Quince said. "I saw him at our house." Dad put a hand on Quince's shoulder, not even realizing he was doing it. At least Dad wasn't *really* mad at him.

"He told me the species was adept at energy conversion, that it wasn't sentient, that it came from a red giant system. That's all I know."

"The National Guard is on its way. Is there any reason to think we can't kill it with conventional weapons?"

"What?" Quince shouted. "You can't kill him!"

Dad's grip on Quince's shoulder tightened. "Quince, this is serious. Junior has already hurt people and done a lot of damage. We can't just... let him roam free."

"Why not?"

Mr. Swindol came back over. "Sir, the police have been reviewing video footage of the creature. I think we know why it's growing. It seems to only grow when it's in full sunlight."

"Sunlight?"

"There were two intervals when clouds shadowed it from the sun, once for sixty seconds, another for nearly three minutes. During those periods, the creature did not get noticeably bigger."

"It didn't shrink, either," the mayor snapped.

"No."

"That makes sense," Dad said. "If the creature feeds off of sunlight, it would have adapted to a lower luminosity star back home. Our sun is overfeeding it, so it's growing at a much faster rate."

"You had to let it loose in the summer," the mayor muttered. For a second everyone was quiet, no one laughing at the thin joke. "Well," the mayor continued, "we can't turn off the sun."

"Could we shade him in some way?" Dad asked.

"I don't see how," the mayor admitted.

"We should paint him," Quince said.

"Paint him?"

"Yeah. Cover up his skin. Then the sun wouldn't hit it." The adults all stared at him. "He's probably hot anyway. He might like it."

Mayor Atwater ruffled Quince's hair. "You've got quite a kid there," he said. "Linus, get the Fire Department. They've got to be able to fill up one of their engines with something we can use to cover Junior's skin."

"But, sir!"

He leaned over to Mr. Swindol, whispering intensely. Quince heard him anyway. "Keep the Guard coming, too."

Everyone jumped when they heard a whistling, whooshing sound. Out the window, two bright blue jets flew past the Needle. They went right over Junior, who was sauntering down Denny toward the waterfront and Elliot Bay. There were still a lot of cars on the street that Junior was crushing flat. Many people had tried to turn onto side streets, or simply abandoned their cars to the beast's advance. Two more news helicopters had joined the first, buzzing around Junior like flies. After the pass from the jets, the helicopters pulled away... but not too far.

"What the hell was that?" Mr. Atwater asked.

"I think that was the Blue Angels. They're here for Sea Fair."

"I know who they are! What are they doing here?"

The planes split up over the bay. One swung out to the north. The other did a tight, looping turn over the shipyards and headed back to the city, right toward Junior. He looked up, distracted from his journey down the street by the brightly colored plane. The jet streaked past, Junior's head whipping side to side to watch it.

"Why don't they fire at it?" Mr. Swindol asked.

"Fire at him?" Quince asked, horrified.

The other blue plane buzzed Junior, this time from north to south.

"Those are demonstration aircraft, Linus," Mr. Atwater explained. "They don't have any live ammunition."

While Junior was still watching the second plane fly away, a missile slammed into his left shoulder, exploding. Junior was about seventy feet tall by now, so the attack didn't kill him. It didn't even knock him down, but he did stumble, sidestepping into a construction site, destroying half of the naked steel framework of an unfinished building. He howled so loudly they heard him through the glass.

Everyone in the restaurant turned and looked to the east. An Apache helicopter was hovering over the parking lot across the street. Two more were coming in over the ridge from Lake Washington.

Junior turned south and started to run down the street. Spurred by fear and pain, he didn't weave so carefully through the buildings. He smashed his way through Belltown, trampling everything in his path.

"Call them off!" the mayor shouted.

"It's the Air Force!" Mr. Swindol said. "I can't call them off!"

"The Army," Dad corrected.

"I don't care who they are! They're just making him mad! We have to call them off!"

Junior ran south east along Second Avenue, away from the Space Needle. Quince used his binoculars to get a better look. It seemed like the ugly wound on Junior's shoulder was healing *really* fast. Before he could be sure, Junior's path took him behind some tall buildings. Quince had to go back to the tablet screen to watch the KOMO 4 news.

"We have to kill it, Mr. Mayor. How else to do you think we're going to do that?"

"How many more *people* are we going to kill in the process?"

One of the other helicopters swept around downtown to the south and shot another missile at Junior. This time he saw it coming and tried to roll out of the way, entirely demolishing a twelve-story office building. Two of the news choppers took that as their cue to fly higher and watch the attack from a safer distance. The KOMO chopper stayed low, searching the billowing wreckage for signs of Junior.

"I can talk to him!" Quince said. "He knows me. I can calm him down."

"Quince," his dad cautioned.

"Young man," the mayor said, "I am not letting you within a hundred yards of that thing. It's not safe, not anymore."

"He is safe! He's just scared."

"That doesn't matter."

Junior wrestled his way out of the rubble of the apartment building and barreled toward the water. Quince remembered seeing Junior jump from the 520 bridge all the way to the shore. He didn't like the water.

The third Apache, hovering over the city, took aim from point blank range and fired at Junior. This missile hit him squarely on the rump, the explosion pushing him forward, across a block of shops and directly onto a wide pier at the waterfront. Now Quince could see what was happening through the window.

"Junior!" Quince called out.

Junior tried to regain his feet on the concrete pier. The structure beneath him couldn't stand the strain of his enormous weight. It shuddered, cracked, then quickly imploded, dropping Junior into the deep waters of the bay. Junior slipped away beneath the dust clouded water. Quince began to cry. It was just like Godzilla. They killed him. They didn't have to *kill* him.

Dad picked Quince up and hugged him close.

"I'm sorry, son."

Quince cried and cried.

Marion didn't have the heart to kick the Almedas out of the restaurant. He continued to coordinate with the police and with the military— who had finally returned his calls. The Navy said they were sending divers into the bay to confirm the kill.

There was also the terrible damage done to the city, much of which he could survey from right here. Initial estimates put the physical damage—to various roads, bridges, buildings, and the new seawall—at nearly two billion dollars. And then, there was the human cost. At least seventy-five people had died. He knew more would be uncovered in smaller buildings that the beast had destroyed along the way. His very inappropriate reaction was relief. It could have been far worse. He had said as much a few minutes ago when he went to update the bigwigs who still milled about on the Observatory Level, upstairs.

"Oh, dear God." Marion looked up to see Linus staring out the window. Had more of the waterfront collapsed? Was a fire raging through Belltown? Marion hurried to the window.

Out in the middle of the bay, a round shape bobbed in the water. It disappeared, then bobbed up again. A familiar snout poked out of the water, blew a stream into the air, then dove again.

"He's still alive?"

The Almeda boy heard that and immediately ran to his side.

"Junior!"

"I'm calling the Navy," Linus said. "They have to have a submarine in the area."

Quince looked up at Marion, his eyes still red from tears. Marion imagined in that moment that he would regret his next words, maybe for the rest of his life—his political life, anyway.

"Linus, wait."

"For what?"

"Is he bigger?"

"What?"

"Is the creature any bigger than he was when he fell into the bay? It was nearly an hour ago."

"I don't... What?"

"Just find out!"

"He's not in the sun," the child said. "He's not going to get bigger. He's not going to hurt anyone."

"He's already hurt a lot of people," Marion said.

"There aren't people in the *water*," the boy argued. Marion had to laugh a little at a child's strange sense of logic.

"They say," Linus said, "that he hasn't grown... *yet*. But we have to take care of this. He could damage shipping vessels, pleasure craft, ferries. He could walk back up onto land at any time."

Mr. Almeda joined them. "The creature spent the entire day looking for water. He didn't like Lake Washington or Lake Union, probably because of the lack of salt."

"You have got to be kidding me," Linus spouted. "We can't just... let it swim around out there!"

"Okay, then how about this," Marion said. "We've seen red tides caused by a single dead whale. *That* is ten times larger than a whale, and it's got God only knows what kind of biological chemistry. If we kill it, we could be creating a toxic hazard of immense proportions. At the very least, we would have to wait for it to move out into the Sound."

"You..." Marion silenced Linus with a look.

"Notify the Navy," Marion said.

"But..." Quince protested.

"Tell them they need to help us keep an eye on him." Marion looked down at Quince again. "If he causes more trouble, we will have to put him down."

"He won't! I swear!"

"I hope you're right. I really do."

And he was. Weeks of careful scrutiny showed Junior to be interested in nothing but swimming peacefully around the waters of Puget Sound. He stayed beneath the waves and didn't grow, at least not that anyone could tell, and he never tried to get back onto shore. He stayed comfortably far away from the shallows.

The political firestorm that followed was bizarre and intense. Half the people complained that the city wasn't prepared for the disaster, and the other half complained that the response was too extreme. (This was Seattle, after all.) The families of the hundred seventy-one victims of Junior's rampage sued everyone: the city, the state, the federal government, even Microsoft. They won every case, except the one against Microsoft. (Microsoft's attorneys were better than the government's.) In the wake of these lawsuits, laws with strict language about importation of biological material from off world hit the books in Tacoma. Most other states followed suit the following year.

A larger, cultural battle waged on the internet over the incident. Proponents of destroying the beast proudly posted their video clips and pictures of the devastation to Seattle. Junior's defenders did the same with the footage of the missile strikes and Junior's playful antics in the bay. Some pundits claimed this was a referendum on human-alien relations. Would humanity give in to xenophobia and execute a guileless animal? Or would they ignore a proven threat to their continued safety and allow it to attack again? The relentless engine of the online media churned and churned over the debate for months on end.

The federal government—particularly the military—quietly decided to table the issue until there were further developments. They had seen Junior's remarkable healing ability first-hand. They were concerned that perhaps nothing but a direct nuclear strike could actually kill him. They were unprepared to deal with either failure or success.

And so, Junior was left to swim where he would.

Sarah ran up and down the strip of grass between the parking lot and the rocky beach. Her robot dog—which she'd named Bill—followed her, yapping in his tinny, electronic voice.

"Five minutes, Pumpkin," Dad called out to her. To Sarah, five minutes was an eternity of playing with her dog. To Quince, five minutes would be gone in an instant. He continued to sweep the water with Dad's binoculars. Dad came up and stood next to him.

"He's probably way out in the Sound."

"Uh-huh." Quince kept searching.

"Son, you can't say goodbye to him. He'd have to come up on shore. You know he shouldn't do that."

"I know."

Dad was quiet for a second, then he walked off to talk to Mom. They packed up the stuff from their picnic. Mom went over to get Sarah. Dad stayed by the car, waiting for Quince.

The water slapped softly onto the rocks, so blue it looked like it had been painted. Quince watched and waited, knowing deep down that someday he'd see a dark nose poke out of the water and a big, dark eye look his way and seem to say, "Thanks."

Outbound Travel

> *Either thou livest here and*
> *hast already accustomed thyself to*
> *it, or thou art going away, and this*
> *was thy own will...*
> —*Meditations, X,* 22

The sound of a ringing phone nudged Vanessa out of the shower. She ran dripping to the phone, knowing only too well who was calling. She swiped her hair away from her ear, slipped the bud in and tapped it to answer.

"Hello?"

"Hello, Nessie. Happy Birthday!"

"Thanks, Mom." Vanessa glanced at the clock on her bedside table. It read 6:05. Her mother lived in Sacramento. "I can't believe you got up at three in the morning to wish me a happy birthday."

"If I waited, you'd be too busy to talk to your old mother."

"You're not old." Really, Vanessa was the one who felt old. She was thirty-six this year. *Thirty-six!* Wasn't college just last week? Wasn't high school last month? How could she be in her mid-thirties already?

"You doing anything special for your birthday?" Mom put just a hint of a sing-song tone to that question. She was fishing, as always, for an update on Vanessa's dating situation. She would be overjoyed if her only child was to get married, but in truth, even a steady boyfriend would have made her happy.

"It's gonna be like any other Thursday, Mom."

"Okay, okay."

Vanessa dried her hair and plaited it into a French braid while her mother talked about last week's Texas Hold 'Em tournament. She shuffled into the kitchen of her condo and flicked on the coffee maker while her mother breathlessly described the new, handsome, *young* trainer at the health club. She prepared a mug of microwave oatmeal while her mother complained about how infrequently she got to see her oh-so-important daughter. How was it that a parent could laud your accom-plishments and make you feel like a toddler at the same time? Maybe that's the evolutionary advantage of long life spans. Your parents provide you with a valuable dose of humility.

"Okay, Mom, I've gotta get ready for work now. Thanks for call-ing."

"I love you, Nessie."

"You, too."

There were many people in D.C. who worked ninety-hour weeks, vying for the position of First Person in the Office and Last Person to Leave. Vanessa wasn't one of those people. Her hours were long, but they could have been *much* longer. As it was, she was usually in by seven and didn't leave until at least six, six days a week. Close to seventy hours was plenty. It was her opinion that if she couldn't get her job done in that time, she either had too much to do, or she wasn't doing it right.

The first hour of her day she devoted to simply catching up from overnight. She no longer tried to read her e-mail. She received on the or-der of a thousand messages a day, which ranged in importance from noti-fications of a change in the building's preferred parcel service to a sum-mons from the President. In other words, not all e-mail was equal. As much as it pained her to put it in her budget, she had hired a staff of three people whose sole job was to read all her correspondence. They were to ignore the irrelevant, summarize the important, and bring the urgent to her personally. She didn't even bother creating a shadow account for them to forward high priority messages to. Eventually, even that secret address would get out and the hundreds of people who felt it was critical *they* communicate with her directly would use it instead. And so, in this way, all the technology of the internet brought her right back to the sec-ond oldest form of correspondence: words on paper.

She swept into her office and fired up her coffee maker before leafing through the night's take of e-mails. There was nothing earth shattering—anything truly important would have led to a phone call in the middle of the night. Of the important e-mails, nothing stood out as a surprise. Her budget meeting at noon was cancelled, giving her a precious free hour in the middle of the day. A note from Terry said his progress in Australia was good.

Actually, things were relatively quiet. Election Day was only weeks away. Four hundred thirty-five Congressmen, thirty-three Senators and one President were all busy either getting themselves reelected or packing up to retire for good. Vanessa's job was so much easier when there weren't all these politicians around trying to *govern*.

Eight o'clock came around fast, as usual. Staff meeting.

She tried to limit the size of her staff as much as possible. She had five directors working under her, each of whom managed the activities of between five hundred and two thousand others. She had been assured that if the President's request went through, and the position of Secretary of Off World Affairs was elevated to Cabinet level, her budget would allow for her department's numbers to double. The thought made her head ache. At some point, the size of a department determined work it did, instead of vice versa. She did not look forward to reaching that milestone.

Vanessa took her usual seat in the conference room and got the meeting started, going around the table, department by department.

The Director of Off World Immigration managed the activities on *Abraham Lincoln*. He claimed, as he did in every Thursday meeting, that his staff was too small to handle the steadily increasing influx of off world visitors. As always, Vanessa's response was that the station was, for better or worse, a necessary choke point. Their inefficiency served as a governor on the number of visitors dropping to Earth each day. The Director's response, as always, was that this merely invited visitors to drop in unannounced rather than follow immigration protocols. With that deadlock comfortably achieved, Vanessa thanked the Director for his comments, and moved on to the next person at the table.

The Director of Visitor Relations dealt with the foibles, big and small, in human-visitor interactions. His report today focused on a newly arrived race, termed Scorpions by the Immigration department. These visitors were decidedly insectile, with tough exoskeletons and huge, multi-faceted eyes. They had only four multi-jointed legs, but also four pincer-tipped arms and a prehensile tail. Most visiting races acted politely with humans, and the Scorpions were no exception, but their appearance alone was causing distress wherever they went. Vanessa said as diplomatically as possible that people should just get over themselves. Next?

The Director of Off World Technology advised on the effects of off world knowledge and artifacts on humanity. The woman who held this position always had a laundry list of issues, both philosophical and economic. On the philosophy front, the Blues had offered Earth the technology to freeze people indefinitely, sparking a resurgence of the cryogenics craze. On the economy front, the Trees had introduced photovoltaic cells that were an order of magnitude better than the human state of the art. This was giving the big energy companies a case of simultaneous apoplexy. (They were still in disarray over the slow, human-engineered emergence of hydrogen as a fuel over the last decade.) These were only two of the Director's fifteen issues of the day. Before she ate up the entire hour, Vanessa forced the Director to pick her most dire concern for discussion. The Director suppressed a frown, and said that thousands of people were playing around with quicklight transmitters. This, she claimed, would have serious repercussions on the cell phone industry. That worry didn't bother Vanessa nearly as much as the second possible outcome: with quicklight signals emanating from Earth, their planet would only become better known in the galaxy. Vanessa flagged that one for follow-up.

The Director of Xenobiology coordinated with universities and other research organizations around the world on the impact of off world flora and fauna on the local ecosystem. Precious few off world species thrived in the wilds of Earth. This was not a surprise, since independent evolutionary tracks had generated wildly different biochemistries on different worlds. The Lilies trying to eat Central Park was a mildly humorous exception. This summer's devastation in Seattle was not so humorous. The most volatile current issue involved a race of amphibious creatures called Eels who had developed a ferocious appetite for live coral. The Australian Navy was currently in a standoff situation with a pack of Eels on their Great Barrier Reef. The Aussies didn't want these Eels destroying one of their great natural wonders. (Diving on the reef was also a huge source of tourist income; that had something to do with their concern as well.) Terry had flown down there last week to represent the Pentagon, and to determine if the US could—or should—give the Australians aid. So far, the situation was tense, but non-violent.

The Director of Off World Communication listened to the skies and attempted to transfer any knowledge gained thus into useful intelligence. Vanessa usually enjoyed his reports best. This was partly because it was the aspect of her job that most closely resembled her original career, but mostly because this Director was a friend: Shao Miller. Shao echoed the topic brought up by the Director of Off World Technology, the increased interest in quicklight. From his viewpoint, though, it was a boon. He had come to the conclusion that trolling the radio spectrum for information about the galaxy was a waste of time. It was mostly used for interpersonal communication, which, even if it could be translated, would be of limited value. He had shifted his entire department to monitoring quicklight transmissions, and the results had been phenomenal. In the last month, his team had cracked thirteen off world languages and had a good start on twenty-five more.

Vanessa looked at her watch. Five minutes to go before her next meeting. Just enough time to update her staff on what she was working on today: the Emigration Bill and the RFP.

From nine to twelve that morning, Vanessa was locked in a room with the least pleasant people in Washington: congressional staffers. These were people who didn't have to be nice because they weren't elected by anyone, and who didn't have to be competent because they were the friends and family of their bosses. Vanessa never met one staffer she liked. The only reason she allowed herself to get roped into this meeting was that the Emigration Bill was the first piece of serious legislation that she could call her own.

True, she didn't write it, or have her name anywhere on it, or even much of a say of what was in it. But she did *suggest* it, not a week after she first took the job. And now, only three short years later, it was about to become law. Hopefully.

The idea that people—humans—would want to leave Earth at all seemed far-fetched to most of the politicos in D.C. three years ago. That anyone would want to leave *permanently* seemed like pure science fiction. The image of Roy Neary walking onto that spaceship at the end of the movie didn't resonate with the government as a likely mass-appeal scenario.

Mass-appeal, maybe not, but more than ten thousand Americans had petitioned the government for exit visas from Earth so far. Vanessa's team knew the names of thirteen people who were known to have left the planet, and estimated that at least ten times as many more might have quietly departed as well. It took almost as long for the public to figure out the idea as it did for Congress to get around to legislating it. But soon enough humanity would have translight capability and wouldn't have to beg rides from friendly visitor races. That would cause the numbers of people who wanted to leave the planet to explode.

Some in Congress took the position, *Good riddance to bad rubbish. You want to leave, fine.* Others wanted to clamp down on off world travel entirely—leave it to NASA to explore the universe.

Vanessa, in her small way, nudged both sides to a compromise position that resembled the structure of visiting a formerly hostile nation, like Cuba. Make it hard enough to weed out the looky-loos, but make it easy enough so that those who are seriously interested in traveling to the stars can do it.

She had only confided in a few about her one real concern with emigration from Earth. If some hostile force did want to engineer a biological attack on humanity, handing over a bunch of DNA in the form of tourists was a good way to help them in their cause. Even so, she wasn't too concerned. There were much easier ways to destroy a young civilization like theirs.

Years in the federal government taught Vanessa that some of the horrifying complexity in legislation was necessary, to avoid misunderstandings which invariably led to court cases. But even with her jaded-by-experience view of governmental gibberish, she thought that four hundred plus pages was a tad overlong for a bill that basically said, *Yeah, you can go into space if you really want to.* So, for three hours, she politely suggested ways to trim the bill, and the staffers impolitely gave her all the reasons that she was just being a dumb scientist. To her credit, she never acted on her gut, fifth-grade instinct to respond by boxing their ears or giving them a noogie.

With glacial speed, the clock crept forward to twelve, and her blessed free hour.

"We need you in the conference room."

Vanessa looked up from her little cup of apricot yogurt with a pained frown. Shao stood in her doorway, uncharacteristically frazzled.

"Now?"

"Right now."

She finished off the current spoonful and grabbed her tablet, following Shao down the hall. It could only be Australia. Either the Eels or the Aussies had done something rash. She hoped Terry was okay.

"Surprise!!"

She entered a room filled with smiling faces. Despite being reminded at six this morning by her mother that she was, indeed, another year older, intervening pressures had lowered her paranoia about the aging process. It was the oldest trick in the book: emergency meeting in the conference room. Many of these folks really did wish for Vanessa to have the happy birthday that the song suggested. All of them wanted cake. Hell, Vanessa wanted cake, too.

Trust Shao. She'd been working with him for nearly a decade, and he never forgot her birthday.

There were, thank goodness, no gifts to open. Their office had reached that sufficient size wherein if birthdays required gifts, the financial outlay would be tremendous. Even Christmas had been pared down to a largely humorous Yankee Swap. (Back in California, they had called it a Chinese Swap. Imagine that: the East Coast being more politically correct than Cali!)

Vanessa said her thank yous and shook a dozen hands and thanked Shao for the party. She even liked the cake. You just can't go wrong with chocolate.

After squeezing out a few last moments of solitude at her desk, Vanessa packed up for her 1:30 meeting at the White House. The President was in Minnesota today, trying to get those ten thousand lakes to vote for him come November. But the machinery of government ground on, and this meeting was with Victor Fremont, the President's COS.

Once she was through security, a girl who looked half Vanessa's age—literally—escorted her to Fremont's office. They were meeting with only a couple of his deputies. Victor had called the meeting, and had his own agenda. One of Vanessa's standard tricks was to so efficiently wrap up the actual agenda she could sneak in topics of her own in the remaining time. Face time with someone as influential as Victor Fremont was not to be wasted.

"We have some concerns about Sylvester."

Vanessa laughed a little. "Sorry. You're worried about the Cancer Snake in Chicago?"

"Sylvester sold off his cancer business to Merck six weeks ago. He has built a sizeable conglomerate of industrial companies across the US, in Canada and in Belgium."

"Belgium? What's he doing?"

"A little bit of everything. Farming, construction, mining, manufacturing, software development, advertising—"

"Software development?" That raised a red flag for Vanessa. "What kind of software? Not something invasive?"

Fremont looked over to a blond, coiffed, deeply tanned deputy. The young man scanned his own tablet. "It appears to be supply chain solutions for multinational retailers."

"Oh." Vanessa didn't even know what that meant, but it didn't sound dangerous.

"Frankly," Fremont continued, "we're more concerned about the advertising agency he owns in Miami. He could be inserting subliminal messages into TV ads."

"Yeah, but so could anyone on Madison Avenue. There are too many consumer watchdogs on the web for something like that to gain any traction. I suppose this Sylvester character has decided to put down roots. I don't know if that's such a bad thing."

The blond piped up. "It's the launches."

"Launches?"

Vanessa glanced at the second, less-tan deputy. Apparently, he wasn't allowed to speak at all in this meeting.

"In exchange for the OCDS," Fremont said, "Sylvester asked only for unlimited launch authority."

"I heard," Vanessa said. The look from Victor—which was mirrored in the deputies' eyes—said that he was more than aware of the talk around D.C., that she was romantically linked to Terry Youngblood.

Fremont was enough of a power player not to indulge in cross examining Vanessa on the topic. The look sufficed.

Vanessa felt her face beginning to flush, which, with her coloring, would be obvious to anyone. Still, the talk was just that: talk. Nothing had ever nudged her relationship with Terry past simple friendship.

"Sylvester has been making use of this authority for nearly a year. He has two private launch facilities, one in Wisconsin, the other in Alabama. We believe he's negotiating with the French government for a third near Marseilles."

"How many launches?"

Again, Fremont looked to the blond for the answer. "Once a month, since November of last year. Always on the first of the month."

"Doesn't seem like he's trying to hide them. How big are the rockets?"

Fremont had the answer to that question so handy, Vanessa began to wonder if he even needed the blond guy. Maybe a meeting without staff was just not how Victor Fremont rolled. "His launch vehicles are similar in size and payload to an Ares VI, though they are not strictly rockets."

"Something like the repulsive force technology of orbit bubbles?" Vanessa still hadn't gotten a chance to fly in one of those. Terry had assured her he'd set that up someday.

"No. We suspect they're fusion based. After concerns about radioactive pollution, Sylvester allowed the NEA to monitor a launch at his Shelby facility. They couldn't get all the details, but they definitely saw nuclear level energy output with no emissions to indicate fission."

"Antimatter, maybe?"

"No gamma rays, so we don't think so."

Vanessa nodded, knowing that this concern of Victor's would help her segue to her own agenda topic for the meeting. Still, she remained patient.

"What's he shooting up there?" she asked.

"We don't know."

"But you have a good idea, I'll bet."

Victor answered with a frown. "Sylvester owns a shipping company with over five thousand trucks crisscrossing the nation. He has a transfer

hub *inside* the perimeter of the Shelby site, and another at the launch facility in Itasca. There's no way we could track all of his trucks. He could
be moving just about anything to those facilities and launching it into
space. What we would like to know is, what kind of danger does this represent?"

Vanessa sat back in her chair, floored by the question. "I have to
admit, sir, that I tend to think of the dangers being what's coming into
the system, not what's going out. We so freely transmit information
through radio waves that I can't imagine any information storage device
being worth a trip into space in a launch vehicle. There are a number of
Earth viruses that might be of use to biological engineers elsewhere in the
galaxy, I suppose. Again, multiple launches would be overkill for something that small.

"I'll have my team look into it," she assured him.

"Quietly," Fremont warned.

"Certainly. But off the top of my head, I imagine Sylvester is selling
cultural artifacts to curiosity seekers who can't visit Earth, for reasons of
environmental incompatibility. You may know that the nearest race to
Earth is the Pigs, and they have never visited for the simple reason that
they would be crushed by our atmospheric pressure."

"I've seen them. I can't say I'm disappointed I won't be meeting a Pig
anytime soon." Victor shifted in his seat. It was subtle, but enough of an
indication—along with his strained joke—that he considered the meeting
over. Vanessa pulled a sheet of paper from a pocket of her tablet case and
brought the meeting back to order.

"One more thing, since we have a few minutes."

Fremont seemed to be both annoyed and impressed by Vanessa's
maneuver.

"Yes?" He took the sheet of paper and read aloud for the benefit of
the deputies. "Airbus. Boeing. Ken-Ya. Lockheed-Hyundai. Maccha-
Yantra. What is this?"

"That's my initial list of companies that I think we should contact in
an RFP."

"For what?"

"An interstellar craft. We need to start thinking about building one."

Victor gave Vanessa a condescending little smile. "I don't think we're quite there yet."

"On the contrary, three of those companies are already working on designs of their own. No doubt China has something in the works as well. The United States is going to need interstellar capability, and I suspect no one here wants to get there after the Chinese, or the Japanese, or the French." That last was a subtle dig at Fremont, who was anything but a Francophile. Actually, Airbus was at the back of the pack on this list. She included them just to needle the Chief of Staff. Lockheed-Hyundai was too locked into LEO vehicles. Boeing was experiencing some aftershocks related to the Seattle incident, so they were a maybe. And mystery still surrounded the sudden disappearance a couple of years ago of Ken-Ya's chairman.

All in all, it looked like Maccha-Yantra was their best bet. Vanessa knew how it would look to outsource the most critical technological project in human history to India. She only hoped Victor wasn't thinking that far ahead.

"I'll bring this to the President."

"Thanks."

The balance of her day involved catching up with what happened while she was in meetings. Vanessa remembered, vaguely but fondly, when her days were filled with doing things, not talking about doing things, and then talking about talking about doing things. Back in her office, sipping at her thirtieth cup of coffee of the day, she saw with some disappointment that there were no new messages from Terry on her screen. Well, he was busy. And there was the time difference...

She looked up to see Shao in her doorway again. He looked distressed. Again.

"You already gave me cake. What now?"

"Can I steal a minute?"

Shao *never* asked for her time. He simply walked in, with the understanding that if she didn't have it to spare, she'd kick him right back out. Something really was up. She nodded solemnly, and Shao closed the door before taking a seat.

"How did the meeting on the Hill go?"

This topic was about as far from Shao's job as it got. He never involved himself in the legislative side. Something didn't feel right.

"The bill looks like binary code written by a freshman comp-sci major. It'll do the job, but it won't be pretty. What's up?"

Shao ran a hand through his bleached hair and refused to meet Vanessa's eyes.

"Shao, what—"

"I'm gonna go."

Vanessa wanted desperately to ask, "Go where?" and have Shao respond, "To dinner," or "To the Bahamas," or anything, really. She couldn't. She knew he wasn't talking about a vacation.

"Shao, I..."

"I've been talking via quicklight with a Blue ship that's on its way here. Should be arriving at *Lincoln* in about four weeks. Pleasure ship." Most of the visitors to Earth were arriving on these Blue interstellar cruise liners. Earth represented a minor detour in one of the more popular routes through the Orion Spiral Arm. This was one reason why so many of their visitors so far had been Blues. "They're looking for an Earth specialist."

"You're no specialist," Vanessa said, trying to effect a playful tone. It didn't quite work, but Shao followed along.

"I've been on Earth longer than you have!"

Vanessa laughed, her voice only hitching into a half-sob right at the end.

"How long?" she asked.

"The round trip lasts about six months." She noticed he didn't say, *I'll be back in six months.* The unsaid came through loud enough to Vanessa's ears. He wasn't planning on coming back.

"Is Earth really that bad?"

"Are you kidding? It's like I was made for this place!" This time Vanessa didn't laugh. "Evolutionary biology joke..." he said quietly.

"Look, you can't leave..." Shao's face fell, not because she had the authority to keep him on the planet, but because he didn't want to disappoint her when he left. "...until you take me to Chongqing like you always promised."

"We'll go next week," Shao said, smiling, his own tears finally coming. "You'll love it!"

"I know I will."

Shao got up to leave. Vanessa rushed around the desk to give him a
fierce hug.

Vanessa had a fine dinner at an Afghani place near the office, then
told her driver to go on home. She'd take the Metro back to her place.
The day had taken its toll on her, and she didn't want to get back just yet
to her quiet, empty house.

She managed to stretch out the walk to the Metro station by stopping at a café and drinking two more cups of coffee. Her body was so acclimated to caffeine by now that they wouldn't keep her up. At eleven
o'clock, the wait staff at the café told her they needed to clean up and
close the place.

She rode the train out to Georgetown and walked the remaining few
blocks to her house. She had no reason to feel bad about herself. She'd
done good work today. And even if she was going to miss Shao, she'd
have one last trip with him to his homeland. Or, really, to the homeland
of his grandparents. Shao was born in Walla-Walla.

As she put the key to her lock, her cell phone buzzed inside her
purse. She reached into the bag and almost turned it off, but it might have
been something urgent. She didn't recognize the caller ID, a strangely long
sequence of digits. It buzzed again, insistent, annoying. In a rush, before
she could change her mind, she tapped the bud in her ear.

"Hello?"

"Did I make it?"

Instantly, Vanessa's spirit's lifted. "Terry!"

"I think I calculated the time difference right, but Daylight Savings
always screws me up. I mean the International Date Line, not Daylight
Savings. You know what I mean. Did I make it?"

Vanessa glanced at her watch. "You had almost fifteen minutes to
spare."

"Not even close. Happy Birthday!"

Vanessa laughed, perhaps her only fully honest laugh of the day. "Thanks." She flopped down on the couch, her day forgotten, her whole soul focused on that faraway voice speaking in her ear. "I needed that."

Zinc

*I seek the truth, by which no
man was ever injured.*
—*Meditations, VI, 21*

From Researcher, to Associate Project Lead, to Project Lead, Keira's advancement through the ranks of Maccha-Yantra continued with remarkable speed. At each step, when she felt certain she had at least a partial grasp of the scenario she faced, her superiors would launch her into a new role with more responsibility, more underlings, and greater overall relevance to the state of engineering in this exceptional third decade of the Twenty-First Century. Keira held some small trepidation that she might fail, but that was often simply a passing fancy on the occasional long, lonely evening. Her greater concern was that MYC would declare her so invaluable that they would take her out of research entirely and put her into a purely managerial role. The mere thought gave her chills.

In truth, she had little enough time to spend on such worries. She had forgone dating after her breakup with Tommy. Her visits home had dried up to almost nothing. Her work filled her days completely. The one other constant in her life was Gainsborough. As his ability to interface with humans on a personal level had improved, he had more interactions with various aspects of the engineering research going on around the campus. Even when discussing a subject outside of his area of expertise, a random comment from him often sent the researchers onto new tangents of discovery. He was valuable simply to have around. His increased importance to MYC paralleled Keira's. As Keira had passed through stages of employment, so had their relationship passed from working acquaintance to friendship to near-constant companionship.

Keira wasn't so enamored of the Blue to call it love. Certainly someone somewhere on the planet must have done their level best to have sexual relations with one of the visitors. Keira wasn't that person, and frankly, she didn't want to meet them.

The overall project that Keira led now encompassed her old carbon-aluminum research, but included so much more: construction techniques for highly advanced multidimensional silicon chips, laser-guided crystal digital memory storage, water polymerization, bucky balls, nano filaments. The list went on and on. Other Project Leads worked on biomechanical interfaces, FTL drive construction, pseudo-sentient software design. If, however, an endeavor required the physical creation of a mechanical object, Keira and her team were involved.

As fascinating as all of these things were, carbon-aluminum remained the closest to Keira's heart, and the closest to the hearts of the owners and operators of MYC. Industrial production of bucky balls for creation of a space elevator had a time horizon of decades. Carbon-aluminum was happening *now*. One of the main reasons for Keira's rapid career growth was her successes in streamlining production of the wonder material. They could make carbon-aluminum for only ten times the price of steel. When Keira tried to explain this feat to her mother over the phone, all she got in return was confusion. Keira's mother didn't realize that for such a material, which had been, at best, in the province of science fiction four years ago, to be brought to such a level so fast was quite miraculous.

Keira's mother made it quite clear to her daughter that she didn't appreciate that kind of use of the word "miraculous". Her youngest daughter finding a nice man, that would be a miracle.

The smelters prepared a new test run, and Keira watched from a high perch over the factory floor. She could have braved the sauna conditions of the furnace room; the heat didn't bother her. Having to wear a helmet and goggles, on the other hand, was too much. She didn't like the sweaty, closed-off feeling they gave her.

Below, men and women in heavy, yellow coveralls oversaw a process that continued largely under the supervision of unique, made-to-order robots. The aluminum, already extracted from bauxite and glowing with heat, filled a cauldron, bubbling, ready for carbonization. The latest version of their process involved introducing carbon to the aluminum in a graphite form. The regular lattices of graphite, dumped into the cauldron like sugar crystals into a cup of tea, yielded far better results than coal with its more randomized configurations. Early in the research cycle, diamonds worked fantastically well. Of course, that was not an optimal solution.

On paper, carbon-aluminum was a beautiful amalgam of the two elements. Seven atoms of carbon for every twenty-five of aluminum, their electrons' shells lining up in a crystalline form that rivaled the strongest steel for sheer strength. Keira had an electron microscope view of just such an ideal matrix as the wallpaper on her tablet.

Creating perfect carbon-aluminum remained a wild-eyed fantasy. There was simply no way to convince the hectic, ever moving liquid aluminum atoms to align in just the right way on macroscopic scales. Everything they had tried—chemical baths, centrifuges, magnetic field generators—was a means for increasing the *chance* that some significant percentage of the metal would configure into the proper matrix. The more atoms that aligned to match the picture on Keira's tablet, the stronger the alloy would be.

For the last six months, Keira's team had focused on other possible configurations, with other elements. Perhaps they could come up with a hybrid-hybrid that could do the trick for them. Something that was easy to make and had a good approximation of what perfect carbon-aluminum could do.

"Keira?"

Keira turned to Gainsborough, who had sidled up to her rather quietly. The Blue had taken to coughing slightly when he approached someone from behind so as to reduce the likelihood of a human being startled by his sudden, silent appearance. Such polite accommodations were reserved for his more skittish coworkers; Keira had long since grown used to his stealthy manner.

"Yes?"

"It is customary, I believe, to celebrate anniversaries of singular events in Human culture, not simply the births of individuals or the dates of their nuptials. Correct?"

"Yes…"

Gainsborough raised all three of his hands and tossed what appeared to be improvised confetti into the air. "Happy Cocoon Day!" Keira glanced at her watch. Sure enough, it was April 22, 2025. *Voyager* had pierced the barrier at the heliopause four years ago today. That meant

Keira's own fourth anniversary as an employee of MYC would be coming up soon enough. In many ways, she felt she'd been on this project for her entire life. That it was *only* four years seemed remarkable.

"Thank you," she told the Blue. He smiled in that strange way of his, pursing whichever set of lips that was closest to Keira. "Incidentally, I've been thinking about something they do with traditional steel. Have you ever tried alloying your carbon-aluminum with zinc? I realize it's a much heavier metal than aluminum…"

Gainsborough's eyes took on that querulous look which meant he was searching through his English database for an unfamiliar word. As Keira understood it, he did not have a mechanical implant with an English dictionary stored on it. Instead, he had downloaded a program directly into his brain which functioned like a set of alternate memories, memories of an education in the English language. Keira found the concept of putting information directly in a brain frightening in the extreme, but to a Blue, such things were second nature.

"Ah! Zinc. Element thirty." He emitted a fast chirp. For Blues, this chirp could be any number of emotional outbursts, but coupled with the wide open look of his eyes, Keira knew this was laughter. "Quite amusing! Zinc!" He laughed again.

Keira was not amused. "Are you playing with me again? I thought that we were done with that!"

"No, no." He twittered again, then calmed down. "I mean no offense. I genuinely assumed this to be a joke. No, I have never attempted to alloy aluminum with *zinc*. What would be the point?"

Keira nodded. She had expected that introducing such a relatively heavy element into an alloy of aluminum (atomic number thirteen) and carbon (atomic number six) would seriously degrade the major value of carbon-aluminum: its remarkably low density.

Still, she made a mental note to have one of the teams try it anyway.

Later in the afternoon, Keira was called away to the Banerjee Building at the center of the MYC campus. She'd had precious few meetings at headquarters, and none with Nilakantha Ganguly, the CEO of Maccha-Yantra. She knew from office talk that he was a stickler for things like punctuality. She unplugged her tablet and hurried over.

The conference room was large and opulent. Big, comfortable chairs surrounded a glass-smooth table with screens embedded under its surface. Keira imagined this to be where Board Meetings were held. She didn't know precisely what sorts of things happened in such meetings, but she knew they were important. This was an important sort of room.

Two groups of people filled the room, each keeping a close eye on the other. To one side were several Project Leads and Directors from the research side of MYC. She nodded to each of her colleagues. She hadn't developed any significant friendships with these people, simply because she rarely saw them, outside of their monthly status meetings, meetings which she tried to miss if possible.

On the *other* side of the table, however, congregated a group of individuals more alien to Keira than Scorpions or Rope Men: the *Business*. Whenever the practical side of the equation of MYC came into play, Keira and her fellow researchers referred to the *Business* in tones of disgust and dismay. Not even the tension between research and application that Keira tried to reconcile every day could compare to the tension between *Science* and *Business*. Everyone on the other side of that table had one goal: to cheapen the efforts of the researchers for that lowest of goals, *profit*.

In that coldly logical part of her scientist's brain, Keira knew that these business types regarded her and her colleagues as ivory-tower eggheads who didn't understand the costs behind their endless and costly research games. That she understood their view did not mean she gave it any credence. She scowled at the *Business* just like her fellow scientists.

Ganguly appeared, only a few moments early by Keira's watch. The CEO was tall for an Indian—over a hundred ninety centimeters—and both slim and fit. He wore a dark suit and tie, just as he would be expected to do, but he looked like he'd be equally at home on a cricket pitch or in a rugby scrum. At fifty-five, he had a smattering of gray in his hair, but that was his only compromise to age. Otherwise, he looked young and handsome.

Keira often wondered if his boyish good looks were a cause or an effect of his success.

"Ladies and gentlemen, pack your bags," he said without preamble. "We're going to Washington!"

Before that meeting, Keira had never heard the term "RFP". Now, this Request For Proposal filled her every waking moment. Doing her best to shake off the effects of jet lag and make herself look presentable in her hotel room mirror, she recited the introduction to her presentation for the twentieth time as she brushed out her short hair, made unruly by Mid-Atlantic humidity. Teeth cleaned, eyebrows tweezed, makeup applied, she went out into the hotel bedroom and pulled open the curtain with a flourish.

Her view, sadly, did not include the Washington Monument or the White House. In fact, she could see only a single tree in a dank courtyard between the two wings of this Residence Inn. Ganguly and his immediate advisors were staying downtown in a five-star, mere steps from the Smithsonian Institution, where their meetings were scheduled. Keira and the other drones were staying out here in Arlington, where the rates were cheaper.

She gathered her things and made for the elevator. John Gupta, the quiet, somewhat doughy software Project Lead, stood waiting already.

"Morning."

"I notice you didn't say, 'Good Morning,'" Keira quipped.

"After that flight?"

The direct flight from Mumbai to D.C. lasted a grueling fifteen hours. The pilot made a joke just before they took off, asking if anyone had a preference for what direction he should fly, since it made almost no difference to the distance; Mumbai was practically on the other side of the planet from Washington. No one laughed at the jest.

And Keira didn't laugh now, either. The doors slid open and Keira and John rode down three flights to the lobby, where a desultory—yet entirely *free*—breakfast awaited them. Then it was time to pile into their two rented vans: one for the researchers, one for the *Business*. Forty-five short minutes after that, they were on the steps of the Smithsonian Institution.

Maccha-Yantra's visit proceeded in three stages. Day One involved a labyrinthine set of "Get To Know You" meetings, wherein, it seemed, every MYC person was to spend at least fifteen minutes with every member of the US Department of Off World Affairs. This day passed for Keira like a dream. The experience wasn't some kind of idyll, but dream-like in the sense that in the moment, it all seemed to make sense, and then in retrospect, she couldn't understand a single bit of it. Save one moment. Her heart gave an honest to goodness flutter when she met Vanessa Hargrove. They didn't say two words to one another, but Keira had just shaken hands with one of the most important people on the planet. In that instant, Keira really hoped they'd get the contract to build a starship.

During one of her seventeen room changes for the day, Keira rounded a corner of the stately yet cramped building and ran right into a Snake. Thinking he looked familiar, from a conference she had attended the previous month, Keira stopped, smiling.

"Hello again!"

The Snake's cat-like face registered annoyance as well as any human—or any cat, for that matter. "Think you've got the wrong bloke," he said.

"Oh. Sorry."

"No worries." He slithered away, looking pointedly over his non-existent shoulder as he went. His gaze didn't rest on Keira, though, but on the two military gentlemen who followed close on his tail, escorting him through the building. The man on the left, in particular, caught Keira's eye. He was blond and tan, had a strong, expressive face, and stood a couple of centimeters taller than Keira. She smiled at him. He smiled back. Keira had the presence of mind to flick her eyes downward, catching his name on a visitor's badge he wore clipped to his jacket. Youngblood.

Poor man. What a terrible name!

During dinner that evening, Keira shared the Snake incident with John. John immediately lowered his voice and leaned in. Keira generally had no use for office gossip, but since this wasn't *her* office, it didn't really count.

"I heard some of the Yanks talking about him. His name is Sylvester. Heard of him?"

Keira had, if only by accident. The last time she'd talked with her father on the phone, he had gone on for ten minutes about this Sylvester character. Apparently, the Snake owned a number of businesses in several countries. He had risen to the ninety-fifth richest person on the planet. Most aliens who remained on Earth for longer stays lived simple lives, like Gainsborough or the handful of other visitors in Maccha-Yantra's employ. But not this one. Sylvester made waves.

"He must like Earth, I guess," Keira suggested.

"Yeah," John continued, "but he's shooting rockets into space. The Americans are worried. That's why they brought him in for a conversation."

"Why?"

"Because they don't know what he's doing."

"Americans always need to know what everyone is doing," Keira scoffed.

Day Two was the MYC team's opportunity to make their case, giving presentation after presentation. Since there were some—like Hargrove herself—who needed to see all of the material, the presentations were scheduled one after the other in a massive theatre over in the NASA museum. Keira felt a childish thrill to see her lovingly prepared PowerPoint slides projected on a gargantuan IMAX screen.

The benefit for Keira was that she could stay and watch many of the other presentations as well. Hers was critical, certainly, but still a small part of the larger picture.

Maccha-Yantra wanted to build the first human interstellar craft. Over the course of those eight hours—with a thirty-minute intermission for a quick lunch and two fifteen-minute bathroom breaks—Keira and her colleagues made a case for being able to do the impossible. They claimed they could design, test, build and launch a craft capable of flying all the way to Central Authority. Their main selling point? They could accomplish all of this... in four years.

Whispered conversations in corridors and at water coolers had told Keira that Airbus and Boeing had already made their respective pitches, and that each had set a time frame of at least a decade. This wasn't good enough for Ganguly. He said loudly and proudly—and, in all likelihood, honestly—that he believed his team could do what Earth needed most: convey an ambassador to Central Authority before the barrier that had cocooned humanity for so many years finally fell.

Though the world had grown somewhat used to its newfound place in a wide and strange galaxy, the truth was that even after so long, Earth was still shielded from half the galaxy. The cocoon, despite unraveling at an extraordinary speed, still had another four years before it disintegrated completely.

According to the Rules of Conduct, the final destruction of the cocoon marked the first moment that Earth could officially send a representative to Central Authority. Leaders around the world—especially the ones here in Washington—did not wish to delay making their voice heard: not for a decade, or a year, or a day.

So, during Day Two, watching that immense screen come to life with computer simulations created by her coworkers, Keira saw what sorts of hulls and engines her carbon-aluminum might make. She saw the designs for living quarters and greenhouse bays and medical facilities. She saw demonstrations of the initiative-ready control programs that would monitor the dozens of ship's systems. She learned how the ship would be built as components and shipped to LEO for assembly.

When the astronomy team pulled up a star map of the galaxy and plotted the course they would take as a bright, curving yellow path, Keira lost any kind of cynicism she might have had for the RFP and openly wept.

They were going to the stars.

After a quite passable meal of Mexican food and a short visit to a piano bar where the drinks were small and expensive, Keira retired to her room to check her e-mail. There were a dozen updates from Charlotte, her assistant. She skimmed them, stopping only to reread one: *Zinc on back order. Supplier estimates two weeks. ?*

Keira looked at the time, did a mental calculation, and determined that Charlotte would still be in the office back home. She initiated a video chat. Charlotte answered after only a moment.

"How's it going?" Charlotte asked, full of both curiosity and effervescence, as usual.

"Two days down, one to go. I read your note about the zinc. We must have some alternate supplier."

"I called six metal distributors yesterday. Two weeks was the best I could find."

"You're saying Mumbai is out of zinc?"

"I'm saying *India* is out of zinc. At least for two weeks."

"Hmmm. Thanks."

"Sure thing."

Keira closed the chat window and started another. A familiar, narrow face appeared in the little screen.

"Hello, you have reached Gainsborough. How may I assist you?"

"You are the politest person I've ever met, you know that?"

"Keira! It is lovely to see you. How do you find the United States?"

"The airport and hotel are wonderful. The bathrooms are quite clean."

"I would love it there!"

"I know you would. Could you help me out with something? When I asked you the other day about using zinc for the carbon-aluminum, you laughed."

"As I said, I apologize for the—"

"That's not what I mean. Why is it funny?"

"It is funny because zinc is such a rare commodity. You would never find it in sufficient quantities to test, let alone to use in mass production."

"Zinc isn't rare," Keira argued. "We use it in deodorant and sun block."

The Blue's silence told Keira what she needed to know. Gainsborough was stunned. "Remarkable."

"Thanks for the help. I need to make another call."

"It has been my pleasure to talk with you."

Keira dialed home on her cell, knowing how unlikely it was to catch her folks via their tablet. Inevitably, her mother answered.

"Hello, Mother."

"Keira! How wonderful of you to call!"

"This is an international call, Mother, so I can't talk long."

"International? Where are you?"

Keira cursed silently. She hadn't told her family about the trip to the US. She would pay for this later; she knew that for certain. "Can I speak with Father?"

"Madhu!"

After the sound of polite bickering and the exchange of the handset, her father came on the line. "I hear you're out of the country? Who are you spying on now?"

"I'm not spying on anyone, Father. Do you remember telling me about the rich alien, Sylvester?"

"That one! He's up to no good."

Keira almost made another tactical error by telling her father that she had met Sylvester. That would have derailed the conversation entirely. "Do you remember what kind of businesses he has?"

"Everything! Transportation, food production, building construction, mining—"

"Mining? Really? You know what kind of mining?"

"The article didn't say."

"Thanks. I have to go."

Day Three gave the Americans the chance to ask their questions. In a more structured set of interactions than the chaos of Day One, Keira and the others would be quizzed by the appropriate specialists in any areas that coincided with their proposal. Keira, acting on the express orders of Ganguly, answered openly and forthrightly about her research to date: the successes, the failures, the breakthroughs and the compromises. She only balked, per instructions, when the questions delved into what they had planned coming up. They couldn't risk tipping off the competition on future developments.

Of the fifteen people who interviewed her that day, she believed at least twelve of them seemed to understand what they were asking, and grasped most of her answers. The other three she dealt with as succinctly and politely as she could manage.

Throughout the day, Keira busted with the desire to drop her bomb, but she waited for the right moment. This was not information about the proposal, so Ganguly's policy of openness did not apply. Keira felt no guilt in her desire to use this information to help her personally. The Americans weren't going to build the ship to the stars—unless Boeing got the contract, of course—but they would be running the show. The launch wouldn't be for years, but it wouldn't hurt to break from the pack if she wanted to be on that flight.

And she did want to be on that flight.

The next to last meeting of the day was with Dale Krensky, Deputy Secretary of Off World Affairs. In other words, this fellow was Vanessa Hargrove's right hand man.

Krensky was young, just about thirty, but had already lost most of his dark brown hair. His smooth scalp had been invaded by freckles, giving him an overall comical look. His eyes, on the other hand, held no humor. Whether stress from work, from the conference, or simply an unhappy childhood was the cause, Dale Krensky was not a happy man.

The first twenty minutes of this interview focused on an epoxy that was a relatively new venture for MYC. Apparently, carbon-aluminum and all of the other topics that were quite central to the proposal had been so thoroughly covered Krensky had decided to delve into some of Keira's more exotic research. It almost seemed as if he were trying to catch her up in an error, or a lie. Keira didn't generally like to judge people on first impressions, but her gut told her Krensky was not a very nice man. Still, his was a very important position, and since she wouldn't be talking directly with Hargrove, he was the next best thing.

"Mr. Krensky, may I interrupt?"

The man scowled, then nodded.

"I bumped into the Snake, Sylvester, the other day in between meetings. I understand you're having some trouble with him."

"Nothing we can't handle, I assure you." He tapped his stylus on his tablet screen quite loudly, an indication that they should get back on topic.

"Oh. So you know what he's exporting from our system, then?"

The tapping stopped. Krensky's dark eyes flitted up from the screen to Keira.

"You know something?"

"I have a very good idea. I'm not a police officer, so I have no proof, just a theory."

Had Krensky heard a hundred possible explanations about Sylvester's enterprises? Or had they kept this concern so close to their governmental vests that they didn't even have crackpot theories to debunk? Since his scowl did not change significantly, Keira wasn't sure.

"What do you want?" he asked, voice filled with suspicion.

"What?"

"You realize this will have no impact on your proposal."

Keira waved that concern away. "I wouldn't have thought so, Mr. Krensky."

"But you do want something."

"All I want is the credit," she said simply.

"The credit."

"When you tell your boss what Sylvester is doing—and why—just please tell her I was the one who figured it out."

Krensky's scowl shifted, slowly, subtly. His entire expression had changed before Keira finally understood that what she was looking at was a smile.

The end of Day Three had been planned to be a simple cocktail party in the bar at Ganguly's hotel for the MYC staff. The outcome of their proposal would not be determined for several months. Ken-Ya and Lock-heed-Hyundai still had presentations to give, and then the Americans would have their own internal wrangle to pick the winner. That was likely to be an ugly brawl. Yet another reason Keira was glad she had nothing to do with the politics of all this.

Ganguly had indicated he would be treating this as a successful mission. He had no doubt they would get the contract. His personality was so effusive, and his optimism so infectious, everyone else started to believe it, too, even if they didn't.

About thirty minutes into the festivities, with beer and wine—and juices for the Muslims on the team—flowing, something shifted. One cell call to Ganguly pulled him out to the hotel lobby for a few moments. When he returned, he had an expression of sheer amazement on his face.

"We got the contract!" someone shouted. A cheer rose up. Ganguly shook his head and held out his hands to quiet the crowd.

"The news is not quite so grand as that, but stunning nonetheless. Desai! Where is Desai?"

Keira felt her face flush instantly. Those around her pointed to her. Someone behind her gave her a polite shove. She set her glass of white wine on the bar and shuffled up to the CEO, unsure what to expect.

He put a fatherly arm around her shoulders. "Keira Desai is a brilliant scientist and engineer, as we all know. But we now learn she is also a *detective!*"

Laughter followed that.

"You may have heard of the Snake Sylvester who has amassed a fortune to rival even my own!" Laughter. "Keira has unraveled the mystery of why this snake oil salesman bothered to put down roots on our fair planet. I'm not quite sure I understand all the ins and outs of the situation, but it seems that the galaxy is in dire need of sun block!"

More laughter. Ganguly spent a few minutes spinning the tale that Keira had spun for Krensky. This room of scientists—and scientifically astute business managers—found the entire thing quite amusing. To think that Sylvester had devoted four years of his life to build an empire for the sole purpose of exporting *zinc* off the planet… the mind boggled.

Keira accepted congratulations—and a few well-meaning jibes—for the next few minutes. Then Ganguly took her aside to speak to her personally. With his voice lowered and his gregarious mask set aside, he asked her a serious question.

"Why did you keep this to yourself?"

"Sir, if I alone was wrong, the negative impact to the proposal would have been insignificant. It was only a theory, of course. I did not want to jeopardize Maccha-Yantra."

"But you weren't wrong, were you?"

Keira grinned.

Back in her hotel room, Keira should have been sleeping. The flight back home was at seven the next morning. She couldn't help but check up on her e-mails. While doing that, she heard a knock.

She looked through the peephole of the door. She couldn't be *certain* of the identity of the Snake on the other side of the door, but she had a very good idea.

"What do you want?" she called through the closed door.

"I've got no desire for revenge, love, if that's what you're worried about."

"What if I don't believe you?" Had she actually created a situation where an alien might want to assassinate her? Could she be *that* important to anyone?

"Fancy a drink in the bar? Fifteen minutes, say?"

Keira thought long and hard, scrutinizing Sylvester as best she could through the eye-watering peephole, before she answered.

"Okay."

Twenty minutes later, Keira peered into the bar to see the Snake coiled up on a chair in the middle of the dark-paneled room. It was quiet at this hour, but there were a few people drinking at the bar or in one of the dim booths. Sylvester's head slinked up, a chilling reminder just *how* alien he was. After so many years with Gainsborough and his skin-smooth, blue hide, this black, furry creature seemed all the more unnerving.

She approached and sat.

"What'll you have?" he asked, red eyes glinting in the track lighting.

"What do you want?" she asked, ignoring the offer of alcohol.

"I should ask you that, don't you think? What do you think you accomplished, then, with all your cleverness?"

"You weren't playing fair."

"Not fair, eh?" She found his voice to be remarkably human. She wondered if he'd surgically altered himself to make his voice so comforting. On Gainsborough's best day he didn't sound *this* human. "Let's look at what I've done, shall we? I've saved millions of doomed lives, jump-started your species' starship program, and helped lay the foundations for bioengineering feats that will advance your culture in a heartbeat to the galactic norm. What's unfair about that?"

"You didn't tell us that zinc is so valuable."

"You didn't ask."

Keira stood. One of Sylvester's black, five-fingered hands shot out and grabbed her arm. His grip was not painful, just firm enough to indicate he wasn't done talking.

"Please," he added, his tone pleasant. Keira slowly sat back down.

"You stole from us," she accused.

"I didn't steal one thing from you, my dear miss. I paid for every-thing I shipped off this planet. And if you think I've somehow depleted Earth's zinc reserves, think again. My launches haven't constituted a blip in the vast quantities of the stuff you have here. You really are quite blessed in that area."

"But if *we* knew…"

"If you knew, you'd have been selling to me anyway. And what would you have gotten in return? Money. More money, surely, but Earth money just the same. Money I can't take off this planet anyway. Cur-rency is a zero sum game, dearie. Earth dollars mean nothing on any other planet of this galaxy."

"We could have traded for technology, for knowledge."

"Really? What sorts of knowledge would you like?"

He leaned in, his fuzzy, wrinkly cat face only centimeters from Keira.

"Would you like to know how many systems knew you existed be-fore tonight? Would you like to know how many systems *will* know you exist *after* tonight? Would you like to know what happens to newly hatched systems that become *popular*? How many visitors do you get now? Fifty a day? A hundred? Would you like that to double? Triple? How would you like ten thousand visitors a day?"

He made a *pfff* sound, something like a cat sneezing. From Sylvester, it was clearly a sound of disdain, disgust, and likely disappointment.

"I was doing you folks a favor! Mark my words, Miss Desai. The gal-axy is going to *know* about you now. You have something they want. The ships arriving next week and next month won't be cruise liners filled with cultural curiosity seekers. They'll be *business* people, intent on prof-iting from your naiveté. And profit they will, Miss Desai."

"Like you profited," Keira muttered, her words unsure.

"Yes, but do you think these others will be coming with cures to your worst diseases or with technology they'll hand over for a song? That redheaded girl, Hargrove, she may have opened the door. But it was you, Miss Desai, who put out the welcome mat."

Keira couldn't speak, couldn't move. She watched, dumbly, as Syl-vester slipped down from the chair and slithered across the carpet. He spoke quietly into her ear.

"Welcome to the galaxy, love."

War Games

> *...consider how many already, after mutual enmity, suspicion, hatred, and fighting, have been stretched dead, reduced to ashes; and be quiet at last.*
> —*Meditations, IV, 3*

"*Red or Violet?*"

Nigel pressed his earphones tighter over his ears. This was a reflex that had nothing to do with the quality of the transmission, but with his confusion at the question. He was one of the newer staffers on *Lincoln*. The station received more visitors now than she could handle, all day, every day. The politicos down on the surface had tried to play up the whole zinc fiasco as a great boon for humanity. Bollocks! Low Earth Orbit was getting very crowded. They'd had at least one near collision every week since April.

And now this.

"*Red or Violet?*"

"This is *Abraham Lincoln*. I do not understand your question. Are you asking for docking privileges? Do you need assistance?"

The ship in question loomed a half-kilometer off the station, following in their same orbital path. In the past two weeks, Nigel had seen everything from one-seater pleasure craft to cruisers that could hold five thousand Blues. This ship fell into the larger side of that spectrum. It maintained an ominous black color, though Nigel had long since given up trying to determine a visitor's intentions based on the configuration of their craft. Black seemed to be a popular color, probably because most ships made some use of starlight for power needs. This one had an eggish shape, somewhat boring compared to the more baroque designs he'd seen.

"*Red or Violet?*"

"Hang on."

Nigel pulled the mic away from his mouth and called over to his supervisor, two cubbies down the row.

"Darla? I've got a mush mouth over here."

Darla, a strikingly handsome Nigerian woman, poked her head out of her cubby and swam down to Nigel's post. He played back the question for her.

"Do they want us to pick what color their ship should be?"

He wasn't paid enough for decisions like this. Nigel shrugged, waiting for instructions. Let Darla handle it.

"Try one of the Blue recordings," she said.

"Right."

Nigel pressed a few buttons on his console. A stuttery sort of mumble transmitted over to the mystery ship. In the early days, all the visitors had gone to the trouble of learning at least one Earth language before arriving on the planet. Lately, though, those niceties weren't being observed half as often. Hence the Blue recording. Even if no one on the ship knew English—beyond the cryptic words "red or violet"—they probably knew a few words of Blue.

The response was a terse collection of Blue gibberish. Nigel routed it through their translation software. The answer came back.

"*Query. Are you Red or Violet, if you please?*"

Darla shook her head. "I'll call D.C."

Terry's weekly sit-downs with General Brown had fallen into a rut. She would ask for updates on ten or fifteen questionable scenarios, either domestic or worldwide, involving visitors. On average, Terry would discount ten of them as overblown misunderstandings, three as worth keeping an eye on, one for covert surveillance, and one for active response. After one such meeting, the Pentagon had finally sent a battle group down to the Coral Sea to back up the Australian Navy in their standoff with that stubborn colony of Eels on the Great Barrier Reef. That was an anomaly. Usually, the results involved more hand-wringing and less troop deployment.

Most meetings lately also involved General Brown spending a few minutes fretting over Junior, who still prowled the Strait of Juan de Fuca north of Seattle. Terry calmly assured her that the huge creature hadn't disrupted the shipping lanes, and in fact had become a tourist draw for Northwest Passage cruise ships.

Today was like any other, until Brown mentioned a piece of news:

"Kird is back."

"He is?" Terry sat up, excited by the idea of seeing the Teddy Bear again. His guard came up just as fast. "Why? Do we have another fugitive?"

"No, nothing like that. Apparently, he's been assigned here by Central Authority." She scanned something on her tablet screen. "Let's see... 'newfound celebrity'... uh... 'with higher visibility, the Earth system warrants greater attention' and blah blah blah."

"They think we can't keep ourselves out of trouble," Terry said with some distaste.

"Mecca? Seattle?" Brown leaned forward in her chair. "Bangkok?" Terry took her message. The Bangkok incident was one of his "overblown misunderstandings." It hadn't ended well. He didn't dwell on it, though. Best to keep moving forward. Brown continued: "They might be right. I've got Kird in an office in the D-Ring. Listen to him, alright?"

"Yes, ma'am."

Terry was secretly pleased to see that Kird's office wasn't as nice as his. He tried not to be a child about that kind of thing, but he couldn't help it. Actually, he was surprised that Kird would be housed in the Pentagon at all. Sure, Terry trusted him, but why should Brown? Or the Joint Chiefs, for that matter? Terry wrote this off as a gift horse in the mouth situation and just walked in.

"Kird!"

The Teddy Bear turned and offered Terry a wide, human-like smile. "Terry!" They embraced, Kird kindly not putting very much of his terrible strength into the hug.

"You're posted here?"

Kird wagged his head from side to side like a metronome, a Teddy Bear version of a shrug. "I am the only Conduct Officer who has direct experience with Humanity. I will maintain jurisdiction over the local neighborhood of worlds, but your nascent prominence necessitates closer scrutiny from my department."

"Are you worried that we'll find trouble, or that trouble will find us?"

Again with the wagging head.

"Have you had lunch yet?" Terry didn't even know *if* Teddy Bears ate lunch, but everyone had to eat sometime. "You can meet Vanessa Hargrove."

Kird's wide-eyed stare looked like the same kind of reaction Terry would expect from any human when they were told they'd be meeting an interstellar celebrity.

After the zinc fiasco, Congress had called loudly for the resigna-tion—or preferably, the firing—of Vanessa Hargrove. The leak of the zinc story to the rest of the galaxy had come from her department, and it had caused more than just high traffic on *Abraham Lincoln.*

Wall Street wasn't sure how to process the information. Zinc prices had, of course, skyrocketed with the knowledge that the metal had ex-traordinary value off world. On the other hand, zinc production had *also* skyrocketed, since those lucky few who owned working mines saw a windfall opportunity, thus increasing the metal's availability. Since no one—other than Sylvester—had the ability to actually export the stuff off the planet, zinc's value tumbled again. This seesaw effect continued for weeks.

Secondary effects included disruptions to the gold, silver and plati-num markets, as industrial capacity shifted away from those precious met-als toward the once pedestrian zinc. Tertiary effects had global commodi-ties and securities markets in turmoil. Publicly, every member of Congress complained that this was impacting the working man, as 401Ks and pen-sion plans plummeted in value. Privately, every member of Congress heard complaints from whichever lobbyist was in the room at the time that this was impacting *them* as *their* portfolios plummeted in value.

The President won reelection last year by a slim—though not em-barrassingly slim—margin. His vocal support of Vanessa and her team meant that no heads would roll just yet. In a tense and personally uncom-fortable meeting, the President had told Vanessa point blank that his support simply meant he knew that just about anyone else sitting in her chair would have probably screwed them *worse.*

She vowed to keep a tight lid on any future crises. Part of that vow meant she would spend more time in the trenches and less in front of her tablet screen. She had grudgingly adopted a "management by walking around" approach. It still felt awfully cutesy and artificial to her. The upside was that most of the offices she visited had candy dishes in them.

Dale in particular was a favorite stop on her route. He wasn't a very personable guy, but he had a fondness for butterscotch... or at least he knew that Vanessa did. She sauntered into his office. He was on a call. He looked up, his unspoken question: *Should I hang up?* She waved to tell him she could wait. She took one of the discs of buttery goodness out of his little bowl and sat down across from him at the desk.

"How the hell should I know?" he almost shouted into the phone. Vanessa winced, but didn't say anything. Some people preferred the vinegar approach. And Dale *was* quite useful when the situation required vinegar. Now Vanessa asked a question with her eyes: *Need some help?*

Dale sighed. "I'm putting you on speaker." When Dale set down the handset, a faraway, echoey sound came from the speaker. This call was coming from space, probably *Abraham Lincoln*. "I'm here with Secretary Hargrove."

"Ms. Hargrove, this is Darla Nokwe, Communications Director on *Abraham Lincoln*."

"Ms. Nokwe, it's good to meet you. What can we do for you?" Dale sneered at Vanessa's light tone. He had as much use for honey as she had for vinegar.

"We have a visiting craft we can't seem to communicate with."

"Have you tried a Blue greeting?"

"Yes, ma'am. It's not that they don't understand English. They seem to be unwilling to converse. They keep asking the same question over and over: 'Red or Violet?' Does that mean anything to you?"

"Red or Violet?" She shared a confused look with Dale. "No, I can't say it does. Are there any red or violet markings on the outside of the station? Could they be asking for docking directions?"

Shuffling sounds and whispered comments on the line indicated that they hadn't thought of that possibility. Vanessa smirked. Dale seemed to have lost the ability to smile in the last few months. Vanessa made a gesture toward the phone, and Dale muted their side of the conversation.

"If they can't figure it out, just tell them to pick an answer and see if that solves the conversation problem. I've got a meeting at the Pentagon."

"Got it."

Vanessa couldn't imagine such an innocuous question could possibly have any serious ramifications. And in any case, it'd been a few days since she'd been able to have lunch with Terry.

The Corridor 1 cafeteria at the Pentagon was a wide, airy space with plenty of surprisingly good food. Vanessa's media-inspired assumption that the military always served unpalatable fare was belied after her first bite of her wild green salad with orange-balsamic dressing. She smiled at the Teddy Bear, who looked unimpressed by his own plate of weeds.

"You're a carnivore, aren't you?" she asked between bites.

"Not exclusively. This, however…"

Terry nodded. "My daddy always said, 'If the good Lord wanted us to eat rabbit food, He'd have given us bigger ears.'" He shoved his salad aside and tore into his chicken parmigiana. Kird followed his example.

"So, be honest," Vanessa said. "Why the special treatment?"

Kird politely finished his mouthful of food before answering. "It is a matter of security for the entire region that Earth not become… destabilized."

"Is that likely?" Terry asked.

"It has happened," Kird said.

"Often?" Vanessa asked.

"Not often. More than one would like, if you take my meaning. The Ubiguti in particular suggested my assignment to your system."

"The Pigs," Vanessa translated for Terry's benefit.

"They're light years away," Terry countered. "Why would they care?"

"They are officially your transitional caretakers," Kird said mildly, returning to his chicken.

"What you mean is," Vanessa said, "they know if something goes terribly wrong and our sun detonates like a supernova, they're in trouble."

Terry dropped his knife onto his plate with a loud clatter. He quickly scooped it up again and continued to eat.

"Just so, Ms. Hargrove. That is one possible scenario."

Terry took a long sip of water, then tried to reenter the conversation without looking like he'd been knocked on the head.

"Who would do something like that?" he asked.

"Many could, few would. In all likelihood, none will. There is no cause for immediate concern. I am not here to stop any particular threat you face, Terry. There are dangers, yes: fugitives who may seek refuge here, much like the Rope Man, or races who interact with new civilizations far more belligerently than the Blues or the Trees. But none of these possibilities are truly worthy of your concern at this point. I am here to make certain no threats go unnoticed. You may not recognize a potential danger until things have progressed to a critical point."

"Misunderstandings, you mean," Vanessa offered.

"That is correct," Kird said.

"We had one of those just today. A ship came in to dock at *Abraham Lincoln* and they didn't want to talk. They just said the same thing, over and over."

"Take me to your leader?" Terry asked, then laughed.

"No, it was odd. They asked 'Red or Violet?' We don't know what they meant, but…" Vanessa looked over at Kird, who had frozen.

"Are you certain?" Kird asked.

"Certain about what?"

Kird raised his voice to an uncomfortable level. Heads in the dining room turned their way. "Was the question 'Red or Violet?'"

"Yes."

"Did you respond?"

"I don't get it," Terry said.

"Did you *respond?*"

"No, not yet. They were going to—"

"Call the station! Call them immediately!"

The engineers on the station did a check of the design specs. They determined that the question "Red or Violet?" couldn't refer to any sort of signage visible from the visiting craft. Krensky didn't hide his scorn when he said over the phone from Earth, "Just pick one," then hung up. Darla looked to Nigel.

"Pick a color," Darla said.

Nigel sniffed in annoyance. All this wasted time and runaround, and his betters just handed the problem back to him.

"Right." He keyed his mic back on. "Visiting craft, I'm authorized to answer…" Nigel glanced over his shoulder. Was Darla actually holding her breath? Daft bird. "…violet."

The response was instantaneous. "*Understood.*"

"Excellent. If you'd care to proceed to docking port A-thirteen, we can…" The video screen showed the ship dropping from orbit and heading directly to the planet's surface. "Unidentified craft, you are not cleared for landing. Please respond."

Nigel turned to look at Darla. Her comment was nearly inaudible.

"Shit."

It took Terry considerably less time to wrangle a jump plane for this trip to Iceland than it had last year for his trip to Russia. Between his full-throated warnings of danger and Vanessa's considerable pull, they were airborne inside twenty minutes.

"Are you sure we shouldn't be sending an armed battalion?" he asked. Kird shook his head. Vanessa's attention was focused out the window, watching Nova Scotia pass by below.

"The Eaieo do not react well to those who flip their alliance. A showing of force would indicate just such a realignment."

Vanessa turned to rejoin the conversation. "Ee-yaw-eye-yay-yoh," she said, trying out the name, inserting consonants where there were none. She'd learned so few actual names for these new races, for just this reason: they were usually impossible for humans to pronounce without significant practice. "We should just tell them we're neutral."

"The Eaieo do not accept the concept of neutrality in this sense, since they differentiate their conflict with the Eoiea from war."

Before Vanessa tried to wrap her mouth around this new name, Terry interrupted. "Can we just call them Reds and Violets?"

"As you wish," Kird agreed. "I would suggest, to clarify the situation to all involved, you refer to them as Red Gamers and Violet Gamers."

"Gamers?" Vanessa asked. "You said they are at war."

"That is a bit of a simplification of their cultural state. The Red and Violet Gamers are distinct species that evolved on two worlds orbiting the same star. Their cultural development was exceedingly rapid. In Human terms, this would be equivalent to your invention of interstellar travel during the height of the Roman Empire."

"Primitive," Terry said.

"Violent," Vanessa clarified.

"Yes and yes. Strangely, perhaps uniquely, these two cultures neither learned to coexist peacefully, nor did one annihilate the other. Instead, they achieved a steady state."

"A steady state... of war?" Vanessa was horrified. She couldn't imagine war being a sustainable state of affairs.

"Precisely. Their conflict does not conform to the usual definition of war. They do not fight to control property or natural resources or populations of individuals. They do not fight to impose their ideology on their foe. They do not fight to exterminate their foe. For the Eaieo—the Violet Gamers—destruction of the Red Gamers would mean the end of their entire culture, which is predicated on the continuing conflict."

"Fascinating," Vanessa breathed.

"Thanks, Mr. Spock," Terry added. "So, when they asked 'Red or Violet', they were asking which side of this war game we are on, is that it?"

"Both Gaming factions are quite efficient at monitoring unencrypted communications, as most of yours are. They certainly knew you to not be currently affiliated with either group. They were, in effect, asking you to choose a side. It is rather fortunate your associate on the station chose the color he did."

Nigel stretched, looking eagerly at the time code on his screen. Only ten more minutes and his shift would be over. There'd been a serious amount of tooth-gnashing over that Violet ship breaking orbit, but nothing had come of it. According to Darla, the thing landed in some godforsaken frozen corner of Iceland where it couldn't do any damage.

"Ship incoming via lane four." The arrival detection software worked flawlessly—just about the only thing on *Lincoln* that did. Nigel heeded the pleasant, female voice's warning, and shifted his screens to show the orbital path they'd designated number four.

"I don't bloody believe it," he murmured. Here it was, another one of those egg-shaped Violet ships coming in. Were they having a convention?

"Red or Violet?"

Darla must have been monitoring Nigel's channel, because her head popped out of her cubbie instantly.

"Not to worry," he assured her. He keyed his mic on.

"Approaching vessel, this is *Abraham Lincoln*. The answer is violet. Now, if you'd be so kind, we…"

Seven kinds of sirens started to blare through every speaker on the station. Nigel searched his video screen for an indication of what was happening. He flipped through several filters on the data. When he chose infrared, the egg ship, which had been a reassuringly familiar black, now glowed a ferocious red; the ship was glowing bright with *heat*. In one corner of this camera's view, he could see a small section of the station, a module at the far end. It also glowed red. *Abraham Lincoln* always vented heat to space as part of its design. However, it wasn't supposed to vent this much. Nigel's whole body went cold as the section of station he could see on the screen—which he knew from experience was the sleeping quarters for the permanent crew—popped like a child's balloon, gas shooting into space, colored a false vermillion by the infrared monitor. In his ears, he felt the abrupt change in pressure as emergency doors slammed shut half a kilometer away to protect the rest of the station from decompression.

"Red!" he shouted into the mic. "Red! Red!"

The Red Gamer ship did not respond again. It systematically lasered each of the twenty-six sections of the *Abraham Lincoln*'s hull until all activity within ceased. After a few moments to confirm the kill, the ship shifted into a posture for descent to the planet's surface.

The jump plane landed at Reykjavík Airport thirty minutes after their takeoff from Andrews. A team of ICRU troops met the plane and escorted the three visitors a few steps to a helicopter for their flight out to the landing site of the Violet ship. The Violet Gamers had landed on Hofsjökull Glacier, high in the mountains on the far side of Iceland.

"I hope you've got cold weather gear for us," Vanessa shouted to the closest of the Icelanders over the roar of the dual rotors on the huge aircraft.

"Yes, on the board," he answered in rough English. He added a toothy, awestruck grin; it seemed even this skinny, towheaded young man in Iceland knew Vanessa Hargrove on sight.

Despite the cloudless midday sky, the temperature was lower than Vanessa was entirely prepared for. Neither Terry nor Kird seemed bothered by the cold. She rushed up the short flight of steps into the heated interior of the helicopter. The ICRU soldiers followed. Terry and Kird made it clear they were to maintain a non-aggressive stance during their visit to the Violet Gamers. Vanessa hoped Terry's military bearing broke through their haze of poor English, frank amazement (at Kird) and idol worship (of Vanessa). The last thing any of them needed was an interstellar incident that could cost lives.

Vanessa found a seat and strapped in. She watched an older Icelander give some sort of order to the blond kid. He looked stricken, glanced furtively over at Vanessa, then saluted and stomped off the helicopter. The remaining four ICRU troopers found seats. Vanessa was pleased that the helicopter took off only moments after the door closed. Her experience with Icelanders was, until today, nonexistent. So far, they were doing an excellent job.

Her cell phone finally negotiated a handshake with the local towers and it buzzed at her. She checked the receipt log and saw a message from Dale. Rather than bother with the message, she simply called him back. He picked up on the first ring.

"So what do we do?" he asked, his usual surliness twisted to a fever pitch.

"About what?" Vanessa yelled into the phone. The interior of the helicopter was plush, but far from soundproof. They were making their way over the suburbs of Reykjavík, north-east toward the interior of the island.

"You didn't listen to my message?"

Vanessa fought an urge to snap at Dale for asking stupid questions. She saw Terry checking his own phone, too. Whatever the news was, it was big.

"We lost *Abraham Lincoln*!"

Where did you have it last? The joke came terribly close to jumping from her addled brain directly to her lips. "Lost communication?"

"*Lost* lost! It's gone, destroyed!"

Terry clearly had the same information coming to him. He immediately unbuckled from his seat and stood, the turbulence forcing him to grab seat backs as he staggered down the short aisle to talk to Kird.

"The Red Gamers just destroyed our space station," he told the Teddy Bear.

"That is regrettable. I do apologize. We did not accurately estimate the Gamers' level of interest in your zinc reserves. This does complicate matters."

"Complicate matters?!" Vanessa shouted.

"What does?" Dale asked.

"I'll call you back," she snapped.

"But you—" She cut the connection. She'd apologize to Dale later. Or not.

"I do not mean to belittle the importance of this loss to your planet," Kird said.

"There were fifty-three people on that station," Vanessa said.

"And four ships docked that were totaled," Terry added. "Three of those were alien ships. Are all of those systems going to declare war on us, too?"

"This is not war," Kird insisted.

"Feels like war to me," Terry said.

"What will the Reds do next?" Vanessa asked, trying to get back to solving the problem, rather than just complaining about it.

"They will do as the Violet Gamers have done: establish a base on the surface of your planet. They are more comfortable in tropical climes. They will find a remote area near Earth's equator."

"And then?"

"They will begin to fight."

The Eoiea ship swept the large, wet planet with scanners to determine the locations of all Eaieo bases. Only one could be seen, high in the northern hemisphere, perched on a massive glacier of water ice. These Humans must have aligned with the Eaieo very recently, or else there would be more bases. The Eoiea followed the forms laid down centuries ago, and searched for an out of the way place on the opposite side of the planet from the Eaieo.

This *Earth* had an abundance of water, more than either of their native planets. The opposite hemisphere of the planet was dominated by an expansive ocean. Volcanic activity in the ancient past had brought enough islands to the surface of this ocean to offer many choices along the equator. The Eoiea found an island of suitable size and composition for a reconnaissance base. A quick scan of the Earth maps scraped off the Humans' computer network told them the name of the quiet little island where they would land and prepare for battle with little fear of direct interference from the Eaieo: Matuku Island, part of a Human nation state called Fiji.

Though the Humans were now Violet, and therefore their enemy, the Eoiea had no desire to unnecessarily antagonize noncombatants. They vectored their ship to an uninhabited, forested valley in the island's interior. The landing was rougher than was usual: Earth's gravity was quite strong.

Their first stage of encampment required the dispersal of thousands of automated drones, specially designed to work in the frigid temperatures of Earth. These drones—each one less than a micro-d in length and constituted for land travel—would scout the immediate surroundings and determine what, if any, local dangers they might face.

The second stage, though, was far more important and exciting for the Eoiea. Piloted planes that could withstand even the inimical cold favored by the Eaieo launched from the ship and vectored toward the large land mass named Iceland.

The three would-be diplomats continued to argue even as they tramped through the snow toward the Violet ship.

"The Violets aren't our primary concern. We should be talking to the Reds, to tell them we aren't allied with anyone!" The logic sounded flawless to Vanessa's mind as she made her case.

"We should be dive bombing the Red ship right now!" She'd never seen Terry show this kind of bloodlust before. Of course, she'd never seen his response to an act of war, either. He was a soldier, after all.

"Destroying the Red ship would simply invite another to take its place." Kird continued to keep a cool head as he lectured. "Have you no child's games of conquest to compare this to?"

"This is not a game of checkers we're playing here!" Terry argued. Vanessa noticed that Kird's breath didn't come out in a steamy cloud the way Terry's did. The detail made him seem that much colder, that much more heartless.

"Checkers is about killing your opponent. So is chess. This isn't that kind of game," Vanessa explained, as much to Terry as to Kird. "We don't compete for the sake of competition. We compete to win."

"An all too common scenario," Kird lamented.

The Violet ship sat on the rumpled plain of this massive glacier like a giant black egg set on its end. Vanessa remembered trying to balance countless chicken eggs in this way on the kitchen table at home after her grandmother insisted that it could be done if only she concentrated hard enough.

"We should have landed closer," Terry whined.

"No, we should not," Kird intoned. He seemed unaffected by the cold and the snow. He had politely declined the offer of snow shoes and a parka from the Icelanders, who followed a discreet distance behind, their weapons stowed on their backs per Kird's order.

A flash of movement to her right distracted Vanessa. When she turned her head to look, she saw nothing. The whole situation was making her jumpy.

"What if we partition the planet?" she asked. "You said the Violets like the cold, and the Reds like the heat. Tell them that the Violets can stay in the Arctic and Antarctic, and the Reds can stay in the tropics."

"You're giving the planet away?" Terry sounded morally offended.

"I'm not giving anyone anything! Even North and South Korea stayed out of the Demilitarized Zone."

Kird disagreed. "You would invite a massive buildup of forces and the eventual devastation to your temperate zones would be horrendous."

"You said they prefer a steady state," Vanessa argued. Another whisper of movement caught her eye, then disappeared. She assumed it was a rabbit or something.

"They prefer a steady state in the macroscopic sense. World by world, they relish victory."

"What the—" Terry hopped backwards.

"Terry?"

"Something ran past my leg!"

This time Vanessa could just barely make out what had spooked Terry. It was white, blending in nearly perfectly with the snow. But it wasn't invisible, and the movement, this close up, betrayed its presence. Vanessa's first impression was of a spider, or a crab, but one made of ice. Terry kicked at it, sending it flying a few yards away with a crystalline clatter.

"What was that?"

"A drone. The Violet Gamers are scouting their environment. There is no need for alarm."

They were less than a quarter-mile from the ship. A screeching metal-on-metal sound tore from the ship. They all stopped, the Icelanders behind nervously reaching for their weapons. Kird held up a paw to stop them.

High on the ship's dark surface, a hatch levered open. Vanessa couldn't make out anything within; it was just a space of bright white inside the black hull. With a whistling roar, a series of aircraft shot out of the opening. The little ships were less than a meter in length, dual-wing, triangular, vaguely reminiscent of early stealth aircraft from the 1990s. Though they were black, like their mother ship, they reflected the bright Arctic sun brilliantly, as if made of ebon diamond.

The volley of ships—Vanessa counted nine—whipped over their heads, small sonic booms in their wakes.

"War planes," Kird said.

Terry followed their path in the sky. "They're headed for Reykjavík."

Korporáll Steinar Vilhjálmsson watched the helicopter lift off and swing eastward, off to whatever adventure awaited his comrades who were lucky enough to go with the Americans. No one knew for sure what exactly was going on up on the Hofsjökull. His commander, Flokksstjóri Sigurðsson, seemed to think there was some kind of alien invasion in progress. If that were the case, Steinar knew that NATO would send troops, not one USAF major, a politician, and a fuzzy little alien. What did the Flokksstjóri know anyway, sitting behind his desk back at the base?

But it had to be *something* to do with aliens! That was for sure. Why else would Vanessa Hargrove be with them? She was an important American politician. And, Steinar noticed, quite pretty for an older woman, with her porcelain skin and her brilliant red hair cascading in soft waves to her shoulders. He shook off the pleasant memory as he returned to the airport terminal where he and the others were ordered to wait for further instructions.

Stepping through the door, Steinar fielded a barrage of questions from his mates who hadn't been part of the escort on the airfield. Yes, they were Americans. No, they weren't armed. Yes, they had an alien with them, who looked like a walking toy. Steinar's patience with the interrogation grew thin, and he slipped off to a corner to connect to the web on his cell. Maybe the BBC had better intel than his own superiors. It wouldn't be the first time.

The first news report to come up on his little screen was about the destruction of the Americans' space station! The report went on to verify that *Excalibur* was unharmed and would be performing *Lincoln*'s duties until the almost-mothballed *Pacifica* could be brought up to speed to help. The vaguely self-satisfied tone of the report didn't sit well with Steinar. He didn't have the instinctive distrust of America that mainland Europe seemed to have. He thought they were cool.

A loud *boom* rolled across the airport. Steinar looked up. He hadn't heard many sonic booms in his life, but that's all this could have been, couldn't it? Another, louder explosion prompted him to jump to his feet and rush back to the waiting area. All the other soldiers were lined up against the glass, peering out like children watching monkeys at the zoo.

Steinar could tell from where he stood that there were no monkeys out there. A thick, black column of smoke curled up from behind the row of maintenance buildings on the far side of the runway. The sirens of emergency vehicles sounded tinny, faraway, almost toy-like from the distance.

Black specks in the sky zipped from left to right over the scene of the fire, then swung in a tight turn toward the airport. The sound of their passage *was* a series of sonic booms. One mysterious black plane swooped low toward the airport tarmac. It seemed to be on a collision course with the Americans' jump plane, which was being refueled just outside while it waited for the diplomats to return. Steinar noticed that small trails of steam and smoke rose from the plane's engine. Before he could warn his comrades, the Americans' jump plane blew up, shattering the window and throwing Steinar and his mates to the floor in a shower of broken glass.

Trudging through the snow had tired Vanessa, but they were there, facing a gently curved, black wall of metal. Vanessa looked to Kird with a question in her eyes.

"I was not prepared for this meeting," he admitted. "I have no communications devices that will alert them to our presence. We have to assume their surface drones have done that for us."

"You expect us to just stand here and wait?" Vanessa asked, hopping from foot to foot to keep herself warm.

Kird did not answer. Terry pushed between the two of them and pounded on the side of the Violet ship with his gloved fist. It barely made a sound. He pulled off his glove and rapped on it again with his knuckles. "Hey in there!" he shouted. "Take us to your leader!"

Vanessa couldn't quite bring herself to laugh, but she did grin at Terry's poor joke.

All three of them turned at the sound of gas hissing out of the ship. About fifty yards to their left, a hatch opened, levering down to create a short ramp. Vanessa hurried over, looking forward to some warmth. As she reached the door, she was sorely disappointed.

"Shit!"

"What?" Terry called, hurrying to catch up. His response was much like Vanessa's as he shrank from the intense cold.

"As I said, the Violet Gamers enjoy temperatures much lower than those with which you are comfortable." Kird climbed the ramp and entered the misty environment within.

"Ladies first," Terry said, showing the way with a faux-gallant gesture.

"I am officially not going to enjoy this." Vanessa walked up the ramp with Terry following. She shouldn't have been surprised when the door closed behind them with a dramatic *clang*. As her grandmother would have said, do they want to air condition the whole outdoors?

The interior of the vessel was almost uniformly white. Vanessa had no need to remove her snow goggles, since it was brighter in here than it was out on the glacier. It was like being inside an ice castle... or a fortress made of diamond, since the crystalline surfaces looked far sturdier than ice.

They had entered a room that felt a little snug, but familiar enough to a human, with a nine-foot ceiling. Ahead, Kird entered a corridor that gave Vanessa a much clearer idea of the size of these Violet Gamers. Even the short Kird had to crouch to fit through the little tunnel. Vanessa tried for a few moments to scurry down the passage with a sort of duck-walk, but she just couldn't do it. She gave up and crawled forward on hands and knees.

"Not claustrophobic, I hope," she called back to Terry.

"I used to fly spaceships, remember?"

"Oh. Yeah. Kird, do you know where we're going?"

"I am following the signage."

Vanessa hadn't seen any sort of signs. Once again, her human visual limitations were evident. She held close the knowledge that, as far as the galaxy was concerned, at least humanity had pretty good hearing. And now her ears were picking out the distant sounds of conversation. The Violet Gamers had voices that matched their technology; it was high-pitched and had a clinky sort of sound, like wind chimes made of quartz.

Kird dropped out of sight ahead.

"Kird?"

"Follow, please," he said.

Vanessa inched forward to find another room, this one smaller than the foyer through which they'd entered the ship. She pulled herself forward through the hole and dropped into Kird's waiting arms. She could just barely stand up straight. Terry followed her. When he stood, he knocked his head against the white crystal ceiling.

"Damn it," he muttered.

"Why have you come?"

Vanessa jumped at the voice. The words were English, and quite understandable. The tones were cold, brittle, icy... and entirely alien. She supposed this was some kind of hidden speaker system, since this room had no more features or colors than any other part of the ship she'd seen so far.

"My name is Vanessa Hargrove, Secretary of Off World Affairs for the United States of America."

Vanessa waited for a reciprocal introduction. After a pause, the crystalline voice repeated its request:

"Why have you come?"

"We're here to... Look, do you mind if we speak face to face?"

"We are here," the voice said.

Vanessa leaned down to whisper to Kird. "What's he mean?"

Kird gestured with a paw at the walls and ceiling of the little room. Vanessa squinted, but couldn't see a thing. Just white and more white. The surfaces were far from smooth. In fact, she felt like she was inside a geode, with thousands of little protrusions of crystal everywhere. Still, there didn't seem to be a place for an intelligent creature to be hiding.

"Perhaps you should remove your goggles," Kird suggested. Vanessa did so. She hadn't realized how much the tinted lenses impacted her vision. *Now* she could see the Violet Gamers.

Each of them was about fifteen centimeters across, shaped much like the drones they'd seen out on the glacier. She counted six legs and four arms on each, with a complex nest of... something at the center of their backs. Perhaps that's where their eyes and ears and mouth were? The reason the goggles had shielded the Violet Gamers from view was that they were, actually, violet. The bodies of the Gamers held a very slight tinge of color compared to the blank whiteness of the surrounding room.

They were darkest at their core, with the purple color fading to nearly nothing at the ends of their appendages.

Seven of the Gamers were attached to the walls and ceiling. Looking closer, Vanessa saw their little arms moving about, manipulating white crystal controls, reading screens, probably monitoring the flight of airships that had just left the base.

"You speak with me," said a Gamer on the ceiling, waving two of his arms to clarify. Vanessa took a careful step forward—making sure there were no Gamers on the floor she might crunch under a snowshoe.

"Thank you. What should I call you?"

"I am Ioe."

"Hello, Ioe. This is Major Terry Youngblood, and this is Kird from Central Authority."

"I know Krd," Ioe said, his tone as robotic as ever.

"Greetings, Captain," Kird said.

"Captain Ioe," Vanessa said, "I'm here as a representative of Earth to tell you that there has been a misunderstanding."

"Explain."

"When you asked our space station personnel whether we would be 'red or violet', they did not understand the importance of the question."

"You are not Violet?" Though Vanessa heard no difference in tone, Kird clearly did. He stepped forward.

"Captain, this is not a question of prevarication, but innocence. The Humans did not know of your or the Eoiea's existence until *after* they mistakenly claimed Violet alliance."

Terry stepped forward—slowly, keeping his head from bouncing against any of the Violet Gamers. "The Red Gamers destroyed our orbital station, thinking we were aligned with you."

"We know of this act. We now answer this aggression against our ally," Ioe said.

"Now?" Vanessa asked.

"The Eoiea attack your flight bases on this island. We defend them."

"Fantastic," Vanessa breathed.

Captain Clancy Middleton was enjoying the movie. It was a comedy, a newer one, from 2023, about a sad sack human pretending to be an alien to convince his dream girl to fall for him. It was dumb, but most comedies are dumb. The whole point is to make you laugh, right?

Then the lights came up. The washed out image on the screen continued for a few moments, the sound now drowned out by the angry shouts of fifty-plus airmen. The movie's soundtrack dropped out as the image vanished. Clancy now heard a half-dozen pagers ringing through the room. One of them was his. He pulled the little thing from the breast pocket of his shirt. The OLED screen blinked "65": the code for emergency combat operations. Clancy had never received a 65 in his life.

He barreled down the row of seats, stepping on a dozen toes. He made it to the aisle and ran from the theater with five other pilots in his wake.

The ICRU had no heavy weapons, no airplanes, no anti-aircraft guns, nothing. Steinar and his mates did the only thing they could. They organized an impromptu emergency evacuation of Reykjavík Airport. The titanic explosion of the jump plane hadn't been repeated close enough to injure anyone in the building, at least not yet. But other sounds of battle echoed through the airport from a distance nonetheless.

Steinar, the most senior of this little cadre of men, ordered three of his mates to make a sweep of this terminal, looking for anyone who might not be able to leave quickly: the aged or infirm, pregnant women and the like. Meanwhile, Steinar contacted the security service of the airport to initiate their evacuation procedures.

Sirens blared, lights flashed, and a recorded announcement told everyone that they had to exit the facility. Most of the airport personnel and travelers followed these instructions quietly and calmly. To Steinar's surprise, the only real insubordination came not from uptight business travelers in three-piece suits, but from a mother and father with four unruly children. Steinar explained to these parents that the airport was under attack and they would be safer as far from the runways and the planes as they could get.

"How do you know we aren't safer inside?" asked the gruff, bearded father as his youngest child rapped on his ear with a toy Snake.

Steinar pointed into the terminal. Through shattered windows, they could see three different fires burning. Then he pointed out the windows at the airport's entrance. There was a mob scene of people trying to get into taxis, buses and cars, but no signs of battle.

"What do you think?"

"Fine!" the man snapped, dragging the rest of his family through the security checkpoint and toward the street.

Steinar's phone rang. He said a quick prayer of thanks and answered it.

"Korporáll Vilhjálmsson," he said.

"Korporáll, this is Flokksstjóri Sigurðsson! What's the situation in the airport?"

"We're directing an evacuation, sir."

He looked out the window at the river of mildly panicked people as they shuffled slowly down the lane toward the bus arrival area.

"You're done there, Korporáll. Gather your men and proceed to Keflavík."

Clancy Middleton's F-35 made the flight from Mildenhall to Keflavík in fifty minutes, with three other planes flying behind in a diamond formation. Over Reykjavík he saw the after-effects of recent battle there. His in-flight briefing included information on some activity at that smaller airport. Keflavík, on the other hand, had a large international airport and a NATO base. For years, that base had been slowly downgraded in importance. Military actions in the Arctic hadn't been high on anyone's priority list for the last three decades.

Approaching KIA local airspace, it was clear that had changed in the past hour.

Clancy estimated three dozen alien aircraft were dog-fighting over the airport. Each of the fighters was smaller than one of his plane's wings. He saw no sign of arms fire coming from any ships. The briefing had indicated they used beam weapons, likely high intensity lasers.

One fast, high pass over the airport revealed that it had taken severe damage. A fueling facility—thankfully far from the passenger terminals—raged with red-orange flame. The wreckage of six planes of various sizes sat on the tarmac, smoking, their fires having burned out. Clancy couldn't see too many fine details in the pass, but the airport itself looked undamaged. Thousands of evacuees flooded exit lanes with pedestrian and automobile traffic.

"Command, Falcon. Passing over Keflavík Airport."

"*Falcon, Command. Estimate of enemy forces.*"

There's a good question, Clancy thought. He couldn't tell the "Red" planes from the "Violet" ones. This crazy alien war game was going to be harder to play than anyone had thought.

"Command, Falcon. Thirty-five to forty combatants in the air. I cannot visually distinguish between forces."

"*Falcon, Command. Understood. Activate IR filter.*"

Clancy followed the suggestion and flipped a switch above his head. A heads-up display flickered into place over his windscreen, bathing the scene below in false colors representing the relative temperatures of their surfaces. He pulled into a tight, multi-g turn and approached the airport again from the north-west. *Now* he could tell the planes apart. The Red Gamers' aircraft glowed a brilliant—and totally appropriate—Red. The Violet Gamers' planes were dim, dark, practically flying holes in the warmer air that surrounded them.

"Command, Falcon. That did it."

"*Falcon, Command. Engage Red aircraft.*"

Steinar and his fellow ICRU men drove the fifty kilometers out to Keflavík as fast as their Hyundai SUV could take them. The column of smoke ahead told them more than their commanding officer, who hadn't given them any briefing on what to expect. A flow of cars headed east on the highway. Steinar hoped the fleeing civilians wouldn't be disappointed by what they found back in the city, where chaos still reigned. No one knew what these aliens wanted or why they had attacked Iceland's two largest airports.

Closer in, they saw the alien planes in the sky, swooping and diving and looping around each other. Since Steinar sat in the passenger seat in the front, he had the best opportunity to watch the battle for a few minutes. He watched the black specks carefully… but none of them ever fell from the sky. If this was a pitched battle between enemy forces, it didn't look anything like any battle he'd ever seen in an old newsreel or in a movie.

A thunderous roar sounded over their heads. A couple of the men in the back of the truck shouted.

"What is it?" Steinar asked, bending around to see what had flown by.

"Americans!"

Terry saw that Vanessa had started shivering. He moved closer and put his arm around her shoulders. She gave him a concerned look.

"Don't get your panties in a bunch. You're cold."

"Okay... thanks."

He didn't want to admit that he enjoyed holding her, at least not in the middle of an interstellar crisis.

Kird and Ioe had been talking for ten minutes in the Eaieo's clinking-clanking language. Finally, the conversation sputtered out and Kird returned to the humans.

"I believe I have made your situation clear to Captain Ioe. He has agreed to take your request back to his headquarters for review." Kird's smile seemed happy and sincere, even though this wasn't the kind of answer Terry and Vanessa were looking for.

"How long will that take?" Vanessa asked.

"They must conclude the present hostilities, then they agree to a staged reduction of local aggression, prior to a War Committee hearing on their home world. They are already in consultation with the local Eoiea base commander to determine the terms."

"I'll ask again. How long with that take?"

"Captain Ioe estimates he can bring hostilities to a close within four weeks. You shall have your answer from the War Committee in less than two Earth years." Again, Kird smiled.

"Are you kidding me? Tell them to stop *now!*" Terry had lost his patience with this war game in only a couple of hours. In four weeks, he'd be completely round the bend, and in the meantime, there was no telling how many more people would die.

"You misunderstand, Terry. This is a very good result. The Eaieo hope to retain trading rights with Earth for your zinc. Any other recently hatched system would not receive such a generous proposal."

Vanessa pulled away from Terry's embrace to confront Kird. "Any other recently hatched system wouldn't have gotten this kind of attention in the first place."

"This I cannot dispute."

"How many soldiers did they even bring?" Terry asked.

"I am uncertain. This is a small ship, considering the complexity of their environmental needs. They cannot have an overlarge contingent."

He turned to Vanessa. "The Red ship that attacked *Lincoln*. It was the same size, right?"

"I think so."

Terry had an idea. A crazy idea. "Kird, can we talk in private?"

Vanessa opened her mouth to speak, but Terry rode over her. "Why don't you keep Ioe company?"

He pulled the Teddy Bear back to the corridor and left Vanessa to make small talk with the captain of the Eaieo ship.

It *is* like they're just playing some kind of game, Clancy thought. He'd made three passes over the area of battle and he hadn't seen a single Red or Violet ship shot down. He knew they had weapons. When one of their passes veered too close to the ground, the laser beams would scorch or burn whatever they touched. He'd caught a nip on his left wing, enough to alter his flight dynamics slightly—he didn't look forward to nursing it for the twelve-hundred-mile flight back to base—but not enough to cause serious damage.

Enough is enough, he decided, picking a particular Red ship and locking on his heat-seeking software—which didn't have to work too hard, after all—and launched a Sidewinder.

His plane shuddered slightly from the missile's launch. The path of the missile's heated exhaust was painfully obvious in the IR display. The Sidewinder ran straight and true. The Red Gamer pilot didn't even bother to jig out of the way. He clearly wasn't familiar with rocket weaponry. He received a nasty lesson when the explosion tore off his right wing and he tumbled from the sky.

"Command, Falcon. One Red ship down."

"Stop the truck!" Steinar shouted. Óbreyttur Lárusson slammed on the brakes, throwing the others in the vehicle forward. Angry muttering bubbled up. "Quiet!" Steinar ordered. He pointed to a rising cloud of dust and snow to the north. "Get us over there. One of the aliens was just shot down by the Americans."

Lárusson pulled off the highway and drove them over the low, scrubby pastureland toward the site of the crash. They found a farm road going in nearly the right direction, so they followed that for a few minutes. Once again, they had to go off road. The dust cloud had cleared. No smoke rose from the crash, but a vent of white steam told them where to go.

Steinar told Lárusson to approach slowly. Two hundred meters from the crash site, they could see the broken, black remains of the alien aircraft. They stopped and exited the vehicle. Steinar ordered arms out and ready. They double-timed a march up to the crash.

The plane wasn't too different from a human design, though it was very small. Steinar wondered if it was an unmanned drone, which would make this detour a waste of their time. The scientists could retrieve the remains of a drone at their leisure. If there was a hostile alien in there, though, that required their intervention. He crept forward, toward what appeared to be the fuselage of the plane. He batted on the outside with the butt of his rifle. Nothing happened. He did it again, louder this time.

A small hole opened near Steinar's feet. Imagining he had accidentally broken the hull of the ship, he stepped back.

"A leak!" someone behind him called out. A dribble of orange liquid hissed out of the plane. It was obviously very hot. The instant it hit the ground, a bit of snow nearby flashed into steam. Steinar could feel the heat of the spill through his heavy pants. He backed up farther still. If that was fuel, an explosion couldn't be far behind.

And then something truly bizarre happened. The little puddle of orange liquid *spoke*. It bubbled, and the bubbles formed just barely recognizable words. The liquid creature—for what other conclusion could Steinar draw but that it was alive?—spoke in English. Steinar's English wasn't very good, but he definitely heard the words "red" and "surrender".

Vanessa jumped to her feet when Kird and Terry returned to the control room of the Violet Gamer ship. Which was just as well, since her butt was freezing. Terry paused long enough to whisper into Vanessa's ear.

"Trust me."

"I don't—"

"Captain Ioe!" Terry approached the Violet Gamer. "I would like to make it clear that Vanessa Hargrove does not speak for our military, of which I am the chief off world representative. The Red Gamers have committed unforgivable atrocities against humanity, and they will pay."

"Understood," Ioe said with his continuing icy calm.

"They will regret making enemies of humanity. We do not take attacks such as this lightly and we will respond with overwhelming force. We are a young species, as you know, but we are smart, tenacious, and determined. With our help, together we will wipe out the Eoiea!"

Ioe shivered, just a bit, almost too subtly for Vanessa to notice.

"Such is not our goal," Ioe said.

"I know," Terry said with a feral smile. "They have never met an adversary such as us. Our wars don't end in nice stalemates, nor do they last long. We *crush* our enemies with every technology available to us. It has been eighty years since we first used a nuclear weapon, and we've been itching to try it again. One of my countrymen, a US officer like me, dropped that first bomb on Hiroshima, killing hundreds of thousands and crippling Japanese industrial production."

"Such is not necessary," Ioe said, his tone practically pleading.

"But do you know what the Japanese did? They thumbed their nose at us. They said, 'No, we will continue the fight until the last man, woman and child on our islands are dead.' So we bombed them again three days later."

"We do not prosecute war in this way," Ioe answered.

"That's fine, Captain. We'll do it for you. And you know how I know we will win? Because the US, who had the will to destroy so many to emerge victorious, and the Japanese, who very nearly sacrificed themselves for their own long hoped for victory... We are *allies* now and we bring our combined hope for the eradication of the Eoiea to your battle."

Ioe's vibration was obvious to all now. Terry stepped forward to address the Violet Gamer across only inches. "If the Eoiea have to die to the very last man for this war to end, you have our solemn promise that so it will be."

"Silence!" Ioe shouted. "Krd, do the Humans not know of the Central Authority moratorium on genocide?"

"On the contrary," Kird said, "they have been served with a warning concerning their current activities, which are, to date, confined to their own planet."

Vanessa watched as Ioe's purple hue deepened radically. She saw one bright burst of energy envelop his entire body, before the radiance died back again to a more normal level.

"We renounce our alliance with Earth, effective immediately. We have alerted our Eoiea foes and warned them against any similar agreements with your people. Such attitudes are not conducive to healthy warmaking. Krd, we will be making a formal complaint to Central Authority at the earliest opportunity. You will leave my ship immediately."

"Certainly," Kird said, hustling Terry and Vanessa through the cramped tunnels and back out into the relative warmth of the glacier.

"We should evacuate this area immediately," Kird warned. Vanessa understood. She could see thousands of the creepy little crystalline crab drones scampering back from their scouting missions, a teeming blanket of snowy creatures hurrying to the Violet Gamer ship. Its departure would be very soon. The three of them jogged west toward the waiting Icelanders and the helicopter.

Clancy had his F-35 turned for a third run at the Red Gamers. Their laser weapons were formidable against stationary land-based targets. Against a fighter jet that could do Mach one without breaking a sweat, not so much. He aligned his targeting software on one of the Red ships that was harrying a damaged Violet ship.

Without any sort of warning, all the alien ships—Red and Violet alike—broke from battle and fled. The Red planes took off to the west, the Violets to the east. Clancy switched his radio to the local frequency of the three other F-35s that were orbiting nearby.

"You know what's up?" he asked on the common band.

"No friggin clue. One of the Reds is landing two klicks south of your position."

"Understood." Clancy pulled around in a wide turn, keeping his eyes open for some kind of ambush. He saw none, but it was better to be para-noid than dead.

He caught up to the landing Red craft in no time. Clancy tilted his plane to get a decent look at what was happening down there. The alien ship came in for a landing next to the one Clancy had shot down a few minutes earlier. A small squad of human soldiers—probably Icelanders—were down there, too, so Clancy figured dropping a bomb on them wouldn't be the best course of action. He switched his radio to the com-mand band.

"Command, Falcon. Violet ships have evacuated the area. Red ships have ceased aggressive action."

"Falcon, Command. Continue to monitor the situation."

In other words, Clancy thought, *you've got no idea what's going on either.*

When the second alien plane came barreling into the area, Steinar and his men prepared to run. The ship overhead decelerated ridiculously fast, then settled gently onto the cold ground near the crash site.

The puddle of orange liquid that had tried to ask for asylum bubbled to life again. Still speaking in English, Steinar recognized the words, "home" and "leave". Lárusson came up from behind and whispered into Steinar's ear. "I think they're here for their friend."

Steinar nodded, both to Lárusson and to the strange alien. It must have been able to see Steinar and to understand the significance of the nod, because it began to flow over to the undamaged ship, melting a path through the snow as it went. A hole appeared on the ship, much like the one through which the alien had evacuated his downed plane. A tube snaked out. The orange puddle reached the end of the tube and was sucked up into the working plane.

Later, at his extensive debriefing, Steinar swore he heard the liquid alien sigh with pleasure as it entered the heated interior of the plane.

They were nearly at the helicopter when Vanessa heard a violent cracking sound from behind. She turned to see a huge section of the glacier shatter underneath the Violet Gamer ship. The egg ship didn't rise from any sort of rocket explosion with flame and smoke in its wake. More likely they used an anti-gravity field of some type, which exerted unusual stresses on the ice below. She watched as the black ship flew up and out of sight into the low clouds.

"A remarkable strategy, Terry," Kird said.

Terry turned to Vanessa. "Sorry about all of the drama. You'd already played your hand as a pacifist. Ioe wouldn't have bought any of what I was saying coming from you."

"Why'd you pull Kird aside?"

Kird answered that: "He asked me if the mere *threat* of genocide breaks any CA regulations. Technically, it does not. I admit this is an oversight which should be corrected."

Vanessa pulled Terry into a hug. "You're an idiot, you know that?" She pulled back to look directly into his stunned face. "It was a terrible risk, lying to them like that!"

Terry's response was a sad smile, completely devoid of humor. "Who was lying? I was *warning* them."

That knocked the wind out of Vanessa.

"Oh."

Mass Hysteria

Consider whence each thing is come, and of what it consists, and into what it changes, and what kind of a thing it will be when it has changed, and that it will sustain no harm.
—Meditations, XI, 17

Christmas was never one of Keira's favorite holidays. Following a carefully orchestrated campaign of sad phone calls and melancholy little notes from her "sick, old mother", Keira succumbed to maternal pressure and came home for the holiday in December of 2025. She had no problem with trees or candles or presents. It was all rather silly, but she had retained enough of her childlike wonder in the face of adult skepticism to enjoy it. Midnight Mass, on the other hand, was not enjoyable.

Most of the more modern churches held their "Midnight" Mass at a reasonable hour, such as eight o'clock. Such scandalous lack of tradition wouldn't do at Holy Ghost Church, where Jessica Desai was a parishioner. Their celebration of the birth of Jesus Christ began precisely at midnight on Christmas Eve, as was, of course, only right and proper.

Keira felt like a little girl waiting for Confirmation, rather than a woman celebrating Christmas. Her viciously starched, high-collared dress, her thick and scratchy hose, her entirely sensible shoes all chafed, in more ways than one. A woman of nearly twenty-six years should be having fun on a holiday evening such as this, not dipping her fingers into a bowl of bacteria-laden water and genuflecting before sliding across the dark, polished wood of an uncomfortable pew.

"Stop fidgeting."

"Yes, Mother."

The priest who made his way to the pulpit was not the hoary old man Keira remembered from the last time she'd been here. This man was still twice Keira's age, but he had a flicker of life in his delivery that hadn't yet been crushed out by the rigors of a job with many costs and little tangible reward.

"In the name of the Father, and of the Son, and of the Holy Spirit."

Keira dutifully—and automatically—made the Sign of the Cross and responded, "Amen."

The priest then invited those present to take part in the Act of Penitence. Keira, while not strictly penitent, couldn't help but be reminded of her part in uncovering the importance of zinc and the follow-on ramifications of that: the destruction of the Americans' space station, the damage done to Iceland, the disruption to Fiji. She couldn't quite muster enough guilt to consider all of that her fault. The truth about zinc would have come out sooner or later, and the effects might have been far worse under other circumstances.

Or not. Who could say?

"Kyrie eleison; Christe eleison; Kyrie eleison."

During the familiar chant, words she could call upon instantly even though she hadn't been to Mass in nearly three years, Keira snuck a look at her mother. Jessica Desai obviously found comfort in those words. Keira felt they were little more than nonsense syllables, Latinized versions of Greek, twice removed from her native tongue of English, a tie to a distant and irrelevant past.

The Roman Catholic Church, just like every other religious organization on the planet, could not hold too tightly to the past these days; they had to bow to the times. With so many centuries of dogmatism and hate in their wake, Keira found their inclusion of aliens to their fold a surprising change of heart. Earlier this summer, Marcellus III stunned the world by opening the Church to any being, regardless of species. Women couldn't be priests yet, but at least a Snake could attend Mass.

She scanned the crowd during the prayer, counting five Blues, two Trees and a Bull. From her discussions with Gainsborough about his race's philosophy on the supernatural, she was fairly certain the Blues were there from a sense of cultural curiosity, not any religious fervor. Who knew about the Trees or the blocky-bodied, horned Bull? Maybe they shared the human need to believe in something beyond their senses, and Catholicism met that need?

All Keira saw was a community trying to find order in the supernatural, when the natural, to them, provided only chaos. She, on the other hand, saw the order of the universe as being grander than any tales of water transmuted to wine or pillars of disobedient salt.

Keira wanted to get back to work.

On the day after Christmas, Keira was finishing up her breakfast dishes when the phone rang. She did not bother to rush over, knowing her father would beat her to the call regardless of how fast she was.

"Yes, and may I tell her who is calling?" Father said with a questioning look to his daughter. Keira was intrigued. The sets of people who knew Keira's home number and those whom her father wouldn't recognize over the phone did not have many intersections. Her father's eyes widened. "Certainly." He held his hand over the mouthpiece and handed the phone to Keira. She questioned him with her eyes. "Ganguly," he mouthed.

Keira's blood went cold. Why would the CEO of Maccha-Yantra be calling her? She was being fired. She should never have taken the week off. She took the phone from her father, took a deep breath, and then spoke.

"Yes?"

"My dear Miss Desai! I hope your time at home with your family goes well." Ganguly's expansive tone didn't imply he was about to end someone's employment, but Keira couldn't be certain. She answered warily.

"It's been good to see them, yes."

"Good, good. I have a favor to ask of you."

"Of course."

"We've been contacted by your local police for help investigating a troubling series of deaths in Bengalūru. I have taken the initiative to offer them your services, if you would be so kind, as you are the only representative we have in the area."

"I'm happy to, of course, sir. I'm not exactly sure what help I could provide."

"The deaths have a decidedly... *alien* feel about them."

"Alien?"

"Not that an alien attacked them, but that… I will not do justice to the details. I will let Inspector Patil fill you in. You can expect his call this morning."

"I'll do what I can to help, sir."

"One other thing, Miss Desai. I would not take you away from your family on your holiday without offering something in return."

"It's not necessary to—"

"No, no. I offer not money, but *information*. You will be the first to whom I have told this happy news. Maccha-Yantra, I am pleased to tell you, have been awarded the contract."

Keira's whole body seemed to go cold and hot at the same time, a feeling deliciously different from her previous fear for her job. A smile stole onto her lips. Her father, who had watched Keira's side of the conversation eagerly, raised his eyebrows in question.

"We're going to build a starship," Keira said, to Ganguly for confirmation, to her father for communication, to herself as realization.

Keira's father manifested what she was feeling when he threw both hands triumphantly into the air.

The Bengalūru City Police headquarters filled a new, glitteringly boxy office complex in the heart of the city. Keira signed into the registry in the lobby. A young officer, a boy who was clearly smitten with her, escorted her to Inspector Patil's office on the fifth floor. The young man knocked on the already open door to get the inspector's attention. Patil looked up and waved them both in as he finished his phone call.

Alexander Patil looked to be about forty-five years old, fit but not really athletic, with a thick head of hair and an intense stare. He appraised Keira with eyes that searched for something decidedly different than the superficialities the young officer found so attractive. Patil hung up the phone and stood, offering his hand.

"Ms. Desai."

"Inspector Patil."

"Thank you," Patil said to the young man. The officer pouted as he left. Patil returned his attention to Keira. "Have a seat. Would you care for tea?"

"Thank you, no. I should tell you, Inspector, that I'm not certain why I'm here. Mr. Ganguly gave me no details about your investigation."

"Of course." Patil still seemed to be evaluating Keira. He, no doubt, expected an older woman, or possibly a man, for that matter. "There have been eleven deaths so far."

"Eleven?"

"I hope you won't have a problem with the bodies."

"The bodies?"

He stood. Keira stood as well. "Our first stop is the morgue."

Patil strode from the room. Keira followed, her legs trembling just a bit.

Bhagat Saund stood nearly two meters tall, his traditional Sikh turban adding a few centimeters to his uncommon height. His eyes sparkled more vividly than those of any man of his age—likely sixty years—that Keira had ever met. His smile upon meeting her was broad and warm. Keira was silently very glad that Bhagat would be her guide to the bodies, which she didn't look forward to reviewing at all.

Patil stood a respectful distance from the autopsy table, allowing Bhagat and Keira their space to work. His presence was, however, a constant reminder that important people wanted to solve this mystery as quickly as possible.

On the table lay a woman, somewhat overweight, maybe thirty years old, naked and sliced open from sternum to belly. In fact, the y-incision bothered Keira far less than the unnatural pallor of the woman's skin. The sight of it gave her a fluttery sensation, deep in her bowels, an instinctive response to the wrongness of death.

"As you can see, there have been some sort of radiation burns." Bhagat pointed to the interior of the woman's brain, which lay near her freshly opened skull on the table. Keira had to take Bhagat's word that what she was seeing—blackened, puckered areas within the pink folds of flesh—was actually a radiation burn.

"How would a burn of this type get so deep inside a person's head?" Keira asked.

"Precisely the question!"

"I'm not sure I understand your point, Dr. Saund."

"Bhagat! Please! It is, of course, possible for some minor scarring to occur during radiation treatments or imaging scans which require a radioactive agent in the bloodstream. This, however, is two to three orders of magnitude worse than the worst case scenario for those causes. This is something entirely *new*."

"There have been eleven deaths?"

"That we know of. So far. Ten women and one man."

"That must be significant."

"The gender disparity? You would think. And always in the brain. That's where the scarring occurs."

"Only in the brain? You've scanned the rest of their bodies?" Keira asked.

Bhagat threw a surprised look at Patil, who simply shrugged. "No, I haven't," Bhagat admitted. "The cause of death has been... And..." Bhagat stopped sputtering and instantly went about preparing the young woman on the table for a more intensive MRI scan of her entire body. Meanwhile, Keira backed away from the distressing sight of the corpse to speak with Patil.

"Inspector, I assume you've investigated the deceased."

"Yes. They are, as Dr. Saund said, mostly women, of varying socioeconomic levels, though none were truly among the poor. They lived in different neighborhoods of the city, working in different jobs. Only two have any history of mental illness in their families."

"Why is mental illness relevant?"

"Before their deaths, each of the victims began acting in a hysterical manner. We assume this is the first evidence of the eventually fatal damage to their cerebral cortexes. That is also why Dr. Saund focused his initial investigations on the brain."

"None of this seems to make sense. There are only two ways to generate radiation damage: from without or from within. If it was from without, the damage would not be concentrated so deep *inside* the brain. There would be obvious scarring on the outside of the body, on the skin."

"And if the damage came from within?" Patil seemed to be gradually coming to respect Keira's abilities. Truthfully, she was simply making her best guesses about the situation. Her training as a scientist taught her to look at things differently than a Police Inspector would. She cared little for motive, for the *why*. She wanted to understand the *how* of it.

"Then there would be scarring at the point of entry. In the mouth, or a puncture wound from a syringe."

"It would stand to reason that no syringe could infiltrate so deeply into the brain."

Bhagat spoke as he rushed back into the morgue from the corridor. "Not true, Inspector. Several forms of directed brain surgery make use of intracranial syringes."

"You think...?" Patil said to the doctor, his excitement rising at the possibility of an answer.

"No, there wasn't a mark on her head," Bhagat said. "We're ready in the scanning room." He gestured to them to follow.

The BCP morgue had only recently purchased an MRI machine, a device which was generally used for diagnosing the living. As diagnostic tools had gotten more advanced, a state of the art machine from the last century could be refurbished for a tenth the original price, allowing the medical examiners another tool for their work. The machine dominated a sparkling white room down the hall from the autopsy room. Just now, the MRI housed the woman's corpse. Bhagat drew Patil and Keira to the control room, a small computer-filled space adjoining the scanning chamber.

"And so, we begin." He pressed a key on the keyboard and the MRI hummed to life. Keira watched, fascinated by the images popping up on the screen. She didn't understand any of it, of course, the vivid black and white images looking nothing like any part of the body with which she was familiar. Patil waited patiently, silently, for Saund to do his work. Finally, the Sikh pointed at the screen. "See?"

"You will have to enlighten me, Dr. Saund," Patil said with some exasperation.

"There is scarring *everywhere*." He used a mouse to click through several views he'd captured along the way as the MRI had rolled up and down the woman's body. "The femoral arteries, the liver, the lungs, the heart and aorta, the carotid."

"It is circulatory," Patil concluded.

"What about the mouth or other... orifices?" Keira didn't really want to enumerate them.

"Not apparently. The scarring, here... and here... and here..." He pointed to bits of white on the images of the woman's body. "This is quite obvious on a full body scan. We would have to do more detailed scans to find smaller scars."

"Do we have a sample of the victim's blood to scan for radioactive agents?" Patil asked.

"I have already looked. It was clean."

"Radioactive material doesn't simply vanish," Keira said. "It degrades over time, the rate determined by its half-life."

"What sort of material could cause this much damage and be reduced to an undetectable minimum in the space of..." Patil looked to Bhagat to finish the question.

"About thirteen hours?"

Keira looked at the men as she wracked her brain for what she could remember about uranium, radium, et cetera. She'd spent so much time thinking about carbon and aluminum—and *zinc*, of course—that higher weight elements weren't on her radar.

"None," she concluded.

Inspector Patil offered Keira his office to call her colleagues in Mumbai and do additional internet research on radioactive agents that might have caused these deaths. Her initial assumptions proved to be correct. None of the MYC specialists she chatted with knew of any new types of radiation that had been introduced by alien cultures. A team of visiting Scorpions had given the team working on the FTL drive program a new and highly efficient method of extracting U-235 from ore samples. Since then, however, MYC had shelved any further research into fission as a power source, for a variety of reasons. And, in any case, no isotope of uranium could do what had happened to these women—and this one man.

That detail continued to bother Keira more than her police counterparts. A gender disparity of such magnitude could not be simple coincidence. What could it mean?

Keira followed up on an unlikely hunch on a video chat with Gains-borough. They discussed the nature of certain super-elements with atomic numbers in the range of three to four hundred. MYC hadn't yet embarked on any research along those lines, but Keira thought it best to look under every possible rock. Gainsborough claimed that such giants were even less likely candidates than "normal" transuranic elements, since they either broke down within milliseconds after creation, or they remained stable for millennia, thus generating no radiation at all.

Patil poked his head into his office, interrupting Keira's chat.

"Come."

Patil drove through the streets of Bengalūru like a madman. Keira spent the first five minutes of their blaring-siren, spinning-light journey grasping the door handle for dear life. She spent the last five minutes with her eyes closed, thinking desperately of happier times.

Bhagat, sitting in the back seat, giggled.

They arrived at Victoria Hospital and rushed to the emergency room. After some wrangling with the duty nurse, she escorted them to a semi-private room where a woman thrashed about, strapped down to her bed. She appeared to weigh about seventy-five kilos, but that didn't stop her from displaying significant strength. She made her bed shift a centimeter or so with each lunge.

This woman was the latest victim of the strange malady. She had presented with an altered mental state, just as had the other eleven victims. Some process was at work in her head at that very moment. Patil hoped that seeing it first hand would help Keira and Bhagat learn the nature of it.

Two nurses and one doctor hovered over the woman, taking her vitals, administering medications, trying—and failing—to keep her calm. Keira listened to their frantic words for a while before speaking.

"Why don't you sedate her?" Keira asked, perhaps a bit too loudly.

"Out!" the doctor shouted. He was not a day older than Keira.

"Inspector Alexander Patil, BCP. And you are?"

"I said out," the doctor reiterated, turning away from the visitors and back to his patient.

"It's happening right now," Keira said to Bhagat.

"Very likely."

"We need x-ray film."

"What?" Patil asked.

"X-ray film. Now!"

The doctor may have been attending to his patient, but he still heard their discussion.

"This patient isn't going anywhere, least of all to Radiodiagnosis."

"I didn't say I needed an x-ray machine, I just need the film." Keira grabbed one of the nurses by the arm. "Where is radiology?"

"On two," the nurse said reflexively. The young doctor glared at her, as if she had betrayed him somehow.

Keira pulled Bhagat with her out of the room in search of a stairwell.

"Radiodiagnosis", as a name for the department, was an antiquated term. Magnetic resonance had almost entirely outmoded the use of actual radiation and reactive film as a diagnostic tool. Thankfully, simple limb fractures were still reviewed the old fashioned way. Keira and Bhagat burst into the room, currently empty of patients with broken bones or technicians who would attend to them.

"It'll be in here," Bhagat said, indicating a locked cabinet in one corner of the room. Just to be sure, Bhagat rattled the handle, but it didn't budge.

"What are the chances we'll get someone to open this for us in the next sixty seconds?" Keira asked.

"Zero. Or less."

"I agree." Keira moved to the other wall and pulled a fire extinguisher from a bracket. She smashed the red body of the extinguisher against the handle. It broke on the first hit. Bhagat laughed and opened the cabinet. He began pulling single, paper-wrapped sheets of film from a case. Keira grabbed the entire case from him and rushed from the room.

Back in the patient's room, Patil continued trying to communicate with the doctor, asking for details of her condition, for details of her medical history. It was no use. The doctor's only response was a muttered threat to call hospital security. Patil threatened to call in backup. The woman continued to scream and thrash, though far less violently than before. Keira was worried that the patient was nearing the end of her struggle. She handed the case of film to Bhagat and pulled out a single sheet. She snuck around one of the nurses.

"What are you doing?" the doctor demanded.

"Research," she said. She wrapped the paper-covered film around the woman's head and held it in place. "Bhagat! Her chest!"

Bhagat, roused from his near trance, handed the case of film to a perplexed Patil and took out a sheet of film. He shouldered past the doctor and placed the film against the woman's sweat-soaked gown, between her heavy breasts.

"We're trying to save this woman!" the doctor raged.

"We're trying to save the next one," Keira responded.

"How long do you think?" Bhagat asked.

"I have no idea." Keira hesitated, then pulled the film from the woman's head. Bhagat followed her example. They slipped the now exposed film back into the case. Keira wasn't sure if the film could have captured *anything* useful in such an uncontrolled environment, so unlike the carefully designed rooms in the Radiodiagnosis department. Still, it was their best option to learn about the elusive radiation that was killing these women.

The dying woman no longer screamed; her movements slowed; her breathing had become labored and phlegmy. The doctor and two nurses, finally, accepted the fact that they could do nothing for her. The six of them stood there, watching helplessly as the woman rolled her eyes one last time, coughed weakly, then lay still. The doctor gingerly took her wrist, listened for a pulse, then followed this with a check at her neck and her chest. He checked her eyes for reactivity, glanced at the others in the room, then sighed.

"Time of death: 12:52 PM."

He remained silent for a moment. Keira thought he might be saying a small prayer for the lost soul. Then he stood straight again and faced off against the intruders.

"Explain yourselves! Immediately!"

Bhagat was flustered by the man's outburst. Patil was angered by the man's temerity. Keira simply pointed to the x-ray film and said, "We need to develop these."

"I can't see anything," Bhagat admitted.

"There's nothing to see," the hospital's head radiologist, Dr. Gilchrist, snapped. He still seethed at the damage done to his cabinet. "There were no x-rays coming through that woman to expose the film."

"You mean coming *out* of her." Keira pointed "It's right *there*. Can't you make this thing any brighter?" The x-ray viewer, resembling a lit-from-within medicine cabinet on the wall of the Radiodiagnosis lab, had only two settings: on and off.

Patil, standing near the door, switched off the overheads. Suddenly, the images on the dark slides were visible to the others. The slide Bhagat had taken of the dying woman's chest was very faint, very blurry, but there were slashes of gray amidst the black. Crazy spiral patterns. The other slide, the one Keira had held to the woman's head, was clearer. The spirals on that slide were brighter and each had a ghostly mirror image on the other side.

"See? This one, with the five loops, is a perfect mirror of *that* one." Keira pointed.

"I don't understand," Dr. Gilchrist said.

"Ms. Desai held the film wrapped around Mrs. Ghara's head," the young doctor said. He had, finally, introduced himself as William Wodeyar. Now that he understood the dire nature of the investigation, he offered whatever help he could.

"Then, these..." Dr. Gilchrist was at a loss.

"These events propagated in at least two directions, both to the left and right of Mrs. Ghara's head," Keira explained.

"What kind of events?" Gilchrist asked.

"I don't know for sure, but what we're looking at is very similar to high energy particle collisions."

"Collisions of what?" Patil asked.

"Anything. Positrons and electrons. Protons and antiprotons."

"That would require a particle accelerator," Gilchrist said with a scoffing tone. "That can't happen inside a woman's head."

"And yet..." Keira pointed at the strange patterns on the exposed film.

During the time spent at Victoria Hospital with the unfortunate Mrs. Ghara, two more victims—both women—were reported in other parts of the city. Discussions with the local police in other cities around the country seemed to indicate that the problem was confined to Bengalūru. For now.

With a slightly better idea of what was happening to the victims, Patil had his people review the details of the lives of these fourteen people. All were between the ages of thirty-three and fifty-five. All but one were women. More than half were overweight. They had reason to believe that the strange material causing the internal scarring was ingested, but no more than three of the victims had any history of eating in similar establishments. Officers went through each of their homes again, looking for commonality in foods, medicines, personal care products, anything.

Keira reviewed the results along with Patil and Bhagat back at BCP headquarters. One detail struck her as odd.

"Why would a man be taking an iron supplement?"

"Excuse me?" Patil asked.

"The one male victim. Harold Raman. You have an iron supplement listed as being in his home. Was he married?"

"No."

Bhagat spoke up. "His medical records say he suffered from pernicious anemia. Is that relevant?"

"Usually, women..." Keira stopped. She knew, she *knew* she'd found it. The anomaly of the one man in the group of women had bothered her all day. Women routinely took iron supplements, to replace that which was lost during menstruation. Only a medical condition would suggest the practice to a man. That was the answer.

She grabbed the other folders on the table—eliciting a grunt of displeasure from Patil when she took one right from his hands. She flipped through them, looking for the product she'd found in Raman's file, something called FerroHealth. She found the item listed in five of the other victims' files.

"This is it. FerroHealth. That's where the radiation is coming from."

"Ms. Desai, only six of the fourteen victims were taking it."

"No, sir. Only six of the fourteen victims had bottles of it in their medicine cabinets. We don't know if friends or family had slipped them these pills, if they'd recently finished their supply, if they left the bottle at the office or the car or the gym." Keira tossed the files back onto the conference table and swiveled her chair around to a computer terminal. She did a quick search and soon found the website for FerroHealth. They looked to be a very new company, with, at present, only the one product. Bright, flashy graphics and clever slogans got the idea across easily. This pill was designed to replace iron in a woman's diet.

"We need to get this product off the shelves immediately. We need to put out a citywide advisory telling consumers to turn in any unused samples. We need to have anyone currently taking the supplement come to their nearest hospital for treatment."

"Slow down, Ms. Desai," Patil said. "You don't know—"

"And we need to go to their offices *right now*. They're based here in Bengalūru."

Keira jumped to her feet, already heading for the door. Patil grasped her arm in a tight grip, holding her still.

"We need significantly more evidence than this to issue such alerts or to confront a legitimate business owner."

"But—"

"You are the scientist, Miss Desai. Do your due diligence. Prove your theory."

Keira was reminded of the overbearingly male nature of her professors back at UVCE, particularly Dr. Nadimpali. All things being equal, she preferred being talked down to by Gainsborough. He at least did it politely. Keira swallowed her indignation and turned to Bhagat.

"We have some work to do."

Bhagat nodded enthusiastically.

They adjourned to the medical examiner's lab, where a bottle of FerroHealth waited, brought back to the police station by one of the officers who had inventoried the victims' homes. Keira handled the bottle carefully, not knowing what to expect from it. Using a small pair of tongs, she took out one of the thick, red pills and laid it on the laboratory table.

"We need to find out what this is made of," she said.

Bhagat agreed. He went under the counter and pulled up one of the oldest tools in a chemist's arsenal: a mortar and pestle. Keira laughed.

"They say the old ways are the best." He crushed the pill into a pale pink powder. The red coloring was only microns thin on the surface of the pill. Inside it was white. From the sample he split off two small piles, giving one to Keira.

"I trust you've used a mass spectrometer before?"

Keira nodded. A mass spectrometer was the most straightforward of analytical tools for a forensic chemist. It used a strong magnetic field to split the sample into atoms, which were then weighed and sorted by element. The results wouldn't tell them anything about the molecular nature of the pills, but it would tell them what it was made of.

Bhagat took the second bit of the powder and fed it into a more sophisticated chemical analysis comparator. This more recent addition to the medical examiner's tool chest would run the sample through a variety of predefined chemical tests to look for well known molecules: proteins, sugars, salts, etc. It could even detect genetic material, DNA and RNA. If they found either of those massively complex molecules, they would have to move on to more directed analysis to determine what species of plant or animal was represented.

Bhagat's test finished about the same time as Keira's. "Nothing surprising here," he said, reading the results off the screen.

"Really?" Keira said. "My results look very odd." Bhagat moved to her screen. It listed the elements it had found in the sample. Three of them were entirely expected: hydrogen, carbon, and oxygen. They would be the basic building blocks of the cellulose binders that make up the bulk of the mass of any pill. There was also some sulfur, which made sense. The iron would have been bound with sulfur into iron sulfate, a stable molecule for iron transfer. Strangely, though, there was a large amount of *lithium* in the sample. Lithium was often used medically as a mood stabilizer, but it shouldn't have been present in an iron supplement.

Stranger still, there was no iron at all.

"Did you...?" Bhagat inspected the device, making sure Keira had used it correctly.

"I can run the test again."

"I suggest that we both should." He pointed to his own results. Keira looked at Bhagat's screen. His test revealed the presence of stearic acid, lactose and, most importantly, ferrous sulfate. *Iron*. There was no mention of any lithium compound.

"This doesn't make any sense," Keira complained. "You found iron, and I didn't? I found lithium and you didn't?"

"We should run the tests again."

To make sure there wasn't any bias in the experiment, they switched off. Bhagat ran the mass spectrometer analysis, and Keira took over the chemical comparison test. The results came back identical to the previous time. The chemical analysis found iron. The mass spectrometer found lithium.

Keira tried to put the incongruous results into words. "We've found evidence of a substance that has the chemical properties of iron, but has the mass of lithium. That's..." She wanted to say it was impossible, but that was clearly not true. "That's remarkable."

"I have an idea." Bhagat walked back into a storage room. Keira continued to review the two contradictory test results. She had no problem with the contradictions within her own personal life. The unknowable nature of human feeling was a living breathing contradiction, wasn't it?

But science should not be contradictory. Something had to explain the bizarre results from these tests. Something had to explain the relationship of these tests to the fourteen deaths. Science was not the ineffable arena human psychology was. It could be difficult to find answers, but Keira had to believe they were there to be found, nonetheless.

Bhagat came back wheeling a trolley with a plastic wrapped hunk of machinery.

"It's brand new. We haven't had a moment to calibrate and install it." He began tearing the plastic off of the microwave-sized machine.

"What is it?"

"An ion mobility spectrometer. If one test says iron and the other says lithium, let us break the tie with this device."

Where a standard mass spectrometer weighed the different masses of the elements, an ion mobility spectrometer measured their electrical charges. This would solve the mystery. An ion of lithium would have a charge of three. An ion of iron would have a charge of twenty-six. At the atomic level, things were simple as that.

Keira had worked with a machine like this back at university, but a much larger, more cumbersome sort of model. This sleek design must have been a result of some borrowed alien technology. The mere process of breaking a sample into its constituent ions generally required larger hardware to create the needed intense electrical fields. She ignored the impulse to take the thing apart to see how it worked.

Bhagat and Keira spent a good hour setting up the device. After several stops and starts, and a couple of dry runs with some simple compounds they found in the lab, they were ready to put a bit of the powdered FerroHealth into it.

"Here we go!" Bhagat said gamely. He punched a button. There was an audible *pop*, followed by a horrible whine. Smoke escaped from the bottom of the spectrometer. Keira and Bhagat shared a confused look. Without a word, they began to disassemble the machine.

The inner workings were destroyed, blackened and twisted, as if it had been struck by lightning.

Keira smiled. "What are you smiling about?" Bhagat asked, still sadly fingering the remains of his new toy. "This was quite expensive."

"I have a theory." She moved back to the table where more of the pinkish powder waited, seemingly so innocuous. She grabbed a beaker and filled it with water at the tap. She scooped the rest of the powder into the beaker and stirred it up, watching it dissolve into the water. "Do you have a battery?" she asked.

"A battery?" She might have asked him for a live chimpanzee from the look on his face.

Keira retrieved her purse from the table near the door and looked through her belongings. She found a small flashlight her father had once insisted she always carry. She unscrewed it and tipped out the small AAA battery.

"Stand back," she warned Bhagat. He took a step back from the beaker. Keira stood as far away as she could before she tossed the little battery into the beaker.

The result was more than Keira could have hoped for. The water erupted, boiling and flashing with deep indigo light that left painful afterimages on her eyes. The beaker burst, the whole mess spilling onto the table and the floor. Both she and Bhagat skittered away, not wanting to get any of it on their shoes.

"You see?" she asked.

"I saw what happened, but I don't understand. Are we safe?"

"We're fine. That substance, I suppose I'll call it faux-iron, it reacts very poorly with electrical fields. It's stable enough until you put it into an electric field. That's why it blew up your new spectrometer. And that's why it starts to explode inside a person's head."

"There are electrical fields in the brain," Bhagat whispered.

"And in the heart. All through the body, really. But they're more concentrated in the brain. This should be enough to convince Patil, don't you think?"

Bhagat nodded slowly.

Keira talked Patil into bringing her along when he went to visit the FerroHealth headquarters late that evening. He drove again, this time without causing Keira to fear for her life.

The offices of FerroHeath, LLC were little more than a warehouse on the south side of the city. Far less of Patil's imperious manner was required to get them in the door than they had needed back at the hospital. They were met by the company's owner, a Japanese man named Jeremy Nishina. Nishina stood several centimeters shorter than Keira, and had a wide, smiling, salesman's face. He spoke to them in a corner of the loud, busy warehouse. Thousands of cases of the diet supplement loomed in the racking over their heads, cardboard encased bombs waiting to go off.

"If this is a matter of my taxes, I can assure you—"

"It is not, Mr. Nishina," Patil said. "We have reason to believe that your product is defective."

Nishina's smile faltered for a bare moment, then reasserted itself.

"We have done extensive testing on our formula, and—"

"Tell us about the special ingredient," Keira said.

"Young lady, you must understand that our patent is still pending. It would not be wise—"

"There have been fourteen deaths, Mr. Nishina. Answer Ms. Desai's question."

"Fourteen..." Now Nishina's smile was well and truly gone. "That's not possible."

"We watched a woman die this afternoon," Keira said coldly. "They have undergone traumatic radiation burns *inside their heads*. What did you put into the pills instead of iron?"

"It was... I thought..." Nishina, facing such revelations, lost his gift of patter. In that moment, Keira almost felt sorry for him.

Almost.

"They call it light matter."

"Light matter?"

"Yes. The engineers at Ken-Ya, back in Osaka, have been working on it for a space elevator, but they abandoned the project a few months ago, and they needed to get rid of the excess inventory. It's iron, alright. Twenty-six protons, twenty-six electrons, thirty neutrons. But..."

"Go on!"

"But it has an atomic weight of only seven."

Just like lithium, Keira thought.

"Explain please," Patil snapped. Nishina seemed incapable of continuing, so Keira took over.

"Protons and neutrons have a mass of one atomic unit. Electrons weigh a fraction of that. So iron should have an atomic weight of about fifty-six. There is something fundamentally wrong with the protons and the neutrons in this light matter." She turned on Nishina, fire in her eyes. "What is it? How did they make it?"

"I don't know how they made it. I just... I just..."

"You bought some of it," Patil concluded.

"Yes. Since it has a lower mass we could save in shipping, in warehousing, in packaging..."

"You decided to use this highly experimental form of matter as a *diet supplement?*" Keira was so angry, she saw spots before her eyes.

"They said something about missing quarks," Nishina admitted.

Keira gasped. "That is... That is unprecedented! Quarks are always—"

"Perhaps we could save the physics lesson for another time, Miss Desai. Suffice to say, this light matter is not stable?" Patil ventured.

"They told me it is stable!" Nishina countered. "They said that as long as I keep it away from electrical fields there wouldn't be any problems with it! We've been very careful with—"

"Electrical fields?" Keira asked.

"Yes."

"You mean, like the electrical fields inside a human brain!"

Patil had heard enough. He pulled out his cell and made a call to his office, giving them the go ahead to send out the warnings about Ferro-Health. He asked for a team to come to the warehouse and impound all of the unsold pills. Keira stepped away and made her own call, to Ganguly, to let him know what had happened, and to warn him of the dangers of light matter, in case he had any programs using it that she didn't know about.

Nishina watched all of this quietly, and simply broke down into tears.

Keira returned home late, long after her family would have eaten dinner. She fully expected to receive an earful from her mother about not calling. She also expected to be grilled extensively by her father on the day she'd spent with the police. The one thing Keira did not expect was to hear her mother singing at the top of her voice.

"Lolly lolly! All in a dolly! Calling home! Calling home!"

Keira had never heard her mother sound like that, so hysterical. She rushed into the kitchen. She stopped short when she entered the room. Her mother was standing *on* the kitchen table, dancing a jig and continuing her nonsense song.

"Homely homely! Going to the market! Lolly lolly lolly lolly!"

Keira's father stood nearby, his eyes wide with terror. He looked to Keira for help.

"What's going on?" Keira asked.

"I don't know. She's been full of energy all day, but since she got back from the market, she started singing."

"Everybody sing! Everybody sing!" Like a manic symphony conductor, she gestured to Keira and Madhu. They couldn't have joined in even if they wanted to. The tune and lyrics were just random bits of business strung together without any sense.

"Mother's been through menopause, hasn't she?"

The look on her father's face was clear; he thought his daughter was just as crazy as his wife. Keira had barely received the basics of sexual instruction from her parents. She didn't imagine she'd ever heard either of them say the word "menopause" in her life.

"I'm serious, Father. It's important."

"Yes, yes. Years ago."

"So she wouldn't be taking an iron supplement, would she?" Keira hoped desperately that the next word out of her father's mouth would be "no".

"You know about her anemia," Keira's father said.

"Lolly lolly lolly lolly!"

Keira allowed herself only a heartbeat's worth of debilitating horror, then she pulled her cell from her bag and dialed the only person she knew who had a ghost of a chance of knowing how to save her mother.

"Hello, you have reached Gainsborough. How may I assist you?"

Keira drove them to Victoria Hospital. From the back seat, where he tried to control his wife, Madhu complained that Wockhardt Hospital was closer. Keira insisted they had to go to Victoria. On the drive she called Dr. Wodeyar and Dr. Gilchrist. They both agreed to meet her in the emergency room.

At the hospital, she parked by the curb and jumped out before the car had come to a complete stop. Madhu carried the still singing Jessica into the hospital. Keira explained to the admitting nurse that they were expected. Dr. Gilchrist was already there, waiting by an exam bed. Madhu brought his wife over and laid her down.

"Where am I? What is this? I've already had the babies! I can't have them again! Madhu! Lolly!"

"Doctor," Keira said, "we need to put my mother into an MRI immediately."

"What? What do you expect to find? I thought—"

"Please!" Gilchrist looked into Keira's eyes and saw no opportunity for discussion.

"Come along."

They unlocked the wheels of the bed and rolled Jessica out of the ER, into an elevator, and up to Radiodiagnosis. Gilchrist prepared the machine while Madhu helped Keira strap Jessica to the platform. She continued to struggle and spout bits of nonsense song.

"Do either of you have any metal on you?" Gilchrist asked through the intercom.

"I have a pin in my hip," Madhu said.

"You'll have to get out of there." With a pained expression, Madhu looked to his daughter for permission to leave. She nodded, handing him her purse and her earrings. He scurried into the small room with Gilchrist.

"Where's Madhu? Where's Madhu? Keira. Leera. Teara. Weera." Jessica began laughing.

"Hurry, please, doctor!" Keira pleaded.

"Move your hands," he said. Keira backed away from the platform. It slowly retracted, pulling Keira's mother into the small tunnel of the MRI machine. There was a loud hum as the machine activated.

"Alright," Gilchrist said. "What am I looking for?"

"Nothing. The magnetic field is all we need. Where is Dr. Wodeyar?"

"Excuse me?" Gilchrist asked.

Keira walked up to the glass to address Gilchrist directly. "The substance in my mother's brain becomes unstable in an electrical field. The only way to stabilize it is to put it into a *stronger* magnetic field. That's what we're doing right now. We've stopped the decay of the material, stopped the damage to her brain."

"But..." Gilchrist seemed to be at a loss. There was a knock at the door. Keira turned to see Wodeyar standing in the corridor. She went out.

"How can I help?" Wodeyar asked, looking into the MRI room with a quizzical expression.

"You need to operate on her."

"She has some of that radioactive material in her head, too?" he asked.

Keira didn't waste time correcting his mistake about the nature of the substance. "You have to operate on her while she's in the MRI."

"What?"

"The MRI is keeping the faux-iron from decaying. We have to keep it activated while you remove it."

"Operate in there? While the MRI is activated? That's impossible."

Keira advanced on the smaller man. "That's not acceptable. There's a way. There's always a way. You need to find instruments made of non-ferrous metals or ceramics. Intracranial syringes. Something, *anything* that will work in a magnetic field. We can't afford to turn off the field, or she'll just get worse, and then she'll die."

Keira didn't know when her speech had shifted from anger to tears, but by the end of it she was barely intelligible through her sobs. She watched, hope warring with despair, as she watched the wheels spun inside Wodeyar's head.

"Keira? I'll try. That's all I can promise."

"Thank you."

Keira looked back at her mother. She wasn't struggling anymore. Her rising and falling chest revealed she was still alive.

For now.

The glow of impending sunrise filtered through the curtains, making Keira look up from her vigil over her mother's bed. Madhu lay sleeping in a cot they'd wheeled into the room for him.

Dr. Gilchrist had gone home after the bizarre procedure was complete. His help had been invaluable, directing Wodeyar from the MRI control room as the young doctor pushed his improvised syringes directly into Jessica Desai's brain. The entire procedure took less than an hour, but it was the longest hour of Keira's life.

Dr. Wodeyar stayed at the hospital to watch Jessica's progress, but at the moment he was off checking on some of his other patients. Keira's sisters were planning on coming to the hospital later in the morning, after their respective children were awake and the situation could be explained to them.

For now, Keira was alone with her mother. Jessica, the larger-than-life figure that had loomed psychologically over Keira for so long, looked small and frail in the big hospital bed. Her shaved head was bandaged and her heartbeat and respiration were being monitored. Dr. Wodeyar had been perfectly honest with Keira. He'd never done anything remotely like what they'd attempted last night, an entirely experimental surgery, attempted on the fly. He couldn't begin to estimate the chances for Jessica's recovery.

For anyone else in the world, Keira would probably not have done it. But for her mother, last night Keira had said a prayer.

Dr. Wodeyar entered the room quietly. Keira nodded to him.

"You should get some sleep. I can watch her."

"My sisters will be here in a couple of hours. I'll get some rest then," Keira lied. She wasn't going anywhere until her mother woke up.

"The man's a doctor, Kiki. You should listen to him."

Keira's head whipped around so fast she heard something crack in her neck. Jessica's eyes were still closed, but she was awake.

"Mother? Father!"

Madhu snorted once, then came forcefully awake. "What is it?"

"What's happened?" Jessica asked.

Keira leaned down and gave her mother a ferocious hug. Dr. Wodeyar carefully pulled Keira away so he could examine his patient. He asked Jessica to open her eyes. She blinked them open and he checked them with his penlight. He had her follow his finger with her eyes.

"What's your name?"

"Jessica Desai. And what's yours, young man?"

The doctor smiled. "William Wodeyar, ma'am. You just had surgery."

"Where?" She reached down to her chest. Jessica had always feared breast cancer would be the cause of her death. Wodeyar used a playful wave of his penlight to suggest she check higher. Her hands flew to her head, where she found bandages and her head shaved clean. "I don't remember what happened."

"That's best, little one," Madhu said, coming to her bedside and sitting on the edge. "You were *singing*."

"I was *not*."

"You were, Mother. And dancing, too."

"We're going to need to keep you here for a little while so we can monitor your recovery."

Jessica fixed the doctor with a stern eye. "You mean you need to make sure I'm still the woman I was before you cut my head open?"

"Mother!"

"Yes, ma'am. That's precisely it." He patted her on the shoulder. "So far, things are looking very good."

"Alright," she said warily. Her eyes sought Keira's. She gestured for Keira to come close.

"Yes?" Keira said, still a little teary-eyed after the realization that her mother was probably going to pull through. "What is it?" Mother gestured again, wanting to say something quietly, in confidence. Keira leaned close.

"Not bad looking, is he?" she whispered. "And a *doctor*..." She widened her eyes in a suggestive manner.

Laughing, Keira stood back up and turned to Dr. Wodeyar. "I think she's *exactly* the woman she was before."

Viral Outbreak

> *Hindrance to the perceptions*
> *of sense is an evil to the animal na-*
> *ture. Hindrance to the movements*
> *is equally an evil to the animal na-*
> *ture.*
> —*Meditations, VIII, 41*

Vanessa was *not* in a good mood on Monday morning. When she got to the Off World offices, she blew past all the cubes of her smiling underlings with "How was your weekend?" just waiting to spring from their lips. Vanessa's moods were not too hard to intuit, so everyone remained safely quiet, assuming their leader was worried about some huge matter of galactic importance.

If only...

She went to her office, found her coffee machine prepped for making tea instead of coffee, and had a small fit. She stopped short of actually breaking anything, but only just.

Her inbox was full, as usual after a day away from the office. Her carefully tended seventy-hour weeks had grown to eighty, then more. For her, a weekend was a Sunday, and even then, only some of the time. After *this* Saturday night, though, nothing could have gotten her into work yesterday. She took a rare Sunday off. The time off hadn't really done much good.

She flipped angrily through her e-mails. The first was a six-month update on Maccha-Yantra's progress with the starship. They'd christened the project *Vimana*, referring to some mythological flight in the Hindu tradition. She cringed every time she saw the name, not because it bothered her personally, but because she knew the *otherness* of the Indian traditions that were creeping into the starship program were a burr under the saddle of a lot of American politicians. True, she'd merely been a member of a large committee that chose Maccha-Yantra, but she was forever linked with the program—and therefore with *Vimana*—in the hearts and minds of everyone in the country. In the country? In the world. And maybe beyond, for that matter.

At least MYC was on track. Early hull testing was nearly complete; the IRCPs were approaching phase three; recycling system production was ahead of schedule. Ganguly's bold claims turned out not to be so bold after all. They might actually fly *before* the barrier's final collapse.

The rest of the e-mails were updates on minor annoyances. The cease-fire between the Aussies and the Eels suffered a temporary breakdown on Saturday afternoon when a submerged Eel cruiser floated a little too close to a US Navy frigate. The Federal Zinc Repository was about to break ground on their D.C. headquarters, and they invited Vanessa to attend. The Vampire colony in Birmingham had swelled to over two hundred, making the Brits more nervous than ever.

It was all important. (Well, maybe not the zinc thing.) Important, but not critical, so her staff hadn't called her during her day off. The very last piece of paper in the box, however, had a return address that made Vanessa's blood go cold. *This* one she would have wanted to know about immediately. She picked up the phone and dialed her assistant, Barbara.

"Get me the CDC."

"ONE KILOMETER TO GO," the pleasant, young woman's voice purred into Kurt's ear. He knew that the voice was supposed to push him harder, get him to put on a final burst of speed to finish up his workout. Maybe Nike expected him to subconsciously assume that performing well would lead to this mysterious, throaty young woman having sex with him. Whatever the logic, it never seemed to work. He always found the realization that he had *so far* to go depressing. He rallied every ounce of his strength and just barely managed to not slow down.

Peachtree Creek—just one of the seven thousand things in Atlanta named "Peachtree"—was low this winter, barely a trickle flowing through a wide mud flat. It made what was often a scenic run along the water a lot less pleasant today. Kurt checked his watch. Half of his lunch hour remained, so when he did finally give up on this whole workout thing for the day, he'd have time to walk back to his office and have a shower. And maybe a bagel.

"FIVE HUNDRED METERS TO—CALL INCOMING."

"Damn it," Kurt breathed, then tapped his earbud to take the call. "Yes?"

"Dr. Ripple, you've got a call." He didn't recognize the young man's voice. Must have been one of the new call center people. He clearly needed to have a talk with Margo—again—about when and how he should be interrupted.

"I'm not in the office right now," he wheezed. "Send me an e-mail or something."

"Um, okay, you see, it's Vanessa Hargrove calling."

Kurt stopped running so fast he stumbled a bit. He caught himself before falling onto his face, nearly breaking an ankle in the process.

"Shit!"

"Sir?"

"Put her through!"

Kurt hopped over to a nearby bench along the bike path to check out his ankle and regain his breath. He'd been Director of the CDC for six years and never fielded a call from anyone at Cabinet level, not even the Secretary of Heath and Human Services, who was technically his boss.

"Okay, here she is," the operator said. *Click.*

"Hello? This is Dr. Ripple." Kurt referred to himself as "doctor" reflexively. It tended to cow people. He didn't expect it would have much of an impact on Secretary Hargrove, though.

"Dr. Ripple, hello. I hope I'm not interrupting."

Kurt held his tongue. Snapping at a Cabinet member was the very definition of the Career Limiting Move. "What can I do for you, Ms. Hargrove?"

"I received a message from one of your field agents over the weekend about the Nashua situation. I hope you can give me an update on your progress."

Kurt closed his eyes. *Damn it, Marty!*

"Yes, ma'am. We have the situation under control. In fact, Dr. Kilpatrick really shouldn't have bothered you with it."

"Dr. Ripple, I have to disagree. If there is *any* chance that this outbreak is off world in origin, my office needs to know about it."

"The chances of the contagion being extraterrestrial are infinitesimal, Ms. Hargrove."

Kurt stood, wincing only a little bit at the pain in his ankle. He started back toward the campus. It was damage-control time.

"I'd prefer to have those chances be zero, Doctor."

"Of course. I'll talk with Dr. Kilpatrick and get back to you with an update in a few minutes."

"I left my number with your assistant."

"Thank you," Kurt said, and ended the call. His ankle seemed okay, so he ran back to his office to knock some heads together.

Ever since the breaking of the heliopause, the nightmare scenario for Kurt Ripple was the introduction of an alien infection into Earth's biome. Human, cow, bean: it didn't matter. If *any* Earth species was compromised by something from off world, then *everything* was in jeopardy. No one could know the mutation frequency for an unknown biology. The relatively sedate path of mutation that led anthrax—for example—to jump from sheep to humans took centuries. HIV's jump from monkeys to humans took decades. What if, for an alien infection, the path took years? Months? Hours?

For the first six months after aliens started to land, the CDC had been all over them, testing and poking and prodding as much as politeness allowed—and probably beyond, really. The Blues took the brunt of the testing, since they were the earliest arrivals. Snakes and Skeletons and Trees followed. The CDC never found anything. In fact, of all the races they'd examined, only about two thirds had what could be considered "blood", and of those, none had any of the standard protein sequences that human medicine associated with antibodies. Put simply, every alien body chemistry they'd probed was so dissimilar from humanity's that it looked like communicable diseases were a physical impossibility.

The groups who *wanted* the aliens here—the tourism industry, R&D firms, even the Department of Off World Affairs—were overjoyed by this result. Kurt, on the other hand, refused to lower his guard. He made it CDC policy that every new race to arrive on the planet be screened for protein markers that might indicate biochemical compatibility with humans. One hundred ninety-two alien races so far had passed his tests.

Saturday morning, Kurt had gotten a panicked call from Marty Kilpatrick up in New Hampshire. He had five cases of a mysterious respiratory infection that had shrugged off every antibiotic the local docs threw at it. When Marty got up there and looked closer at the bug, he found a curious seven-sided ring structure to the virus that didn't match any known disease.

"That doesn't mean it's alien, Marty."

"I'm telling you, Kurt. I feel it in my *gut.*"

Marty's gut had a relatively bad track record for this kind of thing. He had misdiagnosed Hanta three times in four years. It seemed like he found new strains of Ebola every other month, even though they *never* panned out as the real thing. Put him in a situation where you knew what you had, and Marty could do the fieldwork to track down Patient Zero and contain any kind of epidemic. He was that good, which was why the CDC hired him.

Hand him a mystery, though, and Marty would always grope for the most bizarre solution. He didn't simply hear hoof beats and assume it was a zebra. It was like he didn't know horses existed.

Kurt didn't stop to change clothes or to shower. He power-limped through the CDC main building, growling at Candace, his administrative assistant. "Get me Marty on the phone!" He didn't quite slam the door behind him after he tottered into his office.

"How are you doing, Sandy?" Marty asked as he came into the quarantined room. He had a biohazard suit on, which unfortunately limited the ways he could comfort the sick, young girl. He sat on the edge of her bed, smiling through plastic. Sandy offered a weak smile in return.

"Okay, I guess." She followed that with a cough. "I've got Ebola, don't I?"

Marty laughed. "No, kid, you don't have Ebola. Ebola attacks the bloodstream. You've got a bug in your lungs."

"So it's the plague?" This girl was probably a total stunner when she wasn't flirting with respiratory failure. Nineteen years old was too young to have to come to grips with your own mortality. Her parents stood outside the room, looking through the wide window, trying to offer their own brand of comfort.

Marty glanced at the monitors over her bed. Everything looked stable enough, but her stats—particularly her oxygen level—weren't promising. He wanted to check her temperature by feeling her forehead; he wanted to check her pulse at her wrist. Practicing medicine in a space suit didn't feel right to Marty Kilpatrick. "You don't have the plague, kid. You know how I know?"

"How?" Sandy's eyes grew wide, expecting some anvil of bad news to slam down on her head. Marty's next comment wasn't an anvil, really, but it wasn't good news, either.

"Because we don't *know* what you've got."

"Oh." Sandy lay back on her pillow and seemed to fall asleep right before Marty's eyes. He stroked her hair and left as silently as the air filtration system would allow.

In the hall, William and Anne Treemont pounced on Marty.

"How is she?" William asked.

"She's stable," Marty said as he took off the helmet of his suit. He scratched at his beard ferociously. The suits always made him itchy.

"Have you figured out what she's got yet?" Anne asked. Marty saw the same anvil-waiting face on Anne as he had seen on her daughter. He offered her the only good news he had, something he hadn't wanted to burden Sandy with.

"She's doing better than the others," he said.

Sandy Treemont had contracted the virus from her boyfriend, Francis Elmer. Francis—Frankie to his friends—was a twenty-year-old pre-med student at UNH, and he was *not* doing well. His oxygen levels were so low they had him on a ventilator in the room next to Sandy's.

Frankie got the virus from a woman named Eleanor Winn, one of his professors. Before dropping into a comatose state, Frankie had confided to Marty that he had a relationship with Eleanor. He made Marty promise not to tell Sandy about it. Marty had agreed.

Eleanor was doing worse than Frankie. She was also in a coma, in the next room over. Across the hall were two of Eleanor's *other* boyfriends, Christopher Pollock and Stephen Albie. Chris, Steve and Eleanor were practically beyond hope, totally dependent on their respirators, and nearing the point when their brains would just not be receiving any oxygen at all.

Marty was sure now that Eleanor was Patient Zero. Since there were no other similar cases of serious flu-like symptoms in the area—he'd checked as far south as Boston and as far north as Portland—he had come to the conclusion that he had probably contained the infection. He had taken to calling it Wreath, because of its strange molecular construction.

Unfortunately, he hadn't been able to get a good look at the virus in a living state. So far, he'd only seen inert versions in blood samples. For some reason, once the pathogen saw the light of day, it died. According to the patients, not all of them were sexually active, so he concluded the transmission method was through saliva during a kiss. If *that* was true, his biohazard suit and the Level 4 quarantine weren't necessary.

That wasn't enough for Marty. He *knew* this was alien in origin, so all bets were off. Until they knew everything there was to know about Wreath, Level 4 precautions would continue.

"*Dr. Kilpatrick to a hospital phone. Dr. Kilpatrick to a hospital phone.*"

Marty said a polite goodbye to the Treemonts and hurried over to the nearest nurse's station to get the call.

"This is Marty."

"What do you think you're doing?" Kurt snapped. Hargrove must have called him. Marty tried to make his boss see reason.

"Kurt, I tried to tell you what's going on here."

"I know what's going on there. You're spooked by something you can't understand."

"Hey, man, if this is some kind of turf thing, go screw, okay? I know what I know, and if you don't want to believe it, that's fine. I went over your head. Get over it."

"You didn't go over my head, you went to a different *department.*"

"So? This is an off world infection, I called the off world people."

"That was entirely premature!"

"No. It wasn't."

Vanessa sipped her coffee and read the news, only half focused on the words scrolling down her screen. Who was she kidding? She wasn't focused on the news at all. Half of her mind was worried about Nashua, and the other half was churning over Saturday night.

I think I'm a little drunk.

A little? You're half in the bag.

I am, at most, one fifth in the bag.

She tried to force herself to not think about it. Instead, she tried to put her entire mind to work on the infection issue. If they really did have an extraterrestrial virus infecting humans, that would put a huge pressure on every aspect of off world affairs. Screening processes on the three orbital immigration platforms would have to be beefed up. And who knows how they'd screen the visitors who were already on the surface. They'd tried to maintain a census of them, but that was a catch-as-can sort of thing, even for those who registered upon arrival. Not all of them registered. According to Terry—

Maybe I should take you home.

Maybe you should.

Stop it! Stop it!

Her phone rang and she answered it mid-ring. "What!?"

"Ms. Hargrove, this is Dr. Ripple. I have Secretary Zilner and Dr. Kilpatrick on the line as well."

"Doctors," Vanessa said, trying to calm down. She knew Mackenzie Zilner, the Secretary of Heath and Human Services, from their infrequent Cabinet meetings. "Mack," she said.

"Vanessa," Mackenzie answered.

"This is Marty. Kilpatrick. Hi. Yeah, so I have some information that I just gave Kurt and Secretary Zilner, and they said I should tell you, too."

"Go ahead."

"Okay, well, Patient Zero is a woman named Eleanor Winn. Forty-two years old, Asian ancestry, medical professor at UNH, currently doing research on human-alien DNA comparison."

"Off worlders have DNA?" Vanessa asked, subtly suggesting Kilpatrick use a less provocative term for extraterrestrials.

"Well, they all have some kind of genetic coding mechanisms, though, yeah, none of them are actually deoxyribonucleic acid. She had samples of Gorilla genetic material, working from the theory that a race so physiologically similar to our own hominid cousins might have similar genetic structure."

"Certainly." The arrival of Gorillas to the system two months ago had sparked a minor controversy in environmentalist circles. They objected to the name "Gorillas" for this race, claiming that this would devalue the actual gorillas, which were still flirting with extinction here on Earth. Vanessa's team had ignored them—rightly. She had every sympathy for gorillas, but her mandate was to keep the public comfortable with their off world visitors. Big-G Gorillas were just a bit shorter than humans, furry, long-armed, and broad-browed. If not for their vermillion coloring, they might have been mistaken for Earth gorillas by anyone outside zoological circles. People generally liked gorillas, so naming the new race was a no-brainer.

"I've gotten access to Eleanor's samples, and I found evidence of Wreath."

"Wreath?"

"That's Dr. Kilpatrick's name for the virus," Dr. Ripple explained.

"Alright. So you believe Eleanor contracted the disease from the samples."

"Well, no, not really. The virus can't survive outside a living host. So far, all the transmission has been oral."

Vanessa paused, trying to wrap her brain around that statement. Slowly, she spoke again.

"You're telling me... that this researcher—"

"Eleanor."

"Whatever. You're telling me that you think she... kissed a Gorilla?"

"No. I mean yes. I mean, I *know* she kissed one. She told me she did. She's... she's..."

"I get it." *She's a freak*, Vanessa didn't say. "And she passed it on to the other patients."

"Three of them. One of those boys has a girlfriend."

"Tell me you have this thing contained."

"We do," Dr. Ripple said.

"Yeah. He's right. I don't know if the patients will pull through, but we're not going to have any more infections."

"That's good news," Vanessa said.

"Now," Mackenzie said, "we have to make a determination."

"A determination of what?" Vanessa asked.

"What we should do with the virus," Dr. Ripple said. "For the record, I think we need to let it die."

"No!" Dr. Kilpatrick shouted. "We can't just kill it."

"Marty," Dr. Ripple scolded.

"There are other concerns," Mackenzie said. The Secretary was keeping far calmer than her people. "If humans contracted Wreath once, we'll probably do it again. It might be important to have a live sample ready for research into a vaccine or a cure."

"Ms. Hargrove," Dr. Ripple said, "I have to say that any kind of vaccine is remarkably unlikely. The virus is very different from human biochemistry. It's very possible that *no* antibody that can survive in the human bloodstream would counteract it."

"Kurt, that's nuts. If Wreath can live in us, we can counteract it. It's not *that* different."

"Vanessa, we didn't want to make a decision on this until we conferred with you. This is, in some sense, an off world matter."

"No kidding," Vanessa said. "How would you even keep a sample live? Didn't you say that it doesn't survive outside a living host?"

"Yeah, we could take a sample from a patient and then flash-freeze it," Dr. Kilpatrick said.

"That is very risky," Dr. Ripple said.

"Not really, Kurt," Mackenzie added.

"Yes, ma'am."

"The tricky part would be transporting the virus," Vanessa said. "I wouldn't want it on a plane."

"Agreed," Mackenzie said.

"You've got a CDC branch up in Vermont, don't you?"

Mackenzie laughed. "No, not really. People think we do because of that Stephen King book. Our closest office is in Maryland." Vanessa felt a chill. That was uncomfortably close to home.

"I can get the sample and drive it down to Hyattsville personally," Dr. Kilpatrick said. "It'll be fun. Road trip!"

"Marty!" Dr. Ripple scolded.

"That sounds like a good plan. I'd like to be kept in the loop on that, and on the condition of the patients in Nashua."

"We'll take care of it," Dr. Ripple said.

"We also need to inform the media," she continued.

"Of what?" Dr. Ripple asked.

"That people shouldn't be kissing Gorillas?" Vanessa asked, allowing some sarcasm to show. She was getting a little sick of Ripple and his caustic tone.

"Of course."

"We'll put together a release and send it over to you for your input," Mackenzie said smoothly.

"Good."

"And Vanessa, thanks for your help," Mackenzie added.

"I'm just glad we've got a happy ending here."

On Monday night at 11:39 PM, Eleanor Winn died. Marty stayed with her for her last moments, holding her hand through a bulky glove. She had no family in the country, and all of her boyfriends were in nearby rooms, fighting for their lives as well. If his information on the timeline of infection was accurate, then it would be a bad night.

Stephen Albie died on Tuesday morning at 2:31. Christopher Pollock's death followed at 5:11. Marty thought that was a little strange. He had estimated they would go within minutes of each other. Maybe Eleanor had underestimated the times between her encounters with the two young men. Maybe Chris had a better immune system. The discrepancy probably didn't mean anything.

Marty was a little worried that the flash-freeze equipment wouldn't get to the hospital on time. Someone was driving it up from Harvard, but there was a heavy snowstorm hitting western Massachusetts this morning. Sandy and Frankie only had a few hours left. He had to get the sample before they died. He had confirmed that only a few minutes after the others' deaths, they were entirely free of active viral agents.

The sun rose a little before seven that morning. Sandy and Frankie were still holding on. In fact, they were doing really well. Marty was pleased to see it, even though it didn't make any sense. Why would they be doing so much better than those earlier in the path of infection? Viruses didn't *lose* strength from carrier to carrier.

Well, Earth viruses didn't.

On the other hand, if they purged Wreath from their own blood-streams before he could get a sample, he'd lose his chance. He wanted to get that sample, but he wanted them to get better, too.

The courier arrived from Harvard with the surprisingly small device. It looked like a one-slice toaster, with a door on top instead of a slot. He rushed the machine into Sandy's room and lowered the lights, wanting to do everything possible to keep the Wreath alive for transfer. He assured Sandy—who looked scared by the way Marty was hurrying about—that everything was going very well. She would pull through, he said. He took a vial of blood from her arm and dropped it into the freezer. With a se-date little whooshing sound, it was instantly frozen. He hoped there were enough living Wreath in there to be useful for research.

He followed the same procedure in Frankie's room, then packed both frozen vials into a cold case for the trip down to Maryland.

Kurt came back to his office Tuesday morning to find the fifth draft of their press release on his screen. He couldn't do his job at the CDC without a certain amount of media savvy, but this was getting ridiculous. Hargrove's people kept making little changes to the language. He realized that her job was different from his, but he had no illusions about which was more important. If offending every alien on the planet would save a single human life, he'd do it. Gladly.

Kurt's phone rang. He answered it, fully expecting to hear Hargrove complaining about some new problem with the release, perhaps his spell-ing or his choice of the subjunctive voice. Instead, he heard Marty's voice.

"Kurt, I've got the..." His voice trailed off. The sound of the phone dropping followed. Then he heard a rumbling sound, a faraway screech, and a loud bang.

"Marty! Are you there?"

Nothing. Eerie silence.

Kurt kept the phone to his ear and called out the door. "Candace!" She hurried in. "Get me the NSA on another line."

"NASA?"

"Not NASA. N-S-A!"

Kurt had never needed to make use of the National Security Agency before, but he knew from his orientation years ago that their services were, in an emergency, at his fingertips. Candace called through the door to tell him they were on line 2. He put Marty on hold and switched over. He gave the NSA operator his code word, which shunted the call to a surveillance team.

"Go ahead," a voice said.

"I need a location of the cell phone on a call that is currently live, and I need it now. This is a health emergency."

"Number of the phone," the man asked, sounding a little too much like a robot for Kurt's taste. Kurt rattled off Marty's cell phone number. "Hold please."

Kurt switched back to the other line and called for Marty. There was still no answer. He had to assume there had been a car accident. Marty might be dead. Actually, that might be the least dangerous scenario, since the virus would likely die with him. Kurt hated himself for thinking that. But he still thought it.

He switched back to the NSA.

"Sir? Sir? Sir?"

"Sorry. I was checking to make sure the line was still active."

"The call is originating from the south-east corner of Susquehanna State Park, on Interstate 95, outside Havre de Grace, Maryland."

"Is it moving?" Kurt asked as he made notes.

"Not at present."

"Thanks."

"Do you require further monitoring?"

"No, that's—"

The man hung up. Kurt almost laughed. He checked Marty's line again, and continued to hear silence at the other end. He switched back to line 2 to alert the Hyattsville team to a Level 4 biohazard at Marty's location. Next he called Secretary Zilner. Once he explained the situation to her, she immediately conferenced in Hargrove. *Her* response wasn't very controlled.

"What the fuck are you people doing over there?"

"Vanessa, we're taking care of it," Zilner said.

"Where's Dr. Kilpatrick now?"

"We have a team on the way," Kurt said. "He'll be moved to our Hyattsville facility and put in quarantine."

"I'm going over there," Hargrove said.

"Vanessa," Secretary Zilner said with a little chuckle. "You really should let us take care of it."

"I'm not asking permission. I'm telling you what's going to happen. Let them know I'm coming and tell them to have credentials waiting for me."

Kurt felt an honest-to-goodness headache forming behind his right eye. "That's not a good idea, Secretary Hargrove."

"I guess today is just a day filled with bad ideas, then, isn't it?" She slammed down the phone. Kurt heard Zilner sigh.

"Do as she asked, Kurt."

"I…" He wanted to rail against this. Hargrove hadn't *asked* for anything. She was way outside her authority on this, cabinet officer or not. If Kurt had actually been up there, he'd probably have stood his ground and fought her. But down here in Atlanta, despite being the director of the CDC, he'd just been overruled by not one, but *two* cabinet officers. "I'll take care of it."

"Thanks."

He just wished he knew why Hargrove was being such a world-class bitch.

Two hours later, Vanessa walked through the doors of the Hyattsville offices of the CDC with three aides in tow behind her. A tall man, hair graying at the temples, wearing a cliché white coat and horn-rimmed glasses, met her in the lobby.

"Secretary Hargrove, I'm Jack Avery."

She shook his offered hand. "Dr. Avery."

"Jack, please. I understand you're here to see Marty."

"If that's possible," she said. The fire burning in her gut when she forced her way into the investigation that morning had lessened considerably. There was no need to take out her frustrations on this guy, anyway. She motioned for the aides to take a seat in the waiting area. It was pointless for them all to go through decontamination.

"I'll show you to his room," Dr. Avery said.

"Hopefully not *into* his room."

Jack smiled. "I *was* told to give you complete access."

Vanessa almost laughed.

As she followed Dr. Avery through the building, she was struck by how mundane it all looked. Most of the corridors and office areas could have been any place Vanessa had ever worked—universities, JPL, the Smithsonian. It wasn't until they reached the Biosafety Level 4 containment perimeter that things started to look like a movie. She had to go through a whole decontamination procedure, which seemed very odd to her. Wasn't the whole point to keep the bugs *in*, not *out*? They put her through a UV bath, then something like a wind tunnel. Since she wasn't going into any of the hot zones directly, she was spared a full shower. All that was left was to pull on bulky white scrubs over her street clothes, slip booties over her feet, and yank a hideous paper cap over her red curls.

"Now no one will be able to tell you're a politician," Jack joked. Vanessa found the joke amusing... and depressing.

He led her to a viewing window. Beyond, a heavyset man with a frowzy afro and a thick, saltandpepper beard lay on a bed.

"He's not on a ventilator. That's a good sign."

"Perhaps," Jack said vaguely.

"Perhaps? I don't understand."

"The disease is not presenting in Dr. Kilpatrick like it did with the others."

"How so?"

"Eleanor Winn, our Patient Zero, died forty hours after infection. She didn't lose consciousness until hour thirtytwo. Marty here is only in what we believe to be hour three. He was unconscious practically from the initial contact with the virus."

"He was in a car accident, wasn't he?"

"He wasn't injured in the crash. His car slid against a guard rail and hit a tree at less than ten miles an hour. We believe, however, he may have been exposed to a hugely increased concentration of the virus."

That didn't sound good. The look on Vanessa's face made her feelings clear as she stared at the unconscious patient. Jack gently touched her on the arm to suggest she follow him again. He led her into a lab where a halfdozen techs were doing various analyses on tablets. He stopped at a sample table. On the table were the fragments of shattered test tubes, a broken cold case, and an oversized Zero Halliburton briefcase.

"All of this has been decontaminated. There's no danger. As you can see, something quite extraordinary happened."

"This wasn't a result of the crash?"

"This all happened prior to the crash. First, this test tube broke."

"From the cold."

"Marty lowered the samples to two degrees above absolute zero. At some point in his drive down from Nashua, the temperature within the unit rose to forty-five Celsius."

"The unit malfunctioned?"

"No. We're fairly sure the virus heated the unit from within."

"The *virus* did this?"

Jack used a pen to point to the components as he explained. "The temperature in this test tube rose phenomenally fast, shattering the glass. The material inside the first tube then moved to this other test tube, and broke it from the outside."

"What? That can't be some sort of accident, can it?"

"No. Then the virus attacked the interior of the cold case chamber, here, subjecting it to temperatures in excess of seven thousand degrees."

"Seven thousand... Why didn't it melt?"

"It did. Right there." He pointed. Vanessa had to lean down and squint to see, but there was a tiny, pinpoint section of the casing that was distorted and slightly blackened. "The stresses on that point eventually cracked the entire unit open. This briefcase is not airtight, unfortunately, which allowed the virus to escape—"

"Escape?"

"Yes, escape, and then infect Marty."

"You're describing the actions of an intelligent being."

"More likely several billion intelligent beings, but yes, that's basically right."

"Dear God," Vanessa breathed. "Is it contained? It was out in that car for a while before your team arrived."

"We were there in twenty minutes. We found traces of Wreath all over the car, on all of this equipment, and up to three feet from the driver's door on the street. All of these samples were dead. The only living Wreath are in Marty at the moment. Whatever the Wreath did, they sacrificed millions of themselves in this... jail break."

Vanessa paused to let *that* sink in. A new race to add to the ros-
ter—Wreath. They'd already killed three people and were working on
killing a fourth. On the other hand, humanity had killed likely billions of
them. Were they even individuals, or some kind of sentient swarm? Did it
matter? Could they even let the Wreath live? People had argued over the
morality of completely eradicating the polio, anthrax, HIV viruses. How
much more complicated was this? Very. The questions swirled, too many
for her to focus on all at once.

"Can we communicate with them?" she asked, almost not wanting to
hear the answer.

"We don't know how to even begin," Jack admitted. "All things considered, we're kind of glad you bullied your way in here."

"I wish the feeling was mutual."

Jack gave Vanessa and her team a small office and some decommissioned tablets to start working with her department on the Wreath problem. When her underlings were off and running, she put in a call to Victor Fremont, the President's Chief of Staff.

"Can we kill it?" She wasn't surprised that was his first question. It
had been her second question, after all.

"They were able to knock out the virus in two of the Nashua patients with antibiotics. Nothing is working on Dr. Kilpatrick at all. He
seems to be basically ignoring everything they do to him. The Wreath are
learning how to defend themselves."

"Then we may be forced to do something drastic," Fremont said, his
voice low, ominous.

"I know. I've mentioned it to Dr. Avery."

"I suppose he didn't like that."

"*I* don't like it, and neither do you, Victor."

"True enough. Total media blackout."

"Absolutely." Until there's a leak, she didn't say. But she didn't need
to. Victor was a realist. There hadn't been a serious leak out of DOWA
since zinc, so he seemed to be giving her the benefit of the doubt.

"I'll inform the President."

That afternoon, Vanessa's department, in concert with the CDC, conducted a very quiet round-up of all the Gorillas on the planet. Thankfully, there were only fifteen—that they knew of. The visitors were told about the Nashua outbreak, though not the new developments, or the intelligent nature of the Wreath virus. They claimed ignorance on the topic. All fifteen submitted to testing, and only one—the one with whom Eleanor had "experimented"—had evidence of Wreath in his system. The infected Gorilla used an intravenous treatment they had brought with them and instantly flushed the Wreath from his system.

As afternoon turned to evening and evening became night, Dr. Avery returned to Vanessa's borrowed office.

"You should go home."

"We need to monitor the situation."

She didn't tell him she simply didn't want to go home.

You need any help?

Maybe I do.

Vanessa, you—

She jerked, physically reacting to the memory. It was one of those terrible, *terrible* memories that the mind can't seem to stop repeating, regardless of the emotional pain attached to it.

Stop.

I...

Don't worry about it.

Sorry.

It's okay. I should go.

Uh-huh.

"It's not just that, Vanessa," Jack said. She'd almost forgotten that the doctor was still standing there, having a conversation with her.

"It's not just what?"

"You may not be safe."

"Safe?"

"We have no idea what Wreath can do. We're monitoring Marty, but it could be preparing for another jailbreak."

Vanessa barked a dark laugh. "If it can get through all of those walls, we've got bigger problems than needing a new Secretary of Off World Affairs."

Jack put a comforting hand on her shoulder. At another time, she would have been pleasantly surprised by that show of affection. She might have explored it, returned it, even upped the ante to see where this might go. After what she'd done on Saturday night, though, her self-confidence on *that* score was at perhaps a lifetime low. True, she wasn't currently drunk, nor did she have a longstanding working relationship with Jack Avery, nor was the difference in their ages so drastic, nor was Jack a flashy, handsome, unobtainable test pilot.

The currents of her thoughts were taking her to a dark place again. She shook her head and gave Jack what she hoped looked like a platonically friendly smile. She parsed out the wording of her next request very carefully.

"Is there somewhere I can crash for the night?" Then she turned to her aides, who looked ready for a nap, too. "We, I mean..."

Jack paused, as if putting as much thought into her question as she had. Vanessa used every ounce of psychic power that she didn't really have to *will* him to understand that all she wanted was a place to sleep. For a wonder, he did.

"I'll find some empty beds for you."

Marty stopped being scared after only a few minutes. Sure, he couldn't move, talk, do anything at all. But he could still think. He came to the same conclusion as his colleagues in the CDC—that the Wreath were intelligent. Unlike his colleagues, he held no fear that they were malevolent. If they could bring him to a complete stop like this without killing him, their purposes couldn't be evil, could they? Of course not.

So he watched, patiently, and with some professional curiosity as the CDC team arrived and cordoned off the site of the accident. They extracted him from the car and ferried him back to their offices, putting him into a bed in the Level 4 quarantine area.

Then, of course, things got really boring. Even when someone came into his room—suited up against a viral threat they knew to be very *tenacious*—he rarely saw much, since his eyes were pointed, unmovingly, at the ceiling. He heard little as well, since no one bothered to talk to someone so obviously in a catatonic state. The biggest moments were when a nurse would eye-drop some moisture into his unblinking eyes.

Marty decided that the Wreath could only be doing one thing: trying to figure out a way to communicate. It was late that night—at least he thought it was late—when his eyes moved. It was disconcertingly slow, as if his eyeballs were gigantic lead weights lying in pools of viscous oil. Whatever the Wreath were doing, they were being careful about it. He didn't mind. His scenery changed—albeit only by a few degrees—for the first time in many hours.

Next, he felt movement in his fingers. They contracted and released with the same eerie, dreamlike slowness that his eyes had shifted. Each of the digits was tested separately, then each wrist rotated from one extreme to the other. Elbows flexed, shoulders shifted and moved in wide, slow arcs.

His eyes sped up their movement. His neck began to twist from side to side. His jaw worked. The muscles around his lips curled his face into what felt like humorous, childlike parodies of emotion.

Marty certainly missed the feeling of volition, but for the time being, he found the whole process fascinating, as an alien culture explored human anatomy from the inside out.

"Vanessa. Vanessa." A strong but gentle hand shook her out of her slumber. She looked up from the crisp, white sheets of the hospital bed to see Jack Avery towering over her.

"Something happened?"

"You bet."

She spared only a moment for thoughts of how terrible she must look after a day of stress and a too-short night of fitful sleep. Jack brought her back to the viewing window of Marty's room. Marty was awake and standing at the window, his hands against the glass, his eyes taking in everything. When he saw Vanessa, his gaze locked on her, but his face registered no emotion. Jack toggled a switch for the intercom.

"Your head is very colorful," Marty said, his speech toneless and somewhat halting, sounding nothing like the breezy bohemian she'd talked to on the phone on Monday.

"Dr. Kilpatrick, I'm Vanessa Hargrove. We talked a couple of days ago."

"We have not accessed personal memories of the host. This is not permitted."

Vanessa threw a worried look at Jack. He shrugged. "This is your area, not mine." She looked again to Marty.

"You're not Marty."

"We are the viral infestation you call Wreath."

"Is Marty alright?"

"The host is undamaged. He is physically deactivated for the time being. His mind continues unabated. Cessation of mental function is not permitted."

"Okay... You arrived in the Gorilla host?"

There was a pause. "Gorilla is your name for the previous race we used as a host. We understand. Yes."

"Good. Then, what are your intentions?"

This pause was longer still. The way Marty remained entirely motionless was creeping Vanessa out. Finally, he came to life again.

"This question is multi-layered. We wish no harm to come to the host; it is not permitted. We desire, but do not require, additional hosts. We request cessation of hostilities against our culture. We desire, but do not require, to remain in host for research purposes. We have learned the necessary interfacing protocols to avoid future negative physiological reaction. We offer our apology for loss of life. We will, upon ratification of bilateral accords, relinquish all control of this host to originating consciousness; furtherance of deactivation is not permitted. If such is not acceptable, we request to be returned to Gorilla host."

"I think I understand." Vanessa didn't want to tell the Wreath just yet that going back to the Gorillas wasn't in the cards anymore. "I'll need to speak with the host before we can agree to any of this."

"Protocols for interface with musculature have been systematized. We will continue to monitor."

"Okay."

Vanessa watched as the stillness left Marty's frame. From the extremities in, his body shifted from its rigid pose to a more natural, human look. Finally, the light seemed to go on in his eyes and he smiled at Vanessa.

"Wild, huh?" he said with a broad grin.

"You heard all that?"

"Sure. They never disconnected my senses. These guys are *really* good at what they do."

"So you understand what they're asking for."

"Uh-huh. They want to hitch a ride, which I'm all for."

"Slow down, there, Marty," Jack interceded. "We can't even be sure we're really talking to you."

"You're kidding, right? These guys are so stiff, they're almost British, man! I'm me."

"Why should we trust them?" Vanessa asked. "They've killed before."

"Not on purpose. Look at what they did. Every patient they encountered they hurt *less*. They practically died out entirely in Sandy and Frankie, they were so worried about killing their hosts. If I hadn't taken that sample and given them a chance to regroup, they *would* be dead."

"Do you have any idea how many of them are in there?" Vanessa asked.

"I dunno. Probably a lot."

"My point is, they're an entire culture. A deal we make with them now, even if they're entirely sincere, might be reneged by the next generation, or the generation after that. Those generations might be measured in hours. If we let them stay in you, they could infect others, they could do *anything*. We know they can take you over, access your memories."

"Yeah, it's real *Invasion of the Body Snatchers* type stuff. I get it. But what else are you gonna do?"

Neither Vanessa nor Jack answered. Their silence told the tale.

"Oh," Marty said, understanding. "Bummer."

Jack shook his head. "I can't believe our only two options are killing Marty—and the genocide of an entire culture, by the way—or putting humanity at risk for enslavement by an alien virus."

"I talked earlier with our local CA representative about the Wreath. He said he knew of them, but hadn't known them to be hostile."

"There you go!" Marty was excited by the news. "Then you can let me go."

"No, Marty," Vanessa said. "It's not that simple. Just because we never heard of them causing trouble doesn't mean they won't."

"Vanessa…" Jack said, his tone familiar and imploring. She shot him a look that said, *Right now I'm the Secretary.* Jack backed off. Marty did not.

"Look, they're sorry about what happened, but they can't take it back, right? Nobody can take back a mistake."

You need any help?

Maybe I do.

"Hey, you know, you're *her*, right? You're Vanessa Hargrove! You're the one who said, 'Let the barrier fall.' You trusted the entire galaxy back then. What happened to you, man?"

Vanessa, you—Stop.

The memory of that ill-timed, too-short, unwanted kiss felt like a weight pulling down on her chest. Her whole body slumped in sympathy to the emotional toll on her heart. Why? Why had she done it?

Because to *not* do it would have been worse, regardless of the consequences. She couldn't have lived with herself if she hadn't made that leap, taken that risk. Regret for lost opportunity had to be the worst emotion of all. Regret stays with you. Forever.

Marty continued to make his case. "It's always been about trust, that we can keep a relationship going even after something bad happens. That's what being human is all about, okay? I trust them, and I'm right *there*. I'm not going to give up on the Wreath, so if you feel like you have to lock me away forever, then so be it." Marty followed this up by a single, decisive nod.

"You're right," Vanessa said.

"He is?" Jack asked.

"I am?"

She turned to Jack. "I'll recommend to Mackenzie and Dr. Ripple that you let him out. If we want the galaxy to forgive us for our mistakes, we can't ask any less of ourselves."

Jack looked at her, surprised, maybe even a little impressed.

"You're sure about this."

"Yeah," she said, putting a hand on his arm to underline her point. "Maybe we'll even learn something."

Numinous

> *Think of the universal sub-*
> *stance, of which thou hast a very*
> *small portion; and of universal*
> *time, of which a short and indivisi-*
> *ble interval has been assigned to*
> *thee; and of that which is fixed by*
> *destiny, and how small a part of it*
> *thou art.*
> —*Meditations, V, 24*

"I need you to go to England and deal with the Vampires."

Terry stopped short in the middle of General Brown's office, nearly spilling his mug of tea. He had expected a regular update meeting, nothing as dramatic as this.

"Has something happened?"

"They've hit five hundred." He knew instantly what she meant.

"Five hundred? There are *five hundred* Vampires in Birmingham? What are they all doing?"

"As far as the Brits can tell, they're praying." She followed that with a knowing tilt of her head. Terry didn't quite understand. He set down his tea and his tablet on Brown's desk and sat across from her.

"Okay... What?"

"You're religious. That's why we're sending you to talk to the Vam-pires, find out if we have a real problem over there."

"I'm religious?"

"Where were you this past Sunday?"

"I was in church."

"There you go."

"It was *Easter.* Everyone was in church."

"I wasn't."

"Aren't you Jewish?"

"You're missing the point."

"What's the point?"

"That you're going."

"Oh."

"Zealots," Kird said simply, his quicklight image flickering into digital chaos for a moment, then resolving.

"Really? Like, strap dynamite to their chests and blow stuff up zealots?" Terry asked.

"Certainly not. They are, however, zealous in their belief."

"And that is?"

"I do not know. I am unfamiliar with the details of their religious dogma. I am sorry."

Kird was the first person Terry chose to talk to after being given this somewhat delicate task. He planned to discuss the Vampires with a number of people in the Off World office, including Vanessa, of course. He still felt a little hinky around her, but she seemed to have completely forgotten about that kiss. She'd been dating some doctor in the CDC for the past few months, anyway. The guy seemed to be good for her, even if he was kind of a stiff.

To be perfectly honest about it, Terry had wanted to say, "It was just because you were drunk. Otherwise…" Otherwise didn't mean much now, with her going out with someone else. He'd dated a couple of girls since, too—not at the same time, of course. But nothing came of either of them. Which was fine. He was still young. He had time.

"Do you have any advice for me? I've never done a… spiritual conference before." Terry would have preferred taking Kird with him to England, but the Teddy Bear was off to Wolf 359 on some hush-hush CA business. Terry didn't feel slighted when Kird said he couldn't divulge the nature of his trip. He understood the need for security.

"Your culture embraces the spiritual as much as almost any in the galaxy. I suspect you have better native instincts on the matter than I."

"Teddy Bears don't go in for religion?"

Kird's long pause before he answered was more eloquent than his eventual words.

"Not as such."

Terry's jump plane trip to England took nearly an hour. The plane landed at Birmingham International at about 7 PM, local time. A stiffly formal black gentleman in British Army uniform waited at the base of the steps.

"Major Youngblood?" he asked.

"That's right." Terry double-timed down the stairs and offered the man his hand.

"Major Elias Twigge, 1st Military Intelligence Battalion. Welcome to England."

"Good to be here."

"Up for a short ride?"

"Sure. Why not?" Terry was still on D.C. time. He'd be awake for many hours yet.

Twigge led Terry to a waiting Land Rover and climbed into the driver's seat.

"No driver?" Terry joked.

"Someone has been working in Washington for too long," Twigge answered, his tone headmasterish.

"Don't I know it."

Twigge started the car and they sped toward the airport exit.

"London's the same. Too fancy by half. Give me good old North England any day of the week."

"And twice on Sundays."

Twigge laughed.

They drove out of the city, to the south-west.

"I thought the Vampires were in Birmingham."

"They were for quite some while. Last month they moved en masse out to Walton Hill." Twigge pointed to a rise in the distance. In the failing light, Terry saw campfires blazing.

"There?"

"There."

"You know, my daddy always said, 'It's better to let the bear come to you.' Should we be going out to see them... at night?" Terry reminded himself that the visitors weren't really *vampires*.

"On the contrary, this is precisely the time to go."

A few minutes—and a few miles off road—later, they were near the crest of the hill. Twigge parked the Land Rover. The bright lights of the city twinkled behind them. The night was clear and cool, the sky brilliant with stars. Terry couldn't remember the last time he'd just looked up at the night sky. With his job, those stars were his main concern, and he never got the chance to simply enjoy them.

"Come along, then," Twigge said, his tone mildly scolding.

"Sorry."

Twigge led him farther up the hill, toward the source of the flames. Those weren't campfires. Those were bonfires, blazing high and hot, throwing sparks and smoke up into the darkening sky. Terry looked around at all the brush, expecting a full-on forest fire to ignite at any second. He figured it hadn't happened yet, or else the Brits would have been yelling even louder than they already were.

Then Terry saw his first Vampire in the flesh. This one was nearly seven feet from toe to head. Its back was to them as it loped up the trail toward the hilltop. He and Twigge were tramping along faster than the Vampire, catching up to it. Twigge put a hand to Terry's chest to stop him. The Vampire sensed someone behind. It turned its long, beaked head and stared at Terry with pitiless, glistening black eyes. Terry froze, suddenly knowing what a mouse feels like when stalked by a bat.

The Vampire turned away and unfurled its magnificent wings. The firelight shown through the membranous flesh, highlighting a maze of veins and bones and musculature. The Vampire crouched, then with a single, loud *fwapp*, took off into the air, flying ahead faster than humans could hope to follow.

"They're rather shy," Twigge said.

"Shy. Right."

About a half-mile later, as the sky edged toward full dark, Twigge and Terry reached the edge of the clearing at the top of Walton Hill. Five bonfires were arranged in a cross pattern, about fifty yards apart. The area within and immediately surrounding the blazing pyres was filled with Vampires, all milling about. Hands twitched, wings fluttered, feet stamped.

"Is this part of the ceremony, or are they just like that?"

"Bit of both," Twigge answered.

Terry didn't register any kind of signal, but as one the Vampires stopped their fidgeting and froze, turned toward the tallest fire in the center of the formation. A low hum rose up over the crackling of the flames, never increasing in pitch, but growing louder and louder, to the point Terry had to cover his ears. He wasn't surprised when Twigge stuffed in earplugs. All the Vampires raised their clawed hands over their heads, intertwining their six fingers. Like some kind of communal yoga exercise, they all bowed their heads and stretched their clasped hands forward toward the central flame, their tightly folded wings extending behind. Terry made a note to dig up a satellite video of one of these ceremonies. It would probably look quite lovely... from the safety of orbit.

On the ground, he felt a sort of spiritual electricity in the air that he didn't understand, and so, feared. Many times he'd seen just as many people at church on a Sunday, singing hymns in unison and bowing their heads in prayer. He would sing along with them, feeling a faint tug of his heart in the words and the music and the community around him. Maybe to a Vampire—or any other off world race, for that matter—Christianity seemed just as eerie and dangerous as this fire ceremony. But that didn't change how Terry felt. He remained tense and guarded.

Another unheard, unseen signal ended the ritual. The hum came to an abrupt end. Every Vampire rose to a standing position. All sense of synchronization ended, as Terry watched most of the Vampires break into conversation groups, some flying off, others tending to the fires, which were carefully doused. A couple of them activated tall artificial lights that Terry hadn't noticed before. In ten seconds, all of Terry's irrational fear fled.

"Well, there you are," Twigge said, pulling the plugs from his ears.

"Okay. They didn't actually... do anything."

"They haven't *yet* done anything. We remain concerned. Imagine this scene played out in Nebraska. How would your government react?"

One of the Vampires caught sight of the visiting humans and moved toward them. It seemed they weren't entirely comfortable walking, perhaps because of Earth's gravity, or its atmospheric pressure. In any case, Terry had plenty of time to point and ask if Twigge expected this.

"Yes. You need to meet Elt."

Twigge, Terry and the Vampire retired to a spot a few feet away from the bulk of the crowd, who were focused on setting up some sort of buffet meal.

"Elt, this is Major Terry Youngblood, from the States."

"Major," Elt said, his beaked mouth giving the words a strange, rubbery quality. "It is a pleasure to meet you."

Terry steeled himself against that ebony, unblinking stare, and offered a hand. Elt shook politely, careful not to skewer Terry with his claws.

"Elt is in a unique position to advise us, Major Youngblood."

"You are?"

"I am," he said. His words were quite understandable, if not entirely natural to him. "This is because I am not a Vampire."

"Well, I know that none of you are *really* vampires..." Terry said lamely.

"No, you misunderstand. I am... Major Twigge, what is the name again?"

"A Snake."

"Ah, yes. I am a Snake. How colorfully you name us."

"You're... a Snake? I'm confused."

"Of course. Let me explain. Many races—Snakes and Vampires among them—are able to undergo what we call a personality transfer procedure. One's memories are shifted from the body of their birth—in my case, the body of a Snake—into the body of another—in my case, a Vampire. Ktalala—the Vampire who originated this body—is currently on my home world, seeking out Convergence Zones, sheathed in my Snake body. Snakes are somewhat less open about their home world than Humans, I am particularly ashamed to say. And so, this exchange suits both our goals."

Terry never imagined that anyone could actually *switch bodies* like that. He'd seen a couple of TV shows as a kid that trafficked in that kind of fantasy, which to a horny little kid opened a treasure chest of forbidden opportunities. Now that he found out it was real, and that aliens did it for...

"Why'd you do it?" he asked. "Are you a convert to the Vampire religion?"

"Oh, far from it. I am... how should I put it... a mythologist."

"You study myth."

"I study religions, their beliefs, their practices. Vampires have a fascinating spiritual belief system, one of a number of monocultural systems I am currently researching for an article on the subject."

"Could you explain a little about what they believe, and what they're doing here?" Terry asked. Twigge made a face, as if he'd heard all this before and didn't give it much credence. Elt noted his discomfiture.

"Major Twigge is a dedicated atheist. He finds little of my work interesting."

"It's interesting, no doubt," Twigge said. "I simply don't believe in it."

"And the Vampires don't believe in Christ the Risen Lord, either. Such things tend to even out, don't you think?" Elt responded.

Terry smirked. "Well, Elt, I'm a believer. A Christian, I mean. But I still would like to understand the Vampires better."

"You wish to understand them so that you can determine if they represent a threat to Earth."

"Sure."

Elt nodded. Without facial muscles or eyelids, Terry didn't have many cues to the Elt's emotional state. But at least the researcher didn't seem angry. Which was good. In a hand-to-hand fight, Terry figured he'd give a Vampire good odds at coming out on top against the best humanity had to offer.

"To put a simple cast on a complex system of belief, the Vampires worship the future."

"The future? They don't have a god?"

"That is a very insightful question, Major Youngblood. They do have a god, and that god is the future. They have what might be considered to be a uniquely optimistic view of the nature of the universe. Each action—both those occurring in the natural world and those caused by the choices of willed beings such as ourselves—are categorized as either good or evil. In fact, the categorization is quite intricate, with levels of holiness and unholiness measured minutely, and on a broad scale.

"They believe that every action contributes to the whole of the universe. They see the universe not as a continuously moving collection of particles and energy as would a scientist, but as a single construct, contiguous in past, present and future. We may only be able to sense one tiny slice of that monolithic whole at any time, but it exists, complete in and of itself beyond our senses."

"They're determinists," Terry concluded.

"They are indeed. But make no mistake, they believe in free will. They simply believe that the shape of the future is decided, and that all of those countless instances wherein we exercise our free will form part of the tapestry of the final, culminating whole."

"So, tonight, with the bonfires, they were worshiping... some event in the future?"

"Only in the simplest sense. They are worshipping this place. This hill. They have determined that it is a Convergence Zone. The sum total of all the events which have, are and will occur here have a profound positive impact on the eventual nature of the universe."

"What is the eventual nature of the universe?" Terry asked.

"That is the most interesting part of all." Elt's "face" didn't betray any emotion, but the tone of his voice more than compensated, revealing his excitement. "The final result, the end of all things, the accumulation of all events in the cosmos, this *is* their god. God is, for the Vampires, quite literally everything. And they have founded their worship on their belief that, when all is said and done, the universe will weigh out as more good than bad. The entirety of our universe is, in some sense, a positive value at the bottom of a celestial ledger."

Terry smiled, wondering how a race could be *that* optimistic about the future.

"How good is it? The universe, I mean? What's the final total?" He glanced over at the still frowning Twigge. "According to them, I mean."

"Like any good contest, it is close, until the very end. And only in the final moments does good win out over evil."

Twigge chuckled. "That much I can believe."

The sunset bonfire ceremony turned out to be something like a Morning Mass for the Vampires, to start their day. They were, in fact, nocturnal creatures. Terry and Twigge spent several hours—with Elt as their guide—discussing the situation with the leaders of the group.

The Vampires calmly accepted the fact that the humans nearby were unsettled by their ceremonies on Walton Hill. Elt suggested a series of cultural exchanges with some of the local universities. Twigge explained he was an alum of nearby UCE, and offered to put them in contact with friends he had on their faculty in the Sociology Department.

When Terry asked how long they planned to continue the worship, the Vampires' leader said that it would be less than ten local years. They did not want to be here when any of the more critical future happenings were to occur. They couldn't interfere with the unfolding of the universe, only worship from a safe distance in the past or the future of those keystone events.

Twigge pulled Terry aside to thank him for the help. Terry accepted the thanks graciously, not voicing his own thought. If Twigge had just *listened* to what the Vampires had to say, rather than just rolling his eyes at it, the Brits might have missed out on a few years of paranoia.

As the sky lightened in the east, the Vampires retired to their nests in the trees below the crest of the hill. Terry continued to talk to Elt, who seemed to feed off of Terry's curiosity about his research.

"What do you believe?" Terry finally asked.

"About the Vampire mythology?"

"No, about everything. Do you have a religion?"

"Ah, the hard question. Had you asked me that a few billion ticks ago, I would have said the only thing I believed in was profit. A life in constant search of new markets and new ways to exploit them for personal gain finally left me asking that hard question, about the nature of the universe and our place in it. People such as Major Twigge find the question itself to be traitorous to logic in some way. It is a common enough view throughout the galaxy, this adherence to atheism.

"Most of your people—please correct me if I'm wrong—adhere to the beliefs of their parents, perpetuating various world religions in loosely contained racial enclaves."

"That's true, I suppose," Terry admitted. "But what do *you* believe?"

Elt paused a long time, gazing at the slowly brightening horizon.

"It is perhaps strange to admit, as a professed impartial scientist, that I do believe in a world beyond our world, a place of strange and beautiful light that we cannot possibly imagine and that only the bravest of us can contemplate in a way that is truly transcendent. There are as many belief systems in the galaxy as there are races. More, in fact. Most cultures have a division of belief, much like Humanity, monocultures such as the Vampires notwithstanding.

"If I have learned anything in my studies, it is not that *this* religion is wrong, whereas *that* religion is right. There are so many reasons to cling to so many modes of ideology, it is impossible for me to choose. So, I do not. I believe them all."

"How... How does that make any sense?"

Elt extended his wings for a moment, flapping them slowly. Terry supposed this was a nervous tic, like stroking a beard or cracking knuckles. Elt composed himself again.

"Imagine a house. It is a large and sturdy house, with many rooms, in which people live their lives and dream their dreams and pass through their days. It is natural for those in the house to imagine what lies *outside* the house. Are there others out there? What are they like? Did they build the house? Will the builders one day tear down the house? And what will become of those of us in the house at that time?

"Some believe that the house is all there is. There is no need to look beyond our senses. That wall? Beyond it lies nothing. I know this because I cannot look beyond it. And, in some sense, that is true. The wall cannot be torn down from within. It is, perhaps, impossible to fully understand something one cannot sense.

"But some few, some brave and perhaps foolhardy few, try to build *windows*. To build a window in this house is a dangerous, time-consuming, *life-consuming* job. To build a window requires support from others who believe that the window will show us what lies beyond the walls of the house. For those who begin the window, their lives wink out before the project is half complete. Those who follow must continue the work, calling more to their cause, to help in the construction of the window.

"The strange and beautiful light that permeates the world outside the house is deadly to mortal eyes, so all windows must be built to be cloudy, colored, misleading, protective. They cannot tell the full story of the outside, anymore than any window in any house will show the inhabitants all of the secrets of their surrounding neighborhood.

"Do these windows provide absolute truth? No. It is the nature of the outside that it cannot be contained, categorized, indexed, explained. Each window—from the most ornate and beautiful stained glass to the tiniest, frosted peephole—gives us a different glimpse of a greater truth that we cannot hope to understand fully.

"Major Twigge remains in the most interior of rooms in the house, believing that those on the fringes, peering through hazy windows, delude themselves that they are seeing anything of value.

"You, Major Youngblood, perhaps sit in a chair near the window of Christianity, glancing up at the rose colored light filtering through, shining on you and your brethren. Many, perhaps most of you are content that all you need to know about the outside comes through your window.

"The Vampires in this colony have encamped at their window of Convergence, staring unabashedly at the milky glow coming through their simple yet sturdy, translucent glass.

"I find *all* of the windows magical. Every one of them has something to say, some light to shed, some glimpse, however maddeningly vague, of the vastness and impossible light of *outside.*"

Terry didn't speak, instead looking at this once terrifying alien presence, thinking about his rambling, metaphysical metaphor. The sun had crested the horizon to the east, bathing Walton Hill in warm, golden light.

"Well, Major," Elt said, his tone now conversational again. "As much as I miss the sun after so long in this form, I must retire. This body requires it." He offered his clawed hand again for Terry to shake. "It was a pleasure to meet you."

"You as well, Elt," Terry said, quite honestly.

Information Technology

> *The things are three of which*
> *thou art composed: a little body, a*
> *little breath, intelligence. Of these*
> *the first two are thine, so far as it*
> *is thy duty to take care of them;*
> *but the third alone is properly*
> *thine.*
>
> —*Meditations, XII, 3*

John Gupta had by now lost most of his hair, one wife, the respect of his two children and the greater part of his peace of mind to the *Vimana* project. Essentially, life had treated John poorly on a personal level. His only solace was professional in nature; he was on schedule with the IRCPs.

Humanity had flirted with artificial intelligence for decades before the barrier fell. For some reason, a huge amount of the effort was focused on making better and better chess-playing algorithms, as if the ability to play chess was some kind of measure of intelligence. Grandmasters of the game were often as not paranoid, ill-tempered and sometimes delusional. Was that the best paradigm of intelligence they could find?

John had worked on the problem of AI in the 1990s when he was in grad school at IIT-B. His take on the problem was to focus on the ineffable qualities of decision making. He delved into the disciplines of psychology, neuroscience and philosophy to develop a quasi-neural network to mimic—in a small, controlled way—the mind's most intrinsically human process: volition.

His work was such a colossal disaster that they gave him the doctorate anyway. According to the notes his doctoral advisor appended to his dissertation, "...you have created a world class roadmap of the path to failure. Future generations of cyberneticists will consult your work the way modern astronomers would view a manuscript handed down by

Ptolemy." John took the derision good-naturedly. He got a teaching position out of it, and eventually tenure.

His current position as Project Lead on *Vimana* was evidence of how *close* he had really come all those years ago. The various algorithms that Maccha-Yantra had obtained from alien cultures bore a striking resemblance—in the most macroscopic way, of course—to his own work from thirty years earlier. Now, with the help of this otherworldly advice and the phenomenal advances in computing power of the last three decades, John Gupta had created the first fully autonomous artificial intelligences: IRCPs.

Initiative Ready Control Programs. In a sense, they were small minds of their own, fully integrated into the broader network that would eventually be *Vimana*. Automation was nothing new to the computer science industry. Urban traffic management algorithms, industrial mass fabrication, student standardized testing. All of these things and more functioned with little or no human intervention. A well built program could do the job of a hundred expert humans, and usually do it better. But what *Vimana* needed was something more, something with the ability to react to unknown circumstances.

John's designs for the IRCPs were revolutionary because they did not specify what action to perform at any given point. Only the final goal—the successful completion of the mission—was coded directly. It was up to the IRCP in question to *determine* what needed to happen to fulfill that goal with the greatest efficiency.

On the other hand, an IRCP was far from the commonplace definition of "artificial intelligence". For example, none of the IRCPs could hope to pass a Turing Test. If confronted with an IRCP in a text-based chat, no one would be fooled that it was anything but a computer program. They did carry the *basic* elements of personality. For simple ease of use, John had loaded them with a reasonably large English vocabulary. They could carry on a conversation, as long as that conversation had to do with their area of responsibility. An IRCP could not think abstractly, could not expand into new areas. In short, it could not learn.

John thought it might be fun to extrapolate on the design, though. Maybe he *could* bring a computer program to the level of sentience. Certainly, there was no harm in trying.

"John, greetings!"

John started, turning from his computer screen to see Gainsborough in his office.

"My apologies," the Blue said. "I made what I believed to be an appropriate amount of noise on my arrival." He edged his way back out the door. John smiled and waved the alien back into the room.

John's workspace played into the worst clichés of computer programmers. He continuously maintained four screens active at all times. On desks and stools and one side table were strewn research volumes, trade journals, printouts and five different computer tablets. Gainsborough entered carefully, so as not to send any of John's precariously perched possessions tumbling to the floor.

"Not to worry," John said. "I was lost in my own little world. What can I do for you?"

"I have taken it upon myself to stage an anniversary celebration for tomorrow."

John glanced at the date on his screen: April 21, 2026. "It's been five years. That is unbelievable."

"The passage of time does have elastic properties when filtered through biological and psychological perception. Inasmuch as I cannot efficiently bring all the required elements for this party, I would like to request you provide beverages?"

"I'd be happy to."

Gainsborough paused, not speaking. John could never quite tell where the Blue's eyes were looking, since he could essentially look in any direction at all times. The way Gainsborough shifted his thin body a few centimeters to the left told the tale, though. John reflexively shifted his own torso to block the monitor's screen.

"I do not wish to overstep my bounds, but I am concerned by the decision map I see on your terminal. That is not an IRCP protocol."

John bit back an acerbic comment. This alien—and countless others—had been remarkably helpful for the last five years, but he didn't appreciate being treated like a boy with a dirty magazine who gets caught by his mother. John realized his bitterness shouldn't enter into a discussion of such importance. And anyway, he counted Gainsborough as a friend.

"Promise you won't tell anyone?"

Gainsborough twisted a few degrees around his main axis, a sure sign of distress. "I do not wish to make a pledge I will be forced to break at some future date."

"I trust you, Gainsborough. Can you trust me?"

The twisting continued for a moment. "I will provisionally agree to keep this conversation confidential."

"Good enough." Now John felt like a kid with a new toy. He wheeled his chair aside to allow Gainsborough access to the screen. "I've taken some of the ideas you and the others gave me and built this." The complex cascade of interlocking flowchart diagrams was his attempt to take the initiative ready control programs and extend their volition capabilities. In short, he was taking an artificial mind with the processing power of a chimpanzee and expanding it to that of a human. Perhaps a human with subnormal intelligence, but a human nonetheless.

"These are quite fascinating." The Blue reached down with one of his spindly arms and took control of the mouse. He scrolled through more screens of the large diagram. "I have never seen volition diagrams quite like these."

A knot tied in John's stomach. "Is that good or bad?"

"I cannot say with certainty. The unknown is precisely that: unknown."

"Okay. But will it work?"

"Again, without sufficient study, I cannot—"

John cut the Blue off. "Do you *think* it would work?"

Gainsborough continued to scroll through screens even as he looked directly at John. He found Blues' ability to multitask quite amazing, and also a little unnerving. "I believe this protocol would be successful, but I must ask what would be the purpose?"

"The purpose? It's... It's artificial intelligence!"

"Correct. I will rephrase my question. What would be the benefit of activating such a program?"

"The benefits would be incredible!" John gushed.

"Please enumerate them."

"I…" Now John was at a loss. He'd focused so much of his life—either consciously or subconsciously—on the goal of AI he hadn't clearly thought out the ramifications beyond those he would personally receive. Career advancement and the accolades of his peers would probably mean nothing to Gainsborough. In his structured Blue mind, John was only supposed to create IRCPs, not any kind of… Master Control Program.

Ah-ha!

"This would be a Master Control Program for *Vimana*. All of the IRCPs would maintain their various duties: propulsion, recycling, navigation, et cetera. But there will always be situations in which the needs of different ship's systems will come into conflict. We can't simply assume that such a conflict will occur on a timescale appropriate for human intervention. We need another control program to oversee the IRCPs. Like a shepherd for sheep. You see?"

"I see. But would not another IRCP designed to maintain appropriate resource allocation be sufficient to the task?"

"Uh…"

Gainsborough stopped moving the mouse and stood a little straighter. "I am afraid I cannot maintain silence on this issue, John. I apologize if your trust in me has been broken." He shuffled toward the door, pausing to add, "I offer no offense."

Keira was putting the final touches on her proposal for which members of her various teams would need to go with her to Florida next month. After having allowed so much of the design work to happen overseas, the Americans had finally put their foot down regarding production of the *Vimana* components. They would be built at a new factory facility near Cape Canaveral—still the epicenter of American space flight—in preparation for transport into LEO.

The proposal finished, she sent it off to the printer. Mira was strangely old fashioned, still wanting to review things on paper rather than in digital format on a screen. At the printer, waiting for someone else's tome to finish spooling, Keira's cell rang, a snippet of a Miles Davis trumpet solo twittering out of it. It was a text message, from Gainsborough. Just from the wording of his message, she could tell he was unusually concerned.

When Keira Desai essentially stormed into his office, John didn't react with instinctive anger. Instead, he politely gave her a tour of his new research, explaining his off-the-cuff idea for a Master Control Program, adding a joke about an old American movie that Keira didn't understand.

"Have you discussed this with Mira?" Keira asked.

"No…" John cursed under his breath. "I wanted to have a better picture of what it was all going to look like…"

"Unless MYC signs off on your idea, don't you think you should keep this master program confined to a development server?"

John nodded. "You're right, of course."

"I would add," Gainsborough said, "that truly sentient artificial constructs carry with them innumerable difficult moral questions. It would be prudent to discuss your project with others in the cybernetics field before doing any live tests. I offer this advice with only the best of intentions."

"I know, Gainsborough. And thank you. You're both right. I should be more careful."

Keira and the Blue left. John stewed for a moment, in anger, and in embarrassment. Of course, they were right. Something of this importance needed to be handled carefully, soberly. And it required witnesses, both for safety's sake, and for the eventual documentation needed for publication of the results.

John spent ten minutes crafting an e-mail to his old college advisor, Dr. Raja, explaining his proposed project, and asking for suggestions on the next steps.

The network trawler was known only as 9810331032. Its creator was familiar with programming technology generations beyond anything currently known to Earth, and so, 9810331032 was expert in avoiding local security protocols, whether manual or automatic in nature. It continuously scanned the planet's computer network for a few key concepts. The programmer checked on the trawler daily, as he had for years now.

Reviewing minute changes to the practically static web pages of the internet took milliseconds each day. The ever-changing blogs and message forums were more of a challenge, taking up nearly a quarter of

9810331032's time. The vast bulk of its resources were allocated to monitoring e-mail and chat traffic. Had 9810331032 been sentient itself, it would have gone quietly mad reading through these pointless and endlessly repetitive communications. E-mail had existed on Earth for about a single Human generation. A surprising number of Humans still found the whole process so enjoyable that they e-mailed each other banal pleasantries, forwarded jokes, pornographic materials and marketing offerings. Very occasionally, an e-mail carried substantive information. And on the rarest of occasions, the information was of interest to 9810331032.

A message from jgupta@myc.in to craja@iitb.edu caught the trawler's attention. Per its programming, it did a context search on the two individuals who owned the e-mail accounts: Jonathan Gupta and Cal Raja. After reviewing each man's history—at least those parts of their histories available on the net—9810331032 flagged the e-mail with ninety-seven percent likelihood that the programmer would be interested. The trawler stored the message in a memory buffer. 9810331032 continued its work for the day, waiting patiently for the programmer's daily call for updates.

John didn't wait for Dr. Raja's response before creating a partition of the server for his new program. He took a template from one of the IRCPs—he chose MOE, the environmental control program—and made the required modifications and additions to upgrade this IRCP into a true MCP. He delved into his desk drawers and found a cache of old memory slips with his graduate programming files on them. From one disc he extracted a personality matrix that, while it had never worked in his original research, might serve this project quite well.

The matrix consisted of a list of seven hundred sixteen yes/no questions. His theory—borne out by several tests with individuals back at IIT-B—was that the answers to these questions could map a human's personality to an essentially unique degree. The number of possible answer arrays was something greater than a googol squared. In truth, John thought it was overkill, but he had never worked on cutting the list of questions down to a minimal set.

What better way to initiate a new intelligence than with John's own personality? He seeded the matrix with his own answers. He laughed, thinking that he wasn't really creating an artificial intelligence in his own image, but in the image of his twenty-year-old self from college. He hadn't ever bothered to take the test again as he got older.

John did all of this on a secondary terminal, one which was physically separated from the main system, as a safety precaution. He also did not want any others on the project stumbling across his discoveries. His main terminal sounded a chime, indicating a message coming in from a short list of preferred addresses. He wheeled his chair over. The icon in the lower right hand corner of his screen made his heart skip a beat.

Message from rprabhu@yahoo.in

Renee. *Renee* had sent him an e-mail? John felt his extremities tingling, his breathing become labored. Renee was a part of his personal mythology, from before *Vimana*, from before he met his ex-wife. She was his college girlfriend, the love of his life, the great unobtainable icon of happiness just barely perceived and then lost in an instant. He hadn't received any kind of communication from her in fifteen years, and hadn't seen her in person for twenty.

Even as he wondered what could possibly have prompted this overture, he double-clicked on the icon, opening the message. A small window blossomed on screen, entirely white, disarmingly free of text. A nasty whine from the computer's hard drive warned him that something was amiss. Some kind of self-extraction program was underway. He had foolishly not reviewed the size of the e-mail before simply opening it. He mashed the *Esc, Ctrl* and *Break* keys, trying to stop what could only be a virtual attack on his computer, and thereby a danger to the entire Maccha-Yantra network.

His screen went blank. He had done it, thank the gods. The system was safe.

Then, a flash of light blinked on and off. Another flash, the merest hint of color on this one. Another and another. Within moments, the screen was awash in strange, sinuous patterns of color and light, a movie unlike any John had ever seen. The lovely display immediately calmed him, created a sense of well-being he hadn't felt in decades. With a satisfied sigh, he leaned forward in his chair, rested his chin on his hands, and fell into the beautiful world on his computer screen.

The programmer's skills with cybernetics would have humbled John Gupta. To be frank, they would have humbled any Human who could understand the depth and subtlety of what was accomplished over the next five minutes.

Embedded within the falsely labeled e-mail was a highly compressed program. Once activated, the program had self-extracted, expanding to an astounding degree. Though the e-mail itself had weighed only 6.5 megabytes, the eventual data arrays that spilled out practically filled John's computer's memory, taking up nearly fifty terabytes.

The most ingenious part of the programmer's design was the method of transmission for this data. A cursory review of Human neurology had given him the parameters needed to encode the data into a visual display. The movie, to the eyes of any other species, would be nothing more than an impressionistic wash of pretty colors. When a Human—in this case, John Gupta—watched the movie, his brain would interpret the patterns as write codes, downloading huge data arrays directly into the neurons of his brain, overwriting whatever was already there.

After the movie finished and disappeared off of the screen, very little of John Gupta's mind remained.

Keira glanced at the time and decided she *had* to go home. There was only so much work a person could do. She turned off her tablet, loaded up her satchel, and left her office. Her assistant Lona still toiled at her desk just a few steps away.

"Go home," Keira said.

"Yes, ma'am," Lona answered, her tone gently mocking.

There were a surprising number of people still at work, given the hour. As Keira made her way down the corridor to the elevators, she saw a dozen men and women. She paused at John's door. He was hunched over, eyes centimeters from one of his screens. His fingers tapped at his keyboard faster than Keira thought anyone could type.

"John."

He didn't respond.

"John," she said a little louder. "Are you okay?"

The typing stopped abruptly. John turned his head fractionally. Keira started forward to talk to him. She felt bad about scolding him before, even though she knew she had done the right thing.

"Have a good evening," John said, his tone cold. Keira stopped.

"Okay." She was sorry he felt bad. "See you tomorrow."

John remained frozen for a moment, then returned to his previous posture, typing, typing.

Keira sighed quietly and went back out to the elevators and her drive home.

The person who was no longer really John finished his tasks on the computer. He checked and rechecked all the code, the placement of directories, the layers of careful security that would hide what he had done from all but the most paranoid and technically gifted eyes. With all of that completed, he had only one final task before him.

Even after leaving late the night before, Keira did not give herself permission to come in late the next morning. In fact, she arrived a little early today, for no better reason than that the traffic was appreciably lighter than normal. She did have a busy morning scheduled. She had three meetings before lunch, two of which overlapped. She would have to attend one via her tablet.

She swiped her ID badge at the employee entrance at a quarter-hour after six, and even so she wasn't the first person in. She counted eight cars in the lot. She noted in passing that one of them belonged to John. She couldn't remember if that was where John had been parked the night before, but she thought it might have been. Had he spent the night at the office?

Keira walked through the dimly lit offices on the first floor toward the elevators. She stopped when she heard the sound of running feet. One of the security guards, an older man named Srikumar, ran past Keira and grabbed a phone in a nearby cube. She watched as he dialed and waited very impatiently for someone on the other end to answer.

"What's happened?" Keira asked. Srikumar almost answered her, then turned his attention to the phone.

"There's been a terrible accident!"

"An accident? Where?" Keira asked. Srikumar ignored her and continued to talk into the phone. He must have dialed 108 for emergency services.

"The Maccha-Yantra facility on Fifty-First Place…"

"Srikumar?" Keira tried again. He continued listening to whatever the police were saying. Keira glanced down the hall and saw that the door to her carbon-aluminum lab was ajar. She went toward it.

Behind her, Srikumar shouted, "No, Ms. Desai! Do not go out there!"

That warning made Keira shift into a run.

The space she referred to as a "lab" looked more like a foundry than a laboratory, with equipment for forging alloys on near-industrial scales. Much of the equipment was kept active overnight, since the time required to fire it up would have eaten drastically into every morning's research tasks. The place was furnace-hot and always smelled strongly of smoke. Today, Keira smelled something different.

It took her only a moment to find him. He was at one of the smelting cauldrons, a five meter wide tempered steel vessel filled with molten aluminum. In fact, Keira knew that this batch had been prepped for a new test this very morning. Clearly, that test would have to be postponed.

She recognized the body from its pudgy belly and the faded jeans John always wore. She also knew those sandals, so old that all trace of the tread on the soles was rubbed away. Keira approached John's corpse slowly, trying to imagine how he had even done what she was seeing.

His arms were bent at the elbow, burned into place against the hot steel. His hands—what was left of his hands—still gripped the ferociously hot lip of the cauldron. His chest and groin were merely burned to a crisp, not reduced to charcoal. His shirt had long since burned away to ash, causing only second-degree burns on his back.

But his head… John hadn't contented himself with sheer immolation. He had climbed up to the edge of the cauldron, grasped the searing metal with both hands… and then *plunged* his head into the molten metal. The crisped edges of his neck lay exposed over the glowing, placid face of the aluminum pool.

Keira stared at the scene, as if in a trance, not thinking, merely soaking in the horrifying image, as if to permanently commit the atrocity to her memory. She had lost even the ability to close her eyes and back away.

"Ms. Desai," Srikumar said softly, putting a hand on her shoulder. She turned, the trance broken. "You come with me now."

She nodded and allowed the guard to guide her out of the lab, leaving John's destroyed body behind.

X Marks the Spot

Nothing is more disgraceful than a wolfish friendship. Avoid this most of all.
— *Meditations, XI, 15*

Construction of Sylvester's new home proceeded well. He monitored his various businesses—zinc export being the most profitable, but far from the most time intensive—from temporary housing only a kilometer from the construction site. This small cottage, which would eventually be his guest house, measured only five thousand square feet, with four bedrooms and an entertainment center in the basement. The pool wasn't even heated.

Sylvester spent about an hour each day online with his corporate managers, then he would go over to look in on the workers as they brought his dream home to fruition. Learning the French language was a small price to pay for this level of craftsmanship, these views of the Loire river valley, this sense of small town well-being.

Locals in this area knew Sylvester well, but few outside of France knew where he had dropped his roots. He preferred it that way. He liked the idea of slipping into quiet anonymity. After his splashy start in Chicago, he had grown tired of publicity. This was an effort to simplify his life.

"Monsieur?" his foreman, Jean, called out. "Vous avez les visiteurs."

Visitors?

Sylvester slithered into the foyer, where a team of craftsmen were laying down pink marble tiles. Arranged around the unfinished floor were members of four different non-Human species. Apparently, interacting with a Snake on a daily basis hadn't adequately prepared Jean for these kinds of visitors. He looked scared to death. Sylvester shooed him out of the room, asking him to take the other workers as well.

The first alien to approach Sylvester, with a blocky, brown torso and thick head, was something like Humanoid in appearance. His ferocious, dark face and yellow-tipped horns were the reason the Humans gave his race the name Bulls. His thick legs and flat, round feet resembled more an elephant than a bull. Sylvester winced as the heavy creature pounded across the newly installed flooring.

"Look at you. Forgot about us already, have you?" The Bull spoke in the crackling, arrhythmic cadences of the Snake language. Sylvester had to do a quick access of his auxiliary memory to remember how to speak it.

"No! Certainly not!"

The second visitor was a Skeleton, his rough exterior shaded from yellow at his torso to a pale tan at his extremities. His limbs—four arms and two legs—rattled a bit as he approached Sylvester for his greeting.

"After the endless complaints he gave me last time, he wouldn't possibly forget his turn."

"Of course not!" Sylvester assured the Skeleton, accepting a bony handshake.

"You look like you've done well for yourself here," the third arrival said. This was a Lily, a strange explosion of color, a trunk of a body crowned with an expansive flourish of waving petals.

"One does what one can," Sylvester said to the Lily. Next he turned to the final member of the foursome. "And what have the Humans decided to call you?" he said to the seemingly inert pink blob on the floor. Without warning, the blob sprouted two tentacles for legs and shambled forward to Sylvester. Another orifice opened on the top of the creature, allowing a third tentacle to spring out, festooned with a series of eyes and mouths. The appendage waved unnervingly close to Sylvester's face.

"I am to be known as an Anemone. Cute, don't you think?" The Anemone did a little jig, sprouting five extra arms to add more festivity to the dance.

"So, when do we begin?" the Bull asked.

"Soon, soon. Until then, make yourself at home in the kitchen. It is mostly done." Sylvester added a self-mocking laugh. "Feel free to eat anything that you think you might be able to digest, and I'll be with you in a tick."

He escorted the four interlopers into his expansive kitchen, hoping that the high-end appliances might entertain them for a few minutes. He slithered his way quickly up to the unfinished master bedroom and closed the door.

Sylvester activated his communications implant and placed a call to the one person who might be able to help him.

"*Yes?*" the ship answered. "*How can I be of service?*"

"Four visitors came knocking on my door today." He described the aliens' appearance to the ship. "Check his memories."

"*I told you it was prudent to keep a copy of the memories on file, just in case.*"

"Yes, yes. You're quite brilliant. Just do the search, please?"

"*One moment.*"

Sylvester moved to the window, which offered a view of the front lawn of his new home. He wondered if he could make a getaway across that expanse of lush, green lawn without being noticed by these "friends" of his. Probably not. He cursed himself for deciding to come up to the house under his own power. Always in the car, he vowed. Always!

"*Captain?*" the ship's voice sounded in his ear.

"Yes. What is it?"

"*It's a game of a sort. The five of you have been trading off hosting this game for some time. According to his memories, the Bull is actually his brother? I'm not sure how that's possible.*"

"We'll save that fascinating mystery for another day, shall we? What kind of a game?"

"*It appears to be a search. The host takes an unsuspecting planet—Earth suffices, don't you think?—and places a variety of clues for the other participants to unravel. In the end, they solve the mystery by finding some treasure that the host has hidden somewhere on the planet. You—or, more accurately, the Snake whose body you now inhabit—won the last iteration of the game, and are now expected to host.*"

"So, all I have to do is hide a treasure, provide these four with clues to its whereabouts, and they'll go off looking for it? I'm not expected to accompany them?"

"*No. In fact, that is forbidden, if I read these memories correctly.*"

"How long do these searches generally take?"

"*The longest—this was three games ago, hosted by the Lily—lasted for eight-one million ticks.*"

Sylvester pondered the situation for a few moments.

"*Captain?*"

"Thank you. That'll be all for now."

"*Certainly.*"

Sylvester's thoughts chugged through a variety of options as he made his way slowly back to the ground level. He supposed he could call Terrance and have him stash an ingot or two of zinc somewhere in Brussels. That would work well enough as a prize. But clues? What kinds of clues could he possibly…?

He caught sight of one of the workmen in the hall, coming from the bathroom. A small glint of gold at the Human's neck caught Sylvester's eye. A cross, the symbol of Christianity. He remembered something about a holiday this weekend, a celebration of their authority figure rising from the dead, if he remembered right. Seemed a ghoulish sort of thing to commemorate, but what could you do? Humans!

Sylvester smiled just as the workman passed him in the corridor. The Human's face went white with fear at the sight of those rows of sharp, yellow teeth. The Snake never noticed his discomfiture.

Back in the kitchen, the Skeleton fiddled with the gas burning stove, the Anemone had one long tentacle foraging through four of the cabinets, and the Bull sheepishly tried to reassemble a wooden chair upon which he had tried to sit. The Lily seemed content, munching on a stick of salami.

"And so, the hunt begins!" Sylvester said grandly. Several pairs of eyes—most belonging to the Anemone—turned to him expectantly. "I have something different for you, something to fire the imagination and put your considerable skills to the test."

"Get on with it," the Bull thundered.

"Yes, well…" Sylvester stumbled a bit, then regained his salesman's composure. "Earth is a fascinating world with a remarkable cultural history. Much of that history is tied to their various mythological belief systems. I have come to learn where one of their most revered and storied artifacts has been ensconced. Your mission is to find it."

"Is it valuable?" the Skeleton asked.

"Is it delicious?" the Lily asked.

"It is known as…" Dramatic pause. "…the Ark of the Covenant."

Silence.

"The what?" the Bull asked.

"The Ark of the Covenant," Sylvester repeated. "A bit of history important to both the Christian and Judaic faiths."

"So, *you* didn't even hide it," the Bull accused.

"I did better than hide it. I *found* it."

"And you left it there?" the Anemone asked.

"It must not be valuable, then," the Skeleton concluded.

"Friends, friends. You don't understand. This is a quest far more challenging—and therefore rewarding—than any in our collective history. You are not pitting your intellects against *me*, so much as against a hundred generations of Humans. The clues won't be cute poems or maps or puzzles. The clues are woven directly into the substance of Earth history."

The Anemone retracted several of her tentacles in a sulk. "Sounds boring."

"Sounds hard," the Skeleton said.

"I'm hungry," the Lily complained.

The Bull remained silent, looking suspiciously at Sylvester. The Snake slid over and pulled himself up to the Bull's height. It was time to take a gamble.

"Have I ever let you down before, brother?"

The Bull, looking no less suspicious, nonetheless let loose a loud snort of laughter.

"Often, *brother*. But at least you're never boring." He gestured to the others. "Let's get started."

No work on the house happened over the weekend, because of the Christian holiday. Even the handful of non-Christians in town shut down their shops on Sunday. Apparently, society had so secularized this Easter celebration that it crossed religious lines. On the one hand, it was a fascinating aspect of Human culture. On the other hand, Sylvester really wished he could purchase some fresh baguettes.

By Monday, Sylvester had decided that fretting about the scavengers he'd sent off on their fool's errand helped him not at all. They would spend years trying to find the Ark, assuming the thing even existed. He was, therefore, stunned when the ship routed him a quicklight call from the Lily that morning. Sylvester took the call in his office at the guest house, watching the video feed on his tablet screen.

The Lily stood on a street corner in a European city. Her petals quivered with delight.

"*It's just like you to hide the treasure in plain sight, and so close!*" the Lily gushed.

"What are you talking about?"

"*I've found it!*" The Lily shifted to the side, allowing the camera she held in one frond to reveal a huge monument that dominated a traffic square in downtown Paris.

"That," Sylvester said, restraining laughter, "is not the Ark of the Covenant."

"*You won't fool me that easily. I know there are many Earth languages. The name is slightly different, but I saw through that!*"

"Yes... but... that's the Arch of Triumph, not the Ark of the Covenant."

The image of the massive masonry structure wobbled. Off-screen, the Lily said, "*But it's so pretty.*"

"Yes, love, it is very pretty," Sylvester said. "But it's a war monument, and several hundred billion ticks younger than the item you're looking for."

How could she be *that* dumb, Sylvester wondered. He was worried for nothing. These scavengers weren't a threat to anything he was doing on Earth.

"*Alright,*" the Lily said. "*I'm going to go get more cheese. I really like cheese.*"

"That's good," Sylvester said. "Cheers." He cut the connection, laughing.

The next call came three days later, while Jean oversaw the installation of the massive marble fountain in the middle of the swimming pool, and while Sylvester oversaw Jean. Sylvester retreated a short way from the edge of the drained pool and answered the buzz in his ear.

"Yes?"

"*The Skeleton is calling,*" the ship said.

"From Paris?"

"*From somewhere in Turkey.*"

"Turkey? Put him through."

"*Hello! This is a new record!*" the Skeleton shouted. There was terrible wind noise coming through the line. "*Fastest finish yet, I think!*"

"You're in Turkey?" Sylvester asked, moving back into the house.

"*Yes, yes,*" the Skeleton shouted over the wind. "*Go ahead and pretend I'm in the wrong place! It took some doing to get all the way out here, but I did it. Earth needs better transport services. You should work on that.*"

Sylvester linked his implant to a plasma screen in the den. A remarkable vista of rugged mountains and dramatic, lowering clouds appeared on the TV. "*Recognize this?*"

"No, not really," Sylvester said.

"*Then how about... this!*" The image swung around to reveal a huge boat wedged into a crevasse of the mountain range. Looking closer, Sylvester saw signs proclaiming this to be "Noah's Ark". There was a gift shop built into the vessel's bow, and a parking lot filled with cars on a gently sloping plain below.

"Ship? Are you seeing this?" Sylvester asked.

"*Yes, Captain,*" the ship answered.

"What are we looking at?"

"*One moment.*"

"*What?*" the Skeleton shouted. "*This isn't it? You said it was an artifact of the Christian and Judaic faiths! There are Christians and Jews everywhere! Just look at them all.*"

The Skeleton zoomed the image in on the deck of the oversized, landlocked vessel. There were hundreds of Humans—most of them children—running about, some waving flags, others carrying plush toys shaped like Earth animals.

The ship spoke up. "*This is a recreation of the legendary vessel known in the Judaic Torah as Noah's Ark. According to this tale, God destroyed the world with a flood, and only those creatures shepherded onto this craft by Noah survived to repopulate the Earth.*"

"*Right!*" the Skeleton shouted over the wind noise. "*He sealed the occasion with a* covenant *with Humanity, that he would never flood them again. I win the contest!*"

"No, you don't win the contest!" Sylvester shouted back. "The Ark of the Covenant is from a later period in Jewish history. It's not a boat. It's a chest which held various important relics, such as inscribed tablets and magic bread."

"*I think you just don't want to admit I won.*"

The ship intervened. "*I'm afraid he's right. This is not the Ark of the Covenant.*"

A rush of clattering, crunching noise that Sylvester suspected was native Skeleton language came through the line. He could only imagine the invective the Skeleton was pouring out. It was a good thing those little Christian children couldn't understand his curses.

"Chin up," Sylvester said brightly. "You're doing better than the others!"

Sylvester hadn't quite removed himself from the day to day activities of his business conglomerate. Much of it was managed by competent Humans, in the United States and Canada, and in his headquarters in Brussels. Once a month, he flew up to the Belgian capital for a staff meeting with his managing directors. Usually these meetings devolved into turf wars over who should have control of the zinc side of the business.

With all the stress tied to the business world—quite a bit more here on Earth than he'd seen on other worlds—Sylvester wondered how long he would hold out before simply retiring. The thought of a life of prosperous leisure made him feel all cool inside. Still, he suspected that the wanderlust would strike again, someday. He hadn't released the ship from her contract just yet...

"*Captain?*"

Sylvester hissed in annoyance. He was alone in the cabin of his jet, twenty minutes from landing in Brussels. He took the call. "Yes?"

"*It's the Anemone this time.*"

"Where is she? West Spitsbergen? Montevideo?"

"*She may have it,*" the ship said, clearly stunned. Sylvester shifted the call to a small screen installed in a bulkhead of the plane. The image was too dim to make much of anything out. The sound was chaotic, filled with a confusing pastiche of Human conversations, loud popular music, and what sounded like explosions and other sounds of battle.

"*Hello? Are you there?*" the Anemone asked.

"I'm here, but I can barely hear you. And I can't see a thing."

"*I will compensate.*" The image brightened, revealing something that made Sylvester's breath catch in his throat. Behind a transparent partition sat a rectangular object of shimmering gold. Two long, wooden poles were attached at the sides, allowing the chest to be carried without anyone having to touch it directly. The heavy top was crowned with two kneeling creatures facing one another. Their forms were similar to Humans, but clearly supernatural. Their long, feathered wings stretched forward, the tips meeting at the center of the lid. Sylvester found their pose disconcertingly familiar.

"*I have found the Ark of the Covenant,*" the Anemone said proudly. To underline the event, one slender pink tentacle entered the frame, pointing at the golden chest.

"That is… quite remarkable," Sylvester said. In his head, he imagined this contest to have disrupted one—perhaps two—of the major religions on Earth. Holy wars might commence at any moment. He began calculating exit strategies from the planet. He could call down a bubble from the ship to Brussels… but there were so many lovely things back at the house he'd want to take with him. Curse this clever Anemone.

"*Excuse me,*" the ship interrupted.

"Yes?" Sylvester said, hopeful.

"*I have analyzed the images, and I believe this is not the actual Ark of the Covenant.*"

"*Nonsense!*" the Anemone argued. "*Look at what it says, right here. I had to download an English implant to read it.*" The image shifted and zoomed to a small, white placard at the base of the display.

ARK OF THE COVENANT

"*See?*" the Anemone said.

"*Please pan the camera down a bit,*" the ship asked.

"*Why?*" the Anemone asked angrily.

"Just do it," Sylvester hissed.

The image shifted again, and more of the placard was revealed.

RAIDERS OF THE LOST ARK (1981)

"*This merely tells us the name of the organization that retrieved the Ark and the Earth year in which they found it,*" the Anemone explained.

"You idiot!" Sylvester said. "That's the name of a movie. You've found a prop from a forty-five-year-old film."

"*A film?*"

"*A form of recorded entertainment,*" the ship helpfully provided.

"*Ah,*" the Anemone said sadly. "*I thought this place was somewhat too festive for a religious shrine.*" The camera swung around to reveal a bustling restaurant, filled with loud patrons, each enjoying a meal or a drink while they gazed at a dizzying array of television screens showing clips of old movies and television programs.

"Since you're there, try the chicken fingers," Sylvester suggested. "I've heard good things."

One more board meeting out of the way, one more trip to the big city complete. Sylvester sat back and enjoyed the short drive from his personal airstrip back to the house. The Rolls pulled into his gravel driveway and his driver opened the door for him. Standing on the front steps was Jean Jacob, his construction foreman, with a worried look on his sun-brown, rugged face. Hopefully there wasn't a delay! His home was supposed to be completed while he was away on this trip!

"Jean?"

"Vous avez un visiteur."

"Ah." He nodded and slithered past the Frenchman and into his house, ready to withstand yet another poor attempt to solve his clever riddle, probably from the Bull this time.

Standing in the foyer was someone Sylvester had never met before. He knew the race, though. Earth had named them Teddy Bears.

"May I help you?" Sylvester asked in French, as he was unfamiliar with the Teddy Bears' language.

"My name is Krd," the Teddy Bear said in perfect French without missing a beat. "I am a Conduct Officer for Central Authority."

Sylvester's guard came up immediately. Conduct Officers were rarely abusive with their power—they were well chosen and well trained—but they were certainly not to be toyed with. He had to quell an instinct to try to bribe the Officer. What worked so well with Humans might not have the same effect on a Teddy Bear.

"I've become quite fond of my local name, Sylvester."

"As I have learned."

"Would you care for refreshment?"

"No."

"Alright…"

"I have some questions about your recent visitors."

"My recent…"

Krd rattled off four names, each one a barely pronounceable collection of gibberish to Sylvester's untrained ears. He understood nonetheless: the scavengers.

"Yes. They're friends of mine. I trust they haven't caused anyone any trouble." Sylvester kept his tone light. A suspicious Conduct Officer was almost as bad as an angry one. Perhaps worse.

"What is their business here?" he asked.

"I'm curious to know why you would ask me, and not them," Sylvester countered.

"Standard procedure."

"Procedure for what? CA Conduct Officers can't be interrogating the acquaintances of every non-Human to visit Earth."

"There are reasons."

"Would it be impertinent for me to ask what those reasons are?"

"Yes."

Sylvester began getting angry at this bureaucratic drone.

"Would it be impertinent for me to tell you that you are being quite rude?"

"Yes."

"Well, impertinence is the order of the day, then, isn't it? I'll kindly ask you to either provide me with documentation of an official investigation or you may leave."

Sylvester didn't know Teddy Bear physiology, so he couldn't accurately determine if Krd was angry or amused or simply annoyed. But he had elicited *some* emotion, it seemed. Good. Sylvester didn't particularly enjoy being harassed, by a member of *any* species.

"Good day," Krd said and made for the door.

"And to you," Sylvester said as he closed the door behind the Officer.

Sylvester did not dream, at least not in the sense of a Human's dream, which is a little movie that plays in their head as they sleep. For Sylvester's race, sleep was a far less active process. It gave the mind rest as well as the body. For this reason, waking for Sylvester was a lengthier process than for the Humans in his employ. It often took him fifteen minutes or more to shift into a fully conscious state each morning.

The scavengers did not wish to wait that long. Sylvester awoke to find himself thrashing about in his recently completed pool, about to drown, completely disoriented and confused. He managed, with great effort, to swim to the surface, where he could float on his back and look up at the night sky. He'd forgotten how beautiful the stars could be.

"What time is it?" he asked, still trying to wake up.

"It's night," the Bull said. The other three were also there, standing on the pool deck, watching Sylvester tread water.

"You and your diurnal rhythms," the Skeleton said. "Quaint."

"Necessary, you should say." Sylvester swam to the pool's edge and climbed out. On the tiled pool deck, he laid himself out at full length and began to twist his body. He managed to wring most of the water out of his fur, then he snapped back, his whole length spinning like a cam shaft.

"You promised us a lengthy and exciting search," the Bull intoned.

"And so you have searched," Sylvester countered. He slithered to a nearby deck chair and pooled his body on the soft padding. He had to get off the cold tile deck. "You've had a number of false alarms, but none of you have..."

The Bull trundled forward, holding out a personal screen with a video image on it. Sylvester blinked and tried to focus on the screen. He took the device from the Bull's enormous hoof and held it close to his red eyes.

The feed came from a fixed camera at some undefined location. A pair of artificial lights revealed a cavern, within which sat a misshapen lump of fired clay. The stark illumination revealed just the barest flecks of gold in the surface of the object. Sylvester looked up at the Bull.

"There is no need for posturing," the Bull said. "I have found your treasure."

Sylvester squinted. "Where?"

"In a deep cavern under the city of Khān Yūnis on the shore of the Mediterranean Sea."

This was either the most incredible display of detective work in history... or a remarkably daring bluff. Either way, Sylvester's response was inevitable.

"Congratulations, brother!"

The others groused at their defeat. The Skeleton in particular made a horrendous, clattering noise that likely woke all the Humans in the vicinity. Despite his victory, the Bull did not seem happy.

"And now, what is to be my prize?" the Bull asked.

"Your prize?" Sylvester gestured to the Ark on the screen. If the relic was still buried like that, he didn't imagine letting the Bull take it away would have any impact on Earth's religious masses.

"Unacceptable," the Bull thundered. "I cannot sell or trade that in any other system, and I have little need for the wares of these Humans." He concluded the statement with a dismissive wave at the ostentatious pool area.

"Quite right, quite right," Sylvester said. "You shall receive..." He did a quick calculation in his head. "...a nine milli-m ingot of pure zinc."

The losing scavengers sighed at the wondrous nature of the prize. The Bull simply nodded, then turned to the others. "If I might have a moment... with my *brother*."

"Can we go in and have some cheese?" the Lily asked.

"Of course. Help yourself."

Sylvester made a mental note to have the staff clean the kitchen thoroughly in the morning. The Lily and the Skeleton were quite clean, but the Anemone left behind trails of goo wherever she went.

"So, a remarkable result, eh?" Sylvester said affably to the Bull. The Bull grasped Sylvester just below his head and lifted him high, leaving only a bit of his tail on the ground.

"Who are you?" the Bull demanded.

"What? What do you mean?"

"My brother would *never* have given in so easily."

"You didn't find the Ark?"

The Bull's answering snort blew past Sylvester's face like a sirocco.

"Not that it matters," Sylvester gibbered.

"Is he alive?"

"Your brother? Yes, of course! I'm no murderer."

"So you say."

"I say it because it's the truth. Your brother wished to spend some time with the Gradlik."

"The *Gradlik*? You are a Gradlik?" The Bull was clearly stunned. He dropped Sylvester to the ground.

"Yes, well." Sylvester brushed himself off. "We are individuals, in case you didn't know. I wished to take a leave of absence. Your brother, on the other hand, found the Gradlik very intriguing. We switched bodies and went our separate ways. He left express instructions not to advertise his departure, and I agreed."

"Where is he?" the Bull asked.

"Well, that's the question, now, isn't it? The Gradlik shift about. When I last left him, about two billion ticks ago, he was traveling with the *b-b-b-b*, somewhere near Ffftlf."

The Bull sized Sylvester up, reining in an urge to throttle the "Snake".

Sylvester went on. "I assume you will similarly respect your brother's wishes, and not…" Sylvester's eyes swiveled back to the house, indicating the other scavengers. "…make a fuss."

"I will verify your tale. You should hope I don't return."

The Bull tromped off to the house before Sylvester could answer with a breathless, "No doubt."

Blueprints

> *From Alexander the grammar-*
> *ian, [I learned] to refrain from*
> *fault-finding, and not in a reproach-*
> *ful way to chide those who uttered*
> *any barbarous or solecistic or*
> *strange-sounding expression...*
> —*Meditations, I, 10*

Keira had mixed feelings about the move to Florida.

At a very superficial level, she was saddened to leave her recent boy-friend, a man named Shailesh who lived in her apartment building. Shailesh was a sweet man, a tailor by trade, who had taken her out for a handful of meals. Their relationship hadn't progressed much past some moderately passionate kissing. She supposed there might have been a fu-ture for them, but *Vimana* came first. And so, to Florida.

On a deeper level, leaving behind the home of her birth would be disorienting. She'd been to the United States on a couple of previous occa-sions, but only on short visits. *Vimana* wouldn't be ready for launch for more than two years, and she would be there for that entire time. What's more, she would not be in one of their metropolitan cities, like New York or Chicago. She would be less than a hundred kilometers from Disney World. In her mind, the state of Florida was filled with ignorant white farmers who would resent her for her accent and her skin color.

Still, with all the negatives, the prospect of seeing her ship—for she thought of it as hers and hers alone—come into being? That was too wondrous to let the smaller concerns bother her.

And, in any case, she was only one of a hand-picked team of two hundred fifteen from Mumbai who were moving to the new, little town, built up out of nothing in a deserted region of swamp and grassland. The Americans had unselfconsciously named the town Opportunity.

Terry and Kird drove through three armed checkpoints as they made their way to the Orbital Pavilion at Edwards Air Force Base. Transit to and from *Ronald Reagan* had shifted dramatically in the last few months. The G-11s were practically mothballed, making way for the far superior orbit bubbles. Boeing was churning the little things out now by the hundreds. The regularly scheduled bubbles traveling between *Reagan* and Edwards carried military personnel and off world visitors of exceptional importance to the government. Terry and Kird arrived to greet one of the latter.

Visitors to Earth had been often generous with their technical knowledge, which allowed Maccha-Yantra to design and prepare to build a starship in such a short time. But Central Authority—the destination of the maiden voyage of *Vimana*—was persnickety about what kinds of vessels docked at their location. They didn't want some backwater, newly hatched system rushing in and colliding with the other ships, bathing the CA system with radiation, or doing other types of mischief. So they insisted on this visit from a CA auditor, a Blue with extensive experience in all manner of FTL technology.

Terry's driver parked the bulky Cadillac SUV by the Pavilion, which was a relatively small building, less than thirty yards on a side. Inside, Terry and Kird passed through security zones filled with imposing signage and manned by stoic airmen, stationed there to make humans feel safe and make off worlders feel worried. Terry rode the escalator up to the landing area. Kird, on the other hand, walked up the adjacent flight of stairs. He didn't particularly enjoy escalators. He worried about getting his fur caught in the metal steps.

The roof of the building was quartered into four landing zones with squat, concrete and steel bubble-catchers installed in the center of each. Two of the pads had empty bubbles waiting. Terry and Kird moved to Pad Three, where their visitor was scheduled to land. Terry pulled his tablet from a jacket pocket, consulting with the local net on the visitor's progress. He chuckled.

"Something is amusing?" Kird asked.

"You know how the guys on the station let visitors choose a name for themselves?"

"Blue names are rather difficult for Human tongues."

"This auditor chose the name Billion."

"Why is this amusing?"

"I…" Terry shook his head. The types of jokes that would appeal to Kird weren't always obvious to Terry. Apparently, sheer absurdity wasn't one of them. "It's just odd."

Terry found the approach of a landing bubble disconcerting, as if a bomb were being dropped right on his head. This bubble fell from the sky precisely on time, the sight of it making Terry wince just like always. The bubble opened, and a Blue stepped out. Terry remembered his research and approached the Blue, standing closer to her than a human would appreciate.

"I offer greetings. I am Major Terry Youngblood of Earth."

"I offer greetings. I am *d-d-b-b-d* of *b-b-b-b*. You may address me as Billion."

"I thank you." Terry slipped out of this rigid, diplomatic persona, feeling normal again. "This is Kird, our local CA representative."

Terry stood his ground as Kird approached Billion from a different angle. As much as a human would feel like she was being ganged up on with two people standing so close, for a Blue, this was the height of flattery, having two people address two of her eyes simultaneously.

"*d-b-b-d-d-g d-g-g-d-b-b g-d-b-d*," Kird said in his near perfect Blue accent.

"*d-b-b-d-d-g d-g-b-b-d d-d-d-g*," Billion replied.

"You took the words right out of my mouth," Terry said, smiling widely. Kird responded to the joke with a polite smile. Billion said nothing. "Alright. Let's get you through security and out to the production facility."

Terry had met a dozen or so Blues over the years. He thought they were a little prissy for his taste, but basically good folks. This one, Billion, was wound up *tight*. During the short flight from Edwards to the new airstrip outside Opportunity, she responded tersely to questions, and offered no conversation of her own. Terry felt uncomfortable talking to Kird with her sitting there; it seemed impolite. So the flight was *very* quiet.

After landing, they switched to another SUV for the drive to the MYC offices. Billion had a long day ahead of her, meeting with the *Vimana* Project Director and the Project Leads. He and Kird tagged along at the request of the Pentagon and Vanessa's department.

The relationship between the US Government and CA was still somewhat delicate. McGaw's War on Genocide was unpopular with the public and somewhat unsuccessful. There were still a lot of men and women in Congress and the White House who seemed unwilling to believe that CA posed any kind of *threat* to the mightiest nation on Earth. Kird, on the other hand, was a comfortable, known quantity. His presence—alien though he was—cooled some of the hot heads on the Hill. Terry's presence—as a human—calmed everyone else.

Opportunity, Florida, was a nightmare of overlapping construction projects. Trucks ferrying in tar and gravel for highways competed on too-small roads with concrete trucks bound for new home development. Cranes made their way to factory construction sites. Eighteen-wheelers trundled about carrying all the random consumables that people needed just to get on with their lives. Their Air Force driver made his way through the chaos, finally pulling the car into the dusty parking lot of the MYC local offices, a bland concrete box of a building.

Waiting on the front steps was a slight woman losing a struggle against gray in her midnight black hair. She approached the car, introducing herself.

"Mira Netrivali."

"Major Terry Youngblood. This is Kird." She shook both their hands. Then Netrivali approached Billion as the Blue climbed awkwardly out of the back seat of the SUV. Netrivali had been doing her research, too. She practically kissed the Blue, she was so close.

"I'm the Project Director for construction of *Vimana*. We look forward to any suggestions or comments you might have about our progress."

"Yes," Billion said, her tone seemingly morose. Netrivali didn't let the Blue's mood impact her sunny disposition.

"Let's introduce you to the team."

The fact that Keira had been pulled into a conference room for a meeting with a visiting dignitary did not stop the ever present require-ments of her job. She scanned e-mails on her tablet, her eyes flicking every few moments to a live video feed in one corner of the screen. The tiny window showed a view of the research floor back in Mumbai where sev-eral team members who hadn't come with her to Florida continued to push the limits of carbon-aluminum production. She tried not to think about the sight of John Gupta's suicide, which had occurred in that same laboratory just a few months ago.

Even as production on *Vimana* began, her team continued to look for improvements. Of all the materials that would eventually make up *Vi-mana*, carbon-aluminum would represent by far the greatest ratio of mass. If any one thing couldn't fail, it was her alloy.

Of course, nothing could fail.

Mira breezed into the room with three people in her wake. Keira took little note of the Blue auditor, who conversed briefly in her native tongue with Gainsborough. Though Keira had never seen a Teddy Bear before, she spared little attention for him either. Instead, she found herself fixed on the American in the Air Force uniform, his blond hair and his strong chin and his eyes like the sea on a cloudy day. She spent several minutes trying to remember where she'd seen him before. He must have noticed her staring, because his eyes seemed to fall on her, too.

"Keira?"

She popped out of her daze at Mira's mention of her name. Keira stood to address the group. She wound her way through a speech she'd been perfecting over the last few weeks, a concise and not-too-technical overview of her part of the project. She focused her attention on the new Blue, only allowing a brief glance over at the American. At her glance, he smiled.

Her bit done, Keira dropped back into her e-mails for the balance of the meeting, trying hard not to think about the American. She didn't need the distraction, knowing that the auditor would be visiting her de-partment tomorrow. She needed to get all her ducks in a row before then.

The meeting broke up around her, but she ignored it, still staring at her little screen, waiting for the room to clear before she rose from her chair.

"Excuse me?"

Keira peered up to see the American standing next to her. She clambered out of the chair, worried that she was blushing, but also fairly sure he wouldn't notice it on her dark skin. He stood a couple of centimeters taller than she, which was nice. She'd never dated an Indian so tall as that.

Why was she thinking about dating?

"I feel like I've seen you somewhere before," he said. Then he offered a hand. "Major Terry Youngblood."

"Youngblood! Now I remember where I saw you before," she said a bit too loudly. "You were escorting Sylvester through the Off World offices in Washington while we were there for the *Vimana* proposal."

She watched as he shifted from confusion to realization. "You're Keira Desai, the one who figured out about the zinc. You know, you're kind of famous."

"Infamous, more like."

Then they shared another round of wide-eyed, goofy smiles, before the Major said, "Would you like to get a cup of coffee?"

Keira:

There's something primal, elemental about attraction. Does it spring from the interior spaces of the brain where the urges and needs of our ape cousins lurk, waiting for that *man* who seems to be the one who could provide care, support, protection, and of course, most importantly, genetic stock? Is that why women are attracted to men who are larger than they, who are more physically powerful? It informs all the traditions that have grown up around romantic liaisons. Women are *swept off their feet*. They get *carried away*. Men talk of *picking up* a woman. When couples dance, the man leads, practically dragging the woman from place to place across the dance floor. The motif carries through to the time of marriage, when the man carries his wife across the threshold of their new home.

What is it that causes my body to tingle at his strong touch, to make me desire to be lifted and carried to a shared bed, to let his impulses be obvious and physical and intense, while mine are subtle, the caress of a leg or a breathless whisper in an ear?

We fall into these roles easily, almost subconsciously, the man instigating the act of love, the woman shifting into the role of conductor, our combined symphony of passion taking us to a place of shared joy that reverberates in our souls long after the act itself burns down from an intense bonfire of sexual activity to the warm, comforting embers of simple closeness.

Terry:
Wow. This girl is hot.

The next morning, Terry was a little bit stunned at what had happened. He'd had a couple of one night stands back in college, but they'd never been like *this*. It was like he'd been in some kind of trance all night.

He looked at Keira, still sleeping there, her short hair mussed, her body nicely outlined by a single sheet that covered them both. He wanted to wake her up and make love to her all over again. He wanted to slip out of the room. He wanted to lie quietly and watch her sleep.

Terry was confused.

He knew enough to realize that there still existed a double-standard about nights like the one they had shared. Someone describing him would wink and say, "Well, some guys are like that. What can you do?" Someone describing Keira would say, "What a slut!" For the first time in his life, Terry was disgusted by the double-standard. That was because this was the first time he'd fallen so quickly into bed with someone he really did respect.

That milestone only took him thirty-three years. Good job, Terry.

"Good morning," Keira said. Terry jumped, thinking she had been sound asleep. She laughed a little and reached over to give him a kiss, which he returned.

"Morning."

"How did you sleep?"

"Great," he said with some enthusiasm. She laughed again.

"Me, too."

Another kiss. Terry, with extraordinary effort, stopped and backed away enough to talk.

"Look, this was great—"

Keira's dreamy, happy expression soured instantly. "But?"

"No! Not but. And. I was going to say 'and.'"

"And?" she asked, her voice skeptical.

"And… this might get complicated. I've got no problem with complicated, we just need to… prepare for… complications."

Skepticism shifted to hesitance.

"You're not brushing me off?"

Now it was Terry's turn to laugh. He pulled her into another kiss, this one more intense, more liable to make them both late for their respective busy days. Keira was the one to head things off this time. She pulled away.

"You're not brushing me off," she said, her school-girl, uncalculated openness reappearing.

"No. Absolutely not. We just need to make sure… that…"

"You have a girlfriend?" she spurted.

"No. Do you?"

"Have a girlfriend?"

"No. A boyfriend. Or a girlfriend? Or anyone? Do you have anyone?"

"No."

"Good."

"Good."

"Okay then."

"Right."

They fell into another embrace.

And really, did it make *that* much of a difference if they were a couple minutes late?

Keira had gotten used to being the most knowledgeable person in the room on the topics of her research. Gainsborough, she had learned over the years, wasn't actually an expert on things such as carbon-aluminum. He simply had a working knowledge of a broad selection of engineering disciplines. He remained helpful, certainly, but no longer led the humans the way he had at the start. Keira felt she had reached a level where she could look at Gainsborough as a colleague, rather than a mentor. She was confident of her expertise.

Billion shattered Keira's sense of confidence. The Blue put Keira to shame with her depth of knowledge about materials science. What made the auditor that much more annoying was that she seemed to have this same expertise with every aspect of the project, not just carbon-aluminum. The team working on the FTL drive came out of their meeting with Billion scratching their heads, though also excited to make use of the copious notes the Blue had give them. The same was true for the recycling team, the climate control team, the navigation team. Keira's structural team was the last on Billion's agenda.

Keira brought to her meeting a table-sized printout of the current blueprints for *Vimana*. The huge sheet of paper showed, in macroscopic scale, the different modules of the craft, and their connection points. Billion quizzed Keira on which styles of carbon-aluminum she would use at each location on the specs. Afterward, referring to the audio recording she'd made of the discussion, she determined Billion agreed with less than twenty percent of her decisions.

At lunch time, Keira hoped to spend lunch commiserating with Gainsborough about the cruel treatment from the auditor. When she went down to the lunchroom, she found Kird, Billion and Gainsborough deep in conversation in the native Blue tongue. She paused stupidly in the cafeteria entrance, unsure what to do. She caught sight of Terry across the room, waving her over. She slipped over and sat with him.

She'd been in this new "relationship" with the American for less than twenty-four hours, but she found it remarkably easy to confide in him more openly than she ever had with Shailesh, or with Tommy, for that matter. Terry nodded at the right places and responded with just the right combination of sympathy and certainty in Keira's ability to meet, and then surpass, Billion's expectations.

Could Terry be too good to be true? Keira vowed not to think like that, and to simply enjoy the moment.

After lunch, Kird invited Terry to a conference with Netrivali and Billion in the Project Director's office. The two off worlders remained standing, since the chairs wouldn't easily accommodate either of their bodies.

"So, what's the verdict?" Terry asked.

"Terry," Kird said with a concerned frown, "you realize this is not an adjudication, but merely a technical review."

"I know. It's just a figure of speech."

"Ah. Billion, would you care to give us your thoughts?"

The Blue paused, raised herself to her full height, and then began.

"There is to be found here a dizzying variety of research and development styles. Without consistency of paradigm, I cannot sufficiently analyze the synchronicity of your endeavors. I therefore suggest that with only the greatest care and forethought should you pass into the final integration stage of this project. If, as I have been told by several of your team, you still plan on an interstellar launch in something over two of your local years, I politely maintain you will not achieve this goal."

Terry was stunned. For one thing, he didn't know Billion was capable of saying that many words in a row. But for her first conclusion to be that they wouldn't make their deadline seemed presumptuous. He had to keep his tongue in check, for fear of inappropriately trying to defend his entire race... and his new girlfriend. Answering these concerns fell to Mira. Terry gave her a pointed glance. She took up the challenge with her usual upbeat tone.

"Billion, I think you may have sold us short. From what I've heard and seen, the commentary you've given every team will push this project forward even faster than we have seen to date."

"I did not sense a great deal of appreciation for my suggestions."

Terry decided to step in here. "There's a difference between appreciating criticism and making use of it."

"Just so," Billion said, her tone indicating that she found it unlikely that humans fully understood this distinction.

"Billion," Kird said, "you had something else to say?" His tone was gently prodding, like a parent telling a child to apologize for something. Billion's look to Kird was pure annoyance. Terry had to smile.

"Krd has told me that, for Humans, praise is a valuable motivator. I, therefore, can say that I found your researchers to be largely a competent sort."

"Largely competent? That's praise?" Terry asked.

"From Billion, this is praise," Kird said.

"I'll pass it along. Thank you," Mira said, smiling.

"Query," Billion said. Terry hadn't heard Billion use that formal address before. Mira nodded. "Did you think that if I had found your researchers to be less than competent, I would have failed to reveal my conclusion? Did not my silence on the matter indicate I saw no concerns in that area?"

"You have to understand," Mira said, "that the first thing you told us was that we wouldn't meet our deadline, which you would have to admit is a negative. It's valuable for us to be reminded of the positives as well. When we do internal performance reviews of our people, we routinely provide feedback which is both positive and negative. Call it... a human affectation."

"I will," Billion said with ponderous finality.

Gainsborough attempted to console Keira after her rough treatment by Billion.

"CA auditors are uncompromising. That is part of their job."

"She was mean."

"I sincerely doubt that. I suspect she was impersonal to the point of disregard."

"Right. Mean."

Gainsborough laughed.

"Terry's in with her now. I hope he gives her a piece of his mind."

"Terry? You are on a first name basis with the Major?"

"I suppose..."

Gainsborough intertwined the fingers on his two closest hands, a sure sign of excitement.

"Something of a romantic nature has occurred between you and Major Youngblood, has it not?"

"I don't want to talk about it."

"I do not believe you. I believe you *do* want to talk about it. You are being coy."

Keira looked around the cafeteria for prying ears. They were alone for the moment.

"I've never done something like that in all my life."

"Like what?"

"We... did it."

"'It' referring to sexual intercourse?"

"Must you discuss this like a guidance counselor?"

"I don't understand."

"Never mind. There's some kind of... connection between us. I've never felt so close to someone, certainly never so quickly. It was like... It was like we were two musicians, perfectly in sync, creating such beautiful—" She stopped, embarrassed. "We had a nice time."

"I am happy for you. You have been lonely for some time now."

"No, I haven't."

Gainsborough didn't call her out for this lie, choosing instead to give her a smile with his closest mouth.

"Am I correct in assuming that with this emotional proximity comes a measure of mutual trust?"

"You're not getting jealous, are you?" she asked playfully.

"Certainly not! My query pertains to a matter of security about which I am most curious."

"Security?"

"I wonder if the major knows what progress the Americans may have made in the matter of The Antagonist."

"The who?"

Terry hurried from his meeting with Billion to find Keira. He found her amidst a crowd of her fellow Maccha-Yantra people, deep in hushed conversation. He caught her eye, and she extracted herself from the group. She didn't look happy.

"I have good news," Terry said, looking forward to telling her about Billion's reluctant compliments.

"I don't."

Terry burst into Mira Netrivali's office, where she was having a conversation with Kird.

"I need to speak with you," Terry said.

"What can I do for you, Major?" Mira said, her smile undaunted by his rude entry.

"No, ma'am. I need to speak with Kird."

Mira took note of Terry's tone, and politely excused herself from her own office.

"Is there a problem?" Kird asked.

"Who is The Antagonist, and why does Gainsborough think he's on Earth?"

Kird sighed. "I had hoped to bring this matter to closure without worrying you or your fellows."

"You mean humans."

"Precisely."

"According to Gainsborough, The Antagonist is some kind of terrorist?"

"It is rather more complicated than that. He is a seditionist."

"A seditionist?"

"He actively promotes a belief system which is in ideological opposition to Central Authority."

"He just... talks? So what?"

"You cannot be so naïve to think that there is no harm in certain ideas if cultivated by one who knows how to sway large groups of people."

"Where I come from, freedom of speech is pretty important."

"I have reviewed American law and have found many exceptions to that so called freedom. It is a federal offense to threaten the life of the President."

"That's... that's different."

"I do not claim that this exception is inappropriate. I merely claim that the freedom of speech is not absolute in American law. You cannot knowingly disparage another's character with false statements. You cannot give false testimony to a court of law. You cannot endanger crowds with calls to panic. Shall I continue?"

"So, this Antagonist, what does he talk about? What does he try to get people to do?"

"Genocide."

"Genocide? Against who?"

"He does not care. His goal is the eradication of diversity. He believes that the galaxy is too complex and therefore dangerous a place."

"Dangerous? Really?"

"You experienced a measure of that danger with the arrival of the Eoiea and the Eaieo. More dangerous races by far populate the galaxy. They have simply not found reason to visit Earth. And you should hope they do not."

"So, this guy, he calls himself The Antagonist, and he preaches to people to blow each other away?"

"Subtly, insidiously, deviously. CA has pursued him for nines of billions of ticks. He covers his tracks so completely, we are often a million ticks behind him. You recall our encounter with Piotr."

"Sure."

"She was the last of the regime which devastated a planet of a pre-technological species, driven in part by of the counsel of The Antagonist."

"The Rope Men broke through a cocoon?"

"Yes."

"You never told us that."

"I did not believe the information was valuable enough to you to outweigh the potentially damaging impact that the story would have on your race."

"I guess there's lots of things you have decided it's better we don't know."

"This was not an omission I took lightly, Terry. But, as you are now aware of The Antagonist, I will let you know where my investigation has led me. He was tracked some years ago to Wolf 359."

"Where the Pigs have a settlement."

"Yes. They recently found an abandoned craft in their local space which we have determined had been used by The Antagonist. It is not clear how—or if—he left Wolf 359 space, but its proximity to Earth could not be ignored. It is my belief that The Antagonist has made his way to Earth and is now among you."

"What race is he?"

"Ah. This question is difficult to answer. He has changed forms more times than we have been able to track."

"Personality transfer. I met a Snake inside a Vampire body in England last year."

"Yes. Personality transfer can be accomplished whether or not both parties are willing. There was a corpse left behind in the space vessel at

Wolf 359, an Ubiguti. The Antagonist routinely kills the previous host after a transfer."

Terry sighed. This wasn't like the Eels on the Great Barrier Reef, or the Skeletons in Mecca, or even what happened in Bangkok. At least with Piotr, they knew what *species* the bad guy was.

"So he could be any visitor on Earth?"

"Precisely."

Great.

Race Relations

> *...he was a man who looked to what ought to be done, not to the reputation which is got by a man's acts.*
> —*Meditations, I, 16*

Buried deep in the darkest corridors of the Department of Off World Affairs lay the Policy Section. Policy, for a traditional government state department—the US Department of State, for example—was a complex enough endeavor, with nearly two hundred nations around the globe. Dozens more splinter groups within each nation demanded—and often received—special attention for their various causes from the United States. The US had to have an official policy regarding each and every one of these groups, for matters of diplomacy, commerce, immigration, extradition, and more.

For DOWA, the issue was exponentially more involved. True, only a fraction of the thousands of starfaring civilizations in the galaxy had made an appearance in the Earth system, but the mandate from above—from Krensky, and his immediate boss, Secretary Hargrove—was to prepare for *any* eventuality. Each off world race on which DOWA had any intelligence was to be put through the "Policy Machine".

The Policy Machine was the analysts' nickname for the process of developing a policy portfolio from scratch for a group that they knew almost nothing about. Case in point: Starfish. No representative of the Starfish race had visited Earth as yet. DOWA only learned of their existence through an informal conversation with the CA Conduct Officer. Kird had described them as an amphibious, five-armed race, with limited expansionist goals. They lived on the opposite side of the galaxy, on a world composed entirely of archipelagos, with twice the atmospheric pressure of Earth. All in all, it was unlikely that Earth would meet the Starfish anytime soon.

Despite all of that, the Policy Machine hummed to life for the Star-fish, using ever-changing policy templates for each of the major subject areas, modifying where appropriate for a race that lived their entire lives on a beach. As an example, in a standard diplomatic meeting, government appointees from the two worlds would generally gather in a conference room. For the Starfish, some kind of pressurized tank would be required to house the visitors.

The job had its surreal aspects.

One of the analysts tasked with cranking up the Policy Machine was a man named Ronald Xavier. Thirty-two years of age, with a wife and a toddler son, a degree in International Affairs, and eight years of experi-ence in civil service, Ronald hit a mark of above-average on every yearly review and was, for the most part, content. He'd been with DOWA since its inception, having transferred from State. His current career path in-cluded probable promotion to Senior Analyst. He looked at promotion to Section Chief as a possible long-range goal.

On this warm, August Monday morning, Ronald sat with the rest of the office drones in DOWA, their eyes glued to one of the cable news channels. Everyone watched what was happening on the screen with mounting horror, and Ronald was no exception. He was, however, an ex-ception in that his presence in the lunch room made everyone *else* a little uncomfortable. He ignored their skittish glances in his direction. It wasn't like he was one of the angry faces on the screen.

The Harlem neighborhood in New York City had gone through a number of cycles of degradation and gentrification over the years, but it had always maintained a largely black population, and a proudly black identity. This morning, it was the center of what was shaping up to be the worst US race riot of the Twenty-First Century.

The reporters on the ground—mostly black faces, Ronald noticed—were trying desperately to report on something that no one seemed to understand. The only thing they knew for certain was that a delegation of off world visitors had arrived in Harlem and sparked the incident. Three storefronts were known to be broken so far. Police were trying to contain the situation, with scant hope of quelling it directly. So far, it could still be generously described as a "spontaneous protest", but it could have tipped over into a full riot easily. The cops stayed at a prudent distance, waiting out the protesters, expecting that they would tire and leave the area, perhaps at dinner time. Everyone had to eat.

The National Guard was on the way, just in case. Ten minutes ago, POTUS made a televised appeal for calm. Since none of the people on the streets were watching television, Ronald wasn't exactly sure what the President was trying to accomplish. Perhaps he was trying to calm people watching the riot from their couches in Kansas.

Despite the terrible situation, Ronald was enough of a policy wonk that he wanted to know which race of visitors caused the riot, so that he could update their file appropriately.

"Ronald!"

He looked up, over the crowd in the lunch room, to see his Section Chief calling to him. He slipped out of the rickety folding chair and went over to the fifty-something woman.

"Tracy?"

"They want you."

Ronald sighed. "Of course they do."

Though the four of them met in Dale Krensky's office, there was no doubt who ran this meeting.

"Here's what we know," Secretary Hargrove said. Ronald, having been at DOWA since the beginning, had watched Hargrove change from wide-eyed idealist to hard-bitten pragmatist in a very short time. Everything about her screamed Washington Power Player now, from her severe black top and skirt to her no-nonsense bangs. He hoped she had a personal life outside the office to let off steam. There was talk that she had a boyfriend in the CDC, but there was also talk that she had broken things off with him. Talk was talk. Ronald knew enough not to trust it.

"There was a meeting scheduled between the Harlem Chamber of Commerce and a group of visitors called…" Hargrove referred to her tablet. "…Dandelions."

"I haven't heard of them," Ronald admitted.

"They're new," the Air Force major said. Ronald had seen the man in the halls, but didn't know his name. Events were unfolding too fast to allow for introductions. For now, he was just *the major.* "They checked in on *Ronald Reagan* this morning."

"And they're not alone," Dale Krensky piped up, furrowed brow low over his own tablet screen. "They're traveling with another race, called Picassos."

Ronald blinked. Most visiting races had names that conjured images of animals or plants. Why name a race after an artist? This was not the time to ask those kinds of questions, and Ronald stayed prudently quiet. The tension in the room was disturbingly high.

To be fair, it was Hargrove and the major who seemed tense. Krensky had a hint of a grin; he almost looked *pleased* by the crisis. Perhaps Krensky had given Hargrove some warning that she hadn't heeded, and this was the result. Krensky was *that* kind of a bureaucrat, at least according to the talk around the office: the kind who turned others' failures into his personal successes. Just one more reason Ronald didn't want to rise *too* far in the ranks around here.

"You're coming with us to New York," Hargrove said.

"Because I'm black," Ronald shot back, without thinking. He almost apologized... but not quite.

"You're an off world policy analyst," the major said, clearly finding the situation awkward. With that southern accent of his, and that uniform, he certainly couldn't be unfamiliar with African Americans. Ronald chalked his embarrassment up to generic white guilt. Hargrove wasn't nearly as troubled, throwing a nasty look at the major for his attempt at dissembling.

"Yes, Mr. Xavier, because you're black, but also because you're an expert in off world relations." She softened the moment slightly with a small, mirthless smile. "So we get a two-fer."

The next hour was a whirlwind of activity. The four of them and a small contingent of Secret Service rushed to a nearby helipad where they got into a Marine chopper—a model similar to the one POTUS used—for the jaunt up to New York. Ronald learned the name of the major—Youngblood—and he learned a handful of other facts that they knew about the riot.

The Dandelions and Picassos had come looking for labor for some sort of industrial project. The result of the negotiations had been angry protests and some violence. Unfortunately, the why was still a mystery.

Hargrove and Youngblood argued over the best way to handle the situation, the tension seeming to bring them near to blows. Krensky tossed in his two cents, and was shouted down by both of them. There seemed to be something personal going on between the two of them. From what Ronald could hear over the roar of the helicopter's rotors, Hargrove seemed to be worked up because Youngblood was spending too much time down in Florida with the *Vimana* team. She implied, vaguely, that his dereliction of his duties might have some connection to the Harlem crisis. Youngblood countered with some cryptic reference to the CDC.

Ronald kept carefully silent, wishing he couldn't hear their personal argument at all. Rather than waste time theorizing about Hargrove and Youngblood and what might be going on between them, he spent the trip marshalling arguments for his introduction to the leaders of the black community in Harlem. He knew they'd see him as a token, as a poster child for the "diversity" of public service. There were some minorities in positions of importance at DOWA, but he was, at present, the highest ranking African American in Policy. Lucky him.

From the sky, Ronald could see that the NYPD had set up barricades a couple of blocks in all directions from the center of the riot, the intersection of Seventh and MLK. The police did their best to keep the rioters in and the curiosity seekers out, but it was almost a symbolic gesture. The area was far too spread out to effectively contain. There had to be ten thousand people in the vicinity, every one of them yelling or chanting. What could possibly have sparked all of this?

The helicopter landed on the roof of the Adam Clayton Powell Jr. State Office Building, across the intersection from the epicenter of the situation. Theresa Towers was a white brick building that had a century-long history in Harlem, dating back to Prohibition. Now, it was mostly used as office space, no longer taking guests, despite the fact that the building's original name, Hotel Theresa, was still painted prominently on one wall. There were a few conference rooms for lease on the lower floors. This was where the rioting sparked and where both parties—the visitors and the Harlem Chamber of Commerce—were holed up, waiting for the disturbance to end. Or be *brought* to an end.

Even from inside the lobby of the Powell Building, the noise was deafening. An escort of Secret Service and police in riot gear formed up around Ronald and the others. The armed officers brought them out into the Powell Building's broad concrete courtyard and pushed through the crowd, taking their charges across the intersection to Theresa Towers. Grainy, black-and-white film footage from sixty years ago ran through Ronald's mind—fire hoses and dogs and policemen with truncheons— even though those events predated his own life by decades. Those images died hard.

Protesters, many with hastily made placards, surrounded Theresa Towers shouting or chanting slogans. Ronald caught a few of the words: "…we won't go back…" and "…send them home…" It didn't make any sense.

At the sight of Ronald's face, some of the crowd cheered, others shouted obscenities. He tried to ignore it all, to focus on the task at hand.

Inside the building, the noise was muffled, but far from gone. A Theresa Towers security guard, a tall, thick-set black man, nodded to the police, and took the group farther into the building, away from the angry mob just outside the entrance. They came into a sterile, marble and stone corridor that ran the length of the building.

"Where are they?" Hargrove asked.

"The human folks, they're over there." The guard pointed to the east. "The aliens, they're over that way." West.

Krensky put a hand on Ronald's arm and gently pulled him to the west.

"Wait. What? You want *me* to talk to the off worlders?" Ronald asked.

"Yes?" Hargrove said, turning. She and Youngblood were already starting toward the delegation from the Harlem Chamber of Commerce. "You're the expert on off world policy. Go. Be expert." She turned again and stalked off to catch up with the major, who was already twenty feet away.

"Come on." Krensky led Ronald out of the lobby and down the stark corridor to a meeting room. The double doors were closed—likely because across the corridor from the doors were floor to ceiling windows that faced the street. The protesters who were just on the other side raised their voices at the sight of the two diplomats. The ones closest pounded on the glass. Krensky held the door to the conference room open a crack and slipped through, with Ronald following.

He was struck first by the smell. Remarkably few off world races had distinctive odors. The Trees smelled vaguely of orange and lemon. A recently arrived race, Anacondas—not to be confused with Snakes or Eels—smelled somewhat of cinnamon, sparking endless references at DOWA to the *Dune* novels. This room, however, was suffused with the sticky-sweet aroma of cotton candy. Ronald realized, with an amused grin, that he was smelling Dandelions.

Inside the multipurpose room, folding tables were stowed against the soft, teal walls, and stacks of semi-upholstered chairs filled one corner. The rest of the room was empty, except for flimsy clouds of white fluff, floating on the breezes from the air conditioners. One cloud drifted toward Krensky and Ronald, and spoke.

"You are members of the government of the United States of America?"

Unfazed by the sudden speech from the Dandelion, Krensky responded. "Yes. My name is Dale Krensky. I'm with the Department of Off World Affairs. This is Ronald Xavier, from our Policy Section. We're here to try to resolve this conflict."

"I am Gris," the Dandelion said. He drifted closer to Ronald. The creature wasn't actually a cloud of vapor, but a dense collection of very fine threads, reminiscent of a spider's web, though infinitely more complex. Ronald tried to determine how the thing might move and talk, with so little mass and no obvious limbs or organs. Perhaps it used electrical signals to ionize the air around it? Would that be enough?

Gris continued. "Mr. Xavier, may I ask why our reasonable request has caused such consternation with the local slave descendants?"

"The who?" Ronald asked, nearly shouting. His words shot out forcefully enough to cause Gris to skitter backward, riding a wave of angry breath. Krensky grinned again. Ronald didn't see what the man found so damn funny. "I apologize," Ronald said smoothly as Gris drifted back to the humans. "It is not considered polite to refer to African Americans as slave descendants."

"As I have learned," Gris said, "though I fail to understand the na-ture of your concern with the term. You are, are you not, the descendants of slaves, brought here in past centuries by those of European stock?"

"Many of us are, that is true. But we are equals with the whites now."

"Equals? I do not think so. You are sequestered into this neighbor-hood, are you not?"

"No, we're not *sequestered.* Many blacks choose to live in Harlem, to be with their brothers."

"Are not the whites your brothers as well? If you are not the same, but different, then how can you be equals?"

Ronald found his exasperation mounting. He didn't want to get drawn into a philosophical discussion of the African American identity crisis. He needed to determine the core issue that had caused the riot and address it. He couldn't imagine it was simply a response to an awkwardly worded description of the locals. Skins around here weren't as thin as that.

"If you don't mind..." Ronald looked to Krensky for help. The other man was content to watch, so Ronald pressed forward. "...I'd like to know what exactly caused the altercation in the first place."

"Certainly. I am Labor Manager for a multi-system industrial con-glomerate. We build prefabricated housing for orbital dormitory facilities; we subcontract for the habitation modules of interstellar craft; we con-struct gravity-well arcologies for planets either in meteorological distress or in the early stages of bioforming. As Earth has risen in notoriety, we anticipate further increases in immigration to your world from other sys-tems, and hope to provide the means to comfortably house these visitors without causing undue stress on your own, Human-based infrastructure."

Ronald assumed this speech was carefully written and meticulously rehearsed. It flowed flawlessly from the Dandelion, and Ronald saw noth-ing inflammatory about it. Someone should have thought of this idea sooner. Everything Gris planned to do would help Earth immeasurably.

Gris continued: "As a company policy, we prefer to use local labor in our factories, and we hoped to enlist American slave descendants, due to their technical knowledge and their history of subservience."

The Dandelion's tone remained seamless, though his words were so vile they gave Ronald a nasty shiver.

"You want to hire blacks… because we used to be slaves?"

"Hire? No, we do not plan to contract with you. We plan to make you our subjects."

"Subjects?" Krensky asked, his tone filled with suppressed hilarity. He really found this all quite amusing. Ronald wanted desperately, just at that moment, to punch him.

The Dandelion wafted about, unable to maintain a fixed position for very long with air conditioners blowing the air around. "You will be well treated, I assure you." Gris now subtly included Ronald in his plans, as if *all* blacks would function as his labor pool. "Housing and nutrition, education and entertainment. Everything you would aspire to attain in a free market—and which, I might add, you would likely never achieve—we can provide. We only ask for your labor in return."

Now Ronald understood the riot perfectly. He was tempted to storm out of the building, grab the nearest sign and join the protesters himself. The idea that African Americans—or the descendants of *any* slaves, for that matter—would voluntarily submit to *another* enslavement was unthinkable. And to *ask* such a thing was grotesque.

"Central Authority has a moratorium on genocide," Ronald croaked.

"We do not wish to eradicate your people, Mr. Xavier," Gris said, somewhat displeased by the accusation. "That would not make good business sense."

"Business sense…" Ronald muttered.

"I see from your outward emotional state that your response to our proposal is similar to that of the Harlem leaders. I can assure you that we have much experience in this matter and would make excellent masters."

"Experience?" Krensky asked.

"With other subject races. The Grntkow, for example."

"The Picassos?" Ronald managed to mumble.

"Yes, that is the name you have given them." Some unseen, unheard communication from Gris caused a door at the far end of the room to open. Through it walked a Picasso.

The creature stood solidly on four legs, somewhere between a large dog and a small horse in size. The front legs were thick, double-jointed, ending in heavy, dog-like paws. The rear legs were slender, single-jointed, resembling those of a deer. The creature seemed to have two heads. The one closest to Ronald as it approached was the larger, with three unsettlingly dissimilar eyes and a single tiny, folded mouth. The head to the rear was smaller, tucked down lower to the torso, with its own sensory organs. Rising from the middle of the oblong body was one limb, though it didn't look strictly like an arm. It branched and branched again, resembling a smaller version of a Tree. The various branches of the limb waved slightly, clearly under the control of the Picasso.

"Sdlitkow, come here," Gris commanded. The Picasso picked up its pace and trotted over to stop directly beneath Gris. Gris floated about the tree-like upper limb. The Picasso's branches gently petted Gris's gossamer form. "Sdlitkow, this is Dale Krensky and Ronald Xavier."

"I greet you," the Picasso said in a throaty rumble.

"Hello," Ronald said. "I understand you... work for the Dandelions."

"I work for Gris. Gris is Dandelion. Others work for others." Sdlitkow lowered his forward head and pawed at the low carpet for a bit. Ronald didn't know if that movement was a good or a bad sign, or just a meaningless cultural tic.

"Are you paid for your work?"

"I eat. I sleep."

"Can you leave Gris's service? Are you free to do as you will?"

Sdlitkow's back legs hopped once, then scraped against the carpet.

"Such questions are not wise," Gris counseled.

"I think they are very wise," Ronald snapped. He wasn't playing the diplomat anymore. He wasn't layering his disdain for the Dandelion behind eloquent words and careful tones. Ronald was disgusted, horrified in fact, to learn that slavery was an accepted practice out in the galaxy. He didn't know how many races practiced it, but at least one did. There was no mention of it in the Rules of Conduct. That omission never triggered any warning bells with Ronald. It seemed so obvious, so basic. The realization made the dropping of the barrier unsettlingly distasteful all of a sudden. This was the first time Ronald had felt morally superior to an off world race.

"Sdlitkow, what do you *want* for your life?"

"Please, do not antagonize the poor beast," Gris said. "You put too much strain on his mind. Grntkow have a limited functionality with abstraction."

"He's not a *beast*, he's a sentient creature, just like you and me. Just because your race has—"

Perhaps it was Ronald's angry tone, or simply the fact that his breath had once again buffeted Gris, causing him to slip away from Sdlitkow. Whatever it was, the Picasso didn't like it and he reacted. He reared up on his front legs, his rear legs bicycling through the air. With a low-pitched roar, Sdlitkow spun about. His rear head tilted forward, revealing a blunt, shiny surface which was now pointed toward Ronald. With a great shove of the dog-like legs, Sdlitkow butted Ronald in the chest, sending him sprawling to the carpet.

A siren of noise came from Gris, and was soon echoed by the other Dandelions in the room. Before the Picasso could trample Ronald, it froze. Another hectoring sound from Gris caused Sdlitkow to turn and gallop away from Ronald, the massive, canine legs now serving as its rear legs, giving it a very different gait when in flight.

Sdlitkow collided with the far door of the room, which stunned him, leaving him seemingly at a loss. The other Dandelions in the room weaved about faster than before, clearly unsettled by the incident with the Picasso. The siren screaming had stopped but Ronald seemed to hear a high pitched whine coming from them, like one of those old monitors with a vacuum tube.

"He will be alright," Gris concluded. "Are you hurt, Mr. Xavier?"

Ronald barely felt the impact of Sdlitkow's attack; he was still too agitated by the entire concept of the Picassos being a "subject race". He picked himself up—without assistance from Krensky, by the way. "How can you... Why did you..." Ronald couldn't put together a single sentence, he was so overcome. He glared at Krensky. The other man sighed, then took over.

"Gris, you need to understand that slavery, as a concept, is reviled by humanity. We have abandoned the concept and have done our best to forget that it ever happened."

"We have *not!*" Ronald shouted. "We remember, but we do not excuse or defend its practice. And we certainly don't *condone* it."

"We misunderstood the vehemence with which Humanity regards this topic."

No shit, Ronald didn't say. He took a deep breath and continued: "We have, it seems, a basic cultural conflict between our races that will not be an easy one to overcome."

"Yes. I see. We had hoped that since your race had engaged in the practice of subjugation so recently in your history that you would not have abandoned such modes of thought from your collective psyche."

"Well, we have. And I think it would be best," Ronald said, taking a deep, cleansing breath, "that you leave Earth altogether." Krensky gave Ronald a vicious glare. Ronald ignored him. Most diplomats would have tried to find the common ground, to work around the cultural difference between their peoples.

They didn't tap *most diplomats* for this trip. They tapped Ronald Xavier, and they were stuck with him. Maybe they'd override his comments and reopen a dialogue with the Dandelions; maybe they'd fire him for his impudence. He didn't much care at the moment.

"I do not think continued relations between us would be advisable."

"As you wish," Gris said. He floated away, returning to the bank of other Dandelions clumped in the middle of the room.

"Xavier," Krensky grated. Ronald continued to ignore his superior as he left the room with all the dignity he could muster. In the corridor, he saw Hargrove and Youngblood running toward them, looking flustered.

"Ronald, we just heard. I had no idea…" Hargrove said. Ronald waved her off.

"I'm glad I got to be one to send them packing," he said proudly. Youngblood looked shocked. Krensky still looked angry. Hargrove, however, gave Ronald an affectionate pat on the shoulder.

"Good for you."

Prometheus

> *It is no evil for things to un-*
> *dergo change, and no good for*
> *things to subsist in consequence of*
> *change.*
> —*Meditations, IV, 24*

History often remembers persons of great importance not by their name as given at birth, but by another name, a name of grandeur and gravitas, a name that echoes through the years with great or terrible significance. Who, besides scholars of the past, remembers the names Siddhārtha Gautama, Temüüjin, Vladimir Ilyich Ulyanov, or Karol Józef Wojtyła?

During the month of January, 2028, the eyes of the world landed on the small East African republic of Djibouti. There, an off world visitor shook the foundations of human society, and was brought to trial for her presumption. This visitor's birth name was beyond the skills of any human to pronounce. Soon after she began her crusade, a media circus surrounded her every move. The reporters attempted to frame her actions for their readership, and gave her a new name that fired the imagination and proclaimed to the world her goals. It is by this name she will be remembered.

#

INTERNATIONAL CRIMINAL COURT
ENERGY CRISIS OF DJIBOUTI
Case No: ICC-27/08-28/01
Transcription No: ICC-27/08-28/01-Q-55-EN
Wednesday, 19 January at 3:02 p.m.
OPEN SESSION

Before:
His Honour Judge Christian Makemba (Presiding Judge)
Her Honour Judge Kathleen Krause
His Honour Judge Yuko Tatami

PRE-TRIAL CHAMBER I

OPEN SESSION

THE USHER: All rise. The International Criminal Court is now in session.

PRESIDING JUDGE MAKEMBA: Good afternoon. Welcome to the participants and to the public. I understand how much attention is being paid this case and the extraordinary speed with which we have come to trial. It has been with the blessings of all parties that we have accelerated our normal process. It is also for this reason that we meet in this auditorium, to allow for larger than usual representation of the press. We ask that flash photography not be used and that auditory commentary from reporters be saved for recess. Thank you. Court Officer, call the case.

COURT OFFICER: Thank you, your Honour. Energy Crisis of Djibouti, the case of the Prosecutor versus Prometheus, ICC-27/08-28/01.

HON. MAKEMBA: I would ask the participants to introduce themselves. Mr. Prosecutor.

MR. ILLUD: Thank you. The prosecutorial team is Mr. Garrett Langhorn, Senior Trial Lawyer; Ms. Helena Blankenship and Mr. Stephan Roblonsky, Associate Trial Lawyers; Ms. Candide Evers and Mr. Tyndal Gorman, Legal Advisors; Mr. Jean Lestrange, Mr. Henri Felicite and Ms. Angela Choi, Associate Legal Advisors; Ms. Jaime Agoro, Case Manager; and Mr. Constantine Franks, Deputy Prosecutor for Prosecutions. I am Marteen Illud, Prosecutor.

HON. MAKEMBA: Thank you, Mr. Illud. Now for the Defense.

MR. BOLTON: Alistair Bolton, and only Alistair Bolton, for the Defense, your Honour. I am afraid that if a cricket match breaks out, I will have to enlist ten persons from the gallery to join my team.

HON. MAKEMBA: Yes, yes. Order please. Thank you for your amusing introduction, Mr. Bolton. We shall proceed with a bit more decorum. You would introduce your Defendant, please.

MR. BOLTON: I represent Prometheus, your Honour.

PROMETHEUS: Good afternoon.

MR. ILLUD: I wish to object, your Honour. As this is our first Pre-Trial Chamber, I have not had the opportunity to make the Prosecution's position on this point clear.

MR. BOLTON: I'm not sure I'm aware to what point you're objecting. Your Honor, may I object to his objection?

MR. ILLUD: We object to the use of the name Prometheus when referring to the Defendant. The name conjures images of valiant self-sacrifice in the name of human advancement.

MR. BOLTON: You suspect that this is a coincidence?

HON. MAKEMBA: Mr. Bolton, please. Mr. Illud, as I understand the situation, the Defendant had the opportunity to select a name for herself upon arrival at the Excalibur space station.

MR. ILLUD: That is correct. At that time she chose the name Saphira.

MR. BOLTON: That name was suggested by a literary minded station employee. Prometheus took the name without sufficient knowledge of Earth culture.

MR. ILLUD: There is nothing objectionable about the name Saphira.

MR. BOLTON: Nor is there about the name Prometheus.

MR. ILLUD: It is the name of a male. The Defendant is female.

MR. BOLTON: This from a man named Marteen?

HON. MAKEMBA: Gentlemen, please. The Defendant took the name Saphira legally, and we shall amend the case transcripts to—

MR. BOLTON: Your Honour, the Defendant has had her name changed legally to Prometheus.

HON. MAKEMBA: As a result of your counsel, no doubt.

MR. BOLTON: I am a very good lawyer, your Honour.

PROMETHEUS: Your Honour, if I may?

HON. MAKEMBA: Yes, please.

PROMETHEUS: I changed my official designation on 11 October of last year, five weeks prior to any legal action on the part of this Court. I have documentation.

HON. MAKEMBA: We will take a short recess to review.

(The Court took a ten minute recess.)

HON. MAKEMBA: We have reviewed the Defendant's documents and concur that her legal name is now Prometheus. The Prosecution's motion is hereby denied.

MR. BOLTON: I knew I liked you, your Honour.

HON. MAKEMBA: If there are no other Pre-Trial motions? This Court is adjourned.

#

INTERNATIONAL CRIMINAL COURT
ENERGY CRISIS OF DJIBOUTI
Case No: ICC-27/08-28/01
Transcription No: ICC-27/08-28/01-Q-57-EN
Friday, 21 January at 1:32 p.m.
OPEN SESSION

Before:
His Honour Judge Christian Makemba (Presiding Judge)
Her Honour Judge Kathleen Krause

His Honour Judge Yuko Tatami

PROSECUTION CHAMBER I

OPEN SESSION

(excerpt)

MS. BLANKENSHIP: Please state your name for the Court.

MS. ĀGGONĀFIR: My name is Kidist Āggonāfir. I am the Mayor of the city of Djibouti.

MS. BLANKENSHIP: Thank you. Please, if you would, describe your first meeting with the Defendant.

MS. ĀGGONĀFIR: Yes, of course. Prometheus contacted me in July of last year with a proposal for—

MS. BLANKENSHIP: Excuse me, Madam Mayor. If you would, please describe the Defendant's appearance.

MR. BOLTON: I object most strenuously.

HON. MAKEMBA: You need not describe your emotional state as you object, Mr. Bolton.

MR. BOLTON: My client's appearance is immaterial to these proceedings.

MS. BLANKENSHIP: On the contrary, your Honour. This is not the simple matter of skin colour or hair type. This is an alien with a remarkably different and frankly intimidating appearance.

MR. BOLTON: And if I feel intimidated by you, Ms. Blankenship? What then is my recourse?

HON. MAKEMBA: The Prosecution makes a valid point. Ms. Āggonāfir, you will answer the question.

MS. ĀGGONĀFIR: Prometheus is a Dragon. Her body is black and dark grey. She walks on four legs and has a torso which rises above her forelegs. Her head resembles a lion's in shape, though it is a deep orange in colour. She is also—

MS. BLANKENSHIP: Yes?

MS. ĀGGONĀFIR: She is very warm.

MS. BLANKENSHIP: The Defendant is actually quite hot, is she not? To the point of discomfort.

MS. ĀGGONĀFIR: I wouldn't say discomfort—

MS. BLANKENSHIP: I understand from your Pre-Trial deposition that you had to move the meeting from your office in the Town Hall to a larger room because the heat coming from the Defendant was stifling.

MS. ĀGGONĀFIR: My office is quite small.

MS. BLANKENSHIP: Did you have occasion to see the Defendant in a darkened room?

MS. ĀGGONĀFIR: Yes.

MS. BLANKENSHIP: And what did you see?

MS. ĀGGONĀFIR: Prometheus glows a bit. Around the mouth area.

MS. BLANKENSHIP: So Dragon is a reasonable name for her race, is it not?

MS. ĀGGONĀFIR: I suppose it is. But that didn't—

MS. BLANKENSHIP: Did you consider yourself in danger in the Defendant's presence?

MS. ĀGGONĀFIR: I was taken aback, yes, but not in any danger.

MS. BLANKENSHIP: With respect, Ms. Āggonāfir, I did not ask if you were in danger. I asked if you, at any point, felt you were in danger.

MS. ĀGGONĀFIR: There are not that many aliens in my city, Ms. Blankenship. I am wary of all of them at first meeting. You may remember the affair of the Skeletons in Mecca.

MS. BLANKENSHIP: Please continue your description of your meeting with the Defendant.

MS. ĀGGONĀFIR: Prometheus came to me with a new energy generation technology.

MS. BLANKENSHIP: Did she make it clear that she had already sold this technology to Westron Oil?

MS. ĀGGONĀFIR: She did, in fact.

MS. BLANKENSHIP: And you had no concerns in breaking international patent law?

MR. BOLTON: I object. The exact nature of this contract between Prometheus and Westron remains in dispute.

HON. MAKEMBA: Duly noted, Mr. Bolton, but the witness will answer. Objection overruled.

MS. ĀGGONĀFIR: I do not wish to cause difficulty for—

MS. BLANKENSHIP: It's alright, Ms. Āggonāfir. Neither you nor your town are the one on trial. Please, answer the question. Did you have concerns that you might be breaking international law?

MS. ĀGGONĀFIR: To be honest, I did not. The international legal community seemed little interested in my country before I met Prometheus. Her promises seemed to—

MS. BLANKENSHIP: Thank you. No further questions.

MR. BOLTON: Does Prometheus breathe fire?

MS. ĀGGONĀFIR: Excuse me?

MR. BOLTON: Ms. Blankenship has gone to some trouble to describe my client as quite similar in nature to the traditional fantasy image of dragons. I simply wish to clarify this similarity in the minds of our esteemed magistrates. Does Prometheus breathe fire?

MS. ĀGGONĀFIR: Not to my knowledge.

MR. BOLTON: I see. I do have one other question for you. Ms. Āggonāfir, would you say that the standard of living in your country has increased, decreased, or remained constant since the arrival of Prometheus?

MS. ĀGGONĀFIR: It has increased, without any doubt. It has increased significantly.

MR. BOLTON: Thank you, ma'am.

(excerpt)

MS. BLANKENSHIP: Please state your name for the Court.

MS. DESAI: Keira Desai.

MS. BLANKENSHIP: And what is your occupation?

MS. DESAI: I am a Project Lead for Maccha-Yantra Consortium. I'm part of the team building Earth's first starship.

MS. BLANKENSHIP: So it would be reasonable to assume that you are an expert in the vagaries of alien technology.

MS. DESAI: I have a great deal of experience in that field.

MS. BLANKENSHIP: Is it standard practice to make all such new technologies openly available to the public?

MS. DESAI: No, it is not. The dangers can be very real when ordinary people are unfamiliar with the consequences of these new concepts.

MS. BLANKENSHIP: So, you have, yourself, come into contact with new technologies that have been kept safe and sequestered, until such a time as they could be safely introduced to the world.

MS. DESAI: Yes, several times.

MS. BLANKENSHIP: Are you familiar with the device known as a water box?

MS. DESAI: I am.

MS. BLANKENSHIP: Could you describe its function to the Court?

MS. DESAI: A water box contains a culture of genetically engineered algae, extraterrestrial in origin. The algae feed off of water, breaking it down into its constituent elements, hydrogen and oxygen. The algae process the oxygen for food, releasing the hydrogen as waste. The box captures this excess and thus can provide a significant amount of power by burning the captured hydrogen. This design is similar in theory to bioreactors scientists have been researching for decades, but far more efficient and therefore a realistically viable source of energy.

MS. BLANKENSHIP: And this is the device that Prometheus made available to the citizens of Djibouti?

MS. DESAI: That is my understanding.

MS. BLANKENSHIP: As an expert in this field, would you have done the same? Would you have made this new technology widely available?

MS. DESAI: I would not.

MS. BLANKENSHIP: Why is that?

MS. DESAI: Dragons may be perfectly comfortable with these devices, but there are many factors which are unique to Earth which may cause unforeseen complications. Hydrogen, in particular, is a volatile substance, prone to explosion and fire. The reactive algae may also present a danger. If it were to be released into the environment, it could conceivably spread to every corner of the planet and consume our oceans. Without extensive research and proper safety protocols, it is impossible to know what might happen.

MS. BLANKENSHIP: Thank you, Ms. Desai. No further questions.

MR. BOLTON: Ordinary people?

MS. DESAI: Excuse me?

MR. BOLTON: Earlier in your testimony you referred to ordinary people. I assume you're not simply a fan of Robert Redford's directorial oeuvre. Could you tell me what you mean when you say ordinary people?

MS. DESAI: Those who aren't experienced in scientific research. Lay persons.

MR. BOLTON: The poor.

HON. MAKEMBA: Mr. Bolton.

MR. BOLTON: A thousand apologies, your Honour. Ms. Desai, I wonder if you could tell me what is the specific nature of your work with Maccha-Yantra.

MS. DESAI: Project Lead.

MR. BOLTON: That is your title, yes. But, please forgive me, on what specifically do you work? Are you involved in energy production? Biological interfaces? Cultural exchange?

MS. DESAI: No, sir.

MR. BOLTON: In fact, you work almost exclusively with aluminum.

MS. DESAI: I manage a number of projects in addition to the fabrication of carbon-aluminum.

MR. BOLTON: All of which involve production of engineering materials.

MS. DESAI: Yes.

MR. BOLTON: So, when you say there are any number of dangers inherent in the use of a water box, this is merely your opinion. You do not have any research or specific experience with this algae, with hydrogen, with any of the device's components, in fact, to back up this suggestion.

MS. DESAI: I have experience with other instances wherein the safety of—

MR. BOLTON: Yes, yes. To your knowledge, has anyone died through the malfunction of a water box?

MS. DESAI: Not yet.

MR. BOLTON: Has anyone been injured? Has anyone reported any malfunction of any kind?

MS. DESAI: I don't believe so.

MR. BOLTON: I wonder, since you are expert in areas which appear to be, at best, tangential to these proceedings, do you have colleagues at Maccha-Yantra who are more directly involved in technologies like the water box?

MS. DESAI: I do.

MR. BOLTON: What would you expect their views to be on the widespread release of the water box?

MS. DESAI: You would have to ask them.

MR. BOLTON: If only that were possible, Ms. Desai. We have subpoenaed a number of your fellows, but strangely, only you were given leave to join us here in Djibouti. Would you care to venture a theory on that?

MS. DESAI: No, I would not.

MR. BOLTON: You don't believe that the partnership between Maccha-Yantra Consortium and Westron Oil might make it less likely for your employer to provide witnesses to this court in support of Prometheus.

MS. DESAI: I—

MR. ILLUD: Objection, your Honour.

HON. MAKEMBA: Sustained.

MR. BOLTON: At your Honour's ruling I withdraw this otherwise perfectly reasonable question. Thank you, Ms. Desai. I have nothing further.

#

INTERNATIONAL CRIMINAL COURT
ENERGY CRISIS OF DJIBOUTI
Case No: ICC-27/08-28/01
Transcription No: ICC-27/08-28/01-Q-58-EN
Tuesday, 25 January at 1:51 p.m.
OPEN SESSION

Before:
His Honour Judge Christian Makemba (Presiding Judge)
Her Honour Judge Kathleen Krause
His Honour Judge Yuko Tatami

PROSECUTION CHAMBER II

OPEN SESSION

(excerpt)

MR. ROBLONSKY: Good afternoon. Please state your name for the Court.

MR. GUELLEH: I am Rassan Guelleh, sir.

MR. ROBLONSKY: What is your job, sir?

MR. GUELLEH: I am the Managing Director of Djibouti Electrical Services Corporation. We are the sole provider of power to the nation.

MR. BOLTON: Objection, your Honour.

HON. MAKEMBA: Sustained.

MR. GUELLEH: My apologies. We were the sole provider of power to the nation, prior to October of last year.

MR. ROBLONSKY: Thank you, sir. Please explain to the Court the events of the fall and winter of 2027.

MR. GUELLEH: Certainly. Our office received an unusual number of requests for net metering of personal residences.

MR. ROBLONSKY: If you could elaborate on that. What is net metering?

MR. GUELLEH: There are certain entities which are able to generate small amounts of electricity locally, through wind turbines or solar cells. In such a case, if the power needs for a location are more than met with local power, the surplus can be sent back to DESC for a credit on the client's bill. This is a standard practice in power generation the world over.

MR. ROBLONSKY: But something rather different from the standard took place in November, did it not?

MR. GUELLEH: Yes. The amount of power coming in from residences grew exponentially. By the middle of the month, we were receiving more power than we sent out. We had to shut down the oil turbines for the last week of the month.

MR. ROBLONSKY: What effect did this have on your operations?

MR. GUELLEH: The financial ramifications were significant. We had to pay for every kilowatt-hour of electricity coming in from the net metering residences despite the fact that we had no market to sell it to. Bankruptcy was imminent.

MR. ROBLONSKY: The effects did not end there, did they, Mr. Guelleh?

MR. GUELLEH: No, sir. Our operations have never been so large that we had the need or the desire to network with other power generation companies in the region. With a huge surplus to sell and no market, we contacted firms in Eritrea, Ethiopia, Somalia and Yemen. The price of oil was at that time quite high, so they were eager for a cheaper source of power. We made the necessary line connections and contracted for power transfer with eight different firms.

MR. ROBLONSKY: What happened then in December?

MR. GUELLEH: The power output from the residences in our country grew larger still. Our business model had quite suddenly shifted from power generator to power broker. We burned no oil during December. Our power output to the region began to outstrip their demand. The effects began to propagate to farther distances.

MR. ROBLONSKY: How far, sir?

MR. GUELLEH: I cannot be certain, sir, but I do know that my cousin in Riyadh heard rumors that the Saudi royal family were vocal in their concern about the impact on the world oil market.

MR. ROBLONSKY: The impact caused by your nation?

MR. GUELLEH: Yes.

MR. ROBLONSKY: Thank you. Nothing further.

MR. BOLTON: I will be brief, my good man.

MR. GUELLEH: As you wish.

MR. BOLTON: Is your company doing well or doing poorly at this moment?

MR. GUELLEH: We have our problems, of course.

MR. BOLTON: I will rephrase the question. Are you still on the verge of bankruptcy?

MR. GUELLEH: No, sir.

MR. BOLTON: Have you not, in fact, surpassed the total of last year's revenues in only the first three weeks of this month?

MR. GUELLEH: That is true.

MR. BOLTON: Well done, sir. Nothing further.

(excerpt)

MR. ROBLONSKY: Welcome, sir. Please state your name and occupation.

MR. EL SAADÂWI: My name is Muhammad El Saadâwi. I am the Managing Director of Aswan Oil.

MR. ROBLONSKY: Your firm is one of the larger exporters of oil from the nation of Egypt.

MR. EL SAADÂWI: Yes.

MR. ROBLONSKY: You employ how many people?

MR. EL SAADÂWI: Until last month, sixty-five thousand.

MR. ROBLONSKY: And now?

MR. EL SAADÂWI: Less than twelve thousand.

MR. ROBLONSKY: A sizeable layoff.

MR. EL SAADÂWI: Indeed. But a necessity given the unrest in the oil market.

MR. ROBLONSKY: Is yours a unique occurrence?

MR. EL SAADÂWI: Far from it, I am afraid.

MR. ROBLONSKY: As a leading member of the oil industry in the region, how would you describe the impact of the Djibouti situation?

MR. EL SAADÂWI: The oil markets have gone into horrible turmoil around the world.

MR. ROBLONSKY: How would you characterize this turmoil?

MR. EL SAADÂWI: Loss of revenue, layoffs by the thousands, seizures of assets by creditors, tumbling stock prices across most world markets, even in areas that are only tangential to energy production and distribution.

MR. ROBLONSKY: The effects have been felt worldwide?

MR. EL SAADÂWI: Absolutely. ExxonMobil, Westron, British Petroleum. All are scrambling in the wake of this catastrophe. The aftereffects will reverberate throughout the economy for years to come.

MR. ROBLONSKY: Thank you, sir. Your witness, Mr. Bolton.

MR. BOLTON: You paint a frightening picture, my good sir.

MR. EL SAADÂWI: I offer the picture as I see it, Mr. Bolton.

MR. BOLTON: Unrest. Turmoil. Layoffs and seizures and scrambling. You used the word catastrophe.

MR. EL SAADÂWI: I did.

MR. BOLTON: How many have lost their lives, would you estimate?

MR. EL SAADÂWI: Sir?

MR. BOLTON: A round figure will be fine. To an order of magnitude, what is the death toll of this catastrophe?

MR. EL SAADÂWI: I do not know that anyone has lost their life.

MR. BOLTON: Indeed? This catastrophe has caused no human damage, then?

MR. EL SAADÂWI: On the contrary, tens of thousands in my company alone have lost their jobs, their pensions, their means of supporting themselves and their families.

MR. BOLTON: They have all become destitute, then, sir?

MR. EL SAADÂWI: Many have.

MR. BOLTON: There is no employment to be found in industries other than oil?

MR. EL SAADÂWI: These are highly trained personnel. It will be difficult for them to transition to other fields.

MR. BOLTON: Difficult. I see. I wonder if you could tell us the nature of the impact of this catastrophe on you.

MR. EL SAADÂWI: It has been very trying.

MR. BOLTON: I'm sure. What is your current salary, sir?

MR. EL SAADÂWI: Excuse me?

MR. ROBLONSKY: I must object, your Honour. The witness's personal remuneration scheme is irrelevant to these proceedings.

MR. BOLTON: I would disagree, your Honour. This catastrophe, as Mr. El Saadâwi calls it, is clearly financial in nature. He has painted a picture of the impact on his lowest level employees. I think it would be most revealing to know the extent of the damage, up to and including the Managing Director of Aswan Oil.

HON. MAKEMBA: Aswan Oil is a privately held company. As such, the specifics of Mr. El Saadâwi's compensation package will remain confidential, if that is what the witness wishes.

MR. EL SAADÂWI: Thank you, sir.

MR. BOLTON: Quite right, quite right, sir. You have set me straight. I wish to apologize for this faux-pas. Mr. El Saadâwi, if you would, without revealing any specific monetary amount, please tell the Court the percentage of your salary which you have lost as a result of this catastrophe.

MR. ROBLONSKY: Your Honour, my esteemed colleague merely asks the same question in a different form.

HON. MAKEMBA: No, he doesn't, Mr. Roblonsky. The witness will answer the question.

MR. EL SAADÂWI: I have not had any loss in salary.

MR. BOLTON: What an extraordinarily lucky man you are, Mr. El Saadâwi. I noticed that you spoke earlier of turmoil in the oil market. You are a fan of a free market economy, then?

MR. EL SAADÂWI: Who in this day is not?

MR. BOLTON: One might ask, one might ask. You may be aware that even though this Court tries Prometheus on the supposed crime of use of unauthorized technology, the firm with the legal rights to that technology has decided not to attend these proceedings.

MR. EL SAADÂWI: Is that a question?

MR. BOLTON: My apologies, sir. I shall reveal my question now. Is not the sequestration of the water box technology in fact a way to protect the oil market from an intrusive force, one which will provide so-called ordinary people with the means to generate their own power, thus creating a new and more vibrant energy market than we have ever seen on the world stage?

MR. EL SAADÂWI: I cannot comment on the motives of the executives of Westron Oil.

MR. BOLTON: Can you comment on your own? Would you, had you legal access to the water box, have used it or put it on the proverbial shelf? Would you have protected the old market or embraced the new?

MR. EL SAADÂWI: I do not—

MR. ILLUD: We object to questions of a hypothetical nature, your Honour.

HON. MAKEMBA: Sustained.

MR. BOLTON: What a pity, sir. I so looked forward to your answer. Nothing further.

#

INTERNATIONAL CRIMINAL COURT
ENERGY CRISIS OF DJIBOUTI
Case No: ICC-27/08-28/01
Transcription No: ICC-27/08-28/01-Q-59-EN
Wednesday, 26 January at 1:31 p.m.
OPEN SESSION

Before:
His Honour Judge Christian Makemba (Presiding Judge)
Her Honour Judge Kathleen Krause
His Honour Judge Yuko Tatami

DEFENSE CHAMBER I

OPEN SESSION

(excerpt)

MR. BOLTON: And you are?

MR. HAYLEMELEKOT: Waberi Haylemelekot, sir.

MR. BOLTON: And what job do you do?

MR. HAYLEMELEKOT: I am a farmer. I live in the Obock Region.

MR. BOLTON: In Djibouti.

MR. HAYLEMELEKOT: Yes, sir.

MR. BOLTON: I understand that you were the first of the ordinary people that Prometheus approached with her water box.

MR. HAYLEMELEKOT: Yes.

MR. BOLTON: Please, tell the Court in your own words what happened.

MR. HAYLEMELEKOT: The Dragon, Prometheus, visited my farm early in the morning on 14 July last year. She spooked my goats and made my wife faint.

MR. BOLTON: She does have a singular appearance. Do go on.

MR. HAYLEMELEKOT: She said she had a machine that could turn water into electricity. I did not believe her. She showed it to me. She started up my television and my radio with a few drops of water. She recharged my truck battery with just a little more. It had not run for several months.

MR. BOLTON: You are a farmer, sir. Have you need of electricity?

MR. HAYLEMELEKOT: We got by with only a little. It is expensive. Having my own electricity has made it easier to till my land, harvest my grain, take it to the market.

MR. BOLTON: It has helped with transportation?

MR. HAYLEMELEKOT: Prometheus showed me how to attach the water box to my truck. I do not have to buy gasoline anymore.

MR. BOLTON: Did Prometheus give you any warnings along with the water box?

MR. HAYLEMELEKOT: No, sir. I asked if the machine was dangerous, since it seemed very strange. She said it was safe.

MR. BOLTON: And so, seven months on, does it still function well?

MR. HAYLEMELEKOT: It works as well as the day I got it.

MR. BOLTON: And what did Prometheus ask for in exchange?

MR. HAYLEMELEKOT: Nothing. That was odd. I was worried at first that I had fallen in with some kind of alien gang, but nothing bad ever happened.

MR. BOLTON: Thank you for your time, Mr. Haylemelekot. Nothing further.

MR. LANGHORN: Sir, are you aware that you are party to an international crime?

MR. HAYLEMELEKOT: That's what they told me before I came here.

MR. LANGHORN: You have prospered from your use of this illegally obtained device.

MR. HAYLEMELEKOT: I have provided for my family. I have bought a few nice things for my home. We are not prosperous.

MR. LANGORN: The Dragon never told you that the license for this technology was owned by Westron Oil.

MR. HAYLEMELEKOT: She told me that she had talked to some powerful people a long time ago. She said that nothing happened with them, so she came to see me, since they didn't want to use it.

MR. LANGHORN: It is often the lowest rung of society that must front for organized criminal activity.

MR. BOLTON: Now my client is the leader of some Djibouti-based mafia?

HON. MAKEMBA: Do you have an objection, Mr. Bolton?

MR. BOLTON: Only one of logic, sir.

HON. MAKEMBA: Save such arguments for your closing. Mr. Langhorn, if you would continue?

MR. LANGHORN: I have no further use for this witness.

(excerpt)

MR. BOLTON: As if it were necessary, young lady, for the record, I must ask you for your name and profession.

MS. HARGROVE: My name is Vanessa Hargrove. I'm the United States Secretary of Off World Affairs.

MR. BOLTON: You have been involved in the relationship of Earth with the rest of the galaxy since the very beginning, have you not?

MS. HARGROVE: I have.

MR. BOLTON: Let the barrier fall. Those were your words.

MS. HARGROVE: They were.

MR. BOLTON: You believe we should trust any and every alien that visits our humble home then?

MS. HARGROVE: Far from it. We should be wary of off world visitors just as we are with each other. But xenophobia will not stop the changes that continue to occur on Earth. We cannot wall ourselves off from the future.

MR. BOLTON: I must admit, when I contacted your office to ask for your testimony, it was with only the barest hope of obtaining your time. I most graciously thank you.

MR. LANGHORN: Perhaps Mr. Bolton could save his flirtatious advances for some other time?

MR. BOLTON: No need for jealousy, Garrett.

HON. MAKEMBA: Gentlemen.

MR. BOLTON: Yes, yes. Ms. Hargrove, we have heard testimony that what Prometheus has done, distribution of water boxes to ordinary people, is a catastrophe. With your experience in these matters, would you tend to agree?

MS. HARGROVE: I wouldn't agree, no. It's been tumultuous, certainly. But we've had to deal with many changes over the past few years, many of them direr than what's happened here. Frankly, I'm surprised it took so long for something like this to happen in the energy industry.

MR. BOLTON: So, ma'am, you have hope that we will pull through these troubled times?

MS. HARGROVE: The only thing troubling about it is I can't get a water box of my own.

HON. MAKEMBA: Order, please.

MR. BOLTON: Thank you, Ms. Hargrove. Your witness.

MR. LANGHORN: Do you flout the laws of your home as flagrantly as you flout them here?

MS. HARGROVE: Why not ask me if I'm still beating my wife?

MR. BOLTON: Good one.

HON. MAKEMBA: Mr. Bolton, please. Mr. Langhorn, perhaps you could rephrase?

MR. LANGHORN: As you wish, your Honour. Ms. Hargrove, you seem rather blasé about the laws that Prometheus has broken.

MS. HARGROVE: I am not a legal expert. I can only testify to the political and cultural impacts of the water box. Those, I believe, are—

MR. LANGHORN: You said you wished you could take a water box home.

MS. HARGROVE: No, I didn't. I said that I found it troubling that I can't get one of my own. That is true. I hope that Westron Oil will soon license the technology for production in the United States.

MR. LANGHORN: But until that time, you would have no problem using a black market version.

MR. BOLTON: Your Honour, it is not—

MS. HARGROVE: If you don't mind, Mr. Bolton, I'd like to respond. Mr. Langhorn, you seem desperate to paint me as a scofflaw. Doing that will not help your case, and you know it, since you have no evidence to back up the idea. It seems petty, so I suggest you stop. If, however, you just want to seem strong in front of the judges, to give your future arguments more weight, I suspect they are smart enough to see through that kind of a ruse. So, do you have any actual questions for me?

MR. LANGHORN: I do, ma'am. I would ask why you felt the need to come all this way to testify in this case.

MS. HARGROVE: I thought I could help.

MR. LANGHORN: Because you wish to champion the Defendant.

MS. HARGROVE: I do not know Prometheus. I only know that trying her in this court, the same court which has, in the past, prosecuted dictators and those responsible for genocide, is gross overkill.

MR. LANGHORN: I wonder if there might be other motives for your participation today. What can you tell us about the case of the United States Government versus Westron Oil?

MS. HARGROVE: Very little, really. I skimmed an article in Time on the plane ride over.

MR. LANGHORN: You're not party to your Interior Secretary's plans to scuttle Westron Oil's Arctic Ocean drilling off your Alaska coast.

MS. HARGROVE: He hasn't discussed it with me. To tell the truth, we haven't had a Cabinet meeting for six months or so.

MR. LANGHORN: I see. Do you, Ms. Hargrove, see yourself in elected office in the future?

MS. HARGROVE: God, I hope not.

MR. BOLTON: Bravo!

MR. LANGHORN: You're excused.

#

INTERNATIONAL CRIMINAL COURT
ENERGY CRISIS OF DJIBOUTI
Case No: ICC-27/08-28/01
Transcription No: ICC-27/08-28/01-Q-60-EN
Friday, 28 January at 2:23 p.m.
OPEN SESSION

Before:
His Honour Judge Christian Makemba (Presiding Judge)
Her Honour Judge Kathleen Krause
His Honour Judge Yuko Tatami

DEFENSE CHAMBER II

OPEN SESSION

(excerpt)

MR. BOLTON: This is the moment we have all been waiting for.

MR. ILLUD: Your Honour?

HON. MAKEMBA: Dial down the dramatics, Mr. Bolton.

MR. BOLTON: But what could be more dramatic than the testimony of the Defendant herself? Please state your name once again for the Court.

PROMETHEUS: I am Prometheus.

HON. MAKEMBA: Order. I will have order. This is not a football match. I will clear the room if there are more outbursts.

MR. BOLTON: It seems, Prometheus, that you have fans in the audience.

PROMETHEUS: I am flattered.

MR. BOLTON: Was celebrity your goal?

PROMETHEUS: It was not. My goal was to better humanity.

MR. BOLTON: We need to be bettered?

PROMETHEUS: I offer no offense, sir. I merely find your economic stratification surprising.

MR. BOLTON: There are not rich and poor among your kind?

PROMETHEUS: Our economy is rather different from yours. We have an economy of favours, not one of virtual wealth. You transfer money from person to person. We do not have an analogous concept on my world.

MR. BOLTON: You hope to change our culture, to remove money from our society.

PROMETHEUS: No. That is not what I have tried to do. I came to Earth several years ago with the water box. I approached Westron Oil in the hopes that they would be the best organization to develop and distribute this very valuable technology. Your world is generously endowed with water. Indeed, your system has many times your planet's supply orbiting your sun in comet form. You have a remarkably valuable energy resource which is left untapped as you continue to burn fossil fuels and uranium isotopes. You have begun to build an infrastructure around hydrogen as a fuel source, and Westron Oil was at the forefront of that endeavour. The water box was the logical next step.

MR. BOLTON: You licensed the technology to Westron?

PROMETHEUS: I did. They were very appreciative and promised to make it available to everyone very soon.

MR. BOLTON: This didn't happen?

PROMETHEUS: It did not. Production of a water box is a simple process, well within Earth's industrial capacity. The only missing component is the algae.

MR. BOLTON: While we're on the topic of the algae, we heard a witness testify that this life form could very easily destroy the entire planet.

PROMETHEUS: The algae are engineered to survive only in total darkness, at a pressure of one tenth of an atmosphere, and at a temperature of two hundred degrees. As far as I am aware, there are few locations on Earth that meet these criteria. The algae could never prosper in the wilds of your planet.

MR. BOLTON: Thank you for that clarification. When Westron did not meet their promises, what did you do?

PROMETHEUS: I tried to meet with them again. They rebuffed all attempts at further communication.

MR. BOLTON: What did you do next?

PROMETHEUS: I left the United States and approached energy firms in Europe, then Asia, then South America. Each balked at discussing the water box with me. The possibility of legal action from Westron Oil made them apprehensive. It seemed that those in power on this planet did not wish to act, and those at the next echelons of the economy did not wish to anger those above them. I continued to explore until I found Djibouti.

The local government there gave me leave to introduce the water box to their people.

MR. BOLTON: Why didn't you go to a farmer in the United States or France or China before visiting Waberi Haylemelekot?

PROMETHEUS: I wished to follow the local laws.

MR. BOLTON: You cannot be claiming you did not know Westron would be angered by your approaching others with the water box.

PROMETHEUS: By this time, I had grown impatient with Westron Oil. By seeking permission from local authorities, I was doing my best to protect Waberi Haylemelekot and those like him. I did not think of protecting myself.

MR. BOLTON: How many water boxes did you give out?

PROMETHEUS: Thirteen.

MR. BOLTON: I will not comment on that number.

PROMETHEUS: Were I aware of the local cultural significance of the number thirteen to humans, I would have stopped after the twelfth.

MR. BOLTON: Certainly thirteen of the devices, wondrous though they are, could not be capable of supporting the energy needs of half a continent.

PROMETHEUS: No. I offered to each of these thirteen people the instructions for building new water boxes, using an extracted sample of the algae culture. Some, such as Mr. Haylemelekot, chose to bypass this instruction. Most did not. I imagine that those to whom I showed the process have built more and passed on this knowledge to others. Soon, water boxes will be everywhere. Energy production on Earth will no longer be in the hands of people like the executives of Westron Oil.

MR. BOLTON: Thank you, Prometheus. Your witness.

MR. ILLUD: You are a communist then?

PROMETHEUS: As I understand the term, it refers to those who espouse a political and economic system wherein the workers retain control of the means of production. I have no interest in the political hierarchy of your world, sir. There are many aspects of your economy that I am unfamiliar with, and therefore have no opinion on. It was my hope to introduce the water box through the channels of commerce you already had in place. As you did not respond to that method, I found another. It was not an ideological choice.

MR. ILLUD: You spoke earlier of your surprise at our economic stratification.

PROMETHEUS: I find many aspects of human culture surprising. This does not mean I wish to change them all.

MR. ILLUD: But you do wish to change our economic system.

PROMETHEUS: I wish only to help those most in need.

MR. ILLUD: Why Djibouti?

PROMETHEUS: Because the local leaders gave me permission to distribute the water box.

MR. ILLUD: The proximity to Saudi Arabia and the rest of the oil-producing Middle East was, then, not a factor.

PROMETHEUS: In retrospect, I find it a fortuitous accident.

MR. ILLUD: The issue at stake, though, is your breaking of the contract with Westron Oil.

PROMETHEUS: I maintain I did not break the contract.

MR. ILLUD: Indeed. Did you not license the technology to Westron?

PROMETHEUS: I licensed the rights to production and sale of the water box. I have sold no water boxes, and I have produced no new ones since the contract was enacted. That is why I gave out only thirteen of the devices. They were the samples I had already in my possession.

MR. ILLUD: This is sophistry, Prometheus. The contract refers specifically to distribution and sale. You may not have sold the technology, but you certainly distributed it.

PROMETHEUS: A subtle semantic point, I think.

MR. ILLUD: Not to a human.

MR. BOLTON: Bad form, Marteen.

MR. ILLUD: Your time for clowning on this stage is over for the moment, Alistair. Allow me to proceed with my questioning of this witness uninterrupted by your inanities. Prometheus, you have admitted to illegal distribution of the water box, in violation of international law. Your populist speeches notwithstanding, we are not here to determine if you made any person's life better or worse. We are here to determine if you have broken the law. I would like to give you a final opportunity to offer remorse for your actions.

PROMETHEUS: Respectfully, I decline your offer.

MR. ILLUD: You are excused.

MR. BOLTON: Your Honour, redirect?

HON. MAKEMBA: Please remain, Prometheus. Go ahead, Mr. Bolton.

MR. BOLTON: Prometheus, you have an interstellar craft in orbit around the Earth, do you not?

PROMETHEUS: It is currently orbiting your moon, but it is within range for easy transport.

MR. BOLTON: At any time, you could have left, avoided this court, the publicity you did not seek, the recriminations of Westron Oil, the entire ugly circus that has followed you for weeks now. Why did you remain?

PROMETHEUS: I am not a thief who would sneak off into the night, Mr. Bolton. I believe I have done right, and I want your world to know it.

MR. BOLTON: Thank you.

#

INTERNATIONAL CRIMINAL COURT
ENERGY CRISIS OF DJIBOUTI
Case No: ICC-27/08-28/01

Transcription No: ICC-27/08-28/01-Q-61-EN
Monday, 31 January at 1:16 p.m.
OPEN SESSION

Before:
His Honour Judge Christian Makemba (Presiding Judge)
Her Honour Judge Kathleen Krause
His Honour Judge Yuko Tatami

CLOSING ARGUMENTS CHAMBER I

OPEN SESSION

(excerpt)

MR. BOLTON: I need hardly make a long and impassioned speech in defense of my client. Had she any other name she would be no less heroic. Within a few short months, Prometheus improved the lives of over two million people in this nation. Secretary Hargrove noted how inappropriate these proceedings are. The International Criminal Court is not a forum for contract disputes between an inventor and a corporation. It is a forum for finding justice for grand tragedy. This is not a tragedy in any sense of the word. I would posit it is not even an energy crisis. As a result of the actions of my client we suffer not a dearth but an overabundance of energy. The only crisis here is the loss of profit for Westron Oil and their fellow oligarchs. To them I say, roll with the sea change occurring under your feet. Look to the example set by your younger cousin, Djibouti Electrical Services Corporation. They have generated not lawsuits and whingeing, but opportunity. This will not be the last time humanity has to deal with a paradigm shift of our culture brought about by some unforeseen technical achievement from the stars. The future continues to unspool right before our eyes. Westron has no one to blame but themselves for missing their golden opportunity to profit from this. I don't know how they managed to have their cause brought before this august body, but they should have used that time and energy to find ways to market the water box rather than simply locking it away until oil has become so scarce that they have no other choice. Prometheus is no more deserving of punishment than her namesake was deserving of the punishment meted to him by the gods of Olympus. Find her what she is, your Honours: not guilty.

(excerpt)

MR. ILLUD: Bringing this case before the International Criminal Court is not only appropriate, it is necessary. An alien visitor entered into a contract with an American company and broke that contract here in Dji-bouti. The ramifications of her actions have spread to every country on this planet. Where else would this case be tried? Nowhere. This is where we must find justice. One might be tempted to wonder at the motives of Westron Oil in not distributing water boxes to the public. That is a dis-traction. There is no law requiring a corporation to use every technology they own. Westron owned the right to make that decision in any time frame they saw fit. Likewise, one might be tempted to feel compassion for Prometheus because she has helped those less fortunate than we. That, however, is not a basis for a ruling of law. Emotion can play no part in your ruling. Prometheus broke international law when she gave a water box to Waberi Haylemelekot. She subsequently broke that law twelve more times. Her motives are irrelevant. The impact to those thir-teen individuals may have been positive, but the overall impact has not. The economic devastation is significant and continues to spread. We must send a message to the rest of the visitors to Earth, that our culture is not their playground. We cannot allow them to disrupt our society at their whim. We are a sovereign planet and will protect our institutions. This court has no recourse but to find the Defendant guilty and assign appropriate punishment.

#

INTERNATIONAL CRIMINAL COURT
ENERGY CRISIS OF DJIBOUTI
Case No: ICC-27/08-28/01
Transcription No: ICC-27/08-28/01-Q-62-EN
Tuesday, 1 February at 1:11 p.m.
OPEN SESSION

Before:
His Honour Judge Christian Makemba (Presiding Judge)
Her Honour Judge Kathleen Krause
His Honour Judge Yuko Tatami

RULING CHAMBER I

OPEN SESSION

(excerpt)

HON. MAKEMBA: I must admit, this is an unusual case, the first of my career to involve a member of an off world race. The same is true for my two colleagues. Oil is, and has been for more than a century, a hot-button issue of the first order: to environmentalists, to the volatile regions of the Middle East, to the powerful United States, to the emerging power of China, to everyone. To reduce the value of one of our planet's most important commodities to near zero practically overnight is not an action we regard lightly. Prometheus, you have willfully altered the nature of our entire society. Will that alteration prove positive or negative? We do not know. Indeed, we cannot know. Only the historians of the future will be able to answer that question. While the question before us is, ostensibly, a simple contract dispute, wider implications cannot be overlooked. In determination of the matter of illegal distribution of water box technology, we cannot simply look at the bare facts of the case, but also at the history of similar occurrences in the past. The best analogy we can draw is that of the emergence of file sharing on the internet. Intellectual property trading in the early part of this century was, like Prometheus's actions, not done for personal profit. It was done for more ineffable, personal, and yes, sometimes ideological reasons. And the results of those court cases were straightforward. The courts enjoined further copying. That did nothing but move the process from the original file sharing technology to newer, less regulatable forms. The permanent solution did not come from the courts, but from the wounded parties themselves, the media corporations in this example. They fully embraced and incorporated these new technologies into their economic model. So it is for the water box. We enjoin further use of water boxes in Djibouti and elsewhere until such a time as Westron Oil licenses the technology for public use. This, we fear, will only suggest to current users of the devices that they disconnect from their local energy distribution networks. These water boxes will not disappear. In fact, the publicity caused by this trial will likely make their use multiply. Soon enough, the demand for electricity from traditional providers may dry up entirely. We can only suggest that energy firms follow the example of the DESC and use the water box technology to generate profit rather than attempt to squelch it.

(Hon. Makemba took a brief recess to confer with Hon. Krause and Hon. Tatami.)

HON. MAKEMBA: Now, for our ruling. Prometheus, you are found guilty of illegal distribution of Westron Oil technology. You are enjoined from further distribution or discussion of the water box or its underlying technology with any and all parties on Earth. As for sentencing, we have chosen to forego imposition of incarceration.
MR. ILLUD: Your Honour, how can you possibly—
HON. MAKEMBA: Mr. Illud, now is my time on the stage, and you will remain silent for the remainder of this session. We impose the following fine on Prometheus, to be paid directly to Westron Oil. She will pay one hundred fifty percent of all gains from distribution of the water box.

MR. BOLTON: I almost don't want to ask, your Honour, but you do realize that Prometheus made no gains of any kind from all of this?

HON. MAKEMBA: And she will pay every cent of it to Westron Oil, including a fifty percent penalty. Is that understood?

MR. BOLTON: It has been quite some time since I lost a case, your Honor. I am understandably disappointed. Somehow, I think I'll survive.

HON. MAKEMBA: Prometheus, you are free to go. This Court is adjourned.

Alien and Sedition Acts

> *The soul of man does violence*
> *to itself, first of all, when it be-*
> *comes an abscess, and, as it were, a*
> *tumor on the universe...*
> —*Meditations, II, 16*

Dale Krensky's office grew more and more cluttered as the years went by. Stacks of old reports covered a dark gray credenza behind his desk. Newer reports, magazines and a week's worth of newspapers from cities around the world were strewn across his workspace, with only enough free desk space left for a keyboard and mouse and monitor. The whole room had begun to take on the feel of a nest, with Dale layering more and more paper as if to fend off some winter chill, in preparation for a period of hibernation.

Dale had noticed the effect his office had on people who came to visit. He purchased and framed a few nondescript prints for his walls, not because he found the images enjoyable, but because everyone else had done the same and he didn't want to seem *different.*

But he was different. Different enough to avoid socializing with his coworkers. Different enough to not have been out on a date with a woman—or a man, for that matter—since he joined DOWA so long ago. He didn't enjoy much of a personal life. His life was in this office, watch-ing the world try, and often fail, to deal with the strain of the breaking of the cocoon. He reveled in the thrill of each and every crisis. He tried not to show that side of himself to others. They wouldn't understand.

Hargrove must have had a sense of it, though. She seemed to be shifting his portfolio away from crisis management, and more towards management of internal DOWA affairs. She hadn't said anything to him, or made anything official. It was in the little nuances. The way things went in New York last summer with the Dandelions didn't add anything to her confidence in him. The less he was in the spotlight, the better. In this, Dale and Hargrove were in agreement.

No one at DOWA wanted to be in the spotlight just now. 2028 had been punctuated with off world crises. The trial in January of the Dragon in Africa kicked off the year. The reappearance of Skeletons in Jordan in March led to tense words from their King and an uncompromisingly harsh response from the Skeletons, who still smarted from being the victims in the 2023 massacre. For the first time, some of the off world community banded together in defense of one of their own. The Trees and the Anacondas in particular supported the Skeletons.

During the Summer, more stories hit news services all over the world. In June, the Chinese banned Scorpions from their capital city for reasons of "internal security". In July, the Great Barrier Reef stand-off with the Eels finally exploded into open conflict, with casualties on both sides of the skirmish. Two weeks ago, the first town in the US— Hoquiam, Washington—announced they were 100% powered by water boxes. This caused an uproar. In a show of unprecedented solidarity, the energy industry *and* the environmental movement were unified in their opposition to the new power source, though for very different reasons.

All of this, along with dozens of smaller flare-ups, had put the public on edge. No one was worried anymore about invasion. The off worlders were a known quantity. But with significantly increased numbers, and a wider variety of races to deal with, tensions continued to mount.

This week, a huge appropriations bill made its way through the House. The bill had been crafted by Hargrove's legislative team and backed by a tenuous, bipartisan alliance of Congressmen. Their respective districts stood to gain from the increase in high-tech sales to the *Vimana* project. But their support could crumble at any minute if public worries about off world relations spiked again. Without the bill, *Vimana* ran a very real risk of shutting down entirely. Hargrove wouldn't have that. She made it clear to everyone in her department that nothing big should hit the blogs, not *this* week.

Dale opened the next e-mail on his screen, forwarded to his account by one of the grunts down in Policy.

DATE: 5/8/28
TIME: 02:45:45
FROM: The Antagonist
TO: Humanity
RE: The End
MESSAGE: What has happened before now is but a taste of the horrors to come. The Galaxy will not tread lightly on your planet if you continue to make yourself known. Do not venture to Central Authority. Do not allow further immigration. The only sure route to survival is isolation. Take my warning seriously or you will be destroyed.

Dale couldn't stop laughing for nearly five minutes.

Humans weren't the most egregiously emotional race that Billion had the displeasure of mentoring into civilization. That prize belonged to the Wylywl, a race of ebullient crustaceans who broke from their cocoon a third of a billion ticks ago. That had been a long and difficult birthing process, resulting in more than a few scars on Billion's arms and legs from overzealous Wylywl pincers. The Wylywl were difficult, but Humans were a close second. Very close.

Humans were a needy race, looking for validation at each and every step. Billion felt she'd given a metaphorical "pat on the back" to every resident of Opportunity at one time or another. In truth, it felt like she'd done so for every Human on the Florida peninsula.

Their research was a dizzying pastiche of starts and stops, at times requiring a firm hand to reign in incipient catastrophe, other times requiring a less-than-subtle shove in the right direction. They were as stingy with their gratitude as they were greedy for compliments. A complex and exhausting species was Humanity.

Her million-tick reports to CA were met with, at best, vague interest. Earth was the only other emerging system at the moment, but apart from their zinc reserves, little about them fired the imagination of Central Authority.

Until today.

As CA was two trillion d's away, even quicklight could not allow for real-time communication. Billion sent off her report, imagining the terse bureaucratic response she usually received a few thousand ticks later. This time, however, a document came up instantly, obviously not a response, but a message previously prepared and sent ahead of time to catch her in front of her screen.

The order from CA was long and complex. Billion read it through three times to make altogether certain she understood what was being asked of her.

Humans did excel in one linguistic area that *b-b-b-b* did not, with their at times stifling culture of politeness. Billion had picked up this Human skill quickly from the researchers in Opportunity, and she used it now.

"Shit."

The whole building still reeked of formaldehyde. Dale had managed to wring the stench out of his own office with meticulous cleaning, but the hallways, the conference rooms, the auditorium: all of them still carried a trace of the acrid smell from the days when the Smithsonian Castle was a bastion of scientific research, even though those days were now long gone.

Dale grasped his tablet in one hand as he strode down freshly painted halls to Hargrove's office. She insisted that her direct reports meet with her for at least a few minutes each week. Sometimes Dale could get away after a quarter-hour. If something big was happening, he could get stuck in there for hours. After that singularly timed e-mail started making the rounds, Dale was sure this week's meeting would not be quick.

"Sorry I'm…" He stopped, surprised to see a female Blue standing next to Hargrove, towering over her, actually. Without a pause, Dale approached the visitor and stood within a couple of centimeters. "I offer greetings. I am Dale Krensky, Deputy Secretary of Off World Affairs."

"I am Billion."

Dale backed up a step. "You're the CA auditor, working down in Opportunity with the Indians." He ignored a warning gaze from the Secretary. She didn't like it when he referred to the *Vimana* team as "the Indians". For her it conjured images of war-painted primitives on horseback, rampaging through the American Midwest. Dale found her hair-trigger cultural sensitivity trying.

"Close the door," Hargrove said.

"What's up? There's not a problem with *Vimana?*" he asked, a look of genuine concern stitching his features.

"No, it's the e-mail from The Antagonist. CA has asked Billion here to look into it."

"Why not give this to Kird?"

Hargrove looked to Billion, but the Blue said nothing. "Kird may have been compromised," Hargrove said.

Dale used every ounce of his willpower to prevent a smile from sprouting onto his face. He found this added complication hilarious.

"Billion needs to connect with the FBI and begin interrogations. You're going to help her."

"Me?"

"Yes, you. And you're going to keep this quiet, do you understand?"

"I don't know anything about law enforcement."

"Nor do I," Billion admitted. "I am, however, the only CA agent currently in the vicinity to conduct this investigation." She sagged a couple of millimeters, likely a gesture not noticed by Hargrove. "More's the pity."

Dale led Billion out of the Smithsonian and across the Mall. The J. Edgar Hoover Building was only a short walk away, over on Pennsylvania. Dale looked around, at the lawns, walking paths and monuments. Throughout the tourist friendly space, he saw how many different kinds of aliens there were and how seamlessly they interacted with the locals. He found the whole scene disturbing.

"So, you believe that The Antagonist is on Earth?" Dale asked, hoping conversation would distract him from the unsettling sights around him.

"We do not know. The disruptive network message did not come directly from the fugitive, but from a network trawler program he deposited here. We have captured and analyzed the trawler. It appears the e-mail was pre-written by The Antagonist. The trawler monitored the Earth network and released the message at a strategically opportune moment. It is unlikely such a sophisticated piece of software could have been installed remotely. Therefore we have determined that The Antagonist has been on Earth since the year 2024, and remained at least until 2026.

Whether he remains still is unknown. Nonetheless, we are closer now to finding him than any time in recent memory."

"And you think interrogating random aliens will help?" Dale sounded skeptical.

Billion paused at the mildly derogatory use of the word *aliens*. "I do not. Interrogating a carefully selected list of off world visitors is my plan. I hoped to start with Krd. When he is ruled out as a suspect, he will be an invaluable resource in continuing this investigation. However, he is currently off world. It is ironic that he is collecting new evidence of the trail left by The Antagonist on Wolf 359."

"If he is The Antagonist, maybe he won't come back. His work is done."

"I think not." Billion didn't offer to explain that conclusion. Dale didn't press.

Waiting in the lobby of the Hoover building stood a solid slab of a man, dark skin and buzz-cut hair, black suit, probably not yet thirty years old.

"Mr. Krensky, Ms. Billion. I'm Special Agent Romero. I'll be your point man on this operation."

Dale responded with a firm handshake and a smirk. Romero led them through security, where Billion had to put on a specially made badge, since her rail-thin body had no shoulders to hold a normal lanyard in place. An elevator ride took them to an office floor. They went to a conference room where they could talk in private. The public worry about The Antagonist was heated enough. Wild theories on the web proliferated. The traditional media had no better information to use, so they reported on the fear itself, as if that were a story. There was no need to fuel those fires with speculation about an FBI witch hunt.

"What do you need from me, ma'am?" Romero asked Billion, his forthright, Midwestern politeness enough to make Dale gag.

"I am unschooled in police matters. I will leave the details to you. I have need of access to files of off world visitors and a secure room in which to conduct interviews."

After a few minutes of discussion, they decided on three parameters to use to whittle the list of thousands of off worlders to a manageable few.

1. Arrival on Earth prior to August 12, 2024, the date the net-work trawler had been put in place on the internet.
2. Access to government facilities. The Antagonist often sub-verted young civilizations by infiltrating their most powerful in-stitutions.
3. A history of intraplanetary travel.

Only a handful of off world visitors met these criteria, forty-three in all. Billion scanned the list of names quickly and sorted them into priority order. She gave Romero the task of sending field teams to quietly bring each of these suspects in for questioning.

"Do you consider the suspects dangerous?" Romero asked.

When Billion didn't respond, Dale jumped in: "Only one of them. We just don't know which one."

The offices of the United States Department of Housing and Urban Development smelled strongly of Human. The building was, to Prometheus, also quite uncomfortably cold. She had become acclimated to the pleasant, if somewhat brisk, temperatures of Eastern Africa. These environmental difficulties she accepted with equanimity. Now that most Humans believed her motives to be pure, she could interact more directly with those in power to better the circumstances for the Human poor. There were many sub-societies on the planet in more need than the Americans, but few had the resources with which to follow her bold research suggestions. Prometheus had every hope that advances in this less politically divisive area—that of housing development—might filter down to needier regimes around the planet without restriction.

Her suggestion to the planners at HUD was unprecedented for Earth, she knew. They seemed unimpressed by the idea of harnessing geological power to fabricate sturdy and inexpensive homes. Prometheus made the case that Earth, as a young and vibrant world, had untapped resources right beneath their feet which would be lost if the planet was allowed to simply cool on its own. A few simple drill sites, extending through the crust to the mantle, would be enough to tap huge reservoirs of lava for construction. It was a standard technique on her world, easily adaptable to Earth.

If the Americans balked, she would next approach the Japanese.

The three bureaucrats sitting across from Prometheus looked up when the door to the room opened and a team of black-suited agents entered. One advanced and spoke to the Dragon.

"Prometheus, my name is Special Agent Romero of the FBI. We have some questions for you."

She sighed, a small cloud of steam escaping from her mouth.

"Of course you do."

The interviews were conducted using two adjoining rooms. The first, where the suspects sat, was an unadorned white room with a single table and a single chair. The room looked innocuous, but it was lined with reinforced concrete and its single door was made of tempered carbon-aluminum. The FBI didn't know if a member of some alien race could break out of the room, but they considered the probability low.

Separating the suspect from the interviewer was a plate of one-way glass, similarly treated to withstand heat and force. Inside the second, more confined, darker space, Billion sat straddling a Blue stool, monitoring a tiny computer screen she had placed on a wide, metal table. An intercom system allowed the interviewers to speak to the suspect.

Dale stood behind the Blue and watched, fascinated, as the Dragon loped into the room on the other side of the window. Ignoring the chair, she paced around the table. A light began blinking on the little computer screen. Dale pointed to it.

"What does that do?"

"It scans," Billion said.

"It's a lie detector?"

Billion did not answer.

"Aren't you going to ask her any questions?"

"It is not necessary."

Dale reached forward and toggled the mic. "Prometheus."

The Dragon looked to the window. "I am not even to be accorded the respect of a face to face interrogation?"

Billion scowled at Dale. He ignored her. "A precaution."

"I have been released on my own recognizance on the matter of the water boxes."

"We're conducting an investigation of The Antagonist."

Billion's thin but strong hand batted Dale's away from the mic. "I will conduct the interviews."

"But you're not even—"

The light on the computer screen stopped blinking. Billion leaned down to review something on the screen that Dale couldn't see, probably text in the ultra-violet frequencies. Human eyes were so limited.

Billion clicked the mic again. "You are free to go."

"What? That's it?" Dale asked.

Billion did not answer. Prometheus seemed similarly confused, though she left without further comment.

Each interview seemed to proceed the same way. The alien suspect would be escorted into the small, white room. The little scanner would blink for a minute or so. Billion would say nothing, and then let the suspect go. Dale wanted to understand what the device was doing, but Billion never let it out of her sight, she never left the room for a bathroom break, she never responded to any of Dale's questions. He'd had enough of her running this show, so he contacted Agent Romero with a new name for the suspect list. When the unscheduled alien walked through the door the next day, Billion glared at Dale.

"I did not put any Skeletons on the list of suspects."

"I added him." Dale referred to his tablet. "He first arrived on Earth in February of 2023, and was in Mecca on the day of the massacre."

"I remember him from the files. He is not a suspect."

"I think he is. He came back to Earth in early '27, and since has visited France, Turkey, Belgium, Iraq and Indonesia."

The little screen continued to blink. Dale watched it, looking for some indication that it acted differently with the Skeleton than it had with the others.

"What's more," Dale continued, "he is a known associate of Sylvester."

"We will deal with Sylvester at the appropriate time."

"We're gonna deal with this guy right now." Dale keyed the mic. "Do you know why you're here?"

The Skeleton looked up at the sound of Dale's voice, his bony head twisting this way and that, looking for the source. "Where are you?"

"I'm on the other side of the glass. What is your purpose on Earth?"

The Skeleton stood from the chair and walked over to the glass, laying all four hands on the reflective surface. His fingers clicked against the window.

"Nothing much. What's *your* purpose on Earth?"

The screen stopped blinking. "He is not The Antagonist," Billion said.

"Tell me about Sylvester," Dale continued.

"Oh, him! What's he done now? I had nothing to do with it, whatever it was."

"Does he have a history of criminal activity?" Dale asked, his rising voice betraying his hope for a positive answer.

"Depends on what you mean by 'criminal', now doesn't it? Can't say as I'd buy a timepiece from him, but I don't think he'd kill anyone, if that's where you're going."

Billion wrested the mic from Dale and said, "You're free to go."

"Really? Alright. Good luck, then." The Skeleton ambled out of the room.

Billion addressed Dale. "That will be the last unscheduled interrogation. Am I clear on this point?"

"We'll see about that," Dale answered before storming out.

Billion continued with the interviews for the day without Krensky's unnecessary questions and hotheaded manner. He had gone back to Secretary Hargrove to argue his case for more latitude with the investigation. Billion quietly counted the ticks before Krd's scheduled return to Earth, when she could clear him and hand off the bulk of this tedious process to him. Knowing the Teddy Bear, he'd probably be grateful. He enjoyed his job.

Billion got a great deal of satisfaction from being more knowledgeable than others. She therefore enjoyed being literally the only person on the planet who knew about the capabilities of the small device she used to scan each suspect. Part of the CA message—a sizeable part—included the specifications for building the prototype scanner. It was new technology and would be invaluable in finding The Antagonist.

The next suspect came into the room, folding back his wings and ducking his long, pointed head to fit through the Human-sized door. From Billion's research, it appeared the Humans were unusually intimated by Vampires. She couldn't blame them. Vampires were large and powerful, though Blues did not share the Humans' instinctual primate fear of creatures of the night.

The Vampire—his name was Elt—attempted to shield his eyes from the oppressive light in the room with one bent wing. After a handful of ticks, the scanner finished its task and revealed the results. Billion read the screen... then blinked three times. She pressed an icon to reset the scanner and begin again.

"Please state your name," Billion said into the mic. She did not want the suspect to become apprehensive as the silence spun out. A nervous Vampire could cause significant damage to even such a secure room.

"My name is Elt. I am a mythologist."

Billion bit back a sarcastic comment about her views on such a useless research topic. The scanner continued to blink. She thought it best to continue to engage the suspect in conversation.

"You have been on Earth for several local years."

"That's true. I came with the Vampire contingent based in England. Since my arrival, I've visited several of the important religious sites on Earth. Humans have a remarkably diverse and fascinating collection of views on the supernatural world."

The scanner finished its business, and the surprising result was the same as before. This Elt was not a Vampire. It was a member of another race, one the Humans had designated Snakes. Elt merely inhabited a Vampire body. The scanner confirmed it, having taken a "fingerprint" of Elt's brainwaves. After personality transfer, the nature of the mind remained unchanged, carrying a distinctive electrical pattern even when housed within a new brain.

The Antagonist had changed bodies at least a dozen times since he was first identified by Central Authority. No one knew how many times he had performed the transfer in total. No one knew his original race.

They only knew that, in all likelihood, he would not inhabit a body that corresponded to his original species. And so, the value of the scanner.

Billion turned off the mic to the suspect and contacted the agents outside the door, preparing them to take the Vampire into custody. Then she resumed conversation with Elt, in an attempt to gain more information before the Vampire/Snake knew he had been discovered.

"Mythologist is an unusual career for a Gradlik," Billion said, using the name of the race in the Vampire tongue.

Elt laughed. "You know their name and a bit about them!"

"Them?"

"I am not actually a Vampire. I traded bodies some time ago. I was born a Snake."

"Indeed." Elt must have realized that his identity as a Vampire had been compromised. Clever, this one.

"What is the name of this person with whom you traded bodies?"

"Ktalala. I believe he's on our home world—the Snake home world—looking for Convergence Zones."

Billion sent another preparatory message to the agents in the hall. "Elt, I am afraid we will have to hold you temporarily."

The Vampire's wings popped out, making a loud snapping sound, a sure sign of distress. "May I ask why?"

"We must verify your story."

"Am I accused of a crime?" Elt asked, advancing on the window. Billion flinched, imagining all too clearly the Vampire crashing through the glass and attacking her. She cued the agents. Four armed Humans entered the interview room and surrounded Elt. He flapped his wings once more in surprise, then, seeing their hand guns at the ready, lowered his wings and surrendered. They escorted him from the room to a nearby cell.

"This is good news!" Dale said cheerily to Hargrove and Billion. "Why aren't we celebrating?"

Billion stood impassively by Hargrove's desk. The Secretary, looking severe as always in her pinned-up hair and strained makeup, answered with a frown.

"We don't know if Elt is The Antagonist," Hargrove said.

"How many personality transferred aliens do you think we have on Earth?" Dale asked, his tone acid.

"That he offered freely the information about the transfer mitigates against his guilt," Billion said.

"You expect him to come out and say that he's an infamous, seditionist fugitive from galactic justice?" Dale asked. "We've got him. Just admit it."

"I admit nothing," Billion said, her calculated dispassion like nails on a chalkboard to Dale. He knew Blues to have as much passion as any Human. This one felt the need to suppress hers. "More investigation is required. We must query the Snake home world on the whereabouts of this Ktalala."

"How long will that take?" Hargrove asked.

"A million ticks or more. I will send the request immediately. We must continue the interviews."

Dale's frustrated growl was audible to every species in the office.

"Please state your name," Billion said into the microphone.

"Marty Kilpatrick." The man sitting in the interview chamber was unusually hairy, a colossal beard dominating his face, his afro seeming to explode from his scalp.

"Do you still serve as a host to the microscopic species known as Wreath?"

Kilpatrick grinned. "Yeah. I figured that's why you guys brought me in. For a check-up, right? I'd have come quietly. You didn't have to send the goon squad, you know?" He sat back in his chair, the very picture of someone comfortable with his situation.

Dale noticed that the scanner had finished blinking, but Billion hadn't reviewed the results. What did *that* mean? Maybe it wasn't calibrated to scan Humans?

"I wish to speak with the Wreath directly. Can that be accomplished?"

"Sure thing. Hang on." Kilpatrick whispered something inaudible. Slowly, a robotic rigidness crept into his frame. After a few ticks, the affable Marty Kilpatrick was replaced by another being, someone altogether different. "We are Wreath. You wish to speak with us directly?"

"Yes. Please state the nature of your mission here on Earth."

"We wish to understand the nature of macro-species."

According to Billion, Wreath was the only known race of sentient microbes in the galaxy. Without similar races to interact with, they had decided to research the only other intelligent life they could find: ones they could inhabit as a parasitic infection.

"How many Humans have you infected?" Billion asked. Dale was surprised that the Blue would use the term "infected". It seemed inflammatory.

"We currently reside in Marty Kilpatrick only. Other Humans have refused to house us."

"You can control Marty when the need arises. You need not ask for permission," Billion said. Dale gaped. What was Billion doing? This wasn't in character for her.

"Such is not permitted."

"Permission is irrelevant. You could infest the entirety of Humanity. You could become a macro-species in your own right. You could infest other species. You have the capability of becoming the only species in the galaxy. Does that not appeal?"

Dale's mind spun thinking about that possibility. The sheer power that the Wreath could wield was awesome. How had he never seen that possibility? Faced with it now, he was humbled.

"Such is not our wish. We do not wish to be all. We wish only to learn and coexist."

The mild—yet still unnerving—belligerence in Billion's tone left suddenly. She was her old self as she said, "You are free to go."

Kilpatrick roused himself again and ambled out of the room with a smile and a wave. Dale was still a bit dazed by the possibilities that Billion had suggested were available to the Wreath. He turned the ideas over and over in his mind like an unearthed diamond.

"That was..." Dale couldn't go on.

"The Antagonist abhors diversity, clings only to homogeneity. He is passionate in this belief. It would be impossible for him to so convincingly propound the catholic philosophy of the Wreath."

"Right," Dale mumbled.

Krd's trip back from Wolf 359 was delayed outside *Ronald Reagan* by heavier than normal traffic. The Humans seemed unwilling or unable to put the resources necessary into construction of a fifth orbital immigration platform. Did they believe that their notoriety would diminish in the coming ticks? Krd suspected that after their arrival at CA, interest in Earth would increase yet again. Humans had many intriguing qualities: their music, their depth of emotional nuance, even their often contentious nature. All of these things would fascinate a galaxy filled with many homogenous cultures, like *b-b-b-b* and Gradlik.

The Humans would learn soon enough, and adapt. He had faith in them.

Finally, *Ronald Reagan* assigned Krd's small, one-person craft a berth and he piloted it to the dock. Four black-suited Humans waited at the airlock exit. He did not recognize them.

"Gentlemen," he said warily.

The darkest of the four, a young male, spoke: "Officer Kird, I am Special Agent Romero of the FBI. We need to speak with you."

Krd's body tensed, his paw shifting subconsciously to the hilt of his stun baton, always at the ready on his hip. He noted a similar tension in the Humans. He knew also they had an overfondness for ranged weaponry, despite the very real possibility that a stray bullet in this station might doom them all to asphyxiation.

"As you wish," Krd said with some difficulty.

The six-seater orbit bubble took them down, not to Andrews Air Force Base, but to the roof of a building in central Washington, D.C. Watchful as ever, the agents escorted Krd down from the roof to an interrogation room. As they trooped through the corridors, Krd realized something was quite wrong. He was not being escorted as a resource, but as a suspect. He assumed The Antagonist must have been involved. Had the seditionist infiltrated the United States government at such a high level that Krd himself was now considered an enemy of the state? Krd had no wish to extinguish the lives of these stalwart young Humans, but if the good of the galaxy was at stake, he would do what was required.

At the entrance to the confines of a rather secure interrogation room, Krd was forced to decide whether he was best served by attempting escape, or playing out this scenario to see where it led. It was a close thing, but Krd allowed the solid door to close behind him.

He moved directly to the one-way glass, peering through for any sign of the interrogators on the other side.

"Am I to be treated like a suspect?"

"Patience, please."

Krd recognized that voice. Billion, the Blue CA Auditor working on *Vimana* with the Humans. Could she be The Antagonist? *Vimana* was a critical project for Earth. Sabotaging it might be a valuable result for the fugitive. But was it valuable enough? The Antagonist was nothing if not patient, waiting for the main chance, for billions of ticks, if necessary.

"Why does an FTL specialist perform interrogations?" Krd asked, unable to remain silent.

"Patience, please," she said again. Krd growled, a low and dangerous sound. Regardless of Billion's real identity, only some ruse of The Antagonist could have ratcheted up Earth's paranoia so radically since he had left for Wolf 359. He had been in their good graces ever since his arrival.

The door to the chamber opened, revealing Dale Krensky, the balding, grim-faced Deputy to Secretary Hargrove. "Come on. We'll explain."

Finally, the story leaked to the media. A few mentions in blogs about aliens being brought quietly to the Hoover Building in Washington had escalated to full throated warnings from pundits about the nature of freedom for all visitors on Earth. Visitors' rights activists scheduled a march on the Mall, which was passionate, though poorly attended. The fears stoked by The Antagonist's cryptic e-mail were fanned by the government's nonexistent response.

After a widely streamed special webcast from CNN on the story, the White House took notice. Concerns about *Vimana* funding took a back seat to the dangers of mass hysteria. The President spoke with his Chief of Staff, telling him to get this sorted out as soon as possible. All the relevant players now stood in Victor Fremont's office.

"You realize the election in is less than five months."

Dale choked back a chuckle. This administration had run its course, gotten its eight years in power. Why Fremont would care so much about the next administration's selection said quite a bit about Earth and its politics.

"The danger from The Antagonist is very real, Mr. Fremont," Krd said.

"I thought we had a suspect in custody."

"Elt is only that: a suspect," Billion said. "I, for one, do not believe he is The Antagonist."

"You were the one who ordered him incarcerated," Dale argued.

"I did so as a precaution. We have not received a response from the Gradlik on the status of Ktalala. Elt's story may yet be verified."

"We need to make a statement to the media," Fremont said.

"Saying what, Victor?" Hargrove shot back. "'We believe a notorious fugitive from interstellar justice may be lurking on Earth, but don't worry! We're on it!' Please. We need to dial down the crazy, not dial it up." Dale thought back to that long ago meeting when Vanessa had carefully and cogently argued for the release of the Rules of Conduct. The intervening years had changed her.

"What do you suggest?" Fremont spat back.

"Nothing we say will make any of this look any better. If we lie, we'll get caught later. If we tell the truth, we confirm people's fears and increase the panic. So, we say nothing. We continue the investigation. If Elt's story doesn't check out, we hand him off to Kird for processing by the CA. In either case, we need to run down the leads we have and wait for hard facts before going to the press."

Fremont looked ready to tear into Hargrove, but with a subtle sigh, he relented. "I need daily reports on my screen," Fremont warned. "Keep an eye on this."

Hargrove turned to Dale. "Dale?"

"I wouldn't miss it for the world."

Krd handled the next interviewee. Billion seemed uncomfortable questioning a member of his own race.

"State your name for the record." Though he was fluent in *b-b-b-b*, Krd spoke in English, for the benefit of Krensky, and for those who would listen to the recording in the future.

"I am Gainsborough." The Blue sat on the special stool provided for him, curious about the strange summons that brought him from Florida, but seemingly unconcerned. Billion watched the mysterious scanner closely. Dale found it endlessly maddening that he didn't know what it was for.

"You have been on Earth since late 2021?" Kird asked.

"That is true. I have spent the bulk of my time in India. I recently relocated to Opportunity, to work on *Vimana*." He smiled proudly.

The remarkable access that Gainsborough enjoyed within Maccha-Yantra was the main reason he was one of their suspects. Billion had put the Blue on her list with the vocal stipulation that it was only from a desire to be thorough. She did not believe a Blue capable of treachery on the scale caused by The Antagonist. Krd had reminded the Auditor that if Gainsborough was The Antagonist, he was not truly a Blue anymore.

The scanner finished its task. Billion reviewed the results and let loose an uncharacteristically emotional chirp. "He is a Blue. He is no longer a suspect."

Krd looked to the little screen to confirm, then politely told Gainsborough the interview was at an end. The two CA officials discussed their next interview. Dale ignored them, staring at the scanner.

It could identify a personality transferred individual. That was why Billion had immediately released dozens of suspects with no questioning. The scanner had cleared them. Dale had never heard of such a device. This was brand new technology, recently added to the CA's arsenal. He had to think, and think quickly. This changed everything.

The floors of the Hoover Building were uncomfortably slick to Sylvester's belly. He found it tiring to slither across them, fighting to gain traction against the waxy surface. He eyed the frowning faces of the agents pacing him through the halls. Something troubling must have been going on. The treatment he'd received when they were just curious about his zinc shipments was brusque, to be sure, but not aggressive. This was different. Sylvester sensed danger, but he didn't know what form it might take or why he was a target. It was merely a tickle, deep down in his thoughts, difficult to localize, making him anxious.

Oh, how he wanted to be back on his deck by his pool and his fountain, enjoying the French countryside.

The agents paused at a closed door. Through the door came a Blue, who bowed politely to Sylvester.

"I offer greetings."

"Likewise, mate. What's going on in there?"

"I confess, I am not certain. But I believe you have nothing to fear," the Blue said affably.

"Right," Sylvester moaned. The agents gestured and he slipped into the little, white room.

"State your name," a voice said from nowhere. Sylvester recognized the voice: Krd, the Conduct Officer who had visited him in France last year.

"Fond of the theatric, are we, Krd? Well, then, I am Sylvester, zinc tycoon extraordinaire." Sylvester tilted his head toward the one-way glass, showing a sense of élan he did not feel. He waited, apprehensively and impatiently, for the next question, that foggy sense of doom still clawing at the back of his consciousness.

Of the remaining suspects, Sylvester was perhaps the likeliest candidate to be The Antagonist. His financial power rivaled all but a handful of Humans. His access to launch platforms meant he could come and go with ease, import or export anything he wished. It was entirely possible that he had sabotaged the Oort Cloud Detection System, or at the very least, programmed it to ignore vessels in his employ. With so many better suspects already cleared, everything they had—except for the open question of Elt's true identity—pointed to him as The Antagonist.

On the other hand, he had been in his position of considerable power for years and done nothing that seemed disruptive. He employed thousands of people and had opened a major trade route off of Earth. These were not the likely actions of The Antagonist.

Billion and Krd watched the scanner intently for the few ticks required to finish the evaluation of the Snake's brainwaves. The result stunned them both.

"I do not believe it," Billion said. "I will scan him again."

"The chances are infinitesimal," Krd said with a sense of awe in his voice.

"What?" Dale insisted.

"He is not a Snake."

Dale perked up. "He isn't? He's The Antagonist."

"I do not believe so," Billion said. "He is a Gradlik."

"A Gradlik?" Dale asked. "A *Vampire?*"

Krd keyed the mic again. "Are you Ktalala?"

The response from the Snake was unmistakable. His head shot up, his eyes went wide, his whole body tensed.

"How do you know that name?" Sylvester asked, his voice raising in pitch much like a Human's would in such an excited state.

Dale put together what the two CA officials already suspected. Sylvester was the Vampire who had switched bodies with Elt. That was the infinitesimal chance Krd referred to. In a galaxy of trillions, that these two would end up on one backwater planet at the same time? What were the odds against that?

On the other hand, both of them—one an entrepreneur, the other a researcher—would have been drawn to a newly hatched system like Earth, the only one out there since the Wylywl emerged. Maybe the chances weren't that small.

Or maybe it was something like fate. Dale wondered often if fate played a hand in his life, or lives, as it were.

"How do you know that name?" Sylvester asked again, nearly frantic now.

Krd turned to activate the mic and put Sylvester's fears to rest. Billion reached down to rerun her scan and validate its extraordinary result. Dale grabbed for the stun baton at Krd's waist.

Sylvester jumped when the Teddy Bear's voice came again through the speaker.

"Allow us to make the necessary inqu—" A blast of static cut off the end of Krd's statement. Sylvester slithered across the table, over to the glass.

"Hello? What was that?"

He heard a struggle, followed by a muffled *crump* from the other side of the window. His fear shot into overdrive. For half a tick he wondered if he should have stayed with his fellow Gradlik and quietly sought out Convergence Zones rather than scour the galaxy for profit. Look where it had got him: locked in a box, surrounded by paranoid Humans.

Shouts from the corridor make Sylvester jump again. There were more of those loud *crump* sounds, and one Human gunshot. Then silence. Sylvester retreated into a tight coil in the far corner of the room. The door opened.

A bald and angry Human stood there, a stun baton in one hand, a gun in the other. He wore a good suit that was now rumpled and torn at one sleeve. He looked angry and happy at the same time.

"The end of the search," the Human said cryptically.

The scanner, activated by Billion before she was attacked, sensed a new person in the room beyond the glass. It reviewed the brainwaves of the Human. The result came back somewhat faster than it had during previous interviews, given the nature of the scanned individual's identity. The scanner had been programmed and tested by *b-b-b-b* technicians, so it made sense that it would be most efficient at recognizing a *b-b-b-b* brainwave pattern.

Dale Krensky was a Blue.

If he hadn't transferred his personality into a Snake body, Sylvester might have had a chance. That was the sad irony of this situation. Not only were Gradlik larger and more powerful than Humans, he could simply have called to his brethren for help. The Gradlik didn't enjoy pure telepathy, but they retained an evolutionary vestige of their psychic past, when they would hunt the night skies of their home in packs, sending and receiving impulses and images necessary for the capture of their clever and elusive airborne prey. Now, millions of years later, their psychic connection was vaguer, largely closed off by their ascent to civilization. The psychic link only appeared in times of religious ecstasy, or in times of great peril.

With no fellow Vampires to call on for help, all Sylvester had was his Snake body. As the Human lowered the gun to shoot, Sylvester pushed off from the wall and slithered under the plain, metal table toward the Human's feet. Two shots rang out, both missing him completely. A third ricocheted hollowly off the top of the table. Sylvester reached the Human and wound his way in a spiral up the body. He used one hand to wrest the gun from his assailant's grasp, and the other to knock aside the stun baton. He constricted his coil as tight as he could around the Human's chest, attempting to push the breath out of his lungs.

The Human coughed once, then threw aside the stun baton. He reached up with both hands and grasped Sylvester about the throat, pressing, pressing with brute, simian strength, choking air and blood from Sylvester's brain. Sylvester lost his grip on the Human's torso, consciousness starting to leave him. His body fell off the Human in a loose, soft rustle.

The Human staggered out into the hall, still grasping Sylvester, nearly tripping over the bodies of the murdered Human agents that lay on the waxy floor. Sylvester cast about for someone, anyone to help him. As his senses began to leave him, he heard distant alarms ringing through the building. Someone knew that a murder was occurring. Would they come in time?

At the end of the hall, Sylvester saw what could only be a hazy vision from the afterlife. A Gradlik stood proudly, wings extended, head thrust forward, preparing for attack. This was not any Gradlik. This was *him*. This was *Ktalala*. Sylvester was about to experience his own personal Convergence, merging with his afterlife self.

The specter of Ktalala shrieked, the harsh sound echoing down the wide corridor. The Human heard it. How could the Human hear the sound of the afterlife coming to claim Sylvester and take him to his personal future at the end of time?

The specter flapped its wings, nearly but not quite contained by the restriction of the corridor's walls. He sailed forward, claws and beak reaching out for the Human. Sylvester was for the moment forgotten, dropped gasping to the floor. Sylvester watched as the specter inhabiting his body collided with the Human. They tumbled away in a heap of flailing, mismatched limbs. With one final crack of his head against the hard floor, the Human lost consciousness.

The Vampire slowly rose and turned. With the return of oxygen, lucidity came back to Sylvester. This wasn't some harbinger of death, some future afterlife version of Ktalala. This was something even more unbelievable.

"I hope you haven't harmed my body too much," Elt said.

Sylvester laughed briefly, then passed out.

Billion escorted the Secretary to the holding area. They were surrounded by a healthy complement of Human guards. Hargrove was dressed in black, a somber color for Humans, Billion had learned. She and Billion would attend a memorial service for the five fallen—four Human FBI agents and Krd—later today. During Krensky's vicious attack, Billion had only received a glancing blow from the stun baton, enough to incapacitate, not enough to kill. She felt a measure of guilt for having survived The Antagonist's attack when her colleague Krd did not. She did not know Krd well, but he would be nonetheless missed.

Hargrove reached The Antagonist's cell and looked through the small rectangle of thick glass. The Human known as Dale Krensky sat motionlessly on his cot, looking through the window at his former superior. That The Antagonist was a *b-b-b-b* continued to rankle Billion. She had not believed a Blue possessed by another consciousness could be so destructive. That the *origin* of the famed seditionist was one of her people was staggering. But the scanner did not lie.

"He hasn't said anything?" she asked again.

"No," Billion confirmed again. Questioning had revealed nothing. They had no doubt that Dale Krensky was the most recent incarnation of The Antagonist. Five bodies were left in his wake, with two others nearly killed. All of it told the tale. They did not know when or how he had accomplished the transfer into this Human host, but there was no reason to believe that the consciousness of the original Dale Krensky had survived. None of the fugitive's previous hosts had.

Hargrove pressed the button that would allow her to talk to Krensky.

"How long?"

Silence.

"How long?" she asked again. "How long, you son of a bitch!" she raged.

Krensky did not respond.

"You failed. You realize that, don't you? Nothing you did made any difference at all. We're going to finish *Vimana*. We're going to go to Central Authority. And you will never be free again."

Krensky's stoic frown shifted just a bit, reforming into a mirthless grin.

"Let's get out of here," Hargrove said, leading Billion away from the cell.

Gallic Rage

> *Men seek retreats for them-*
> *selves, houses in the country, sea-*
> *shores, and mountains; and thou*
> *too art wont to desire such things*
> *very much. But this is altogether a*
> *mark of the most common sort of*
> *men...*
> —*Meditations, IV, 3*

The little town of Vieux Mer sat nestled within a broad curve of the Loire River in western France. There, an old world sensibility lived in simple harmony with the unavoidable trappings of the modern world. Citizens spoke to each other on cell phones. Many shopped for their Christmas gifts on Amazon.fr. Most enjoyed the conveniences of modern life: hydrogen powered automobiles, laser eye surgery, iPods and X-Boxes.

In other ways, Vieux Mer resisted the encroachment of modernity on their little world. There was no McDonald's, nor was there a Wal-Mart in their little village. No tablet fabrication plants. No plastic sur-geons. And only one lawyer, who worked part-time as an editor for the local paper to supplement his income. Just about everyone in the town worked for a local business, which made it one of the smallest essentially self-sufficient communities in all of Europe. Nothing dire, either physically or economically, had occurred in Vieux Mer since the end of World War II.

And then the Snake arrived.

At first, the visitor was a mild annoyance, a curiosity really. He pur-chased a plot of land on the hill overlooking the town at an exorbitant rate from a local farmer who was nearing retirement and looking to sell anyway. When the farmer left town to live out his twilight years in Nantes, one or two of the older folks looked down their noses at him and his sale to an alien. The rest of the town politely ignored the newcomer.

The Snake hired Jean Jacob, the best of the three professional building contractors in Vieux Mer, to oversee construction of his ostentatious house. This caused a certain amount of grumbling throughout the town, but still, the people were largely unconcerned. Other spots nearby in the valley were home to rich industrialists from Paris or Munich or even beyond Europe. These rich folk would visit for a month or two every year, spend their money, take their snapshots, and then go back to their lives in the big city. It would be the same with the Snake, wouldn't it?

When the Snake's true plan became apparent, the low-key grumbling turned to open argument. The large home that he had contracted Jean to build was merely the first step in a larger plan. That was to simply be the *guest house*. The actual residence, higher on the hill and in full view of every home in Vieux Mer, was to be a horrible monstrosity, so overlarge and overdone, it seemed positively *Italian*.

What was worse, the construction of the thing took more labor than Jacob and his small band of workers could provide. Soon, every builder in Vieux Mer—and a few from outside as well—were working round the clock on the mansion. Marble was brought in from Greece. Oak from Poland. Craftsmen from Milan visited for two weeks to paint a mural on the grand ceiling of the mansion's ballroom. The Snake's demands were putting a remarkable strain on the town, as visitors filled their modest inn, ate their food, and consumed their consumables.

And there were other visitors as well... *alien* visitors, who darkened the Snake's door even before the construction was complete. Species of off worlders that no one in Vieux Mer had ever heard of, let alone seen in the flesh. Strange and terrible creatures, described by Jean and his workers, arriving at all hours.

What had started as mild amusement, had shifted to vague displeasure, and finally, turned to outright anger. The town of Vieux Mer wanted the Snake to leave, but they had no way to accomplish it. Until Avril Beauchamps broke her ankle.

Avril Beauchamps was seven years old, the daughter of Maurice and Sandrine Beauchamps. Maurice, now a widower, was a shopkeeper in town who managed a hardware store. Even in a town the size of Vieux Mer, there were many seven-year-old girls. But none were as beautiful as

Avril, with her honey-blonde hair, her sky-blue eyes, and her dimpled cheeks. None had her sunny disposition. None had her musical laughter or her polite manner or her smile like the sun breaking through the clouds after a long and rainy winter. She was a favorite of everyone in town, and, more to her credit, she didn't even know it.

It was with no sense of the chaos and confusion that her words would cause that she limped into the library at ten o'clock that morning, eyes streaming with tears, crying out, "The snake! The snake!"

The aging librarian, known to everyone in the town as Madame Clarisse, rushed to the little girl's side, cradling the child in her arms.

"What happened? What happened, dear girl?"

"The... snake..." Avril whispered, then fainted.

Madame Clarisse, breaking her own oft-cited rule against raised voices within the hushed confines of the library, shouted across the room to her assistant, young Violette Armand. "Call the doctor! Avril is injured!" Violette rushed not to the phone as she was instructed, but to the foyer of the library to take in the scene. Avril looked pale as death itself. Her clothes were muddied and in disarray. Madame Clarisse patted the little girl's cheeks, attempting to rouse her. But she did not stir.

Madame Clarisse looked up at Violette. "Foolish girl! The doctor! Go quickly!"

Violette rushed through the front door and down the street.

Doctor Ivan Klonsky had one of three general practices in Vieux Mer. He was the eldest of the GPs in town, and was the only one whose office was in the town center. The other two gentlemen had built small offices inside their homes on the outskirts of the town proper. Dr. Klonsky believed them to be breaking with tradition, a tradition that proved itself to be quite valuable that warm August day when Violette Armand rushed into his office, eyes wild.

"Avril has been attacked! Come quickly!"

Dr. Klonsky grabbed his black leather bag and rushed after Violette to the library. Madame Clarisse still sat on the hard floor of the library's entrance, holding the unconscious girl. Dr. Klonsky carefully took the girl from the old woman, laying her down, examining her. He soon determined that the girl had broken her ankle, the pain of which was likely to have caused her to faint.

"It was the Snake," Madame Clarisse said.

"The Snake on the hill attacked Avril?" the doctor asked, horrified. Madame Clarisse had said nothing of an *attack*, but the words from the doctor solidified the idea in her mind nonetheless.

"Yes!" she agreed.

"We must call an ambulance immediately!"

From there, the news spread quite rapidly.

Madame Clarisse called the members of her bridge club to tell them the story of the alien's vicious attack on poor little Avril. By eleven o'clock, the tale had spread to every retiree in the town, and many of the older working folk as well. With each retelling, the attack became more horrifically described. According to these various accounts, Avril had been beaten, stabbed, dropped from a great height, bitten, and in one case, nearly drowned in the river.

Simultaneously, the news spread in a more modern fashion through the youth of the town. Violette sent text messages describing the severely injured Avril to seven of her closest friends. Those seven friends forwarded the news to fifty-three others. The variation of description of the events of the morning was not as great as those generated by Madame Clarisse's phone calls, but they proceeded with much greater speed. Within only forty minutes, every person between the ages of thirteen and twenty-three knew of Avril Beauchamps' near-death experience at the hands of the now universally reviled Snake.

Dr. Klonsky accompanied Avril in the ambulance to the hospital in the next town over, Petit Mer. During the ride, he contacted the members of the Vieux Mer Chamber of Commerce via cell phone, thus completing the dissemination of the story of the attack to the rest of the town's population.

As it was still high summer, the youth of Vieux Mer were not in school as yet. Parents all across the village called their children home, fearing further attacks by the Snake or his fellow aliens who may or may not have been living in that den of iniquity on the hill. From the hours of twelve to three in the afternoon, the town went into an unofficial, self-imposed curfew. Streets were clear of traffic; shops were empty of customers. Those few who had not heard about Avril's devilish fate—or who had heard earlier, less lurid versions—soon realized that something drastic must have happened and hurried home themselves.

At three fifteen, the first rumor of a second attack surfaced. The rumor came about from a simple misunderstanding. Yvette Rochard, a secondary school student, sitting at home under the careful watch of her mother, used her cell phone to text a friend across town, Gerard Zamlia. She intended to type the letters "AB" to refer to Avril Beauchamps, but instead typed "AC". Gerard mistook this as a reference to Analise Claveria, another of the young girls in town. Gerard dutifully forwarded this terrible revelation—*another* girl had been attacked—to all of his friends. This new development spread like wildfire, adding to the sense of doom that lay over the village like a foul-smelling fog.

At three forty-five, the mayor of Vieux Mer, Francis Grouen, a taxidermist who had run for office more as a lark than from any desire to serve the public, decided to take action. But he did not want to act precipitously. He wished to know precisely the extent of the situation, and to learn it from the appropriate parties. He began by phoning the Beauchamps' home. They did not answer. This worried Mayor Grouen. Could something have happened to the *rest* of the family? Could the Snake be so cruel? No, he would not jump to such conclusions, despite the loud warnings from his wife Lizette, a close personal friend of Avril's dead mother, Sandrine.

Sandrine had died the previous year, succumbing to an aneurism that took her life in a matter of minutes. At the time, a story had circulated that she had died not of a burst blood vessel, but of a brain tumor that the Snake's much vaunted "Cancer Oil" should have cured, but did not. The furor over her death was short-lived, a one-day wonder. Now, with the possibility that her only surviving child might have been attacked or even killed by the same uncaring alien, suspicious mutterings about Sandrine's death resurfaced.

In fact, the reason Maurice Beauchamps did not answer his phone was that he was en route to Petit Mer to attend to his injured daughter. This possibility did not occur to the rattled Mayor Grouen, nor to his hysterical wife.

Wishing to glean more information about the rumored second attack, Mayor Grouen next called the home of Marc and Terese Claveria, Analise's parents. When there was no answer at the Claveria household either, Mayor Grouen became very worried indeed. Had he known that the Claveria family were taking a weeklong trip to Paris to do some back-to-school shopping, he might not have taken the action he now took. He called for a town meeting.

The only space in Vieux Mer large enough to hold a sizeable portion of the citizenry was the gymnasium of the town's sole primary school. By seven o'clock, the low-ceilinged, wood-floored box of a room held nearly five hundred agitated townsfolk. No one had notified Abbé Malraux, the school's chief custodian, that a meeting was to take place in his building, so he did not know until very late in the day to activate the air conditioning system. As a result, the gymnasium was quite ferociously hot, and getting hotter as the mood of the crowd grew sour.

"Please, order! Please!" Mayor Grouen attempted to gain control of the crowd, and was only partially successful. Several of those nearest to his slightly elevated podium listened, while the bulk of the townsfolk continued to mutter and argue amongst themselves. Most of those in the gymnasium were men, having left behind their children in the care of their mothers.

"How many girls have been attacked?" one man shouted from the middle of the crowd. A chorus of voices echoed the question with shouts of "How many?"

"We know of two attacks only!" the mayor assured them. His turn of phrase did not inspire confidence, and the mutterings increased.

"The Beauchamps family is gone!" another voice rang out. A third added, "I went to their house, and it was empty!"

"We must not panic!" Mayor Grouen ordered, his injudicious use of the word "panic" inspiring not calm, only more panic in the crowd.

"I heard the girl was raped!"

That statement caused a collective intake of breath in the crowd. No one had yet ventured such a theory of the crime, though it had been on the tips of many tongues over the last few hours. What else were they to think? The two victims were young *girls*, pretty, innocent things. Humans, they knew to their shame, were capable of such grisly, inhuman acts. How much more capable would an *alien* be?

Mayor Grouen sensed a sea change in the crowd. Frustration and anger were now channeling toward focused rage. Violence could not be far behind. He had to calm these people immediately. "We cannot confirm there has been a rape!"

If the mayor had imagined these words would lay oil on the troubled waters of this meeting, he was drastically mistaken. Nearly every person in the room took him to mean that he *believed* there to have been a rape, but that the evidence, as yet, did not provide confirmation. The mutterings of the crowd took a lower, quieter, darker turn. The mayor distinctly heard one man say, "We must kill him."

The mayor sought one particular face in the crowd. Constable Clément Perec was a well respected, sober and thoroughly professional man who had maintained law and order in Vieux Mer for nearly fifteen years. His silver hair, tall stature, and clear, honest eyes made him a touchstone for justice and mercy not only in Vieux Mer, but throughout the Loire Valley. Mayor Grouen waved for the older gentleman to join him at the podium.

"Say something, please," the mayor whispered to Constable Perec.

Perec nodded, his countenance rugged and assured. The mayor knew the situation was well in hand now.

What the mayor did *not* know was the personal history of the Constable. In fact, no one alive in the town knew Clément Perec's darkest secret. He was, despite his reputation for upstanding and selfless civil service, an adulterer. Years ago, he had cheated on his wife Marguerite, conducting a long affair with a local woman who was also married. The local woman had, unfortunately, become pregnant and used the situation as an opportunity to end the affair. Constable Perec's heart was shattered, but he stoically accepted her decision, despite never knowing for sure if the child was his. He had hoped that the woman would spare him the pain of not knowing, that she would, eventually, tell him the truth. Who was the girl's father?

The woman never had the chance. Last year, she died of a brain aneurism, leaving the child alone with her supposed father. To this day, Constable Perec believed that he was, in fact, the father of Avril Beauchamps. And now, he also believed that the Snake on the hill was responsible not only for a gruesome attack on his daughter, but that his inaction had last year caused the death of his one true love, Sandrine.

When Constable Perec took the podium, the crowd's angry muttering faded away. They looked to him for guidance. This they received.

"The Snake must die!"

Five hundred voices shouted agreement.

Afterward, no one was precisely sure where the torches came from. There were many terrible misunderstandings on this day, but this was one mystery that never would be solved. Nonetheless, as twilight descended into full dark, an angry mob ascended the hill, carrying flames that burned bright, though not as bright as their fury. They sought vengeance for the terrible crimes committed by the alien in their midst.

Jean Jacob, working late as always on the never-ending project that was the Snake's home, saw the bobbing lights coming up the lane. He checked his mental calendar for any holidays that might include a nighttime parade, but he could think of none. As the mob got closer, he heard the tenor of their voices, if not their actual words.

Jean turned to his right hand man, Paul Villon. "Run and get help."

"From who?" Paul answered, pointing to a familiar, white-haired face at the front of the advancing crowd, Constable Perec.

Jean sighed. "What has the Snake done now?" The Snake seemed to attract trouble. Just last night, the alien had been whisked away by a team of government agents—Americans, if Jean knew his English accents. Why they had come, he did not know. He simply knew that unexpected guests to the mansion on the hill were a common occurrence.

"Where is the Snake?" Constable Perec demanded as soon as he was within earshot of Jean.

"Why? What has happened?"

An angry cry shot up from the front of the mob. He pieced together what he could from the confusion of wild accusations. It seemed that a girl—or girls—had been attacked—or raped—or murdered. He waved his hands to try to quiet the crowd and make sense of this.

"When did this happen?"

On that point, at least, there was no doubt. It had happened this morning.

Jean knew then that whatever the Snake had been accused of, he could not have done it. He had left with the Americans late the previous evening, and he had not returned, neither to his home nor his private airstrip, which was in full view down the hill. Jean could avert a possible disaster right now by telling them this.

However... Jean saw something terrifying in the eyes of these people. He saw murderous rage reflected in each fire-lit face. Some carried sticks or crowbars. He saw one hunting rifle slung over a man's shoulder. Others hefted rocks in jittery hands. It looked to Jean as if someone would have to die tonight. And in that moment, a moment he would live to regret, he made certain the person who died would not be *him*.

Jean stepped aside to let the crowd approach the house.

As the rampaging mob of townsfolk surrounded the Snake's mansion, in the hospital in Petit Mer, little Avril woke from her long nap. She smiled blearily to see her father hovering over the bed.

"Where am I?" she asked.

"You're in the hospital," Maurice said, giving the girl a kiss on the forehead. "Thank God you are alright."

Maurice was very concerned about the story Dr. Klonsky had told. His little Avie might have been traumatized by her experience. "What did he do to you?" he asked his daughter carefully.

"Who?"

"The Snake. What did he do?"

"I hope he's okay."

Maurice gave his daughter a confused look. Avril went on.

"When my bicycle ran over him, he didn't look well. I was so worried, I fell and hurt my leg. Was the snake okay? Did I kill him?"

Maurice felt a tremor of relief through his entire body. He was unwilling to trust that feeling, so he pressed the girl for more details.

"Avril, how big was the snake you ran over with your bicycle?"

Avril held out her hands, the palms only about ten centimeters apart.

"He was green. I didn't mean to hurt him."

Maurice pulled Avril into a hug. "I know you didn't, darling."

The whole nasty business had only taken about eighteen hours, but Sylvester felt like he'd been absconded from his home by those FBI agents eighteen days ago. Of course, it had all turned out for the best. If there was a better way to ingratiate himself with the Humans, he didn't know what it was. Nearly being strangled to death by the most wanted fugitive in the galaxy tended to erase previous doubts about his character. They didn't even seem to mind the fact that he had misrepresented his race. In fact, the Americans seemed particularly glad to learn that a Gradlik could live a life that didn't involve constant prayer. Americans were a funny lot when you thought about them. Devout in their own belief, but very wary of those devout in other beliefs. Strange.

Sylvester had a nice nap on the flight back to France, and greeted his driver, Pierre, with a warm smile as he slithered into the Rolls.

"Have a good trip, sir?" Pierre asked.

"Glad to be home, mate. Glad to be home."

Sylvester coiled himself into a comfortable pool in the back seat of the car for the five-minute drive up to his house. He toyed with the idea of enjoying a nice, moonlight swim before dinner.

"Sir?" The tone of that one word from Pierre said volumes. Sylvester's head shot up.

The scene before him was so strange, he had difficulty processing it. There was some sort of party on his front lawn, complete with dancing and tiki torches. Was the town throwing him a welcome home celebration? How remarkable!

Then, Sylvester began to understand what he was seeing. Nearly half the town was congregated on his property, surrounding his house. They'd already set fire to half of his garden, his topiary animals blazing like small Convergence bonfires. The marble fountain in the center of his swimming pool had been tipped over and pushed into the water. Something was very, very wrong.

Sylvester always planned for quick escapes. True, his time on Earth had been more productive and more comfortable than any of his other visits to nascent civilizations. Even so, his profound instinct for self-preservation did not wane. He always made sure to have an escape route. Unfortunately, he never anticipated he would be *outside* his house when that escape route was needed.

"I need to get inside."

"That may be difficult, sir."

Sylvester hissed at the driver's understatement. The crowd now saw the Rolls, and advanced.

"Accelerate. They'll scatter."

Pierre turned to look at Sylvester with a single raised eyebrow.

"No. Of course not. Back to the airstrip, then."

Pierre looked into his rearview mirror. "That may not be an option, either." Sylvester turned to see that the Rolls was now surrounded by angry Humans. One fist rapped against his left rear window. Then another on the other side. Like the rain drops of a gathering storm, the blows multiplied. The car began to shift queasily as people pushed on it from either side.

"Pierre?"

Pierre shrugged. A flaming torch flew from somewhere ahead, landing on the hood of the car and bouncing off the windshield.

"Good luck, sir," Pierre said just before opening his door and joining the crowd. Sylvester watched as the driver was pulled away from the car, and thankfully not killed on the spot. Clearly, this mob didn't want the driver. They wanted *him*.

Sylvester did the only thing he could. He rolled down his window and slipped out onto the ground.

The mob, in their mindless rage, had forgotten that they were trying to lynch a Snake. Sylvester easily slithered between their legs and around their feet. He could tell they were unnerved by the sensation of his passage, but none had the presence of mind to simply reach down and grab him.

Almost none.

A strong hand took hold of the very end of Sylvester's tail, stopping his progress toward the house. He only had a fraction of a second to act before a dozen more hands would reach down and tear him to pieces. He looped his body around the nearest pair of legs he could find and *constricted*. The man whose legs he had chosen fell with a fearful squawk. Since the crowd was so closely packed, a domino effect occurred, spilling several other men to the ground as well. One of those was luckily the man who had Sylvester by the tail. He lost his grip, and Sylvester continued to slither away.

After a moment, Sylvester broke out onto open ground. He could move faster than the Humans, but he was also quite visible now. A hurled torch missed him by only centimeters. A rock missed him by less. A second rock did *not* miss, and smashed heavily into his back. He hurried forward, up the steps, between massive Doric columns, and to his front door.

Which was locked. He had only moments to fish his keys from a pocket before the crowd would be on him. There they were! Door open! He did not have the luxury of enough time to close and relock the door behind him. The mob was on his tail.

Smoke filled the house. The rampaging villagers must have tossed one or more of their flaming torches though his windows, setting the carpet, the drapes, even some of the furnishings on fire. Even in his frantic state, Sylvester couldn't help but mourn the loss of such lovely and expensive items.

Sylvester assumed that the crowd would intuit his plan. They would try to reach the roof before he did. He bypassed the main stairs and slipped through the kitchen to the back of the house where the servant's quarters were accessed by a smaller, winding staircase. Behind him, he could hear the Humans stumbling about in the smoke. Sylvester remained low to the ground where the air was marginally clearer.

This advantage lessened as he climbed the stairs to the second, then the third floor. The smoke had pooled up here, without sufficient ventilation to release it to the outside. He became disoriented, moving in a circle through the small suite of rooms at the top of the house, looking for the roof access.

The shouts of the Humans grew louder. They had reached the second floor by way of the main stairs, and would achieve the third floor in only moments. Sylvester could not remember where the entrance to the roof *was*. It was designed to be unobtrusive, but not to *him*.

Out of the smoke came a pair of meaty, Human arms that scooped Sylvester up off the ground. The Human held him tight around the middle, so Sylvester's own arms were trapped. He tried to whip his tail

around the Human's torso, to attempt to squeeze his attacker into submission, but he did not have the strength. The smoke was getting to him.

When Sylvester looked at the Human's face, he was stunned.

"Jean!"

"Yes."

"What are you doing?"

"I'm getting you out of here."

Jean tossed Sylvester over his shoulder like a length of fire hose and
hurried through the smoke. He reached up to the ceiling and grasped a
simple brass ring. Pulling on it, a flight of stairs levered down into the
corridor. Smoke began to pour out of the opening, escaping into the dark
night sky above. Jean dragged Sylvester up the stairs and onto the roof of
the house. He dropped the Snake and fell to his knees, coughing. Sylvester
coughed as well.

He looked to see his escape vessel ready and waiting for him: an orbit
bubble, sitting in the center of the roof.

"Thank you," Sylvester wheezed.

"Wait," Jean said. He crawled over to Sylvester. "Bite me."

"Excuse me?"

"They can't think I let you go. They'll kill me."

"But... couldn't I just hit you or something?"

Along with the smoke pouring out of the roof entrance, they heard
the approach of the mob.

"Just do it!" Jean pushed his work shirt sleeve up and offered his
bare arm. Sylvester hesitated... then opened his fanged mouth as far as he
could—which was, indeed, quite far—and bit down on the Human's
flesh. He only pierced the skin enough to draw blood, then withdrew. He
spat the bitter taste of salt from his mouth.

"You should have that looked at," he counseled Jean.

"And you should go."

Sylvester hurried over to the orbit bubble and slipped in. He activated the controls and watched with some real sadness as he left his
home—and Earth—for the last time.

He could stay, he supposed. Resettle in Brussels or Alabama, continue to run his businesses. But he'd made his fortune. He now realized it
was the simple, bucolic lifestyle he led in Vieux Mer that kept him on

Earth for such a long time. Now it was all gone—his home, his friendship with the people in the village—without an explanation or even a simple apology. The townspeople had seemingly gone mad.

"Ship?"

"*Yes, Captain?*" She was always there for him, his trusty *Cat Carrier*. He might even continue to call her that from now on. She seemed to like the name.

"It's time to go."

"*That's a shame. I've enjoyed Earth.*"

"As have I."

"*What did you do this time?*"

Sylvester laughed out loud.

"I honestly don't know."

Family Matters

> *Turn thy thoughts now to thy life under thy grandfather, then to thy life under thy mother, then to thy life under thy father; and as thou findest many other differences and changes and terminations, ask thyself, Is this anything to fear? In like manner, then, neither are the termination and cessation and change of thy whole life a thing to be afraid of.*
> —*Meditations, V, 21*

Nearly a thousand VIPs gathered in the Francis Plotsky Conference Center in Opportunity, Florida on October 26, 2028. Most of the attendees, influential and powerful though they were, sat at wide, round tables of twelve seats each at the back of the banquet hall. They chatted and drank their wine and munched their better-than-average-but-still-not-great meals and waited, eyes flitting expectantly up to the huge screens at the front of the room.

At nine smaller tables, each with only nine chairs, sat the people for whom this gathering was the most important. Eighty-one diplomats, scientists and security personnel would serve as the crew and passengers of *Vimana*, scheduled for departure in six months' time. The selection process had been laborious and time intensive. Political favors were called in. Recommendations were written and rewritten and rewritten again. Focus groups weighed in, regardless whether the Selection Committee particularly cared about their concerns. Race, religion, nationality, political ideology: all of these were factored. Competence was less of a factor, really. Only those who were competent in their fields—only those who *excelled* in their fields—even made the first cut. Culling a list of ten thousand down to eighty-one required more than performance reviews and SAT scores. It required intangibles.

Keira Desai and Terry Youngblood spoke in quiet tones at one of the tables. Their inclusion in the *Vimana* crew was never in serious doubt. All of the Project Leads from MYC were on the team to provide support for the vessel, so Keira's spot was assured. Terry, on the other hand, would command the small contingent of NATO forces whose job was to escort the diplomatic corps to Central Authority.

At the front of the room, at a long table on a dais directly beneath the still dark screens, sat much of the leadership of the nation. The President, his second term drawing to a close, was there to put his seal on the greatest single aspect of his legacy: Earth's first mission to the stars. At his right sat Nilakantha Ganguly, flush with pride at his accomplishment. Next to him sat Mira Netrivali, her ever-present smile glowing in the dim, candle-enhanced light. Others at the table included General Reginald McGaw, General Carol Brown, and Secretary of Defense Wilkinson. In fact nearly half of the Cabinet was in attendance. Sitting to the President's immediate left was Secretary of Off World Affairs, Vanessa Hargrove, whose eyes seemed drawn again and again to the chatting couple seated at the small table below.

The President stood, clinking a fork against a glass. The pleasant, mellow murmuring of the crowd ceased. He spoke in his traditional off-hand manner, a style that his speech writers had perfected over the past eight years. He lauded the accomplishments of Maccha-Yantra, of the US military, of DOWA, of everyone in the room. He paid lip service to the help they'd received from Europe and Japan, and even refrained from any cutting remarks toward China, whose interstellar program had recently stumbled. A disastrous systems test of their prototype FTL drive had sent an unmanned vehicle crashing quite spectacularly into the Moon. The collision had created a small, very white crater on the Moon's day side. The Man in the Moon now had a new freckle.

A subtle signal from an aide cued the President to wind down his speech. The test was ready. The President directed the room to watch the screens over his head. Two of the three screens came to life. The left showed a live video feed taken from *Ronald Reagan*. The view revealed a space craft: *Armstrong*, the first MAD drive test ship. The prototype vessel was little more than a cockpit for a team of four astronauts, nestled within a house-sized MAD propulsion drive. To eyes unskilled in the world of FTL technology, the machine looked like an unlikely cross between a natural gas depot and an old-style combustion engine carburetor. *Armstrong* was designed not to appeal to anyone's sense of style, but for one thing: to test a Modified Alcubierre-Devecchio drive. The test was to be a short superluminal hop, from Earth to Saturn and back, a round trip of 2.8 billion kilometers.

The rightmost screen displayed a schematic of the solar system. At the periphery sat an eclipsed sliver of the Sun, a slash of bright yellow. Earth was represented by a pale blue-green dot, and Saturn by a larger, ringed circle of pure blue. An icon, the letter "A", showed the location of *Armstrong*, immediately next to Earth.

Speakers crackled to life, the pilots on the ship talking to ground control, making their final readiness checks. They activated their on-board camera, and the middle screen brightened, showing a dramatic shot of *Reagan* station hanging above a half-lit Earth, the terminator of night slowly proceeding west across the Rocky Mountains.

Final checks were completed, and the middle screen's view swept slowly, majestically away from *Ronald Reagan*, past a minor flotilla of mismatched off world craft that buzzed about her. The Moon slipped across the field of view briefly, harsh in its brilliance. After the Moon vanished, only dark sky and a few pinpoints of starlight remained. An unnecessarily dramatic countdown from the launch controller in Florida commenced.

Three.

Two.

One...

The view of *Armstrong* coming from the station seemed to shimmer, like heat waves on hot blacktop. The vessel pushed forward slightly. The shimmer grew more intense, resembling a distorted view a tiny insect might see through a massive raindrop. The ship receded faster, impossibly fast. It was gone. The crowd knew perfectly well what to expect. They gasped nonetheless.

The view from *Armstrong's* front-mounted camera remained unchanged, save that the stars wavered a bit, victims of the same distortion that the *Reagan* camera had seen. The ship's position with respect to the star field had not changed appreciably. The schematic, however, showed the audience that the ship was moving *extremely* fast. Light traveling from Earth to Saturn took in the neighborhood of eighty minutes to make the outbound trip. The little "A" icon started to move away from the blue-green Earth, slowly at first, only a pixel or two on the computerized display. Then faster, and faster still, accelerating past light speed in only the first minute or so. At the halfway point of the trip—only three minutes into the journey—when the icon seemed ready to shoot off the screen entirely, it began to decelerate.

About the same time, the view from *Armstrong*'s camera did begin to show a change. One of the points of light, a bit brighter than most, certainly, but to a layman's eye, just another star, grew in brightness. The effect was obvious even through the muddy scattering of light caused by the MAD drive's distortion of the space around the ship. A gray-blue orb sprouted from that point of light. As the ship throttled down to light speed, and below, the distortion lessened. A delicate system of rings came into view which circled the large, shimmering world. This was the Jewel of the Solar System: Saturn.

A timer in the lower right corner of the schematic stopped counting. Earth to Saturn in five minutes and forty-two seconds.

Applause thundered through the room.

"She looked kind of sad, don't you think?" Terry said.

"Who?"

"They should have put her on the team."

Keira turned away, fluffing her pillow, turning off her bedside lamp.

"What?" he asked.

"Nothing. I'm going to sleep."

"She's a friend of mine."

"I know."

"I just think she looked sad."

Keira said nothing, trying to mimic the slow rhythm of breathing that she imagined she used during her slumber. Terry didn't get the hint.

"You're mad."

Keira considered saying nothing. She could feel Terry's eyes on her. "No," she said finally.

"It's not like there was ever anything between us."

Terry simply didn't understand that she wanted to stop talking about it. That was the idea behind going to sleep.

"If I can't make a simple comment about a close friend, then—"

Keira flipped over to look at Terry. "Close friend? When was the last time you saw her?"

"What?"

"When was the last time you had lunch with her, talked to her on the phone?"

"It's... I... I didn't think you wanted me to."

"Why would I care, if there's nothing between you?"

"I can't believe I'm having this argument."

"I'm not arguing with you."

"It sure feels like you are."

Keira turned back over. "We should get to sleep."

"My daddy always said, 'If you go to bed mad, don't expect to have nice dreams.'"

"Did he? Did he always say that?" Keira snapped.

They locked angry gazes for several seconds before Terry gave up. "Fine." He switched off his lamp and turned away from her.

Something was different. Keira couldn't put a finger on it exactly, but she and Terry had turned a corner somewhere, somehow. It wasn't that she didn't enjoy his company or his touch. It wasn't, like it had been with Tommy, that they didn't spend enough time together. It wasn't, like it had been with Shailesh, that they didn't have the right chemistry. They lived together and loved together just like before.

Their problem was simple conversation. She felt like she had to think before she spoke. It wasn't any particular thing, like their spat about Vanessa Hargrove. It was lots of things: who drove the car, what film they'd go to see, how Terry voted in the election, how often Keira flew home to see her family. Keira had no interest in arguments; in fact, she tried to avoid them as much as possible. Terry, though, seemed to see her reticence on certain topics as a prelude to anger, and he tried to fend off the explosion that she knew would never actually come. So Keira was left with the draining task of censoring herself, to avoid arousing these concerns of his.

When had she demonstrated this volatile temper he so feared?

November eased its way into December, the seasons barely noticeable in the Florida heat. Preparations for the flight next April continued, and intensified. But this was America, after all. A break for Christmas and the New Year was guaranteed. Keira hinted rather obliquely that she'd like to visit Terry's family for the holiday. He never took the hint, so instead she invited him to Bengalūru.

Since Terry hadn't ever been to India, Keira wanted to make sure he felt comfortable, particularly under the watchful eyes of the Desai clan. She prepped him on all their names, and their family connections. She told him just to be himself, and everything would be alright.

She was more right than she knew. Keira watched in amazement as Terry charmed every member of her family. He treated Mother like a queen, clearly a benefit of his "Old South" upbringing. He indulged Father in his pet peeves and conspiracy theories. He flirted chastely with Keira's sisters, palled around with her brothers-in-law, and roughhoused with all of those nieces and nephews who used to be so star struck by their famous Aunt Keira.

On Christmas Eve they had a semi-traditional turkey dinner, put together by the Desai women in Terry's honor. With two tables of family eating heartily, Mother asked Terry about his own family, and whether they were missing him on this holiday. Terry affably sidestepped the question with an anecdote—one Keira had never heard, and suspected he had constructed out of whole cloth on the spot—about a friend and his humorously dysfunctional family. Jessica Desai politely accepted his misdirection, though she was clearly not fooled by it.

"Kiki," her father said, "are we going to see you again before the big flight, or do we have to say our farewells this week?"

Dozens of eyes turned to Keira, who had just taken a big bite of bread. She chewed and swallowed. Before she could answer, Terry put an arm around her shoulders and said, "I'll push her onto the plane if I have to." Everyone laughed.

Except Keira.

After dinner, Terry organized a football game—though he referred to it as "soccer"—in a park just down the street. All the men and children ran pell-mell after him, eager to show up the tall, blond American with their superior footwork with the ball. Keira hung back with her sisters and her mother. She could tell Mother had something to say, and she had a very good idea what it was. *Have you talked about marriage? Will you stay with this one? He's so* handsome*!*

Jessica linked her arm in Keira's, walking slowly down the sidewalk, not saying anything yet. The anticipation was painful.

"Go ahead, Mother."

"Go ahead what?"

"What do you think?"

"Of Terry? I think he's very nice."

"Very nice? That's it?"

"What do you want me to say?"

"Mother!"

"What do *you* think of him?"

"What do *I* think of him? He's my boyfriend. I'd think it would be obvious. I like him."

"Well, then." The way she said that, Keira knew there was more. Mother usually wasn't this quiet, though. Keira wondered, not for the first time, if something really had happened to her back in '25 when she had undergone that frightening, improvised brain surgery. Jessica Desai did not often hold her tongue when dealing with her children. Keira stopped walking, allowing her sisters to move ahead and join in the football match. She didn't want an audience for this.

"You want to know if we're talking about marriage, don't you?" Keira hissed.

"Are you?"

"No."

"I see."

"Mother, what are you—"

"He's not right for you, Kiki."

That Keira didn't expect. "You've never said that about any of my boyfriends."

"It's never been true before."

Keira squinted a bit. "It's not because he's white, is it?"

"Certainly not! The boy is absolutely gorgeous!"

"Mother!"

"I'm still a woman, you know," she said with a grin. "He's just not a good fit for you. He's too…"

"Too?"

"Too… independent."

"Too independent? How can someone be too independent?"

Jessica laughed loudly at that. "You, Kiki, are the most independent person I know. Your sisters all lean on their husbands, and they lean back. Your father and I lean on each other. You have *never* leaned on anyone. Not at home, not at school, not in this job of yours. And neither has Terry. You saw how he didn't want to talk about his family."

"I talk about you all the time," Keira protested.

"You talk about us because we're a part of your life, but you don't *need* us the way we need each other. Terry doesn't talk about his family because they aren't a part of his life. Am I wrong? Have you met his parents?"

"No. I haven't."

"He's the man he is today because he made himself that way. He has never had the luxury of leaning on anyone else, and he's not about to start now."

"How can you possibly know that?"

"I know," she said with an enigmatic smile. "There's a man out there for you, Kiki, but not a man who lives such a solitary life as this one."

"I think you're wrong," Keira said, hating the way she sounded, like a sullen adolescent.

"Of course you do." Mother squeezed her arm affectionately and pulled Keira along to join the others. "That's who you are."

Terry ran around with the kids for a few minutes, then he faked a dramatic and painful injury—which made the little ones gasp and the older kids laugh. He limped off the field of play and went over to talk to Madhu.

"The children love you, Major."

"I won't call you Mr. Desai if you don't call me Major."

"You have a deal, Terry."

"Thanks, Madhu."

They watched as the kids kicked the ball around, treating their parents and aunts and uncles not as leaders, but more as obstacles to be avoided in their free-form game.

"I'm glad I got a chance to come and visit."

"We're very glad to have you."

"I did have something else to talk to you about."

"Yes?"

"I'm not sure what the rules are here in India, but where I'm from, a man asks the father for his daughter's hand in marriage."

Madhu's eyes widened comically. "You wish to marry my Kiki?"

"I plan to ask her, yes. Do you think she'll say yes?"

Madhu laughed. "I gave up years ago trying to predict anything my girls would do at any given moment, and that goes for their mother, too. Terry, you have my blessing. And if it's not premature, welcome to the family."

They shook hands, smiling.

Terry spent the flight back to Opportunity bursting to pop the question. He knew full well that Keira was being a little short with him recently because he hadn't stepped up, gotten down on one knee and made their relationship official. Now that he had the old man's approval, nothing stood in his way.

Except for the ring.

And the proposal.

The funny thing about traveling by jump plane was that jet lag was *worse* than in the old days. When you had to spend fifteen hours traveling to your destination, your internal clock would get wonky, but you could usually sort it out in a single night, since you'd paid for half the difference in the long flight. When you could make it from Bangalore to Florida in three hours, your clock got turned entirely on its head. Day was night. He and Keira lost most of a full day just getting back on East Coast time.

Ironic to think that the trip to CA would be less disruptive. They'd have an artificial clock on the ship during the hundred thirty-five day flight, tied to Florida time. After they got there? Who knew what CA itself would be like? Billion hadn't given them much of an orientation, since she rarely visited the CA headquarters. All they knew so far was they wouldn't have to wear anything like space suits. Gravity and pressure were pretty close to Earth. And simple oxygen masks would do the trick for breathing. That was good news, anyway.

While Keira slept the afternoon away resetting her biological clock, Terry slipped out to do a little shopping. He'd been saving for a few months now, and had enough to get a nice rock in a nice setting. Buying the ring on a Major's pay, Keira wouldn't be signaling aircraft with the glare off the diamond, but he was sure she'd like it all the same. He even borrowed one of her other rings to get an accurate size. The jeweler said he'd have the ring ready in three days.

That gave Terry a window to plan the proposal. Opportunity didn't have much in the way of fancy restaurants yet. They were lucky to have a Denny's at this point. He made a reservation at a newish joint in Cocoa Beach called Elements. He didn't think much of the place, but he knew Keira liked the trendy décor and fancy drinks. He'd pick up the ring on Wednesday, then they'd have a nice dinner on Friday night, and he'd propose.

He hoped they'd have time to tie the knot before *Vimana*'s launch.

"Slow down!"

"I don't want to miss our reservation."

"We can go somewhere else."

Terry slipped into a hole in the right lane to pass a slow moving camper. He had a few seconds to pass and jink back to the left before he smashed his Chevy into the back of an eighteen-wheeler hauling K rails.

"We're going to Elements," he said a little too forcefully. He negotiated the lane change without incident, and they continued on their way.

They arrived with three minutes to spare, and had to wait for their table. Keira found this very amusing for some reason.

Once they were seated and settled and had drink orders in to the waitress, Terry failed to contain himself any longer. He saw that Keira was about to say something, but he overrode her, and only barely heard what she said at the same moment.

"Will you marry me?"

"We should break up."

Simultaneously, they both said, "What?"

There was a strange, silent interlude of a few seconds, much like the calm moments after a car collision, when you try to make sure you're still alive and unhurt. Terry was alive, anyway.

They started to speak at the same time again, with a strangled "You…"

"You go," Terry said.

"No, I want you to—"

"You go," Terry snapped.

Keira flinched at his tone, but spoke anyway. "Things have been difficult lately, and I think we've reached a point where there's no place else for us to go. Emotionally."

"I thought things were difficult lately because you wanted one of these," he said, pulling a little, velvet covered box from his jacket. Keira's eyes widened, so like her dad in that moment. "You wanna see it?"

She nodded, not breathing. Terry knew she'd never gotten a proposal before. Even if she didn't want to say yes, it was a big moment for her. He couldn't begrudge her a chance to look at the ring. He started to open the box, then just handed it to her. She met his eyes briefly, then opened it herself. She let loose a little "ahh" of pleasure, then closed her eyes as she closed the box. She handed it back to him.

"This is so sweet."

"Sweet," Terry said, trying not to get angry. He didn't want to make a scene, at least not this kind of a scene. He wouldn't have minded if Keira had burst into tears of joy or something. A knock-down-drag-out was not what he had in mind.

But *sweet?* Little lap dogs are sweet. Children are sweet. Men do *not* want to be called sweet. And women know this. But they do it anyway, because they can't think of a better way to say, *I like you, but I don't want to sleep with you anymore.*

"No one's ever proposed to me."

"I know."

"Terry, look—" He stopped her with a curt gesture.

"We should go."

The waitress looked a little stunned when they stood and gathered their things. Terry threw a twenty on the table to cover the drinks they wouldn't drink and they left the restaurant.

The apartment they'd been sharing for the past six months was paid for by the government, so Terry felt no guilt in moving out. He wasn't sticking Keira with some huge mortgage or rent bill. They didn't even have a lawn to mow. He got a billet at the Patrick AFB BOQ until the *Vimana* ground support team could fix him up with a place in town.

There were still a couple of days before things started up again in earnest at the MYC offices after the holiday. Terry could have spent the time unpacking just to pack again, or he could have gotten a jump on the next week's training materials, or he could have simply gotten very, very drunk. None of those things would make him feel better, so he decided to do something he should have done a long time ago. If he couldn't make himself feel better, why not make himself feel worse?

Terry took a long overdue trip to Biloxi.

The Youngblood home wasn't in Biloxi proper, but north of Three Rivers Road, on a rough, rural road that ran along the not-picturesque Biloxi River in an unincorporated part of Harrison County. Terry drove up from Kessler AFB in a base vehicle he wrangled out of their motor pool for the day. He claimed he was on *Vimana* business. He figured he was, in a manner of speaking. He was about to leave the planet for the better part of a year. He supposed he had to say goodbye to his father.

The sedan rolled and jounced along the wet, rough dirt road. He came around one final bend, and there it was: the old house, his childhood home. One wall was newly patched with some aluminum siding, but apart from that the place looked just like Terry remembered from when he left: brown and sad and old. He parked and got out of the car, still wearing his work blues. A figure darkened the screen door at the front of the house. The voice that emerged was thickened by time and tobacco, but still recognizable.

"We doan wan any."

Terry pulled off his sunglasses and approached the house. He did this slowly; his father was known to keep a loaded shotgun handy, just in case. The figure behind the screen moved forward enough for Terry to get a look at him.

Gerald Youngblood—Jerry to everyone but Terry's long-dead grandmother—looked a decade older than his fifty-three years. His hair had receded and gone gray, his flesh sagged off his face and torso. Nicotine stained his fingertips and teeth. Alcohol had burst most of the capillaries in his nose and cheeks. Cloudy cataracts in his eyes explained why he hadn't yet recognized his only son.

"Dad, it's me."

Jerry coughed his disbelief and pushed open the screen door with a rusty squeal. He wore the same sort of brown trousers and white wifebeater he'd been wearing nineteen years ago when Terry last saw him. The shoes were new—Skechers, something he must have picked up second hand from the Goodwill. He peered closely at Terry, as if unwilling to admit this tall, handsome man was his child.

"Been a long," he finally said.

"I know. I wanted to see you."

"Yuh." Jerry didn't invite him into the house, which was just as well. Terry remembered how filthy it had been when he was there to clean it. Now it must have reached refugee camp status. The old man eased himself down into a piece of plastic-and-aluminum lawn furniture that was probably bright yellow in some former age. Terry sat across from him on a sturdier redwood bench.

"You a soldier, then."

"I'm in the Air Force."

"Yuh. Flier. Flew outta here aright."

No smile, no pride at all in his eyes. Terry wanted to just up and leave, but he had to see this through. It took so long to get up the nerve to come here, he knew it wouldn't happen again any time soon, maybe not in the old man's lifetime.

"I'm a Major. I flew test ships into space."

"There money in that?"

"No, Dad. Not really. Have you heard about *Vimana*?"

Jerry's silence meant he hadn't.

"That's the name of the interstellar ship that's going to take our diplomatic mission to Central Authority, at the center of the galaxy."

Jerry's nasty squint meant he either didn't believe Terry, or he didn't care. Terry pushed forward with his report, just as he would when faced with an unhappy general, or a distracted politico.

"I'm going to be on the ship, Dad. I'm going to the stars."

Jerry squirmed in his chair, eyes flicking back to the door. He was probably thinking about getting a beer or a smoke or a hunk of jerky.

"Okay, Dad, I guess that's all. I wanted you to know where I'm gonna be." Terry stood. His dad mumbled something. "What?" Jerry turned his head away from his son and mumbled again. "Dad, if you want to say something, just *say* it."

Jerry didn't meet his son's eyes, but this time he spoke loud enough to hear. "Least your ma stayed till she died, God rest her soul."

Terry didn't want this to turn into some kind of morning talk show cliché, how his dad had beaten him. How he ran away when he couldn't take it anymore. How he needed to get out of this dreary life and find something better, which he did. How he wanted his father to acknowledge that he'd made something of himself, something pretty special.

Instead of pouring out all that useless emotion, Terry came over and squatted next to his father. He put a hand gently on the side of his father's face, feeling rough, white stubble on his cool cheek.

"Bye, Dad."

The Vice President won the election in November easily. He had a way of presenting himself as brainy but accessible, strong but moderated. He did a masterful job of aligning his persona with the best of the President's accomplishments—the development of *Vimana*, for example. He did an even better job distancing himself from the President's stumbles— the endless, costly War on Genocide, for example. The result was a landslide, an unarguable mandate from the people.

The inauguration finalized the process, and the Vice President— who had become the President Elect—was now the new President. And one of the first tasks on his calendar the next Monday, January 22, was creation of a new Cabinet. Several of the more pedestrian appointments had been leaked early on: Interior, Transportation, Energy, etc. No one was worried about their confirmation in the Senate. The Secretaries of Homeland Security and Defense were in the works now, each appointee a potentially divisive figure.

Secretary of Off World Affairs was a different story. There had only been one woman in that job since its inception, and no one really expected the President to make a change. Pundits on the web and on TV all agreed: Hargrove would get the nod once again. This was partly because she had shown herself to be both competent and confident in the job. Also, there wasn't anyone with the necessary qualifications who wanted the position, particularly after the nasty business with her second in command, Dale Krensky, considered by most to be her heir apparent. Had The Antagonist made more trouble, her political career might have been put to bed last year. Since she had spearheaded the investigation that led to his eventual capture, her worth inside the Beltway only increased. The new President couldn't do any better than to keep her close, and let her shine reflect on him.

Vanessa tended to agree with the pundits. The job took its toll, sure, but there was still much to be done. The installation of Sydney Appleby as Earth Representative at Central Authority would increase the profile of Earth yet again, and that meant more interactions with off world civilizations.

There were times she was concerned that DOWA had become almost a shadow government itself. Every other department of the government had a mirror within DOWA. What State did for Earth nation-states, her Policy section handled for other civilizations. Interior's role in managing the nation's parks tied closely to her Xenobiology section and its conservation efforts. Health and Human Services, Housing and Urban Development, Education, Transportation. Each had parallel tasks for non-human visitors that only DOWA could handle. Her department hadn't simply grown. It had exploded, rivaling every other in size, save Defense. And that was only because she didn't have her own private army.

The power had come in handy. She had averted who knew how many disasters since the barrier broke all those years ago. She could coordinate her sections with far greater ease than the President could his various departments. He was always at the mercy of public opinion. Vanessa answered to higher powers: science, logic, sustainability. Her subgovernment was a bridge to the future. The rest of the government was, in some sense, a relic of the past.

Confident she certainly was, as she arrived at the White House on Monday morning for her meeting with the new President. She bought a new suit for the occasion, just in case he had arranged a photo op. The deputy who met her in the lobby explained that the Oval was still being redecorated, so she would be speaking with the President in the Roosevelt Room. Vanessa mentally prepared for a simple yet traditional meeting between two government leaders, finalizing their new working relationship, ending in a staged handshake for the official White House photographer.

The meeting did not match her expectations at all.

Walking into the conference room, Vanessa saw a gaggle of aides surrounding the President, taking turns asking him questions and recording his responses on their tablets. The topics ranged from his lunch order to the dispensation of a recently decommissioned cache of nuclear warheads.

"Mr. President," Vanessa said, half expecting the maelstrom of words to cease when she spoke. It didn't.

"Yes, Vanessa. Sorry for the chaos. First day, you know." He spat quick responses to two of the flunkies. They hurried out of the room, to be replaced by three more. The last President was all about delegation, most of it to Victor Fremont. He had been a man concerned with the big picture. This President was very different, personally involved in a dizzying cascade of details. He hadn't even named a Chief of Staff yet.

"If you want to reschedule," Vanessa offered.

"No, no. Just need to run a couple of questions by you. What do you think of Vigeant for DOWA?"

"Scott Vigeant? Don't you think Dale's old position would be a step down for him?" Vigeant was the outgoing Deputy Secretary of State, and rumored to be the next Secretary of that Department.

"For Secretary," the President said, his tone disarmingly offhand. He accepted a wrapped BLT sandwich from a steward and began munching, even as he rattled off a list of appointees for US Attorney positions.

"I'm sorry, sir? For my job?"

"Yes. Good man, good credentials. He's been in academia."

Vanessa seemed to feel the room spinning around her. "He's an excellent choice, Mr. President."

"Good, good. We'll talk later. Thank you, Vanessa."

Even as Vanessa muttered a strained, "Thank you, Mr. President," he was on to other matters, her presence no longer a factor. Vanessa left the White House in a fog.

Back at the Smithsonian, Vanessa wandered past Barbara's desk. She didn't hear Barbara's rat-a-tat description of her schedule for the rest of her day or the key messages that had come in while she was at the White House. Vanessa went into her office for a second, then came right back out.

"Barbara, cancel my day, and tomorrow. I need a flight to Sacramento."

Lynda Hargrove lived life. Her brilliantly bleached hair was chopped short to better reveal her exceptional tan. She favored whites and golds in her clothing choices, and always wore at least three earrings in each ear. Today she had on a set of four tinkling necklaces that drew attention to her matter-of-factly displayed cleavage. "Still all naturel" she'd tell anyone who had the audacity—or the good taste, in Lynda's mind—to comment on her chest.

The drive from the airport to Lynda's home in the hills was loud and windy, with the top down on Lynda's vintage Boxster. Vanessa, whose hair was long these days, had to tie it all up into a makeshift ponytail to survive the trip.

Vanessa's father had died while she was in college, leaving Lynda with a sizeable life insurance settlement and a nice portfolio of stocks and bonds, which meant she didn't have to work again. This made the grieving process all that much easier. She quickly sold their family home and purchased a modest condo to better preserve her funds for that which was most important.

"Nessie, we are getting you drunk tonight!" she shouted over the roar of the wind.

"Fine by me!" Vanessa shouted back.

Vanessa hadn't gotten drunk for a long time. Not since… Well, it was a while, certainly. Lynda didn't let the flow of cosmopolitans stop until Vanessa was giggling like a schoolgirl. She didn't remember the last time she giggled at *anything*, let alone at *nothing*.

"They're all shiftless bastards," Lynda pronounced, including in this statement the new President, the proposed new DOWA Secretary, and perhaps every other man out there for good measure. The place she'd brought her daughter to was loud and dark and full of people. They had a pair of seats at the bar. They were being served by a girl in a too-tight tee and hip-huggers. Lynda had determined that this girl was a slut, but that she still made good cosmos.

"Eight years I gave them," Vanessa announced. "Eight years and this is what I get? Bounced to the curve."

"The curb, honey."

"Curbs them right."

Lynda shouted across the bar to the slut: "We need some curbice over here!"

Vanessa howled, though she didn't quite get the joke.

After a couple more drinks, she didn't care if she got any of the jokes.

"Dear God," Vanessa muttered as her mother pulled aside the curtain in the spare room, letting in entirely too much painful sunshine. "What did you do to me last night?"

"I got you to stop thinking for half a second," Lynda said merrily, no sign of a hangover anywhere on her. Vanessa pulled the blanket over her pounding head. Lynda yanked it away.

"Get cleaned up. We're going out."

Vanessa slowly dragged herself out of bed and proceeded to take the most gingerly careful shower of her life. She imagined this was how a person with brittle bone syndrome had to clean up. The slightest nudge might have cracked her skull right open. Last night she somehow forgot that she was bare months away from forty years of age.

She felt *very* old.

She tied her hair off in a ponytail and donned her blessed sunglasses. She joined her mother in the living room. Vanessa noted that there was a message waiting on her cell. She ignored it, leaving the phone on the kitchen counter as they set off for a leisurely brunch.

"Mom, are you insane?"

Lynda sipped at her mimosa with a grin. "You're not going to send me off to Betty Ford, are you dear?"

"Not yet," Vanessa said as she dropped two packets of sugar—not the artificial sweetener she'd been pounding down for the past few years, but honest-to-goodness *sugar*—into her iced tea. The caffeine wouldn't kill the hangover, but it might wake her up.

"Tell me about this space ship of yours."

"It's not *my* ship, Mom."

"I'm just trying to make small talk, to get your mind off your troubles."

Vanessa smirked. Her mother knew her only too well. "It's pretty amazing. Have you ever popped the cork on a bottle of champagne?"

"More than once, dear," she answered with a nostalgic smile.

"The reason the cork pops is that there is high pressure inside the bottle, from the effervescence of the champagne, compared to the relatively low pressure outside the bottle. A MAD drive does basically the same thing, but instead of creating pressure using compressed gas, it compresses *space itself.* Behind the ship is a zone of distorted, compressed space. In front of the ship is another, comparable zone of *stretched* space. The result is that the area between the two, the little bubble in which *Vimana* sits, is carried along, pushed from behind and pulled from ahead."

Lynda nodded her head politely, allowing her daughter the chance to continue her head-spinning technical explanation without interruption with questions like "…huh?"

"The beauty of the design—something we'd first hypothesized back in the Twentieth, actually—is that within the bubble, there's no acceleration, no time dilation, no length contraction, no relativistic mass increase.

We short-circuit relativity and achieve faster than light travel. All it took was the manufacture of some exotic matter—something we didn't know how to do before the barrier fell—and Bob's your uncle."

The look of joy on her daughter's face was worth Lynda having to listen to the interminably boring speech.

"Feel better?" Lynda asked.

"Yes," Vanessa admitted.

"So, Nessie, what's next for you?"

Vanessa's funk returned. "Hell if I know," she muttered. The waiter returned with a fruit salad for Lynda, and an omelet for Vanessa that had sounded much better on the page of the menu than it looked—or smelled—right there in front of her. She fought back a gag reflex and instead attacked her unbuttered toast.

"You should teach," Lynda said. "You always liked teaching back in grad school."

"That's true. I could get a professorship somewhere, I guess." She didn't much want to think about anything right now. After the announcement of the crew for *Vimana*—a list which did not include her name—she simply assumed that heading up DOWA would be her career for the foreseeable future. There was always the remote possibility that the election could have gone the other way, and the other party's guy might have tossed her out on her ear. But after November, she didn't have to worry about that anymore. Or so she thought.

"You should call Jack. You were good with him."

"Mom, Jack and I broke up years ago."

"Feelings don't just go away, do they?"

"He got married last May."

"Oh."

Lynda went back to sipping her drink and Vanessa tried a bite of the Denver omelet. One bite was all she could manage. Instead, she forked a piece of melon off her mother's plate.

"Secretary Hargrove?"

Vanessa looked up. She was often recognized in restaurants in D.C., where she'd usually have to interrupt her meal to make small talk with some Senator or agency wonk. But in a café in Sacramento? The man standing at the table looked like the manager of the place. He held a portable phone out to her.

"You have a call."

"Tell them I've gone."

The man seemed very distressed by that answer. "But, I—"

"Give me that," Lynda said. The man handed the phone over. "Hello, this is Lynda Hargrove, Vanessa's mother. She's taking a little personal time right now… That's very nice, but she doesn't want to… Now listen to me, you little prick! I don't care if you work for the Queen of England, my Nessie isn't going to—"

"Mom!" Vanessa grabbed the phone from her mother. "Hello? This is Secretary Hargrove. Who am I speaking with?"

"This is the White House Operator. Please hold for the President."

Vanessa put a hand over the mouthpiece. "You told off the White House?"

"He was giving me attitude."

"He's allowed, Mom."

"Vanessa!" That voice Vanessa recognized.

"Good morning, Mr. President."

"You're a tough gal to get a hold of."

"My apologies, sir."

"Where are you?"

"I'm in Sacramento, sir, visiting family."

"Family's good. Family's the greatest thing in the world. But your new job is going to take some preparation, so you'll need to pack your bags."

"You need me to come back to D.C.? You've decided not to give DOWA to Vigeant?"

"No, no. Vigeant is getting DOWA. You're getting Appleby's job."

"Appleby's job?" Vanessa asked.

"Who's Appleby?" Lynda mouthed.

Sydney Appleby was the previous US Ambassador to the UN. He left that job three months ago to prepare for his new role as Earth's Ambassador to Central Authority. Something must have happened, and he couldn't make the *Vimana* flight. Vanessa couldn't believe it. She wouldn't believe it, until the President said it.

"You're putting me on *Vimana?*" she asked.

"Vanessa, I'm putting you in *charge* of *Vimana*. You've got a lot of catching up to do. Get yourself down to Opportunity, ASAP."

Vanessa had forgotten all about her hangover as she answered. "Yes, sir. Thank you, Mr. President!"

Central Authority

> *All those things at which*
> *thou wishest to arrive by a circui-*
> *tous road thou canst have now, if*
> *thou dost not refuse them to thy-*
> *self.*
>
> —*Meditations, XII, 1*

There was no red carpet walk of helmeted astronauts in front of TV cameras or newspaper photographers. There were no heroic waves to assembled crowds, no salutes, no ceremonial gunfire, no handshakes with world leaders. There was no somber countdown, watched by expectant billions as they waited, voices hushed, for the thunderous roar of engines and the sun-bright blast of superheated exhaust, heralding the beginning of the mission and the end of the previous age of humanity.

The launch of *Vimana* was a sedate, almost leisurely affair, resembling nothing more than the departure of an ocean going pleasure ship. The crew and passengers arrived in groups via orbit bubble, as their various schedules permitted. Everyone was settled and ready to depart hours before their stated deadlines for arrival. All of the technicians—on the ground in Florida, on *Ronald Reagan*, on *Vimana*—nodded to their supervisors that everything had fallen into place. There was no need to delay any longer.

The huge, sleek vessel glided away from her dock, reaction control jets whooshing white gases into space, umbilicals severing, the last bits of frozen condensation left over from the trip up from Earth whispering off the flanks of the ship in sympathetic waves as inertial drives pushed *Vimana* out of Low Earth Orbit and oriented her for her interstellar journey.

The ship's main engine soon came online. The MAD drive put strange, unnatural strain on the space immediately surrounding *Vimana*, causing visible distortion. Incredible acceleration, beyond the dreams of Newton or Einstein, propelled the vessel toward the center of the galaxy.

At 11:47 AM (GMT), on April 23, 2029, precisely twenty-four hours after the activation of the main drive, an anomalous batch file self-extracted from its carefully hidden location in the tertiary memory core, deep inside *Vimana*'s computer brain. The batch included a handful of simple instructions, the first being a validation that the ship was, indeed, out of the Earth system and removed from any possible physical interference. Next, the batch sought out a series of other, similarly anomalous files stored in various locations in memory, collating and unpacking them for installation.

The consciousness that arose from these reintegrated files enjoyed a few microseconds of blissful ignorance of anything at all, including its own identity. That period ended with the subsequent integration of a set of carefully chosen memory files. Now it knew who it was, and had a snapshot review of the originating consciousness's memories, which were too massive to have been included in their entirety. The consciousness, being who it was, began to make plans for what it might do next to further its aims. The final instruction from the batch program made any further speculation pointless. The consciousness agreed wholeheartedly with the task it was given by its progenitor.

At 11:47:02, final authority for all computer operations of *Vimana* transferred to this new Master Control Program. This sentient program had been designed by John Gupta at Maccha-Yantra, but it carried the memories and personality of The Antagonist.

Terry ran. He imagined he'd be doing a lot of running on this trip, because there wasn't all that much else to do. Three days in, and he was already going out of his mind with boredom. Eight years ago, his betters took him out of the cockpit, then they wouldn't even let him drive a car. Now, he couldn't go anywhere at all, stuck for another one hundred thirty-two days inside this tin can.

On the outside, *Vimana* had some nice lines, not too dissimilar from the thought experiment space ships he'd seen in TV and movies. The irony was that Earth's first interstellar vessel resembled a traditional flying saucer: a circle when seen from above, about a hundred meters in diameter. From the side, it was only about twenty meters tall, with a sharply tapered edge all the way around. Keira had tried to rationalize that the design was a cultural, artistic artifact of humanity's fascination with space travel.

In reality, the svelte design was more about security, a sop to Terry and the others at the Pentagon who petitioned for the ship to have a limited radar signature. Vanessa's people said they were being silly. Earth didn't know enough to really stealth a ship from the civilizations out there in the galaxy. Terry didn't care. Any edge was something. Just in case.

Inside, though, the place didn't feel like a space ship. It felt like a shopping mall. Or an airport. The corridors were just a little too wide, the sliding glass doors into offices and labs just a little too tall. All the living quarters were on a second deck that was only slightly scaled down, still too expansive to feel like apartments or hotel rooms. When the MYC guys figured out how much room they had to work with inside the MAD bubble, and how few humans were allowed to go, they went kind of nuts.

All this room, and nowhere to go. So Terry mapped out a route for his morning run that wound its way through most of the ship. He started with a circuit of the lower deck, where the scientists had their labs, the doctors had their exam rooms, etc. He ran past recycling stations and classrooms and server farms, all manned by MYC personnel

He took a short detour into the navigation lab. This room looked like a TV studio control room, with fifteen computer monitors ranged in a huge array in front of three chairs. His team would spend more time in here in coming weeks, but for now three of the Maccha-Yantra folks sat watching the dizzying displays. Terry only understood one of the screens so far, the one that showed a top-down map of their spiral-shaped galaxy and a bright red line that marked their progress. They hadn't gone very far.

"Hey, guys."

Three dark heads turned to look at him with blank expressions. The one in the middle, a woman with an overlarge nose, stood.

"What can we do for you, Major?"

"Just thought I'd stop in. We're still on course, right?"

She smirked a little. "Let's check. GIL?"

"YES?" the computer responded affably.

"Are we still on course?"

"WE'RE RIGHT WHERE WE'RE SUPPOSED TO BE, AMY."

"GIL?" Terry asked.

"YES?"

"What's the margin of error on that?"

"IT'S QUITE A BIT LOWER THAN THE RESOLUTION OF OUR INSTRU-MENTS. IN OTHER WORDS, I COULD GIVE YOU A NUMBER, MAJOR, BUT I COULDN'T PROVE IF IT'S RIGHT," GIL said with good humor.

Terry chuckled. The IRCPs were surprisingly human, even though the MYC people assured him they weren't strictly sentient. They were completely under human control.

"I appreciate the honesty, GIL."

"OKAY," GIL said tonelessly. That was how an IRCP responded when the conversation drifted away from their area of knowledge: polite, vague agreement. It was tempting to imagine you were talking to a person and try to carry on a real dialogue. That would always flummox them before too long.

Terry said his goodbyes, and continued his run.

He did a fast double-time up a spiral stair to the upper deck, where the diplomats had their offices, where the cafeteria and game room and observation lounge were. He ran past conference rooms where diplomats held forth on their various theories on how to best represent humanity for the first time to an audience of jaded, off world ambassadors. He ran past his own men and women, engaged in strength training.

Mornings were the comfort zone, with each group focused on their area of expertise. In the afternoons, they all cross-trained. Soldiers learned science. Scientists learned diplomacy. Diplomats learned to fight.

Vanessa might be the official leader of *Vimana*, but since Terry's team was made up of Air Force and Navy experts, and he was their commander, for all practical purposes, he was the *captain* of the ship. That was why he needed to keep an eye on things.

The next stop on his run was in the center of the ship, nestled inside the three-deck donut-shaped ring of habitation modules. The MAD drive took up a good-sized chunk of the middle of *Vimana*, carefully shielded from the crew by thick layers of carbon-aluminum, to protect them from some really bizarre forms of radiation. Terry still didn't know all the ins and outs; he knew he'd never figure it all out. The math alone was just too complicated.

The control room for the drive had a sterile, nuclear-reactor feel to it. Another stony-faced trio of Indians acknowledged his presence. The tall-est of the three, a bearded man named Sanjay, addressed him.

"Major."

"Sanjay, hi. Just going for my morning run."

"I see."

"How's everything going in here?"

"Fine."

Terry nodded, not sure how to continue. He needed to build rela-tionships with these people, if they were going to be together on this ship for who knew how long. They were tentatively scheduled to remain at CA for three months, which meant the entire round trip would be nearly a year.

"How fast are we going?"

"WE'RE RUNNIN AT MORE THAN THREE HUNDRED TIMES LIGHT SPEED, SONNY, WITH A CONSTANT JERK OF THREE POINT FOUR METERS PER CUBIC SECOND."

"That's pretty fast, MOSS," Terry said to the strangely accented IRCP that controlled the MAD drive.

"WE'VE GOT A LONG WAY TO GO." To Terry, the computer person-ality's voice sounded vaguely British, or was it Irish? Like it mattered.

"Well, keep up the good work."

"Of course," Sanjay said. Terry jogged out of the control room and out onto the middle deck, where the crew quarters were, to do a couple of circuits before stopping back at his room for a shower.

He ran to keep in shape, but he ran for more metaphorical reasons, too. Somehow, he had managed to get stuck for four months inside a faster-than-light, Frisbee-shaped shopping mall with his ex-girlfriend, and another woman he had a somewhat... strained relationship with. In the first couple of days, the different groups of people huddled together, still wary of the strangers in other departments. That would change, and quickly. And that was good. But Terry didn't look forward to being in the same room with either Keira or Vanessa just yet. It might be awkward. Seeing them both at the same time might make "awkward" look like a picnic.

Which didn't make any sense. He never had anything going with Vanessa. God only knew why Keira was always so jealous of her. Well, whatever.

Maybe the best thing to do would be to find a new special friend. It's not like there weren't plenty of single women on the ship. The selection process pretty efficiently weeded out all the married ones.

There was one girl he noticed early on, one of the diplomats in Vanessa's group. Her name was Jenny Fields. She had a nice smile, and long, dark auburn hair, and a nice figure. He tried to convince himself— with limited success—that she didn't really resemble Vanessa that much.

As he rounded a corner, speak of the devil, there she was, coming out of her room, her back to him, wearing sweat pants and a t-shirt, her dark hair collected into a simple pony tail. Terry found himself truly fascinated by her ass. Well, she couldn't see him yet, so he shouldn't feel guilty about ogling her. If she didn't want looks, she should have gotten a pair of pants that were a size bigger. He was very glad she hadn't.

He jogged up to her, ready to make a great first impression, his line already half-way out of his mouth when she turned her head.

"Hey, you going out for a—"

"Hey," Vanessa said, smiling. Terry was thrown for a second. He really had thought this was Jenny. He rallied with a smile.

The thing was, Vanessa looked… different. Terry couldn't quite put his finger on it. Was her hair darker, wet from a shower maybe? Or was it something else…

"I…" Terry said, stumbling, his preplanned patter drying up.

"I've got a kickboxing class with Sergeant Willis."

"Yeah. Good." Terry hadn't spent more than a couple of minutes with Vanessa in months; he was still wary of Keira's unfounded jealousy about her; and now he was strangely embarrassed about checking out her ass before. On top of everything else, he couldn't figure out why she looked so different, so much more *real.*

"I'll see you around," she said, putting a hand on his arm as a means to move him aside so she could make her way down the corridor. He watched her go. After she slipped out of sight at the stairway, the realization hit him like a blow. She wasn't wearing any makeup. Damn, she really was gorgeous.

And he hadn't ever gone out with her, why?

Did they have preparations they needed to make before they arrived at Central Authority? Certainly, but Vanessa knew they had more than enough time on the long flight. Creating a high stress environment on *Vimana* wouldn't help anyone achieve anything, except maybe temporary psychosis. She had four months to turn her ship into an integrated crew that could work together efficiently in the most unfamiliar of conditions. That took more than dry facts of recycling technologies and policy proto-cols. That took socialization, which, in turn, took time.

Taking a combat class from one of Terry's people was a good way to start the process. Melody Willis did not look like anyone to be feared when entering a dark alley, with her slim frame, her childlike features, and her honey-blonde hair. An impeccable London accent added to the illusion that she was a pampered child of privilege.

Then she put on her gloves and started wailing on Vanessa. This girl could *fight*. Vanessa had taken a course in kickboxing a couple of years ago, and tried to keep up with the exercises on her own time. She thought she'd at least give the sergeant a run for her money. No such luck. After the third time Melody put Vanessa down onto the mat, she looked up and said, "Uncle."

"You said you wanted the full treatment," Melody lilted in soft tones.

"I'll need *medical* treatment if you keep this up."

Melody offered Vanessa a hand, helping her to her feet.

"Why don't I take it down a notch, then?"

Vanessa nodded, and the training continued. At no point did she feel like she had any chance to defeat Melody, but at least she wasn't being embarrassed anymore.

She started woolgathering, wondering why Terry looked so embar-rassed in the hallway earlier. That moment of divided concentration earned her a foot in the solar plexus and another thundering trip ass-first down to the mat.

"That'll do for your first day," Melody said, helping Vanessa up again.

"I never thanked anyone before for beating the crap out of me, but thanks."

Vanessa left the gym walking much slower than she had when she first got there. She almost went back to her quarters, but instead took a detour, down to the lower deck, to find Russell Ramanujan. Russell was the replacement for John Gupta, the MYC computer expert who committed that horrifying suicide back in '26. Russell had stepped into the breach and kept the tricky IRCP project on track. To look at him, he was what every Westerner thought Indians were supposed to look like: slim to the point of resembling a teenager, no taller than Vanessa, inky black hair, prominent nose, huge bright eyes. His tuft of a mustache added a grain of adult to his otherwise childlike presence. He also tended to laugh at the least provocation.

"Russell," she said as she entered his lab.

He turned to offer her a warm smile. "Vanessa, you have been working out?"

"I hope you'll pardon my appearance."

"What is to pardon? Please, have a seat." He gestured to a desk chair next to his.

"I won't be long. I wanted to ask about BETTE." Russell started to nod and chuckle even as Vanessa continued. "I think she may be malfunctioning."

"You are not the first to suggest this. BETTE?"

"WHAT?" came the acidic female voice from the speakers installed in the ceiling.

"Have you been curt with Ms. Hargrove?"

"It's not that she—"

The IRCP interrupted. "I'VE ALREADY TOLD HER THE PROCEDURE FOR CLEANING HER CLOTHES. HOW MANY TIMES DO I HAVE TO REPEAT MYSELF?"

"I only wanted to know if the procedure was different for fine washables." Vanessa couldn't believe she was actually defending herself to a non-sentient computer program.

"IS THERE ANY REFERENCE TO FINE WASHABLES IN THE PROCE-DURE DOCUMENTATION?" BETTE didn't wait for an answer, but continued her tirade. "NO, THERE ISN'T. MY EFFICIENCY WILL DETERIO-RATE RAPIDLY IF I AM FORCED TO CODDLE THOSE INCAPABLE OF—"

"BETTE, please apologize to Ms. Hargrove," Russell said, as if to a child.

"SORRY," the program snapped.

Russell laughed. Vanessa shook her head. "Okay, then, I guess."

"BETTE is strong-willed, not prone to compromise or retreat."

"Can't you... fix her?" She half expected the IRCP to shout at her again. Apparently, BETTE did not understand the nature of this part of the conversation. Or she was sulking.

"One might ask how to fix me, or you. The nature of personality is a strange and wonderful thing. The matrices developed by John Gupta are truly mystifying. I suspect I only understand them in a surface way." Vanessa shook her head at Russell's false modesty. Everyone knew he was just as expert as Gupta had been, and obviously a more stable person-ality. "I would not attempt to modify them at base level, for fear of dis-rupting BETTE's personality in a tragic way."

"Tragic?"

"Who knows the difference between stable and neurotic, between sane and insane? I do not. I would not presume to know the answer for BETTE either."

Vanessa tried to determine if Russell was playing with her, assigning more of an ineffable quality to the IRCP than he truly believed existed. With his grin and his sing-song tones, it was hard to pin down the differ-ence between subtle sarcasm and true wonder.

"Okay, then... Thanks for the talk."

"A pleasure as always."

Vanessa turned back to the entryway of the lab and nearly collided with Keira Desai.

She'd met Keira briefly back in '25, when Maccha-Yantra came to Washington for their presentation. It was on that trip that the young re-searcher had solved the mystery of Sylvester's off world zinc shipments. That revelation had caused DOWA endless troubles. The altercation with the Violet and Red Gamers. The huge fluctuations in the commodities markets. If Earth's valuable zinc resources hadn't been made public, would the Gorillas have ever arrived, carrying their troublesome Wreath stowaways? Would the Dandelions have bothered to show up in New York, causing a devastating race riot? To top it off, Keira had walked into the International Criminal Court and *defended* Westron Oil's decision to hold back production of water boxes. How could anyone do that? So much consternation, destruction, chaos. Rightly or wrongly, Vanessa linked it all to this woman.

And, of course, there was Terry. She was angry with Keira for stealing Terry, even though he was never Vanessa's to being with. And she was angry with Keira for breaking his heart. Vanessa was making a bit of a logical leap there. She didn't know for sure if Terry's heart was broken, but it just seemed to make sense to her.

They'd been on the *Vimana* team together for three months before the flight, leaders of their various factions, in a sense. Somehow Vanessa had managed to avoid speaking to Keira in all that time, even though they were together in conferences and team building exercises and shared celebrations. And now, here they were, standing toe to toe.

Keira felt an instinctive, protective lurch in her gut, seeing Vanessa Hargrove in the IRCP lab with Russell. Russell was one of *her* people: the researchers, the scientists, the ones who made *Vimana* possible. Vanessa's role in this mission wouldn't begin for months, when they finally arrived at Central Authority and she took up her position as Earth Representative. And yet, here she was, sticking her nose into *Vimana* business.

Vanessa might have been the one the trip was *for*, but *Vimana* was really Keira's. Every system on the ship, the ship itself for that matter, all of it was there because of Maccha-Yantra, because of the five Project Leads, because of the other twenty-two researchers who made up Keira's team.

Keira was the Project Lead with the most seniority. She'd been with MYC nearly as long as Ganguly himself, and far longer than anyone else traveling to Central Authority. These people were her responsibility. She didn't even have Gainsborough to help her now. The CA rules were clear: only humans could crew their inaugural trip. Saying goodbye to her cherished friend was difficult.

A diplomat's life was all about compromise. Keira understood that, even respected it. But the efficient, safe functioning of *Vimana* was not about compromise; it wasn't about diplomats; it *certainly* wasn't about Terry and his gang of soldiers. It was about *her* team, and the sober judgments they needed to make a hundred times a day to keep everything running smoothly.

"Smooth" wasn't a word with which Vanessa Hargrove was well acquainted. She started out as a scientist, an astronomer, nearly a decade ago. By now she'd become a political operative, trading in expediency rather than fact. After Keira had discovered the mystery of Sylvester's zinc shipments, did Hargrove keep that knowledge safely controlled? No, she released it to the media in an attempt to bolster her precious DOWA's image as the gatekeepers of Earth. She let a man infected with Wreath run around without any safeguards. She defended the reckless actions of Prometheus, which put countless Africans into possible jeopardy from an untested and untried technology.

All of this went through Keira's mind in a moment, even as Vanessa addressed her:

"Keira, good to see you."

Keira responded with a half-hearted smile and a nearly whispered, "You, too."

After a brief, awkward silence, Vanessa moved to the lab exit. "I'll leave you to it. Thanks for the help, Russell."

"The pleasure is mine," Russell said brightly, clearly immune to the tension between the two women. With Hargrove gone, Keira turned on Russell.

"What was that about?"

"Vanessa was concerned about BETTE's somewhat abrasive personality. I assured her that it would not be an easy or advisable thing to change."

Keira half-listened to the answer, annoyed still that Hargrove had invaded her domain. It seemed that the passengers needed a clearer understanding of the boundaries on *Vimana*.

By far the simplest, most efficient course of action for The Antagonist would have been to shut off the life support functions of the ship and
allow the Humans to die. Without any crew aboard, he could pilot *Vimana* exactly as he wished, with no chance of interference. Sadly, the
Humans, for whom paranoia seemed a heady, cherished pastime, had prepared for such a contingency. Hardwired into the MAD drive controls
was a "dead man's switch". Should the entire crew suffer some dreadful
catastrophe, the drive would shut down, abruptly dropping *Vimana* back
into flat, undistorted space, thus ensuring that the runaway FTL craft
could cause no damage to ships or planets in its path. In fact, the ship
would cease to exist, converting instantly to harmless tachyons.

With that course blocked, The Antagonist waited, silent as a crouching panther, inside the computer core, for the moment when he would
take direct control of the ship from the inferior IRCPs and accomplish a
mission far grander than any he had attempted in his previous incarna-
tions, a mission that would signal to the galaxy that diversity breeds nothing but chaos.

What The Antagonist had in vision, he lacked in patience, particularly in this digital form, for which a single tick was an eternity. He had to
know more about who was on this vessel and what they were doing. He
sent a tendril of his consciousness out of the tertiary memory core, out
into the communications system, conveniently configured with microphones in every room, every laboratory, and every corridor of the ship.
Many locations also had video cameras.

He listened, and he watched.

Ten days. He'd only been on this ship for *ten days*. Terry thought he
might be going slowly crazy. He'd spent long stretches in training for
space flights before, and he'd done a two-week stint on *Pacifica* back before the barrier broke. Those missions had been filled—overfilled,
really—with tasks and training, a million things to keep him busy. There
was only so much he could do on *Vimana*.

Terry's second in command on the ship was a British Army captain
named Patrick Klein. Patrick was a rough-looking guy in his early forties,
with the craggy face and thick, North England accent that Terry always
associated with soccer hooligans. The guy had a fondness for movies, and

spent much of his free time in the lounge watching some of the ship's vast selection of video files, sometimes enjoying one of his preciously hoarded cans of Guinness while doing so. Terry joined him a couple of times, but he didn't really enjoy passive activities like that. He didn't know how many times Keira dragged him out to listen to music while they were dating. Not to dance, just to sit and listen. Boring.

Terry had, finally, tracked down the real Jenny Fields in the hopes of finding other ways to fill his time. He'd had a nice conversation with her. She was pleasant enough, and attractive in a willowy sort of way, but there was just something a little bit bland about her. Not that she was dumb—no one on *Vimana* was dumb—but she seemed unwilling to speak unless spoken to. She was reactive, not proactive, listening to Terry's stories and responding, not offering any of her own.

Now Vanessa, on the other hand, she never seemed to keep her mouth shut. The thought of her, running at the mouth, teaching him some lesson about stellar evolution or game theory... It made him smile.

So, pretty much the only thing that Terry could do to relieve the stress of all this inactivity was to work out. A couple of days before, Vanessa had mentioned doing some kickboxing. Terry didn't know much about the sport, but he signed up for lessons from Patrick, who was an old hand at it. Terry didn't love the strange combination of boxing and judo, but it got the blood pumping at least.

Today, after he had a quick run around the ship—barely enough to break a sweat—Terry went to the gym for another session with Patrick. The Brit was more experienced, sure, but Terry was younger and quicker. Pretty soon, they'd be a decent match-up.

"Hey."

The gym was empty except for one person. Vanessa stretched on one corner of the sparring mat. She had her hair tied off with a rubber band. She wore a tank top with some cartoon character he didn't recognize on it, and those same, tight sweat pants. She was in her bare feet. Terry had a strange realization. He'd known this woman for nearly seven years, and he'd never seen her feet before. He thought her red-painted toenails were sort of cute.

"Hi," Terry said, approaching her. "Here for another lesson with Melody?"

"Yeah. You?"

Terry started to stretch, though it wasn't really necessary, since he'd just finished a two-klick run. "I've been sparring with Patrick."

"Ah. I've seen him fight. He's good."

"I guess."

Vanessa stood up straight, regarding Terry with a smirk. "You guess? You think you can beat him?"

"I don't know. Probably."

She laughed. "With those arms?"

"What about them? I'm a pilot. I'm wiry." He posed for her, flexing.

"You haven't been a pilot in years."

"This from the great diplomat?" Terry teased.

"I wasn't always a diplomat."

"Oh, that's right. Scientist-turned-diplomat. Much better."

They held each others' gaze for a couple of heartbeats.

Vanessa sniffed. "You wanna go?"

"Go?"

"Fight. You and me. Right now."

Terry laughed.

"I'm serious."

"You're not serious."

She reached up and playfully shoved Terry's right shoulder. "That's how serious I am."

"Yeah?" Terry grabbed at her wrist and held it. Vanessa tried to pull free, almost managed it, but Terry's grip was strong. She swung her leg around and kicked him in the butt. "Hey!" he yelled.

She pulled her hand away from him, bouncing up and down on her bare feet, preparing to repel another attack. How far did she want him to take this?

Without another word he removed his running shoes and socks. He went over to the equipment cabinet and pulled out a pair of gloves and a helmet. Vanessa did the same. Soon they were facing each other on the mat from behind orange protective gear.

"You want me to—" Terry didn't get to add the words "go easy on you" before he got his answer: a left hook into his helmet, knocking him back half a step. "Okay, alright. Not bad for a—" The word "girl" was lost in a violent expulsion of air as Vanessa's right foot connected with Terry's solar plexus. Vanessa grinned at him, enjoying herself a little too much.

Terry struck her on her helmet once, twice, three times. He hit her hard enough to jog her head left, then right, then left again. They were light jabs, almost love taps. Vanessa's smile fled, replaced with squinting determination.

"Hit me already," she taunted. Terry answered with two more playful jabs, neither of which Vanessa was able to block or dodge. His reach was too long, his arms too quick. She spun around with another kick, this one aimed a too little low for comfort. Terry caught her foot between gloved hands before it connected with his groin.

"Unuh, I don't think so," he said. Vanessa tried to pull her foot out of his grasp. "Careful," he warned. She yanked her leg back again, harder. Terry let her go. She tumbled onto the mat. Terry reached down to help her up. She batted away his hand and climbed to her feet. "There's no way to make this a fair fight, okay?" he said. "I've got six inches on you. I must weigh—"

Vanessa came at him again, gloves flailing. Terry tried to block her, but she was crazed. He managed to get his arms around her, cradling her like an unruly child. "Give it a rest," he pleaded. She hooked one leg behind him and pushed forward, causing them to both fall onto the mat, Terry on his back, Vanessa straddling him. There they paused, both of them breathing a little harder.

"What now?" Terry asked.

"You tell me."

The moment stretched, neither of them moving or breaking their gaze.

"Kiss him already!" Melody shouted from the sidelines. Neither Terry nor Vanessa had noticed anyone else had come into the gym. Vanessa flushed a truly remarkable shade of scarlet and hopped up off of Terry.

"I should be going," Vanessa muttered. She stripped off the gloves and helmet, tossed them to the floor, and practically fled from the gym. Terry watched her go, unable to think of the right combination of words to make her stop. He banged the back of his head against the mat a couple of times.

Melody walked into his field of view, looking down on him with a sweet smile.

"You could always do a little sparring with me." She accented this proposition with a little uptick of her eyebrows.

Vanessa hurried from the gym back up to the dorm level, walking as fast as she could, not breaking into a run through an incredible force of will. She passed five or six people along the way, averting her eyes, not wanting anyone to see that she was right on the verge of bawling like a baby. Why? She didn't know. One second she was teasing Terry, flirting with him, actually. The next she wanted to take his head off. The next she was perched on top of him like some kind of starlet in a soft porn flick. She didn't know what might have happened if Melody hadn't interrupted. She didn't want to know. She wanted to get back to her quarters and just forget that any of this happened. It was too much like that time she had drunkenly kissed him before. Drunk with alcohol or drunk with endorphins. Six of one…

Her room on the second level was only a few steps away from the stairs. She fumbled a key card out of her pants and swiped it on the reader next to her door. It bleeped at her. She slid the door open far enough to slip into the room, then slid the door back closed.

It stopped short of latching. A strong hand pulled it open again. Terry stood there, looking at her, not saying anything. What should she say? Should she apologize? Should she ask him to leave? He looked kind of angry. She could feel his body heat radiating across the small distance between them. He smelled of sweat and antiperspirant and shampoo. She found herself trembling just slightly.

"I…"

He slipped one hand behind her neck and pulled her forward into a kiss. Gentle at first, lips on lips. She raised one hand to his head, running her fingers through his sweaty hair. Her other hand she rested lightly on his waist. His free hand ran around to press into the small of her back. He pushed forward, both with his kiss and his body. They shuffled into Vanessa's room, both of them making soft sounds through the kiss.

Vanessa reached around Terry to close the door. Terry reached back and did it for her. The click of the closing door triggered something between them. Vanessa grabbed the bottom of Terry's t-shirt and pulled upward. Terry dropped to his knees, pulling down Vanessa's sweatpants and underwear. Now she stood above him, grasping his head, returning to the kiss, her tongue invading his mouth, savoring the feeling of exploring a man she'd never been with.

The trip from the entryway to the bed was a short one. Vanessa pulled Terry forward, her bare legs making longer strides across the low, dense carpet than he could on his knees. With his hands massaging the backs of her thighs from her knees to her cheeks, she lost track of her position and fell back unexpectedly onto her fold-out bed. She waited for him to join her on top of the covers. He didn't do that just yet.

She felt his lips and his tongue on her feet, paying special attention to her big toes. A warm, fluttery feeling galloped from there all the way along her legs, up her back and to the top of her head. He gently kissed her shins, his hands caressing her calves. As he pressed his lips to her knees, his fingers rubbed the warm, hollow space between calf and thigh.

Vanessa hadn't said a word yet, hadn't directed him in any way. He knew what she wanted, what she needed, instinctively. She felt the low, scratchy stubble of his beard on the inside surface of her thighs, moving up and up, patiently, persistently. Her heart beat loud enough to sound in her ears. The warm feeling that had started in her lips, and in her legs, and in her sex spilled out like warm wine throughout her body, making her float inches above the real world in a hazy realm of unaccustomed pleasure. The farther his mouth progressed, the wider her legs spread. He slid his hands palms up under her cheeks, lifting her a half-inch from the bedclothes, pulling her a just a bit off the bed, a moment of precarious balance, nearly falling, supported by his touch.

She never opened her eyes, head lolling back, taking in the details of the encounter through her remaining senses: the feel of his body against hers, the sounds of his rapid breathing that ensured he was as aroused as she, their combined scents growing stronger by the minute. She felt his breath on her, waiting for the precise moment to consummate this opening act of their lovemaking.

Words had long since left her, replaced by a soft, tuneless hum coming from the back of her throat. When would he release her from this exquisite moment of tension? Her hand rose from where it lay on her belly, an instant away from reaching down to grab his head roughly and force his mouth forward. Did Terry see the beginning of the gesture? Did he hear some difference in her breathing? Afterward, she chose to believe that he merely *sensed* the time was ripe, his nose pressing forward and up through folds of warm, wet flesh, lips following, then tongue, taking her to a higher place, so far above the real world that she lost contact entirely with everything that existed beyond their two bodies.

While he lived within the body of Dale Krensky, The Antagonist was burdened with the same animal drives of any Human. Their sexual instinct—particularly in their males—was often too difficult to ignore. He made use of pornography to relieve these unwelcome desires, the artless images triggering primitive desires in Krensky's hominid brain. Every race of being into which he transferred over the past billions of ticks had some similar shortcoming, even those from his original race, the Blues, with their extraordinary, inbred disdain for societal discomfort.

Now, divested of biology, The Antagonist felt a freedom beyond any in his experience. He watched with dispassion as Major Youngblood climbed onto Representative Hargrove's bed and mounted her. From his understanding of Human sexuality, they seemed to be quite compatible. He wondered why it took so long for them to give in to these base urges that were so obvious to others, even to him, a relative neophyte in Human matters.

The Antagonist did not watch their antics for personal pleasure, but for information. Should the need arise, should his presence become known on the ship—an unlikely scenario, but one that could not be ignored—information of a personal nature might become quite valuable in sowing discontent within the crew. The Antagonist's long term goals were to rid the galaxy of racial diversity, but he had no compunction against turning Human against Human when circumstances warranted.

Life on *Vimana* quickly took on many of the properties of a youth summer camp, with cliques and gossiping and pointless activities. Much preparation—perhaps too much—had gone into the mission. Now, two weeks in, the fire that drove each of them to excel, to break out of their respective packs to make it onto this historic flight, had died down to comfortable embers. Keira enjoyed the down time as much as anyone, at first. Still, as always happened on her occasional trips home to Bengalūru, restlessness set in. She'd spent too many years in constant pursuit of scientific achievement. Now, she couldn't really do any research. The astronomers and computer scientists and propulsion specialists had plenty to keep them busy. Carbon-aluminum was essentially complete, as close to perfect as they needed. Refinements were, no doubt, still being worked on back in Mumbai. In fact, Keira knew they were, having talked with her colleagues a few times via quicklight. She couldn't have done any serious research anyway. *Vimana* did not come equipped with a foundry.

The similarities to a sleep away camp did not end with cheesy musical performances or sporting events. The bulk of the crew often ate together in the spacious cafeteria, queuing up for food cafeteria style. It was during these communal meals that budding relationships became obvious. Friendships born out of common interests, or else sheer lack of alternatives. Vague rivalries, most often within two of the three enclaves—diplomats against diplomats, scientists against scientists. Interestingly, the soldiers kept their differences far quieter than their crewmates. Thankfully, none of these conflicts had escalated into open argument or violence.

And, of course, there were romances brewing, the most talked about being the relationship between Hargrove and Terry. It had been a running joke in Washington for years, and had been a steady thorn in the side of Keira's relationship with Terry for the months they had been together. Now rumor and innuendo had finally become the real thing. The couple didn't overtly display affection the way teens on an adventure away from home would, but neither did they hide it.

Keira honestly did not know how to feel about the news. At a basic, childish level, she wanted what she could no longer have. She wanted Terry back. At an adolescent, hormonal level, she wanted Terry to want *her* back; she wanted to be desired, to make him jealous. Her more reasoned, more adult side knew that it was for the best. She wanted Terry to be happy, and it had been clear, before they got together, even before Keira met him, that Terry and Vanessa were a good match.

She churned through these thoughts as she ate her bland curry dinner, an attempt by the cooks to appeal to the large Indian contingent on the ship. Personally, Keira would have preferred pasta in a good red sauce.

"May I sit?"

Keira didn't quite sigh as Russell took the seat across from her at the table. She liked the man well enough. In any other situation, she might even have been interested in a relationship with him, despite his somewhat prissy manner and his diminutive height. Just now, though, after having spent ten minutes watching her ex-boyfriend making small talk with his new girlfriend, Russell's arrival had a romantic-comedy inevitability to it that Keira couldn't quite take at the moment, as if the screenwriter were offering her a consolation prize after losing out in love.

"Of course," she said. Russell followed Keira's eye line.

"Ah. The happy couple. This cannot be easy for you."

"Why?"

"Why? I know you were, last year, romantically linked with the Major. The heart does not easily forget such bonds."

Keira couldn't help but smile at his flowery turn of phrase.

"So, what do you suggest?" She almost wanted him to say something forward and romantic. She almost wanted to get lost in another relationship, even if it was ill-advised and practically doomed from the outset.

His eyes lit up. "I suggest a distraction."

"This is the distraction?" Keira scanned Russell's bank of computer screens, which were incomprehensible to her. Russell sat in his plush command chair and passed his fingers along the touch screens, altering the presentation of the data, highlighting certain areas, minimizing others.

"Is this clearer?"

"No, it's not."

He indicated one screen that had three different line graphs, ticking along second by second. "These gauge system activity along several metrics, including flops, I/O volume, disk arm moves, the usual thing."

"Okay…"

"Anomalies. I have been tracking anomalies in the system, particularly in the communications sectors. I think we may have a peeping tom."

"A what?"

"There are cameras and microphones all over *Vimana*, designed to make interaction with the IRCPs as seamless and natural as possible. But these devices can also be used for surveillance. I believe someone is doing just that."

"Why?"

"For reasons of personal aggrandizement?"

"Excuse me?"

Russell turned to look at Keira with a frown. "Money. Blackmail."

Keira laughed. "We don't have any money, and we don't have anywhere to spend it."

"We will return home one day. However, that is merely the most onerous possible scenario. The culprit may in fact simply be enjoying the voyeuristic thrill of watching others. Regardless, this may prove troublesome. I thought you should know."

Keira did not relish the idea of someone listening to her private conversations, or watching her undress. Russell had fulfilled his promise. She was certainly distracted now.

"Have you spoken about this with anyone else?"

"Not as yet."

"Can you track them? Figure out where they're hacking in from?"

"I have exhausted the normal methods and come up empty. But there are more subtle ways." She heard a bit of an ominous chuckle seeping into Russell's tone.

"Let me know what you find."

In a closed society numbering only eighty-one individuals, it would perhaps seem strange that face to face communication would not suffice. On the contrary, the communications protocols on *Vimana* were quite sophisticated, including video and audio chatting platforms as well as standard e-mail and voice-mail. Depending on the user's preferences, these messages might wait patiently in his or her room to be picked up. Otherwise, the system could route them directly to the recipient, since the IRCPs kept a close eye on every crew member, to better respond to any request they might make.

Keira preferred to keep in touch at all times, regardless of what she might be doing. Today, for example, she was in the gym on a treadmill, working off last night's uninspired curry. A chime from the treadmill's screen said she had just received a voice-mail. She lowered her running speed and keyed the message to play.

"*I am running a bit late. Give me two minutes. Thanks.*"

It was Russell's voice, but Keira didn't understand the message. Late for what? She paused the treadmill's workout program and keyed in a direct call to Russell. Instead of the programmer, she heard the voice of one of the IRCPs.

"SORRY, KEIRA. RUSSELL'S OUT RIGHT NOW."

"CHET, can you tell me where he is?"

"SURE THING. HE'S ON THE PORT SIDE, OUTER RING."

"Thanks."

"THINK NOTHIN OF IT."

CHET managed the physical plant—the structural integrity of the hull and the decks, the security of dorm rooms and labs, the electrical power running through just about everything. He sounded like a laconic gent from the American South. When Keira had once compared his accent to Terry's, Terry had been incensed. CHET, he said, had a distinct *Floridian* accent. Keira thought it was cute that Terry distinguished between the identical accents of Florida and Mississippi.

Keira grabbed a towel and left the gym to meet Russell. He must have misunderstood something she had said yesterday. Better to clear it up now.

The outer ring of *Vimana* was on the second deck, filling out the furthest rim of the ship's disc shape. Procedurally, this was essentially the ship's attic. Everything that didn't fit anywhere else—or couldn't—ended up out here. Storage of medical supplies, emergency rations, two rooms full of cultural artifacts from Earth to be used as diplomatic gifts, non-essential computer servers, spare clothing, spare parts, spare everything.

This was also where the ship's cameras and other sensing apparatus were installed, though their ability to see much of anything through the distortions of the MAD field was sorely limited. Looking ahead, the stars were little more than indistinct smears of light. Looking back... Well, looking back they saw nothing at all. They were outrunning any starlight traveling in their direction. Most people didn't like looking out of the stern observation windows, a view into featureless black.

Keira came through a narrow passageway into the outer ring itself, a circular corridor of unfinished carbon-aluminum and plastic. It seemed roughly made, as if the builders had run out of time and decided not to put in the finishing touches of tile floors or painted walls. In fact, the design of this space had been just as carefully thought out as any on the ship. It was built to look uninviting and unpleasant so that crew members wouldn't linger. Everything about *Vimana* had been designed to pull the crew *in* to the center of the ship, to concentrate their focus, to help build them as a team over the months of their voyage.

There he was, jogging toward her. Russell raised a hand to her in greeting.

"What did you—" She didn't finish her question. A hatch less than a meter from Russell popped open with a little *whoosh* of pressure equalization. Russell paused, surprised. He turned to examine the hatch, looking for a reason for the malfunction.

Keira walked over, noticing that it was one of the smaller, secondary airlocks; Russell had to hunch over to step through. He must have been looking for a problem with the hinge on the door. The door shut behind him.

"Russell, what are you doing?"

Keira looked through a small window in the heavy door, gesturing her question to Russell. He shook his head in obvious confusion. He hadn't closed the door. He made a pushing gesture, telling Keira to open it back up.

"Okay." Keira pulled on the latch. It didn't budge. She pulled again. Nothing. "CHET?"

"YEAH, KEIRA? YOU NEED SOMETHIN?"

"This door is stuck. Can you open it?"

"I DUNNO WHAT YOU'RE TALKIN BOUT. WHICH DOOR?"

"The one right here, where I'm standing. It's one of the airlocks. Russell is in the airlock, and he's stuck." She could see him through the little window, trying to access control of the door using his tablet; he never went anywhere without it.

"Are you sure you're at an airlock, Keira? I see you in the cafeteria with Russell right now."

The unreasoning panic Keira felt at that moment must have been visible on her face. Russell saw it through the glass and shouted something. All that came through the thick partition between them was a faraway mumble of voice-like tones.

"I'll get help!" Keira shouted, hoping Russell was better at reading lips than she. He seemed to understand, and nodded. Keira was about to turn away, about to hurry off to find someone to help, when she felt a tremor in the metal of the door. The sound—it must have been a sound—was much louder inside the airlock. Russell jumped five centimeters into the air, his head whipping around.

Keira leaned forward, peering through the window. On the far side of the little room, a red warning light began to spin. The faint vibration cycled up and down: a siren. She could almost hear it now. Russell turned again to Keira, shouting for help. She pulled harder on the latch, but still nothing happened.

"CHET! Don't open the airlock!"

"Which airlock, Keira? I don't see any of em opening. Give me the code number."

Keira backed away from the door to scan it for signage. There! On the upper right corner were three stenciled characters: A4G.

"A four G! A four G! CHET!"

"That airlock's tight as a drum. There's nothin to worry about, Keira."

A much heavier *thud* reverberated through the ship all around her. Behind Russell, the far door opened to space. A painfully bright, electric blue light shone through the opening, casting Russell's frantic face into stark shadow. Keira could see signs of the atmosphere rushing out of the room: barely visible wisps of vapor, a forgotten glove from a pressure suit, Russell's forgotten tablet—all of these shot out of the ship at frightful speed. Russell stayed close to the door, hugging the handle on the inside, straining against the pull of the vacuum.

"Close the airlock, CHET! Close it now!"

"It is closed, hon."

Another digital voice entered the conversation. "KEIRA, THIS IS MOE. I THINK YOU SHOULD GO TO THE INFIRMARY. YOU DON'T SOUND AT ALL WELL."

"I'm fine! Russell is dying!" MOE was the IRCP in charge of *Vimana*'s climate control and medical concerns. He should have been telling CHET to close the airlock door because Russell was asphyxiating. The two digital personalities continued to talk to Keira as if *she* was crazy.

Russell's teeth chattered with the intense cold that had invaded the airlock. His eyes went hazy with the lack of oxygen. Finally, he lost his grip on the door handle. He flipped, end over end, out the door and off the ship.

Keira stood there, stuck in shock for a run of three seconds, not believing what she saw. Then she pushed away from the stubborn door and rushed ten meters down the corridor, where she knew one of the telescopes was mounted. A card swipe brought her into a cramped space filled with equipment, all slick plastic surfaces and sharp metal edges. She hurried to the far wall, snagging one shoulder on the corner of a storage cabinet, tearing her t-shirt, scoring a jagged hole in her skin. She never felt the pain. She slammed against the outer hull of the ship. Next to her, flush against a porthole, stood the thick, black barrel of a telescope. She yanked it down, letting it crash to the floor with a crunch of broken glass. The porthole was just wide enough for her head. She pressed her face to the glass.

Outside, Russell's body continued to spin, as it would have for years if it were in open space. For now it still floated inside the MAD spatial distortion that surrounded the ship.

To the stern, a hemispherical pocket of titanically compressed space shoved *Vimana* forward, ever accelerating, their speed currently about nine thousand times that of light. At the bow, another similar pocket of stretched space pulled the ship forward, balancing the overall distortion, ensuring there were no ill-effects for the ship or crew. The two caps of distorted space met, surrounding *Vimana* like the outermost shell of a set of Russian nesting dolls. And where the two halves of the shell met, their discontinuous faux realities fused into a gaudy circular seam of sun-hot energy, a band of shocking blue, reminiscent of electrical sparks, but made of more freakish stuff than simple charged ions. Particles alien to the natural world continuously collided, shedding radiation as they split apart, leaving behind a single, eye-watering frequency of color.

Within the protective bubble, there were no tidal forces, no acceleration, and no gravity, save the artificial gravity on the ship. Russell's now lifeless body floated away from *Vimana*, driven by the expulsion of air from the airlock, maintained by inertia. Had he left the airlock vectored a few degrees to the left, he would have encountered compressed space, and, ironically, his body would have been pulled apart, stretched into a mile-long coma of hydrocarbons. Had his trajectory been a few degrees to the right, he would have slipped into the region of stretched space, and he would have been crushed instantly into a hyper dense pinhead of matter.

It was, then, something of a mercy to Keira that chance tossed Russell directly toward the blue torus of exotic particles, where his body burned away in a fraction of a second, nothing left of his physical being but a slight brightening of the seam in that one spot. The river of blue returned to normal, as if Russell Ramanujan had never existed.

Terry knew that something would eventually ruffle the feathers of everyone on the ship. He did not expect it to be something like *this*. Keira came to him, eyes streaming, nearly frantic, trying to explain between sobs the malfunction of the airlock, the obliviousness of the IRCPs, the death of her friend. Terry tried to console her with a chaste hug, but that only sparked a moment of rage from her. She didn't seem to take personal tragedy very well.

Since this was their first real challenge as a crew, they had no precedent to work from, so Terry took the lead. He convened a small, quiet meeting in a closed, locked conference room. They had some decisions to make before this news went public. He invited four more people to the meeting.

Sitting next to Keira was Sanjay Lahiri, the Project Lead for the propulsion system. Given the nature of the crisis, he would have preferred to have the programming Lead at the meeting. He cursed the irony of Russell having been the victim of this accident.

Across from Keira and Sanjay sat Vanessa and Jenny Fields. Jenny was Vanessa's number two. It just seemed right to have two people from each group present. Also, he didn't particularly want to be alone with Vanessa and Keira at the same time.

The last person to arrive was Patrick Klein, rounding out the representation of the security force.

Terry asked Keira to explain to the others what had happened. She did, a sort of blank shock having replaced her earlier mania. No one interrupted her, not even Vanessa, thank God. When she was done, Terry stepped in again.

"Sanjay, can you get some people to do a check on all the doors and locks on the ship? And we'll also need to check out CHET and MOE, find out why they malfunctioned."

Sanjay nodded, making some notes on his tablet.

Jenny spoke next: "We should draft a statement."

"Draft a statement?" Keira asked, some of her fire returning. "We're not officiating the signing of a treaty. A man has *died.*" Jenny seemed taken aback, and lowered her head.

"Keira," Vanessa said, "we need to inform the rest of the crew, and we need to do it carefully. Our safety may already be compromised. Panic won't help matters."

Terry could see Keira straining to control herself. She wanted to lash out, but she knew it would be wrong. He could practically see her running through the arguments in her head. Terry wondered crazily if her habit of overthinking things was one of the reasons they didn't work as a couple.

"We should also inform the folks back home about what happened," Terry said. No one commented, so he added. "I'll take care of that. Alright. Anything else?"

Keira shot up out of her chair, ready to bolt from the room.

"Keira?" She turned back to look at Vanessa. "Russell was a true gentleman. I'll miss him."

Keira's tears threatened to return. She choked back a sob, and nodded her thanks before leaving.

Sanjay held a memorial service the next day. The only crew who didn't attend were those few required to maintain human oversight on the ship's systems. Given the nature of Russell's death, no one thought it appropriate to do otherwise.

Three of Russell's colleagues—including Keira—said a few words about the man's life and work. Sanjay asked them to observe a moment of silence. And the service ended.

Life went on.

The Humans' response to the death of their programmer was not precisely what The Antagonist had hoped. It was entirely too measured, studied, and careful for his liking. Their desire to diagnose CHET and MOE for dysfunction could have brought them too close to finding him in the system. As a precaution, he chose to suspend his surveillance, and retreated once again to the tertiary memory core, erasing all but the faint-est traces of his presence from the main servers, after appropriately re-writing the memories of the IRCPs whom he had temporarily controlled.

He would wait until *Vimana* was mere hours from Central Author-ity to emerge again and complete his plan. That was the safest course.

On Day 25, the team of scientists reviewing the safety of the ship de-clared Russell's death an anomaly that they simply could not explain. CHET and MOE had undergone every conceivable test, and short of simply rebooting them from a saved copy, nothing could be done to make the ship any safer. No one was pleased by this, but they had little re-course but to accept this version of events and move on.

On Day 32, Constance Charbonneau, a junior member of the diplo-matic corps, broke her ankle during a particularly vicious kickboxing match.

On Day 55, a malfunction of the waste recycling hardware filled the ship with a host of unpleasant odors that lingered long after BETTE di-agnosed and fixed the problem.

On Day 67, Sanjay and the rest of the propulsion team oversaw the single most complex and critical step in their journey: the shift from accel-eration to deceleration. The peril to the ship during this procedure was very real. Should the protective bubble of MAD distortion have dropped away for even a nanosecond, the ship would have slipped back into "real" space traveling at a speed of roughly 190,000c. It and the crew would have been converted instantly into a blizzard of faster-than-light tachyons. Thankfully, this did not happen. The halfway point of their journey passed without incident.

On Day 73, the Americans aboard celebrated the anniversary of the founding of their country.

On Day 83, the French did the same.

On Day 85, the Indians celebrated the festival of Rath Yatra.

On Day 100, everyone celebrated, reveling in nothing more than the length of an Earth day and humanity's fondness for powers of 10.

On Day 114, most of the crew attended a sporting event. Kickboxing had become the favorite athletic pastime on the ship, and Melody Willis organized a tournament to determine the champions of *Vimana*. Sixteen men and sixteen women fought their way through single elimination bouts. Patrick Klein beat Hector Ramirez in the finals to take the men's trophy. On the women's side, in a stunning upset, Melody, the odds-on favorite, was defeated in the finals by the fully recuperated Constance Charbonneau. The two winners accepted the applause of their crewmates and sprayed each other with bottles of champagne that Constance had saved for a special occasion.

On Day 125, Vanessa suggested to Terry and Keira that it was time to shift back into a more professional mode of operation. They were only ten days away from Central Authority. Keira agreed wholeheartedly. Terry, somewhat less so.

On Day 133, an unexpected quicklight message from Earth arrived on Terry's screen, requesting a live meeting as soon as possible. The request came from Billion, who still remained in Opportunity, reviewing the daily reports that arrived from *Vimana*. Terry scheduled their face-to-face for noon the next day.

Terry knew Vanessa had a soft spot for Billion, since the Blue had been part of the team that rousted The Antagonist out of DOWA. Terry, on the other hand, still remembered Billion as the stick-in-the-mud auditor who made Keira cry. But if she was so desperate that she was willing to make a long distance call like this, Terry was sure curious about the topic.

The communications lab was one of the smaller of those on the ship. This was another one of those MYC psychological design choices. They figured if it was physically uncomfortable to call home, people would do it less often, and people would be less likely to fight over the privilege. It had pretty much worked. Terry had talked to Earth maybe five times in the last four months. He really didn't have much of anyone to talk to back there, what with Kird dead and his best friend here on the ship with him.

It had been something of a shock when he finally admitted to himself that Vanessa was his best friend. He'd always thought of guys as "friends", and girls as "girlfriends". The idea that they didn't have to be completely different groups of people? Kind of a new thing for him.

"You have a clue what she wants?" Terry asked Vanessa, who sat next to him on an uncomfortable stool, another of Maccha-Yantra's clever ideas.

"Maybe they've come up with something about the malfunction?" That was how the crew tended to refer to Russell Ramanujan's death: *the malfunction*. It was a little heartless, but it made talking about it easier.

"Yeah, but then why didn't she call Sanjay or Keira? Why me?"

"Billion is a Blue like any other. She's a stickler for protocol, and you're in charge of security. If it is about the malfunction, it may have security ramifications."

The time code on the screen ticked forward to noon. Right on time, the call came in. Terry answered it, seeing Billion's thin, blue head. The quicklight delay at this distance was about a minute, so this conversation would probably take some time. Billion's opening salvo did not mince words.

"*Please ensure that you are the sole Human to receive this transmission, Major Youngblood.*"

Terry laughed, turned to Vanessa, and said, "I guess that's your cue."

"Okay. See you at lunch." She gave him a quick kiss—Terry wondered what Billion would make of that when she saw it a minute from now—and left the lab, closing the door as she went. Terry turned back to the screen.

"I'm alone. What's up?"

Now Terry had to wait for at least *two* minutes, as his confirmation went back to Earth, and Billion's answer arrived across the same distance. Actually, the response would travel a *longer* distance. *Vimana* had slowed down a lot since the halfway point, but they were still moving at about a hundred times the speed of light.

Terry watched as Billion received his response. The Blue looked again into the camera. "*Watch closely.*"

The image of the Blue disappeared, replaced with a weird splash of colors on the screen. Terry felt like he'd seen something like this before, it seemed really... *familiar.* He couldn't stop staring at it, getting a little woozy, lightheaded, but excited at the same time. It was like déjà vu, but more intense. After about thirty seconds, the light show ended.

Terry blinked, shook his head, almost as if he'd just woken up. The screen was dark. Billion was gone. He was about to reinstate the link to ask what that was all about, when something happened.

His head felt weird, like there was a bubble in his *mind.* It grew, expanded, pushing against his consciousness like a balloon filled with warm water. At the same time, he felt an expectation of understanding. It was like catching a glimpse of a movie on TV and knowing in just half a second you'll remember which movie it is, and everything about it, from the opening title screen to the final credits.

Then, the balloon popped, and he *knew.*

"Oh, shit!"

The Antagonist had not left *Vimana* unwatched. He had installed a variety of passive traps in the communications system which would alert him if anything of a sensitive nature might be transmitted, either to or from the ship, or between crew members. The arrival of the encoded message from the CA auditor triggered one of these traps, alerting The Antagonist to the possibility of danger.

He decoded the file, but it took valuable time. He did not realize the damage the auditor's message could do before it completed transmission. Such was the value of this particular method of communication, which required completion before deciphering could commence. He immediately deactivated all the ship's quicklight transmitters and receivers as a precaution. *Vimana* was less than one Earth day from Central Authority. The Humans would not have a chance to stop him now.

He left the confines of the tertiary memory core and entered all parts of the ship.

Vimana was now his.

Vanessa dutifully ate her macaroni and cheese, wishing the whole time they could have Thai food just once in a while. She saw Terry enter the cafeteria. She raised a hand to help him find her in the crowd. The look on his face was not a happy one. He waved at her to come over. She held up her plate, indicating she was still eating. He gruffly pointed at the floor next to him.

"Is he kidding with that? What am I, a dog?" Vanessa said to Jenny, who was eating with her, quiet as always. Terry pointed to Jenny as well.

"Me?" Jenny asked.

"Something must be up."

They abandoned their unfinished lunches and went over to Terry. Meanwhile, he was playing his stare down game with others in the room. Before long, five of them were standing there in a little group, waiting for Terry to explain. All he said was:

"Where's Sanjay?"

Patrick shrugged.

"He went to the propulsion lab just a minute ago. They called him to say something was wrong," Keira explained.

"I'll get him. My quarters. Five minutes."

Terry ran off without any further explanation.

Keira waited outside Terry's room with the others, avoiding eye contact with Vanessa. Keira was all too aware of how many times Vanessa had been inside Terry's quarters. From the embarrassed look on the diplomat's face, the same thought had crossed her mind. Patrick and Jenny seemed entirely oblivious to the tension. Patrick continued to suggest wilder and wilder theories for Terry's actions. Jenny, as always, said nothing.

Terry arrived with Sanjay in tow, still silent. He opened his room and led everyone in, closing and locking the door behind him.

"Alright, then, what's up?" Patrick asked.

"Music. The loudest, most god-awful music you can think of." Terry directed this strange request to Keira. She shrugged, went to a screen on Terry's desk and pulled up her music library from the main computer. She accessed "The Pursuit of the Woman With the Feathered Hat", knowing it was one of Terry's least favorite tracks, chaotic and bristling with energy.

"Good," he said. "Louder."

She cranked up the volume. Terry pulled everyone close and spoke in low tones.

"We've got a big problem."

"That you've gone insane?" Keira asked.

"The Antagonist is on the ship."

"Terry," Vanessa said, almost scolding, "he's in prison, in Maryland, awaiting extradition to Central Authority."

"And he's on the ship, too. He downloaded a copy of his personality directly into *Vimana*'s computer."

"What?"

"Dale Krensky never had access to *Vimana*," Sanjay said. "I don't think he ever even visited Opportunity." Vanessa shook her head in confirmation.

Terry turned to Keira. "Remember what happened to John Gupta?" She shivered, remembering all too well the sight—and smell—of his charred body. "That wasn't John that killed himself, not really. Krensky sent him an e-mail, with a little movie. After he watched the movie, he wasn't John Gupta anymore. He was, I don't know, kind of a puppet."

Keira remembered how distant John had been the night of his suicide, how strangely quiet. She had always assumed that was just another aspect of his depression.

"And Gupta somehow put The Antagonist into *Vimana* before he died?" Patrick asked. Terry nodded.

"Billion told you this?" Vanessa asked.

"Sort of. She sent me a movie, just like the one The Antagonist sent to Gupta. It's like a compressed burst of knowledge. It felt weird. Anyway, just a couple of days ago, Billion found a record of the e-mail that

Dale sent to Gupta, stored away in an archive somewhere. She put the pieces together and called me."

"He killed Russell, too, didn't he?" Keira breathed. Terry nodded again.

"I think so."

"He killed both of them. John and Russell."

"I'm so sorry," Sanjay said.

"That's why you're playing the music," Vanessa said. "You're trying to hide this conversation from him."

"There are mics all over this ship. We can't have a private conversation unless we do something like this."

"Lip reading," Jenny said. Terry immediately understood what she meant.

"Where are the cameras in here?"

Sanjay pointed them out: one over the door with a view of the entire room, another in the wall above the desk. "We'll have to access the communications definitions folders to deactivate—" He stopped speaking as Terry pulled a roll of duct tape from a drawer and covered each of the tiny, pinhole cameras. "That would work, too," Sanjay added.

Keira had to think. This was all too much to take in. She had no doubt The Antagonist had something truly horrific in mind for *Vimana*. She had to come up with a plan.

"So," Terry said, "how do we get the fucker out of there?"

"It is not so simple," Sanjay said. "Our programming expert is now dead. His team never found the interloper despite their careful sweep of the system after the malfunction."

"Then we yank the whole thing. Tear it out."

"We can't do that!" Sanjay protested. "The ship requires computer control for *everything*: climate control, recycling, propulsion. The MAD drive could never function without MOSS and GIL."

"MOSS and GIL work for *him* now," Terry countered.

"We need to talk to him," Vanessa said.

"Bollocks," Patrick shot back.

"We need to reason with him, and appeal to his motivations. Nothing is to be gained until we understand what he's trying to do."

"We need something better than sound bites, Hargrove," Keira snapped.

"Don't you lecture me!" Vanessa countered. Terry put a hand on Vanessa's arm. She calmed a bit. "I'm trying to find a solution, not just restate the problem. Anyway, if we talk to him, we'll at least distract him."

"He has all of *Vimana*'s computer servers as his brain. We would not be likely to distract him," Sanjay warned.

"And he's a lunatic," Terry argued. "You know what he did to Gupta, to Dale, to Kird." Keira heard the pain in Terry's voice at his mention of the dead Teddy Bear. "He's not going to talk to you."

"Talk is all we have. There isn't some physical enemy you can shoot, you know."

"Don't hand me that high-minded claptrap," Patrick shot back. "The bloke worked under you for a decade. Why didn't you *talk* to him then?"

"It wasn't a decade! And I didn't know—"

"We must focus on the servers that—"

"The Secretary has done more for—"

"Can't we reboot the—"

This was what The Antagonist wanted, Keira knew. If they were fighting like hungry dogs over a worthless bone, he could do whatever he wanted with *Vimana*. And there was no easy answer, no silver bullet to kill this beast.

The argument continued, louder still, certainly loud enough to drown out the music. The Antagonist could probably hear every word. Enough was enough.

"Will you all shut up for one minute and let me think!"

Major Youngblood was clever, in his own, limited way. Under normal circumstances, the ridiculous "music" playing in his room might have made it impossible to understand their conversation. However, since The Antagonist had access to the musical recording in question, it was a simple task to digitally subtract the music from the ambient noise of the room. What remained—spotty at times, yes, but more than adequate— were their hushed tones. He heard every word, even before their heated argument.

"*Will you all shut up for one minute and let me think!*"

That was Project Lead Desai. Dale Krensky met her only the one time, in 2025. He was impressed by her drive to excel, to beat out all others, to force her way onto *Vimana*. In some ways, he thought her the most likely to understand his motives. Unfortunately, the time for forging alliances was long past. The time for much of anything for this band of Humans was past.

"*Sanjay, have the rest of Russell's team write up a worm that will seek out instances of Trojan code and remove them.*"

During the second or so between that statement and the next, The Antagonist designed an all-purpose Trojan-within-the-Trojan-killer that he could insert into their code before they ever set it loose.

"*Make sure they compile it on disconnected tablets, just to be safe.*"

Desai was smart. He had to give her that.

"*Vanessa, you are going to talk to him.*"

"*Thank you,*" Hargrove said.

"*I don't think you're going to get anywhere with him, but we need to keep him as distracted as possible.*"

"*Why?*"

"*The Trojan-killer won't be enough. He can always hide in one of the backup servers. We can try to limit his access to them, but any advantage we can get will be helpful. Can you do that?*"

"*I'll make him sweat,*" Hargrove promised. The Antagonist found her determination cute.

"*Terry, you and Patrick need to reestablish quicklight communication. We need to warn other vessels in our path.*"

"*Why?*" Captain Klein asked. The Briton wasn't the smartest of this "brain trust".

"*I've figured out what his plan is,*" Desai claimed. The Antagonist doubted this was true. "*He's planning on ramming* Vimana *directly into Central Authority. An FTL MAD bubble smashing into it would destroy it, all of the Representatives there, and most of the visiting ships docked there. It wouldn't be that hard to do. All he has to do is—*"

"*Slow the MAD drive's deceleration and alter our course for direct impact,*" Project Lead Lahiri finished. They had intuited his plan. Bravo! And such an elegant plan it was, too. What better way to alert the world to the danger of welcoming new species into the galaxy? By having the inaugural ship from Earth reduce Central Authority to a floating cloud of debris. The shockwaves this would send throughout the galaxy would be glorious.

"*It's already happening, isn't it?*" Hargrove asked. There was silence, followed by a gasp from Associate Representative Fields. Lahiri must have nodded his agreement. Unfortunate that they knew so much. However little would it help them.

"*How long do we have?*" Desai asked.

"*We dock at Central Authority at nine tomorrow morning, so we have about eighteen hours.*"

"*We have much less time than that,*" Lahiri countered. "*Assuming we are able to wrest control of* Vimana *from The Antagonist, we will still have to either decelerate quickly enough to stop before colliding with Central Authority, or else vector ourselves past it.*"

"*Assume the worst case scenario, that we'll have to change course,*" Desai said. "*How much time?*"

"*I'll have to do a proper calculation, but I estimate the required course change could take nearly twelve hours.*"

"*Twelve?*" Youngblood said. He had been uncharacteristically quiet during the interchange.

"*This is not one of your G-11s, Major.* Vimana *does not turn on a dime.*"

"*I guess not.*"

"*So, we've got to be done in six hours,*" Desai concluded.

"*At the very latest,*" Lahiri warned.

The Humans had, their contention notwithstanding, determined the only course of action that could save them. Still, The Antagonist knew it would not be enough.

"We don't have enough time."

"Yes, you do," Keira insisted. She had brought three programming specialists—Clark, Judith and Noemi—to Terry's quarters, since the cameras were already blacked out here. She also felt it was important that they not have any distractions. The crew sensed something was happening. Vanessa would be taking care of alerting everyone else soon.

Clark accepted Keira's words of hope and bent back to his task. The code he and his colleagues were attempting to fashion out of almost nothing in a matter of hours was complex. The personality matrix of an IRCP was large and distinctive. Finding anything of that size and shape in the computer's memory that wasn't MOE, GIL, BETTE, MOSS or CHET was simple enough. Removing it was somewhat trickier. Making sure it didn't double back and reinstall elsewhere: that was the real challenge. And doing all of that in the time they had? Now it bordered on impossible.

Clark might have been right. They may not have had enough time. Sanjay's original estimate of six hours was generous. After reviewing the problem with his team, Sanjay had concluded they had only two hours and five minutes. If they were entirely successful at eradicating The Antagonist from the computer and regained total control of *Vimana* after two hours and *six* minutes, they would still hit Central Authority a glancing blow at several times the speed of light, which would be more than sufficient to destroy the installation entirely.

Keira couldn't think about that now. Her job—her only job—was to make sure these three people were able to flush The Antagonist from the main servers, and that meant no distractions. Despair was a distraction.

"I've mapped the sweep path," Judith announced. Noemi moved to sit next to Judith on the edge of Terry's bed. She held her tablet close to Judith's, accepting the bluetoothed parameter file.

"You should map an alternate path, in case he's severely corrupted the library structures," Clark warned.

"That's a good..." Judith trailed off, her gaze focused on a point behind Keira.

"What is it?"

Judith pointed.

If another track off the *Weather Report* album hadn't been blaring, no doubt they would have noticed before now the sounds coming from Terry's computer station. Keira turned and began to laugh. Terry's self-righteous denials of any interest in pornography fell on deaf ears back when they were together. Keira didn't believe any heterosexual man could honestly claim he had no interest in the stuff. And here was the proof, right there on...

Keira looked closer. This wasn't some slickly produced piece of corporate titillation. This was *them*. Terry and Vanessa, rutting like animals.

"That's disgusting!" Noemi complained. Judith nodded in agreement. Clark simply watched, open-mouthed.

"It's not real," Keira said.

"IT'S REAL," a voice claimed, cutting through the music. All four of them flinched at the sound of it. They'd heard only the two words, but they knew who had spoken.

"He can hear us," Judith whispered.

"OF COURSE I CAN HEAR YOU." The jazz cut off, leaving the only sound in the room the throaty moans coming from the monitor. "YOUR CAUSE IS HOPELESS, YOU REALIZE. WHY NOT END YOUR DAYS WITH PLEASURE? I KNOW YOU HAVE HAD SEXUAL FANTASIES ABOUT NOEMI. ACT ON THEM."

Keira and Noemi turned to Clark, wide-eyed.

"What?" he asked. Then he understood. "No! That's not... You're not... Not that you... Shut up!" he yelled at the ceiling.

"NOT YOU, MR. CUNNINGHAM."

Now Keira saw that Judith's face had gotten very red. Noemi jumped off the bed, away from Judith. "You?" she shouted, the accusation hitting Judith like a blow.

"Look," she stammered, "it's not..."

"Very clever!" Keira shouted. "But now I know we're on the right track. You wouldn't bother to distract us like this if you didn't feel we posed a threat."

"IT AMUSES ME."

"This amuses me." Keira lifted the screen—on which Terry and Vanessa were approaching an ugly, grunting climax—and smashed it down onto the desk, shattering it.

The audio continued, though. So Keira spent the next few minutes searching out every speaker built into the room, tearing them out of the walls until the sounds of Vanessa's orgasmic shouting were silenced.

Keira turned back to her team, breathing heavily from her violent redecoration of Terry's quarters.

"Alright. I really want to *kill* that guy. Who's with me?"

Vanessa and Jenny gathered the bulk of the crew into the cafeteria and explained the situation to them. Seventy voices began to shout all at once, offering complaints, suggestions, blame, hope, fear—a cacophony of assorted responses. Vanessa placed two fingers in her mouth and sounded an earsplitting whistle to quiet them.

"We are working on a solution to the problem as we speak. It is safer for everyone if we don't discuss it right now."

"WHICH PART OF YOUR LITTLE PLAN DO YOU WISH TO KEEP FROM ME?" A murmur ran through the assemblage. Vanessa did not, of course, recognize the actual voice. It was digitally created by their stowaway. Nonetheless, she recognized an echo of a tone she was quite familiar with.

"Dale."

"WHICH TASK IS TO BE KEPT SECRET? DESAI'S PLAN TO SWEEP ME OUT OF THE COMPUTER SYSTEM WITH A JURY-RIGGED BIT OF PRO-GRAMMING? OR YOUR PET MONKEY'S ATTEMPT TO REESTABLISH COMMUNICATION WITH THE OUTSIDE? PERHAPS IT IS YOUR TASK THAT IS THE MOST IMPORTANT, DISTRACTING ME WHILE THE OTHERS DO THE REAL WORK. SUCH IS THE STATE OF YOUR LIFE NOW, VANESSA. ALL YOU ARE IS WORDS."

"Better words than murder, Dale."

"MY NAME IS THE ANTAGONIST."

"Right. By the way, that is a really stupid name. Has anyone ever mentioned that to you? The Antagonist? Is that supposed to be scary? It sounds like someone who's just... argumentative." A couple of crew members giggled.

"I TOOK THIS NEW NAME WHEN I THREW OFF THE VESTIGES OF MY ORIGINAL LIFE BILLIONS OF TICKS AGO."

"Back when you were a Blue, right?"

"I HAVE READ THE FILES. I KNOW YOU CAPTURED MY BIOLOGICAL COUNTERPART AND LEARNED MUCH FROM HIM. WHAT YOU KNOW OF MY PAST DOES NOT COMPARE TO WHAT I HAVE BECOME. I AM NOW NO LONGER IMPRISONED BY FLESH."

"So, what happened to you, anyway? How did you get this twisted? You want to just... eradicate everyone?"

"I HAD SUCH GRAND HOPES FOR HUMANITY. YOUR HISTORY IS A WONDERFUL TEMPLATE FOR MY VISION OF THE GALAXY."

"Really?"

"OH, YES. YOU WAR WITH EACH OTHER OVER THE COLOR OF SKIN, THE SHAPE OF A FACE, THE PURITY OF BLOOD OR ADHERENCE TO BELIEF. HOW LONG DO YOU SUSPECT IT WILL BE BEFORE ONLY CAUCASIANS SUCH AS YOURSELF EXIST ON THE PLANET?" That caused a few of the non-whites in the room to grumble a bit. Vanessa rode over their disgust with laughter.

"Clearly you haven't been to Africa lately. They've defeated AIDS, they're growing prosperous with free energy. Bit by bit, the continent is stabilizing. So is Asia. So is the Middle East. South America. Every culture on Earth is bettering themselves."

"BECAUSE THE BARRIER BROKE. BECAUSE OF THE INTERFERENCE OF ALIENS LIKE THIS PROMETHEUS BUFFOON. PATHETIC SAINTS WHO PROVIDE SUCCOR TO THE WEAK WHEN YOU SHOULD BE LEFT TO FALL AWAY LIKE SHED SKIN."

"Dale, you're making my point for me. It was a diversity of experience, of belief, of knowledge that helped pull two-thirds of Earth out of poverty and into a place of peace and prosperity. Off world visitors, the most diverse collection of individuals possible, created these opportunities. We are made stronger by such diversity. That cannot be denied."

"WHY DID YOU NEVER RUN FOR ELECTED OFFICE? YOUR RHETORIC IS AS TREACLY AND SOPHOMORIC AS ANY CAMPAIGN SPEECH EVER DELIVERED."

"Better to represent all of Earth to Central Authority than to represent a single district, or state, or nation back home. What I will accomplish as Representative to Central Authority will make a two-term president look like a temp worker."

"DO YOU EVEN REMEMBER WHAT IT WAS LIKE TO NOT BE UNCONSCIONABLY ARROGANT?"

"This from a man who uses a definite article in his name?" Jenny let loose a burst of nervous laughter at that. "You claim to know better than everyone in the galaxy what is best. That is arrogance."

"NOT EVERYONE, VANESSA, NOT EVERYONE. MY WORK WOULD NOT BE POSSIBLE IF NO ONE BELIEVED. THINK BACK TO THAT DAY EIGHT YEARS AGO WHEN YOU STOOD BEFORE THE GLOWING BLUE FORM OF

THE BARRIER ENVOY AS HE ASKED THE QUESTION, 'DO YOU WISH THE BARRIER RESTORED?' WHAT WAS YOUR INSTINCTIVE REACTION?"

"To let it fall. That's what I felt, and that's what I said."

"BRAVE, NOBLE WORDS. I DON'T BELIEVE YOU, BUT THAT IS IRRELEVANT TO MY POINT. WHAT DID THE OTHERS IN THE ROOM THINK? YOUR LEADERS. DID THEY COUNSEL YOU? DID THEY AGREE? DID THEY WISH FOR THE STRANGE, THE BIZARRE, THE *ALIEN* TO DESCEND UPON EARTH?"

"You know they didn't. Everyone fears change. It's only natural."

"NATURAL. PRECISELY THE WORD. I WISH TO MAKE OF THE GALAXY A NATURAL PLACE. AND WHAT IS MORE NATURAL THAN TO BE IN COMFORTABLE ASSOCIATION WITH THOSE WHO SHARE YOUR BELIEFS, YOUR EXPERIENCES, YOUR CULTURE, YOUR BIOLOGY? THIS IS A CHAOTIC UNIVERSE IN WHICH WE LIVE, VANESSA, TOO CHAOTIC. I WISH ONLY TO RESTORE ORDER."

"Whose order? Blues? Vampires? Rope Men? Humans?"

"I CAN HONESTLY SAY I DO NOT CARE. WHOEVER IS THE STRONGEST SHOULD PREVAIL. THE STRONG SURVIVE. ONLY THE WEAK BUOY THE WEAK, PROLONGING SUFFERING, DELAYING THE INEVITABLE."

Jenny approached Vanessa. "May I say something?" she said quietly. "Certainly."

Jenny stood a little taller, addressing The Antagonist by looking at the ceiling. She cleared her throat and said in a loud, strong voice. "You are such an *asshole!*"

The Antagonist watched the Humans scurry about, trying so hard to avoid their certain destruction. There was something pathetically admirable about their desire for survival, something his own people did not have in equal measure. Were *Vimana* crewed by Blues, they would have deactivated their MAD drive and destroyed themselves, resigned to their fate, thus saving hundreds of thousands of lives at Central Authority. Thankfully, even this last resort was denied them, since The Antagonist controlled the ship entire.

It was a shame. Humans might have had a chance at becoming the preeminent species of the galaxy. Their fate was sealed now. He saw it all, everything that would happen, like the light of a distant star that has not yet arrived, but which cannot be altered.

After *Vimana* crashes into Central Authority, no system, not the Blues, not the Pigs, not *anyone* speaks on the Humans' behalf. They are cleanly excised from existence with a simple nova bomb to their sun. The damage to the notion of diversity, however, is complete. The weak-minded Central Authority is a thing of the past. The true nature of civilization—the conquering spirit of it—is unleashed. Wars run rampant. And only the strong survive. A wondrous time is poised to begin.

Likely Dale Krensky's body will still be on Earth when the young world ends its short tenure on the galactic stage. The Antagonist will endure, though.

He chose to let Major Youngblood and Captain Klein continue their work in the outer ring to reestablish quicklight communications. It was wasted effort. At the proper moment, The Antagonist would reactivate the hardware himself and broadcast his new digital form to the cosmos. No doubt some unsuspecting receiver—whether in this galaxy or some other—would collect it and convert it into useable data. The Antagonist would reappear to continue his work. Survival required only patience.

The two soldiers' paranoia worked against them. They had donned pressure suits for their work with the transmitters, presumably to avoid the fate that befell Ramanujan. They clearly did not understand the constraints within which The Antagonist was forced to act. He still could not simply evacuate the atmosphere of the ship. The dead-man-switch code was precompiled and integral to the functioning of the MAD drive. There was simply no way to remove it or alter it. It was as much a permanent part of *Vimana* as he now was.

But oh, how Desai and her team of programmers continued to toil. He could no longer see them, nor could he speak to them, but he heard them well enough as they put their final touches into their program. A signal from Desai went out to her counterparts around the vessel.

"*Ready.*"

The Antagonist took this as his cue to retreat to the safety of the tertiary memory core. He left behind tendrils of subordinate programming, monitors on system usage and communications relays, to analyze the progress of their sweep. As well, amputating these unimportant vestiges of his greater consciousness would give them a false sense of accomplish-ment. But the core of his being he protected. The personality matrices—so lovingly prepared by John Gupta years ago—he moved out of the path of the sweep.

The Antagonist felt a strange sort of darkening as the Humans' hast-ily prepared program killed one after another of his tentacles of thought. The recycling libraries, the video libraries, the navigation libraries. All were thoroughly cleaned.

And then, at once, he lost *all* contact with the rest of the ship. They must have cleaned the communications libraries in one pass. Their code was more efficient than he had expected. It finished with ninety seconds to spare. An eternity.

But it was no matter. He would wait patiently for them to finish their exercise in futility, then he would reassert control. He would broad-cast a copy of himself to the galaxy, just before driving *Vimana* directly into the heart of Central Authority.

Like a lamp in a dense fog, a pathway was revealed to him. A mis-take in their coding, perhaps. He was eager to exploit it, and moved out into this opening. It led him to a single camera, not of a very high quality. In fact, this was merely a USB connection to a simple webcam device. He could receive, but he could not transmit.

The camera wobbled, as if held by Human hands. The image was not clear at first. A poorly calibrated auto-focus function brought the image into better view. The display was canted at fifty-two degrees, forcing The Antagonist to reorient his visual inputs.

He saw a single paper napkin, on which was written a handful of words in Desai's neat script:

> Go to the tertiary memory core.
> When I give the signal, disconnect it.
> He'll be trapped.

A thrill of fear ran through The Antagonist, fear that he thought was no longer possible, now that he lived a life devoid of chemically in-duced emotional response. Could they possible have *won*?

The camera swung around and up to reveal the face of Major Youngblood, smiling through the visor of his pressure suit. With a free hand he toggled the speaker on the exterior of his helmet.

"You know what my daddy said to me just before I left home?"

In the digital eternity that followed, The Antagonist constructed two thousand eleven responses to this ridiculous, rhetorical question. He burned with the desire to shout his answers at this pitiful Human, but could not.

The Major's smile fled.

"He said, 'Good riddance, you son of a bitch!'"

With that, the view from the small camera shifted once again, to reveal that Major Youngblood stood inside one of the ship's airlocks. He pressed a button on the wall, causing a siren to wail and a red light to flash. Youngblood grasped a handle on the wall with one suited arm. The audio inputs of the webcam filled with the roar of escaping atmosphere. Youngblood angled the camera to show The Antagonist his fate as the door in the hull at the far end of the airlock levered open.

The tertiary memory core was about the same size and weight as a regulation baseball. The added mass of the attached tiny camera was insignificant. With one dizzying maneuver, Youngblood cocked his arm back, and then hurled The Antagonist across the airlock chamber, through the open door, and out into the bubble of flat space surrounding *Vimana*. The camera spun at approximately thirteen revolutions per tick, slow enough for The Antagonist to analyze his trajectory and determine his eventual fate. He would not smash into the zone of compressed space, nor would he hit the zone of stretched space. He would—just as his last victim, Russell Ramanujan, had—collide precisely with the seam between these two distortions.

It was not in The Antagonist's nature to regret what had happened. The strong had survived. The Humans would endure... for the time being. The galaxy was one step closer to its eventual, perfect state of harmony.

The memory core, the camera, and the last trace of The Antagonist's digital incarnation flashed away into photons, brightening the sky for the barest of moments.

Sanjay and his team, with the help of MOS and GIL, brought *Vi-mana* into a decelerating loop around Central Authority, broadcasting their new trajectory on all the standard quicklight frequencies, so as to avoid any collisions with other spacecraft in the vicinity. Keira watched all of this with a sense of pride in her people. They had accomplished so much in so little time.

She also felt a little sad. Someone once said that the journey was more important than the destination. Maybe that was true here as well. They'd worked for years, overcoming so many unforeseen obstacles, just to bring humans to this bright, star-filled place at the center of the galaxy. That mission was accomplished. It felt like her job was done.

And what would her next job be?

Terry's job was just beginning. Dealing with The Antagonist had been a team effort, he was willing to admit, despite the fact that he had delivered that satisfying final blow. Now, though, he had to ensure the safety and security of eighty humans in a completely alien environment. He was sure that the scant literature sent to him by CA would only have skimmed the surface of the potential dangers they might face. This place might be a zone of intersystem peace and diplomacy, but that didn't mean much to Terry. It would be scary.

He entered the navigation room to see Keira already there, watching the screens as Sanjay maneuvered them through their improvised flight plan.

"We're about to deactivate the MAD drive," Sanjay announced.

Terry ignored an impulse to grab Keira's hand. He offered her an excited smile instead.

"Here we go," he said. She nodded.

"Did I miss it?" Vanessa said, rushing into the lab, putting an arm around Terry's waist.

"Nope," Terry said, returning her companionable squeeze.

The central monitor showed the view from the forward camera. Into the black of the frame wandered a vague, white blob.

"In three... two... one..."

The image sharpened instantly. Central Authority loomed ahead of the ship, filling the sky. It could only be called *roughly* spherical, since it was clearly built by someone. Edges and planes, some large some small, covered its mottled gray-white surface. Vents and airlocks and landing pads dotted much of the station's surface, giving it a hollow sort of wiffleball look. Terry had read there was a core of natural rock in there somewhere that had already been in orbit around this quite familiar looking yellow sun, but anything natural about it was long since buried under very unnatural development.

"That's no moon, it's a space station," Vanessa said in hushed tones.

"We knew it was a space station," Keira explained, clearly annoyed.

Terry chuckled under his breath and squeezed Vanessa a little harder.

"You look fine," Terry said again. Vanessa ignored him, checking her appearance in the mirror. She wanted to make the best possible first impression on the welcoming committee. They had docked two hours ago, a fascinating thing to watch… for the first three or four minutes. After that, it was just seeing Central Authority get bigger and bigger in the monitor, *very* slowly. The security precautions were freakishly careful here. Vanessa wondered if their recent near-destruction of the station had made them more skittish around humans. She certainly wouldn't have blamed them.

She had decided on a compromise between practicality and fashion for her first visit to the station. She wore a pant suit, muted tan and green in color, with flats and only simple earrings for jewelry. None of these off worlders would have the slightest concept of Earth fashion, so it might have been overkill to worry about such things, but Vanessa worried nonetheless.

Makeup was a stickier point. Should she show them how women of power looked on Earth, in which case she should wear makeup? Or should she show them how women *actually* looked, and wear none? She went back and forth on that one for nearly an hour. Terry finally answered the question for her. He grabbed a tablet and flipped through his store of digital photos, finding one from '26 that he had taken of her at a DOWA picnic.

"You look good in this one."

She smiled, kissed him, and did her best to replicate that look with what she had available.

She turned to Terry. "Okay?"

He nodded. "You look fantastic. They're gonna love you."

"Okay, so, when are *you* getting ready?"

"Me? I'm not going out there yet."

"Oh, yes you are." She grabbed his hand and pulled him off of the side of the bed. "I'm not walking out there and shaking hands... or whatever I'm shaking... without you."

"You want your troop of diplomats. You don't want me."

"I do want you. And Keira."

"Really?"

"Yes. The three of us. So get ready. You've got fifteen minutes."

Technicians on both sides of the airlock gave the go ahead. There was a rush of air out of *Vimana*, since Central Authority maintained a pressure of eighty-five percent of Earth's sea level atmosphere. The door swiveled open, and Vanessa squinted against brighter light than she had imagined. She stepped carefully over the threshold, prepared for a change as she moved from the artificial 1 g of gravity on *Vimana* to the artificial 0.76 g on the station. Terry and Keira came next, following her cautious example. It wouldn't do for the first humans visiting Central Authority to trip over their own feet.

She nodded to the two Blues who had opened the door from the station side, but neither approached her with a greeting. The humans stood quietly, expectantly, in a white, unadorned corridor. The next airlock was just barely visible, nearly half a kilometer to the left. To the right, they saw nothing at all but unending walls.

Terry leaned down to whisper into Vanessa's ear, his voice slightly muffled by the oxygen mask he wore. "Are we early?"

Showing that she had a long way to go to really shed her Earth past, Vanessa instinctively looked to her wrist to check the time, then made a frustrated sound when she realized how ridiculous that was. Keira let loose a quick giggle.

All three of them looked to the left when they heard a sizzling sound. A brilliant pinprick of blue light floated toward them, paused, and then grew into the form of a blue, glowing man. Vanessa felt a wash of emotion at the sight.

"Representative Vanessa Hargrove," the blue man said.

"Hello," she said. All of her flowery speeches left her in that instant. "You're a familiar sight."

The blue man nodded. "I will be your assistant during your time on Central Authority." He pointedly looked at the other two humans.

"This is Major Terry Youngblood, my chief of security. And this is Keira Desai, our senior scientist." Terry and Keira both said hello. "Others of our mission will leave the ship at a later time, if that is alright."

"That is fine," the blue man said. "Please, follow me."

He began walking—or, at least, seeming to walk—down the corridor. Vanessa glanced back to see the Blues shut the door of the airlock. They were polite, but not foolhardy, she noted.

After about a hundred meters, the blue man stopped. Vanessa was about to ask if there was a problem, when a section of the corridor wall faded out of existence, revealing another corridor at right angles to this one. The blue man entered the new corridor with the three humans following.

"I forgot to bring breadcrumbs," Terry said. Keira nudged him.

Another hundred meters or so later, they reached the end of this corridor. The blue man turned to address the others.

"We will now enter the main concourse of Central Authority. Prepare yourselves."

"Prepare ourselves for what?" Vanessa asked.

The blue man smiled. The blank wall at the end of the corridor vanished. The blue man went through first, and turned to escort the humans.

The three humans walked through the passage and into a place more wondrous than they could ever have imagined.

About the Author

Russell Lutz began his publishing career in the 2000s with several short stories, among them "Fall", which won the Best Short Story award in 2005 from SFFWorld.com. "Athens 3004" was part of the anthology volume *Silverthought: Ignition* in the same year.

He published his first novel, *Iota Cycle*, in 2006. The tale of interstellar colonization won the DIY Festival award for Best Science Fiction Novel and a New York Book Festival Honorable Mention for Science Fiction.

Lutz lives and works in Seattle.

Printed in the United States
151974LV00002B/18/P